# One Night Standard

A NOVEL

# E. F. DODD

One Night Standard

Copyright ©2024 by E. F. Dodd

Published by

Sugar Beaver
BOOKS

Paperback ISBN: 979-8-9862880-8-6

eISBN: 979-8-9862880-9-3

Cover Illustration: Patrick Driscoll

Editor: Jen Reads Romance, LLC

Copyediting: Revision Division, LLC

Cover and Interior Design: GKS Creative

Project Management: The Cadence Group

For my Granny, who was even more magical than mermaids.
I miss you every day.

# chapter one

## CORAL

As each bag that wasn't mine tumbled its way down the somewhat dented slope of Baggage Claim 5 in the Harry Reid International Airport, anxiety wrapped its spindly fingers around a higher branch in the paranoia tree taking root in my brain. Pretty soon it was going to be perched at the top and breathing into a paper bag. Suitcases, duffle bags, and one too many disturbingly duct taped cardboard boxes tripped, flipped, and toppled their way into the waiting arms of their owners. Neither of my bags made an appearance.

My phone trilled from inside the recesses of my crossbody purse. Fishing around for it, I kept my eyes on the conveyor belt and committed the cardinal sin of answering without checking the screen first.

"Hello?"

"Hey, there, Coral baby," my mother cooed into the phone.

I bit back a groan and continued to watch my luggage not appear. One of my bags I could live without. It only had clothes and other replaceable items in it. But the other . . . losing it would be a nightmare of epic proportions. My stomach knotted tighter at the thought, and I could feel myself starting to sweat. Which, since I'd just landed in Vegas, was to be expected; however, this was sweat of the flop variety rather than anything heat induced. I *had* to have that bag! My job at L'Atelier started on Monday and everything I needed was in that bag. And none of it could be replaced in the span of forty-eight hours.

"Coral, are you there?" Despite never living any farther south than the state of Tennessee, my mother always sounded like she was auditioning for some sort of period drama set in the Deep South. Like if cotton candy could talk but wasn't in too big a hurry about it.

Resigned to my fate, I grabbed my earbuds from the side pocket of my purse and shoved them in place. "Yes, Mom, sorry. I'm at the airp—"

"I'm so glad I caught you," she said, her voice breathy with excitement over her news with no hint of interest in my whereabouts. Which was nothing new since I'd moved out at eighteen. I knew what was coming next before she spoke and rolled my eyes, before snapping them back to the baggage claim, desperate to see my luggage.

God, I should've just shipped it! But the cost was ungodly and the insurance they offered would've done diddly squat for me if they lost it. Because again, my new job starting in two days left no time to replace anything.

"Coral, are you listening to me?"

I popped the knuckles of my left hand against my chest while drumming the fingers of my right against my jean-clad thigh. I hadn't been listening, but that didn't matter, since I'd heard some version of what she'd said since elementary school.

"You met someone," I said, trying to slow my breathing and keep calm, but I was close to completely freaking out. Bags were still coming out, I told myself as Mom continued gushing about her new man. All hope was not yet lost. And then, I saw the flash of purple fringe waving jauntily from the handle of my bag.

"So, when can you come for dinner and meet Tex?"

"Tex?" I repeated, shouldering my way between an elderly couple and a group of frat bros with a muttered, "Excuse me." It was no surprise my being within an hour's drive of her for the first time in a decade only mattered to my mother if it could assist her dogged pursuit of husband number two. Assuming Tex was a man and not a German Shepherd.

I grabbed for the handle of my suitcase and hauled it off the conveyor while keeping my eyes locked on the top of the carousel for my other bag. I fought the urge to gnaw on my cuticle. Both because I loved my new seafoam green manicure and because, well, airport germs.

"I knew you weren't listening to me, Coral Elizabeth," Mom whined into my ear.

"Sure, I was," I lied.

She huffed in frustration, and I wanted to scream with irritation. But hanging up wasn't an option, since she'd just call back until I answered. My mother saw no reason to text when calling incessantly would guarantee her the attention she wanted. "If that's true, then where did I meet Tex?"

*At the dog park?* I wondered silently. My mother, I knew, met men at one of two places—work or a bar—and it was a fifty-fifty shot on either being right. I dreaded the day she dipped a pink painted toe into the online dating pool. Keeping up with her love life was hard enough in analog. The digital version would be a nightmare. I briefly considered the meeting spots for Tex's three most recent predecessors and went with my best bet.

"You met him at work," I said.

Mom harrumphed, which meant I was right and had denied her the ability to berate me for not hanging on her every word, but she didn't pout long—too eager to regale me with her meet cute with the newest Mr. Right. "Can you believe he just dropped into my lap at Trims? Like it was fate, I'm telling you."

It was harder for me to believe my mother worked at a place called Tight Trims, a barbershop owned by a degenerate who hadn't updated his lovely slang for lady parts since the early seventies. Out loud I said, "Certainly sounds that way."

And then I saw it. Haloed by the stark fluorescent overhead lighting was my last and most important bag. I didn't even need the matching purple fringe on the handle to recognize it, as its shape was unique enough. Palpable waves of relief rolled over me as my jaw unclenched and my shoulders detached themselves from their anxious hunch at my earlobes. I didn't even need one last knuckle popping release of tension now that the bag holding thirty pounds of irreplaceable, hand-crafted silicone mermaid tail was within my reach.

"Mom, I have to go. I'll call you later, okay?"

I hung up on her last plea of, "But what about dinner with Tex?" and hustled closer to the luggage belt. Getting my hands on the tailbag wasn't as easy as I'd hoped, since its triangular dimensions and over-weighted top made handling it difficult enough without the added bonus of the crush of people hovering around the baggage carousel. It took me three tries, one of which earned me a dirty look from the elderly couple next to me, before I was cradling it awkwardly against my chest. There was no way for me to maneuver the straps onto my shoulders in this crowd, so I grabbed my suitcase with one hand and side-shuffled to the slightly more open space to my left where a few people stood holding signs scrawled with names and looking for the person to whom they belonged.

Grateful for the additional room to move, I paid them little heed as I checked the straps of my bag to make sure nothing had torn or loosened during the flight. Satisfied all was well, I slid one arm through a strap and hefted the heavy bag onto my back. At least, I tried to.

# JAMIE

The kaleidoscope of chirps, dings, clangs and clicks of slot machines tickled my ears as I made my way through the crowded baggage claim area. *Ah, Vegas.* Even with the dark cloud surrounding my visit out here, I felt my spirits lift with the musical sounds of hope springing eternal from the brightly lit machines. I raised a hand to the black suited man standing between baggage claims four and five to acknowledge I was the Jameson Standard on the placard he was holding. Focused on reaching him, I didn't see the woman hefting a giant canvas bag until it collided solidly with my chest. Whatever was in that thing had to weigh at least forty pounds. Forty pounds that had just slammed into my solar plexus.

All of the air left my lungs in a strangled grunt, and I doubled over. Hell, my knees went weak and for a horrific second I wondered if I were about to keel over.

"Oh my God! Shit, I'm so sorry! Are you okay?" The voice was female and completely panicked. Ironic, since I was the one on the verge of nausea, not her.

Eyes watering and struggling to inhale, I managed another monosyllabic sound that somehow came out as a question. "Guh?"

"Shit, shit, shit!" A hand landed on my shoulder in a tentative hold. "I'm so, *so* sorry. I didn't see you. Not that I was really looking behind me. Even though I probably should've been. Oh, God, are you all right?"

Blinking slowly, I concentrated on blowing out a full breath to get my diaphragm to relax enough to pull air into my lungs. It was the only time I'd been thankful for the body shots Davidson managed to land when we sparred at the gym. Shots he claimed were errant, but I wasn't buying it. Either way, without them, I would've been completely floored by this unexpected airport sucker punch instead of momentarily winded. Okay, momentarily and extremely painfully winded.

Drawing in an experimental breath and pleased when I didn't vomit, I pushed myself up to stand. The hand on my shoulder dropped away when I shifted to face my apologetic assailant. I'm not sure who I'd been expecting to see, but the tall—as in just below my own few inches over six feet—lithe redhead with fluttering hands and full lips turned down into a worried frown wasn't it.

Yes, I'd known from the voice she'd be female, but the rest of her was wholly unexpected. Every part of her seemed to be in motion, from her hands, which vacillated between clasped to almost touching her face to plucking at the hem of her shirt, to the wild coils of vibrant red hair that seemed to operate with their own sense of both gravity and direction separate from the rest of her. It was a wild, unruly tangle of various shades of copper framing an angular expressive face, the most interesting feature of which were wide-set blue eyes so dark they bordered on gray. She was, without a doubt, the most uniquely striking woman I'd ever seen. Who was still talking.

"I'm sorry," I said, cutting into her stream of words. "What did you say?"

She stilled at the interruption, hands frozen at her waist with her fingers splayed wide. Even her hair seemed startled by my question, curls quivering against the freckled slope of her shoulders revealed by the filmy green top she wore.

"Oh," she said, sounding uncertain. "I . . . well, that is, I think . . ." Her words drifted off, and she twisted both hands into a palm up gesture and laughed. "Honestly, I couldn't tell you half of whatever it was I was saying. That happens to me sometimes when I get flustered. I ramble and then can't remember a single word of it."

"Not your first time gut punching someone in an airport, then?"

"Oh, God." She groaned, dragging her hands down her face, and showcasing her manicure. Not something I'd normally notice, but then again I'd never seen that particular shade of green on a woman's fingernails before. It brought to mind lime sherbet and summertime.

*What the fuck?* Had she hit me in the head too? Lime sherbet and summertime? For fuck's sake, my blood sugar had to be low or something for me to be thinking about weird shit like that.

She was talking again. "I swear, I've never hit anyone in an airport before."

I laughed. "But you've committed assault in other areas? Is it just public transit that gets your inner Celtic warrior fired up, or does the urge to attack strike at random?"

Her lips twisted in a less than successful attempt to hide a grin. "Celtic warrior?"

I gestured vaguely toward her hair. "Red hair and rampant bloodlust toward your fellow man. I figured it was a safe guess."

"I don't know if I should be flattered or offended," she said, letting the grin break through.

"Flattered, definitely," I said with a grave nod. "It's not every day you fell a grown man with one blow. Your ancestors would be proud." I delivered this last bit in a terrible brogue broader than the English Channel and earned another smile that came with a huff of laughter.

"What's in that thing, anyway?" I asked, pointing at the oddly shaped bag she'd planted into my gut.

"It's my ta—" She stopped and cleared her throat. "It's for my new job."

"Ah, top secret, is it?" I asked. "Going around flattening people in airports isn't very low-key for a spy, you know."

"I'll keep that in mind." Her brows dipped in concern. "Are you sure you're okay?"

I tapped my abdomen . . . lightly. "I'm fine, I promise. Just got the wind knocked out of me, that's all."

"Okay, well, then . . ." She hesitated, chewing her bottom lip. "If we're all good and you promise you're not going to try and sue me or anything, I'll let you get on with your day."

I raised my hands. "I hereby waive all rights and claims resulting from you trying to use your interestingly shaped suitcase of secrets to remove most of my internal organs."

Laughing, she reached for the bag in question. Its strap shifted in her hand and her body jerked in response to the surprise movement.

Reflexively, I grabbed for it. "Here, let me help with tha—"

My help was ill-timed with her readjusting the bag onto her shoulder. Which meant instead of the side of her bag, my fingers caught the zipper of the front pocket. Her hip twist met my pull, and the zipper sailed open. Catapulting out of the bag and onto the floor between us was the largest bottle of Astroglide personal lubricant I'd ever seen.

For the longest few seconds, both of us stared down at it. Me in total confusion and a good dose of awe and her with what I could only assume was abject horror at her supersized lube container falling out of the bag she needed "for her new job" in front of a complete stranger.

I reached for it. "Let me get that for y—"

"No!" Her refusal was quick, sharp and a bit too loud for the space, drawing several pairs of curious eyeballs our way. Which, given we were in Vegas, was a real feat. Cheeks flaming, she stooped down and snatched up the—bottle? gallon? vat?—and shoved it back into her bag.

Rising from the floor, she looked at me and opened her mouth. Only to close it without saying a word. Because, really, what was the right thing to say just then?

Never one to shy away from a challenge, I decided to at least try. "Astroglide, huh?"

Lifting her chin and meeting my eyes with a defiant gray gaze, she said, "Crucial for that tight tail squeeze."

As my mouth dropped open, she hiked her bag higher onto her shoulder and walked away, leaving me staring after her with thoughts of tight tails and squeezes. *Ah, Vegas.*

# chapter two

## CORAL

The image of my lube bottle tumbling to the floor in front of the blond Adonis wearing a custom suit was on constant repeat in my head on the ride to my hotel. Well, almost constant. It was interspersed with the memory of his resulting smirk. Smirk didn't capture the expression, though, because it hadn't been smug. It was more of a lip quirk, or an attempt to hold back a grin. Whatever you wanted to call it, it looked unfairly good on him.

Although, I was reasonably certain a face like his could wear any expression and still be considered attractive. With bright blue eyes above cheekbones that would've made models jealous and a jawline that could've been used in any math class to demonstrate the perfect right angle . . . yeah, he was hot. Even doubled over and gasping for breath.

I cringed a little at the memory. He'd seemed fine with it, though. At least once he was able to breathe again. He'd been funny, too. And before the lube interruption, I'd considered asking if he wanted to meet for a drink later. It was Vegas after all, the land of the harmless hookup. But after Astroglide slid into the conversation, there was no way I was going there. I mean, there were expectations for Vegas and then there were expectations covered in personal lubricant.

Sure, I could've explained it was to help me wiggle into my tail. But that in and of itself would only have raised more questions. For all I knew Airport Guy was a mervert—yes, you read that correctly, "pervert" with an "m"—of the highest order. Experience taught me it was best to leave the behind-the-scenes part of being a professional mermaid firmly on the other side of the tank until you could be sure how someone would react. Not that he'd given off any sort of skeevy vibe. And after being a mermaid in the entertainment business since my early twenties, my skeeve radar was as reliable as they came.

The car slowed, the click of a turn signal drawing my attention back to the present and away from the memory of that devilish half smile. Glancing out my window, I saw the shimmering façade of the L'Atelier Hotel. Excitement lanced through me at the sight of it. Although it had only opened last year, it was steadily becoming known as *the* place to stay on the Strip.

Its dual towers rose up toward the sky like sparkling sentinels, their metal turret tops connected by an arching glass walkway that offered, according to the hotel's website, stunning views of the Strip below and the mountains beyond. It also housed the already notorious Skybar, an exclusive all-glass—including the floor—lounge that offered panoramic views of Vegas. And the glamorously dressed couples in the photos on the website certainly seemed to enjoy it. Giant palm trees lined the cobblestoned drive of the hotel, their expansive fronds reflecting off the mirrored surface in a wash of lush green. February in Vegas was a far cry from my apartment back in Rhode Island and I welcomed the kiss of bright sunlight through the car window.

We circled past the central fountain with its four rearing horses seeming to erupt out of the water, hooves the size of dinner plates arcing forward and their bronze muscles gleaming in the sunlight. I took a quick snap and posted it to my story on Instagram, tagging L'Atelier and adding #VegasBaby! A neatly dressed bellman opened my door once the car pulled to a stop in front of the hotel's entrance. I stepped out into the mild midmorning warmth and sighed with happiness.

"Welcome to L'Atelier, miss," the bellman said with a smile. "Checking in?"

"Sort of," I said. "I'm not a guest, though."

His smile never wavered. "Ah, here for the casino, then?" He looked quizzically at my bags. "We can certainly store those here at the bell desk if you need."

"No, no," I said, hastening to correct his impression. "I'm a performer. I'm here for a job."

One of the perks of this new gig was that lodging was included, which meant I didn't have to give up the lease on my apartment. Being a working mermaid had its perks; however, job security wasn't one of them. A four month "sure thing" could end in two weeks if things didn't go well. Like the time my summer at sea with a certain cruise line ended after two weeks because of a salmonella incident. A failsafe was always important, no matter how good an opportunity sounded on the front end. So, I'd kept my apartment just in case, refusing to give in to anything more than cautious optimism about my new gig in Vegas.

Understanding dawned in his eyes. "Ah, I see. The front desk will have your name, then. They can direct you to the performers' quarters. Did you need help with your bags?"

"No, but thanks," I said, sliding a few bills into his hand.

I slung my tailbag onto my shoulder, after making sure there was no one behind me, and headed into the hotel. Its interior was as elegant as the exterior. Gleaming white stone columns draped in plush fabric the color of crushed mulberries encircled the expansive marble floor, inlaid with a compass design. The glass ceiling pitched above me in a steep arch, offering another glimpse of the hotel's dual towers and the clear blue sky.

All of the glass made me think of a fish tank, with the hotel guests in their flamboyant Vegas attire the equivalent of tropical fish.

And speaking of tropical fish, a glance to my right revealed the mammoth aquarium featured prominently in L'Atelier's website images. A shiver of excitement skidded across my skin when I saw it. Resting atop a limestone base interspersed with shells and carvings of mermaids and sailors, the tank itself rose twenty feet in a sweeping curve of plexiglass, dwarfing those walking by it. All manner of fish in multiple hues swam through intricate coral archways and around rock outcroppings.

Dropping my bag, I grabbed my phone and opened Instagram. I'd yet to discuss the promotion angle of this job, but social media had been a mainstay of my career since its inception. Follower engagement was key to the success of a professional mermaid. Keeping all of them hooked on each new career path was pivotal for me. Selecting my story, I angled the phone to capture me and the tank behind me.

"Hi y'all! I made it to Vegas! And check out this tank! Can you believe I'll be swimming in that soon? And that's just the beginning here at L'Atelier! I cannot wait for you all to see what we're going to create!" Blowing a kiss, I clicked off, selected a filter, and posted the video.

Shouldering my bag once more, I headed to the front desk to grab my key, along with the winding directions to my room near the back of the main building sandwiched between the two towers.

I'd been expecting something similar in size to the studio apartment I'd rented before moving in with Cam last fall. Not cramped, but not spacious. Efficiency over luxury. That was not how L'Atelier did things, though.

I couldn't hold back my smile as I took in the gorgeously appointed room, with its plush sofa and funky lamps in the living area situated between the entry and the queen beds, as I'd requested, with deep purple comforters and piles of pillows against the far wall. To my left was the bathroom with a long granite countertop, and, most importantly, a giant walk-in shower. You can't really appreciate the wonders of such a shower until you've had to rinse seawater, sweat and lube remnants out of a forty-five-pound silicone mermaid tail in the average hotel bathroom.

I carried my bag over to the beds, finally noticing the gift nestled between the pillows on one of them. Wrapped in lavender cellophane was a wicker basket holding numerous hand towels, lubricating eye gel drops, extra neoprene scuba socks and, most impressive of all, a small portable fan. Opening the small envelope scrawled with my name in a bold, looping script, I read the note written in the same hand.

*Coral,*

*Welcome to the L'Atelier family! These are just a few of the tools of a professional mermaid, as I understand it. I thought you might appreciate them more than flowers or some other toss away welcome gift. If there's anything else you need, please let me know.*

*Also, would love to say a quick (informal) hello in person tomorrow around eleven. The front desk can direct you to my office.*
*Jocelyn Standard*

As the new hospitality manager at L'Atelier and, from what Google said, one of the youngest at a hotel its size, Jocelyn Standard wanted to make a name for herself in a town already known to push boundaries and embrace the spectacle of extravagance. Which meant she needed something, as she'd told me on the phone a few weeks ago, "More than unique. And that's where you come in, Coral."

"Me?" I couldn't keep the incredulity from my voice at being chosen for something like this. I had confidence in my skills in the water, but to be approached not just to perform, but help craft an entire show was an unbelievable opportunity.

"You," she said with an unequivocal certainty that I felt in my very bones. "I've seen your social media feed and YouTube has some of your performances with the Sea Sirens. You're a showstopper in those, as evidenced by the number of views, likes and shares they get. And those are just videos put out by you or one of the other members of your . . . troupe?"

"Pod," I corrected, trying to keep my breathing even as my excitement built. "A group of mermaids is a pod."

"Good to know," Jocelyn said easily. "My point, though, is that if you're garnering so much attention with, and I don't mean any offense when I say this, amateur video, imagine what you could do with a real budget? Real cameras and professionals behind the lens? This is Vegas, Coral. Which means bigger, bolder and brighter than anything you've done thus far. It could catapult you into the spotlight."

What she described to me—a live action mermaid show that ran year-round with multiple performers—was a rarity within the United States. The largest one I knew of was at Atlantis in the Bahamas and required work visas and so much red tape that most of the performers I knew who'd done it hadn't stayed past a few months.

To be involved in the creation of this type of show in a place like Vegas was a dream come true. After years of kids' parties, Renaissance Faires and way too many private parties that verged on creepy, I'd made it into a job with real potential. This wasn't a themed cruise or a short-term festival where I had to get dressed behind a curtain made of old towels. This job could provide a stability that I'd long coveted but had yet to experience.

In my career and, if I were honest, any other aspect of my life either. My work wasn't stationary. It required as much travel as tenacity. I had to go where the work was, which meant since making the choice to mermaid my sophomore year in college, I'd been up and down the Eastern

Seaboard, as well as a stint in California. Renting or subletting while holding down just about every part-time job you could think of along the way.

Furniture wasn't portable, which meant I didn't even have my own bed, always opting for fully furnished units. Relationships with anyone outside the mermaid community were even less permanent when your schedule was unstructured, and you were always looking for that next job or big break. It didn't help that most guys I'd met viewed my career as something of a lark. I'd heard the question "That's a real job?" more times than I could count.

My last semi-relationship had been with a guy named Doug, who'd thought dating a mermaid was cool until his mother wanted to meet me. "Well, you can't tell her you're a mermaid," he'd said with a grimace. "There's no way she'll believe that." Needless to say, I never met the woman.

Everything had an end date, it seemed, so it was best not to set your hopes on anything long-lasting. It was a lesson I'd learned early on. Growing up, I'd seen how ephemeral promises were all on their own. More often than not, promises of fidelity and faithful devotion weren't promises at all. They were shiny lures tossed out in well-placed casts designed to entice and attract, but also camouflage true intentions of temporary seduction. Intentions not seen until it was too late, and you were already caught, only to be eventually tossed back with the other discarded, used up trophies and just the scar of the hook as a reminder of what you thought you had. Of how you weren't enough, weren't worthy of a permanent place.

With a groan, I scrubbed my hands over my face. I wasn't going to let my mom's call and the arrival of her latest version of Mr. Right take away from this moment. Because here, in Vegas of all places, the place that truly defined fleeting and temporary, I had a chance at something permanent. At least careerwise.

I didn't let myself linger too long on that line of thought either, though, because it wasn't a sure thing yet. I had to prove Jocelyn's instincts weren't wrong. I had to earn my chance at prolonged happiness by helping create a show that would bring in enough people to make it not just worth funding, but worth expanding to its full potential and achieve the vision Jocelyn initially described to me. I wouldn't be an underpaid and overworked performer anymore. I'd be part of something here. *If* it all worked out.

My cell chimed with an incoming FaceTime call. Pushing aside all negative thoughts, I slapped a grin onto my face and slid my finger over the screen to answer Cam's call.

"Hey, girl!" she chirped, brown eyes bright with excitement. "Instagram tells me you made it to Vegas."

"Yes," I said, panning the phone around to show her the room. "I think it's safe to say I've made it."

Mocha tinted lips pursed as she let out a low whistle and shook her head, glossy dark curls bouncing along her shoulders. "I'll say so. Damn, girl. That looks amazing."

My heart lifted at her excitement. "And it has a giant shower!"

"No way," she said, returning my grin. "You've officially hit the mermaid lottery."

"It certainly feels that way," I admitted, glad to be able to share the moment with someone who'd understand. I met Cam eight years ago at tryouts for the Dive Bar in Sacramento. We'd formed an instant friendship when I'd loaned her some aqua socks after she discovered a hole in one of hers.

"I need someone to pinch me, so I know this isn't a dream." I shook my head. "On second thought, no, I don't. If this is a dream, I have no desire to wake up."

"And find yourself back in the shallow end of things?" Cam laughed. "Where you are now makes that birthday party gig from years ago seem like an all too distant memory."

I flopped onto one of the beds with a sigh. "God, do you remember that pool? And I use the term 'pool' very, very loosely."

She shuddered. "How could I forget it? Or the fungus that got inside my tail from it."

We gagged simultaneously at the memory. "Yeah, I'm hoping problems like that are firmly in the rearview now."

Cam nodded. "Agreed. But seeing your room makes me all the more bummed I'm not there!"

"Ugh, I know! I mean, I'm glad your Miami job came in, but the timing of it sucks."

"I feel the same, believe me," she agreed. "But a girl's gotta pay the bills. Even if it is by swimming in a tank made to look like a giant bottle of vodka."

I laughed. Promotional jobs, like the one Cam signed on for in Miami, had seen us through some leaner years. Full-time, long-term jobs, like the ones we'd gotten at L'Atelier were few and far between. So, in the interim, you took whatever jobs you could to make ends meet. And once you got one, you didn't flake on it. Which explained why Cam was finishing out her vodka job in Miami instead of coming straight to Vegas with me.

"You'll be here soon, though," I soothed. "And then it's you and me in Vegas, baby!"

Cam squealed and did a little shimmy. "Like you said, if I'm dreaming, no one better wake me."

# JAMIE

I keyed open the door of my room and smiled, reaching for my phone.

Jamie: *Really rolled out the red carpet for your big brother.*

Bubbles appeared immediately at the bottom of my screen.

Jocelyn: *What can I say? I'm the baby of the family, which means I have a constant unquenchable thirst to prove myself to the rest of you.*

I glanced around the well-appointed suite, noting the exotic black-and-white prints above the couch and a touch panel by the door that would make NASA envious. The living room wall was floor to ceiling glass with a view of the bustling Vegas Strip beyond an expansive balcony. In the bedroom, I found a bed that made the term "king-size" seem inadequate. Emperor- size, maybe? *Perfect for someone with long legs and arms in constant motion.*

I shook my head to clear the thought, but not before an image pressed itself into my subconscious. The redhead from the airport reclining against the stacks of pillows all long limbs and graceful lines. My phone buzzed with another text, pulling me from the thought.

Jocelyn: *I take it you've gotten to your room and it's all good?*

Jamie: *It's perfect, Sis. You didn't have to put me up in the penthouse.*

My phone rang then, Jocelyn's number flashing on the screen. She was already talking when I put the phone to my ear.

"I love that you think that much of yourself, Jamie," she said, laughter in her tone. "Vacationing older brothers merit our concierge level suites. The penthouses are reserved for high rollers."

"I beg your pardon," I said in mock offense. "What am I if not a high roller?"

"What you are," she replied, "is taking advantage of the fact your baby sister has a cool job at the swankiest new hotel in Vegas."

"And here I thought I'd just come to visit my beautiful baby sister in her new hometown. My mistake."

"Oh, please." She snorted. "You started angling for an invitation out here the minute you heard I got this job six months ago."

"Took you long enough to extend one," I retorted, which only made her laugh.

"So . . . what do you think of the artwork?"

"The . . . artwork?" I glanced back at the walls, confused by her question. The black-and-white prints were beautifully done close-ups of what I assumed were flowers. "I mean, it looks good to me, Joss. But then again I don—"

My answer ended midstream as my eyes landed on the frame directly opposite the bed. A frame that didn't match the placement of others or contain any sort of floral image.

*Meet Jameson Standard—Boston's Bad Boy of Business* screamed the headline from the framed article in *Boston Commons* magazine. And right below it was a picture of me, shirtless and sweating, in the boxing ring at my gym.

"Oh, fuck," I said, which elicited a cackle from my pain in the ass sister.

"I thought that one piece would catch your attention," she said, still laughing.

"Not cool, Joss," I grumbled, rubbing a hand over my face and turning away from the article that had plagued me for the last few days.

"Oh, really?" she asked, and I knew what was coming next.

"Joss, I'm not in the moo—"

"Not in the mood to hear that article is your own fault and could've totally been avoided if you'd, oh, I don't know . . . *listened* to me when I told you not to trust that reporter."

"'I told you so' isn't exactly what I want to hear right now," I said.

Jocelyn exploded. "Abigail Johnson is a gossip columnist, Jamie, not a freaking news reporter. She probably thinks green sustainable development is a new sort of colon cleanse. Why in God's name would you agree to an interview with her? Where was Davidson in all this? How could he not vet this like he does with literally everything else?"

Davidson Brooks was one of my partners at Standard Development and also its general counsel. He'd never met a T he didn't cross fervently and then double-check. And he'd told me he thought the *Boston Commons* piece was suspect when I'd first been approached to be a part of their February issue.

"Isn't that magazine for the ladies who lunch crowd? Why would they want to do an article on you?" he'd asked, brow furrowed and fingers steepled as he looked at me across his desk. "We're developers, not designers with a new line of resort wear. What's the article about?"

"Resort wear?" I asked, lifting a brow.

Davidson's frown deepened. "Fashion is broader than tailored suits and workout gear, Jamie."

"For you, maybe," I said with a grin that only made his lips turn even further down as he scowled at me.

"Back to my question," he said. "Why do they want to feature you in a magazine that is essentially glorified ad copy?"

I shrugged. "It's some sort of Forty Under Forty thing."

"You're one of forty guys in Boston they've approached? And you're thirty-nine. Aren't you a bit old for an 'under forty' article?"

I shook my head. "No, that's just how they described it. There's no set number, but they want to key in on men under forty." I narrowed my eyes at him. "And last time I checked, thirty-nine was still under forty."

"That's like saying the Panthers played football last season. It's true in a technical sense, but only just barely."

"Anyway," I said. "It could be good publicity for the firm. Highlight what we do, showcase our emphasis on incorporating green space into our developments."

"In the same magazine that touts the latest wrinkle reducer and chemical peels? Seems a little off brand to me."

"Jamie," Jocelyn prompted me from the memory of my conversation with Davidson. "Davidson *did* review this, didn't he?"

"Of course he did," I said. "And he . . . questioned it, but eventually said it was my call."

"Oh, Jamie," she said, and I winced at the irritated sympathy in her voice.

"Yeah, yeah," I said. "I know. Believe me, I know, okay?"

The humiliation of being duped into the story washed over in its own version of a chemical peel, my own stupidity flaying me open once again. It stung to hear how easily everyone else—including my baby sister who lived across the country—had seen something I'd totally missed. That their skepticism had been well deserved, and I'd just glossed over it in my eagerness to be seen as one of Boston's new business elite.

The article was a piece on men under forty—successful *single* men under forty. *Modern Day Rakes, Corporate Raider Rogues and Salacious Stock Market Scoundrels—A Guide to the Playboys of Boston's Business Elite* read like a who's who of the current and upcoming generations of men helming most industries in Boston. Told from the point of view of ex-girlfriends, former lovers and any other person with a less than favorable bias the reporter could find.

It was a wholly ridiculous article that made me look ridiculous by being included in it. Especially the pictures. Pictures of which I hadn't agreed to be the subject. But no reader would know that, nor would they know about the interview I'd given that focused on Standard Development. They'd just see the photos and read the snippets of conversation, coupled with a few quotes from ghosts of girlfriends past, plucked by the writer to create the image of me she could best use to sell copies or get clicks.

After a brief pause, Jocelyn said, "Well, the pics are great. Or should I say your 'pecs' look great? Like a modern-day gladiator gearing up for battle in the boardroom."

I smothered a groan, knowing full well she'd take any acknowledgment of her teasing as a sign of weakness.

"Tell me," she went on, and I could hear her delighted grin through the phone. "Did they add the perfectly placed rivulets of sweat with Photoshop, or is that just your natural male essence leaking from your invisible pores?"

I tried not to laugh, but it was a lost cause. It actually felt good to laugh about it, instead of cringe in abject embarrassment or grind my teeth in frustration, both of which I'd been alternating between since the article came out last week. That and avoiding Davidson's occasional "I told you so" looks.

The women interviewed about their relationships with me categorized our time together as "just another business deal." One had gone so far as saying, "Jamie views everything as transactional, whether it's in the boardroom or the bedroom." All in all, it painted an unflattering image that didn't match the one I had of myself. Sure, I was driven and focused with little time for anything other than my work, but that didn't equate to the cold, somewhat heartless person the article described. Did it?

Since the article's publication, I'd been questioning whether there was more truth in the fluff piece than I cared to admit. It was an unsettling thought that had taken up residence in my head in the past few weeks. One that stretched and flapped from its perch in the corner of my mind during the wee hours of the morning.

And yet when faced with my sister's irreverence over the whole thing, I couldn't help but chuckle.

"You're entirely too good at being an asshole," I said with no real heat to it.

"I learned from the best," Jocelyn chirped back.

"Well, I guess we can discuss my gullibility along with my natural male essence over drinks tonight."

"As disgustingly awful as that sounds, Jamie, I'm afraid I can't tonight. I've got a meeting this afternoon that is most likely going to morph into a working dinner. But I've got you on my schedule for lunch tomorrow. You can tell me the whole story then."

I grinned at that, more than a little proud of how well Jocelyn was doing so early in her career. Her becoming the hospitality manager of the newest luxury hotel on the Vegas Strip at the ripe old age of thirty-two was beyond impressive. But that flash of pride wasn't going to keep me from giving her a distinct ration of shit about it.

"Damn, now I have to get on your schedule? When did you become such a badass, available by appointment only?"

"Again, I learned from the best. Or have you forgotten the time you had to 'pencil in' my college graduation? But look at it this way, I've given your name at every bar in this joint, so your tab is on me tonight. Have fun, but not so much you're too hungover for lunch tomorrow."

I laughed. "Not to worry, sis. I'll make sure to drink this bottle of fifteen dollar water by my bed to avoid any hangover."

"It's made from actual angel's tears, so it's worth the expense and guaranteed to purge all the sins of the evening from your bloodstream. Have fun and I'll see you tomorrow. And we'll chat about this article and why so many women from your past think you're some sort of callous Casanova when I know that's not the man our mother raised."

Buoyed by her faith in my character, I smiled. "Thanks, sis."

"Love you, brother. I'll see you tomorrow."

Once she'd disconnected, I tapped my phone against my palm and considered my options. Dining solo wasn't an issue for me. With my travel schedule, I'd grabbed meals alone in almost every state. I wanted simple for tonight, though, which was more complicated in a hotel that erred on the side of extravagant.

Pulling up the hotel app, I perused the restaurant offerings. The five-star linen tablecloth French restaurant was definitely not what I was looking for, nor was the upscale Asian fusion place, or the admittedly delicious sounding Italian spot. I wanted something low-key and easy. Something like the L'Andier Grill that boasted thick cuts of steak and an impressive wine list, while avoiding the "place to be seen" vibe of the other culinary offerings. I could grab a spot at its wide oak bar, have a meal and a bold red, and obey my sister's—and Davidson's—instructions of fun, but not too much fun.

# chapter three

## CORAL

I couldn't have been more than six years old the first time I saw the movie *Splash* thanks to Saturday morning cable reruns. TBS and TNT were excellent babysitters that introduced me to mermaids. Not the cartoon variety, but real mermaids living in the actual ocean. It didn't hurt that the movie opened with a girl mermaid about my age. One watch of it and I was hooked, pardon the pun, on the idea that I could be a part of that underwater world. In that moment, on a worn blue couch in mountains of rural Virginia watching Tom Hanks dive overboard for Daryl Hannah, I knew that I would be a mermaid one day.

My favorite scene from *Splash* is the one where the heroine dumps a vat of Morton's salt into the hero's bathtub to turn back into a mermaid. She sinks down into the water and her mermaid's body rejoices. Her legs are gone, and her tail is back, its beautiful, winglike fluke unfurling over the lip of the bathtub in full relaxation.

That scene remains the first thing I think of when I unpack any of my own tails. Yes, they're silicone and once I aged past ten, I did know I'd never be a real mermaid. But when my flukes unfurl from their confinement in all their glory, the same spark of excitement I first experienced through *Splash* fizzes up my spine.

This afternoon was no different. Unzipping my tailbag, I reached inside to carefully draw out the heavy folds of silicone in undulating shades of teal from bright aquamarine all the way to a deep metallic blue-green known as "Empress." Gently, I laid it flat on the bed I didn't plan to sleep in, careful to arrange the feathered fluke so that none of pieces were folded or bent under one another. It gleamed in the sunlight streaming through the window, the rays of natural light bouncing off the special finish designed to make it shimmer.

My fizzing excitement went from a champagne bubbly feeling to that of a lit fuse as I stroked a hand down the side of my tail. This job was my big break. I wouldn't just be performing in someone else's show. I'd be one of the architects of the show itself! From the music to the choreography to who knew what else, I'd be helping create it all.

Plus, to drum up interest, I'd soon be the main attraction—other than the multiple species of tropical fish—in the center of the hotel lobby. Before the show opened, we'd—that is Jocelyn and I—decided I'd do some solo swims in the tank to generate publicity and create buzz for the upcoming debut of the full mermaid show. Sort of a preview of coming attractions. The idea of it made me positively giddy.

As much as I loved my tail though, holing up with it and ordering room service wasn't the right way to celebrate my arrival in Vegas or this fabulous new job. This chance deserved to be commemorated as the start of something. Something I'd worked years to achieve and was now within my grasp.

A celebration required food and drink, and, if I played my cards right, company of the sexy male variety. Too bad my lube had ruined any thought I'd had to ask Airport Guy to drinks. He would've filled that last item very nicely.

"No matter," I told the empty hotel room. "This is Vegas, baby." Food, drink and male companionship were a dime a dozen around here. The first two I knew, thanks to my review of L'Atelier's helpful app, were offered in abundance right under the roof of my hotel. And, given my quick glance around on the way to my room, the male companionship angle shouldn't be a problem either. But first, I needed the right outfit to wear for my party of one. The right outfit and the right *shoes*.

As a woman who stood five foot eleven inches tall in just her socks, there were some who argued flats were the only right shoes for me. On more than one occasion, I'd been asked why I'd want to "emphasize" my height. Like being tall and wearing heels was the equivalent of using a pink highlighter to draw an arrow to a fresh pimple on my cheek.

What they failed to understand was being a tall person with lady parts was not some strange affliction or condition that required me to be sequestered from humankind aka the male portion of humankind who preferred their women pocket-size. My height was, in a word, amazing. In two words—fucking amazing.

I could reach anything on any shelf anywhere. It was nearly impossible for anyone to talk down to me, as that was extremely difficult to accomplish when you had to crane your neck to look up at someone. It also helped with online dating, since I was a living, breathing example of what "just under" or "almost" six feet tall looks like. A hint on that? It looked very, *very* different from five foot nine.

Did it also come with its share of weirdos? Sure, but that was the case for any woman—petite, tall, average—who had the courage to put up an online dating profile. We all attracted our share of weirdos. I just got the ones with creatively disgusting feelings for tall ladies.

I'd never let other people's opinions of my height dictate any aspect of my wardrobe, and I damn sure wasn't going to start tonight. It was Saturday night in Vegas, I was celebrating, and I was going to do it in the sexiest pair of high heels I owned.

## JAMIE

"Right this way, Mr. Standard," the hostess at L'Andier said with a smile.

I returned her smile and followed her to a low table marked as "Reserved" and tucked into a corner to the left of the bar. It was private without being isolated and provided a view of the entire interior of the restaurant. So much for grabbing dinner at the bar. I should've known Jocelyn would have other plans for me even if she weren't here. Briefly, I wondered if there were small tables like this with reserved signs at each of the restaurants in the hotel.

"Thank you," I said, accepting the menu and wine list from the hostess.

"My pleasure," she responded. "Andreas will be your server this evening and he'll be right with you."

Once she was gone, I set the menu aside and relaxed back in my seat to survey the place. Force of habit had me analyzing the table count and seating layout. Based on my quick assessment, it appeared efficiently organized with enough space between tables for diners to feel comfortable and not crowded, but close enough to make the restaurant appear bustling and busy.

*Nice work, Joss,* I mentally congratulated my sister.

My eyes traveled toward the bar that took up the center of the restaurant. Highbacked barstools in buttery upholstered leather lined the bar top, each one occupied with a patron. Again, they weren't clustered or shoved in too close, but placed evenly to give people space. Space they could choose to close or use to keep their distance, depending on the customer.

Customers all of whom appeared to be enjoying themselves. My gaze traveled down the line of the bar to the corner where it snagged on the longest, loveliest set of legs I'd ever seen. Tanned, muscular and so long it would take all night to work your way up if you started at the ankle strap of the heeled sandals she wore. But good God what a journey that would be up those miles and miles of satiny skin. These were the pair of legs ZZ Top sang about, the set of stems that would've made Christian look twice in *Clueless*, and that could've been the model for the lamp in *A Christmas Story*.

A starched white shirt came in between me and the object of my ogle. "Good evening, sir, I'm Andreas and I'll be your server tonight. Can I get you something to drink?"

The back of my neck heated with embarrassment at being caught drooling over the poor, unsuspecting woman. Not that the waiter knew either the object or the direction of my thoughts, but still, staring like some horny teenager was pathetic even if only I knew I'd been doing it.

I cleared my throat, keeping my eyes firmly on his broadly smiling face. "Yes, thanks. I'll have a glass of the Leviathan red blend, please."

"Certainly, sir. I'll get that for you and be back to discuss the specials."

*Is one of them seated at the corner of the bar?* I gave myself a mental shake. *Get a hold of yourself, Jamie. Jesus.* What was wrong with me today? I blamed the lube incident at the airport. That, and its beguiling owner, had thrown me off my game and put me in a suggestible headspace, open to thoughts of long legs, smooth skin and . . .

*Dammit!*

Even as I chastised myself, my eyes returned to the bar. This time, however, they made it beyond the legs that had tripped them up before. Up the slope of her thigh, over the hem of the royal blue shorts she wore, across the fitted black tank top, to the smooth sheet of . . . red hair that rippled over her shoulders. Her face was angled away from me, but I felt a tug in my subconscious at the sight of all that hair.

I shook my head, convinced I was being ridiculous. What were the odds I'd run into the woman from the airport here? Not good, even in Vegas. Plus, her hair had been wild and unruly. A rioting curly mass of copper waves. This woman's hair was straight and sleek. Yeah, it was long, but there was no way it could be the same pers—

She turned to signal the bartender, which let me see her full profile. Her angular profile with its sharp cheekbones and resolute chin I knew from that morning would jut out a bit when she was challenged. She laughed in response to something the bartender said, tilting her head back and smiling wide. The movement let the light catch on her face just enough to highlight wide-set eyes and confirm it. The lube connoisseur from the airport was the owner of the legs of my dreams, and her tight little tail was sitting across the bar from me.

I hesitated. My trip to see Jocelyn was well timed, given the havoc that stupid article could wreak on a development deal I'd spent the better part of the last year working toward. I'd eaten, slept and breathed the Union Square project and had been putting the final touches on the last of it—a tricky piece of land acquisition—when *Boston Commons* published the *Rakes* article. Given Gabriel Shattucks was the party from whom we needed to acquire the land, Davidson, Gideon—our third partner at Standard—and I decided it was best that I took a step back for the moment while we waited to see if there would be any real fallout.

Shattucks was old Boston money, Brahmin to the core. Which meant there were only three times it was acceptable to be mentioned in the paper—when you're born, married and once you die. Shirtless, sweating and under the label of "bad boy" or the wonderfully alliterative "Developer Dandy" fell into none of those categories. Which meant at the moment I wasn't the right person to helm the Union Square project. A fact we'd all agreed on before I left for Vegas.

"Just until things calm down enough to get everything back on track," Davidson had said in his mediator's voice, low and reassuring.

The decision left me on one of my first nonworking vacations since we'd started Standard Development. It was eerie not having to constantly check my phone, or dial in to a conference call or any other number of things I'd done every other time I was out of the office. There was nothing relaxing to me about not being needed. The rush of the deal was something I lived for and being sidelined during one of the biggest of my career ate at me. As in, it took big, honking bites out of my insides. It left me restless and uneasy, even though I knew my stepping away was the right thing to do. Knowing it didn't make being cast out any easier to accept. The Union Square development was my baby, my brainchild. I'd spent the last several months crafting a well-honed plan to approach Shattucks about selling to us. An approach that might now be made by someone other than me.

My seat on the proverbial sidelines also put a big damper on what would've been my normal course of action at a second chance with a woman I found as intriguing as this one. Hesitation would not have been my first reaction, but for the fact I'd promised to keep a low profile and stay out of trouble while in Vegas. I could hear Davidson's voice in my head confirming that yes, a woman who traveled with odd-size luggage that weighed a ton and from which spilled huge containers of personal lubricant was in fact the exact sort of trouble he wanted me to avoid.

And yet . . . those legs. Those legs that were currently swiveling back and forth on a stool, jauntily wiggling one sandaled foot.

I could relate to those poor bulls and their reaction to red capes, because the desire to charge forward and claim the seat next to her stampeded through me with an acute urgency. Each little flip of her foot equivalent to a taunting flick of red fabric.

"Your wine, sir," Andreas said, setting the stemware in front of me without a single slosh of the ruby red liquid within it. I'd have been impressed, if I hadn't been so annoyed at his once again blocking my view.

"We have several specials tonight," he continued, oblivious to my trying to see through him to the bar. He rattled off several items that I failed to hear, because through the crook of his arm, I'd seen a man approach the bar and take the seat next to her. *Fuck.*

"Perhaps you'd care for something from the regular menu, then?"

Andreas's question made me realize he'd stopped listing specials and was waiting for my response to them. For any response, really, since I'd sat there mutely for longer than socially appropriate.

"Uh, I'll have the filet, please."

"Very good, sir," Andreas said, and, after several more questions related to temperature, accompaniment, and side choice, he left and cleared my view of the bar once again. Only this time, I didn't like anything about it.

The guy I'd seen on approach now leaned toward my airport angel in an all too possessive way. Her responsive shift in posture signaled she didn't much care for it either. The way her legs were now crossed in the opposite direction, her foot stilled from its previously relaxed bouncing and the slight stiffening of her shoulders transmitted her disinterest in the guy's intrusion as loudly as if she'd screamed it. Given his failure to pick up on her body language, it seemed like she might have to. Whether his ignorance of it was willful or not, his shifting his stool closer and putting his hand on the back of hers had me rising from my seat and moving toward the bar without any further conscious thought.

But she was faster, swinging those muscular legs of hers around with enough force to push her stool back from the bar and knock his hand away. Sliding gracefully to her feet, she rose to her full height and frowned down at him. Though I was still too far to hear, I saw the sharp sting of her words land in the way the guy flinched when she spoke. Flinched and then frowned, his skin going a mottled red as he pushed off his own stool to square off with her.

Only, there was nothing square or even about the two of them facing off. She'd been tall at the airport, but in heels she was a statuesque gladiator ready to smite the guy who'd been stupid enough to challenge her. He took a step back, bumping into his chair. Her brow arched and she crossed her arms, staring down at him imperiously.

I was now close enough to hear her snap, "Nothing else to say, then?"

Recovering somewhat from his obvious surprise at being towered over by a woman, he spluttered, "I was just trying to pay you a compliment, Jesus."

"That would imply that I am in any way interested in what you think of me, which, as we've established, I am not."

"You don't have to be such a bit—"

"Is there a problem here?" I interjected, cutting in before he could finish, and I'd have to beat the crap out of him. A barfight in my little sister's hotel would not qualify as lying low.

The redhead turned, already speaking, "You mean other than this . . ." Blue-gray eyes went wide at the sight of me, and her words tapered off as her brows shot up. "What are you doing here?"

"We meet again," I said, smiling at her. "Lucky for me since I didn't catch your name at the airport." Tilting my head back toward my table,

I went on. "I was having dinner and noticed your . . . altercation and wanted to make sure everything was all right."

The idiot decided to answer for her. "Everything was fine until she got all bitchy about someone trying to be nice to her. It's like you can't even be nice to a woman anymore without them trying t—GAH!"

"That," I said, pressing my thumb harder at the point just above the bend of his elbow, "is a pressure point." I let my fingers wrap around his arm, digging my thumb in further and eliciting a weaker whimpering sound from him as his forearm drooped uselessly at his side.

I leaned back to take in his face, pale beneath its tan with a bit of sweat beading on his forehead. "This may be hard for you to grasp," I pushed in again and he squeaked. "But you don't have the right to talk to a woman simply because you happen to think she's attractive. If you do, she has every right to tell you to fuck off. That doesn't make her a bitch, it makes her a human being entitled to enjoy her evening without you encroaching into it unbidden. And your only response to her request for you to fuck off should be, 'Sorry I bothered you.' And then, know what you do next?"

I relaxed my grip on his arm, hoping he might know the correct answer. When he didn't immediately respond, I pressed in harder. "I asked you a question, sir. What do you do when a woman tells you to fuck off?"

He licked his lips, a bead of sweat sliding down his face. "I f-f-f-fuck off," he stammered.

"Now you're getting it," I said, with a robust clap to his back. I stepped back, still gripping his arm, but no longer putting any pressure on the nerve. I nodded toward the luxuriously tall redhead, whose brows remained close to her hairline. "What do you say to the nice lady?"

"S-s-sorry I bothered you." I wondered if his stammer would be permanent and then found I didn't give a shit.

"Very good," I said, as though speaking to a petulant child. I released him and he staggered back, clutching at his arm and staring at me with fear so palpable I could taste it. "You managed Part A of our lesson," I said. "But you're still struggling with Part B."

When he simply continued to stare without moving, I leaned closer. He blanched and took a step back. I sighed. "And here I thought you understood." Baring my teeth in a snarl-like smile, I said, "Fuck. Off."

# chapter four

## CORAL

I watched the entitled man-child scurry off like a rat back to its dark corner, thrilled and a bit appalled by whatever it was that just happened. The thrill was winning by a landslide, though. The appalled part was more on principal than any real objection to Airport Guy stepping in to hand the little weasel his ass. I'd had the situation under control . . . but damn, it had been nice for him to ride to the rescue and finish the job.

"Are you all right?"

The question brought my gaze back to the man I'd semi-met in the airport earlier that day. The man who'd used some version of the Vulcan death grip powerful enough to make the creep from the bar scuttle back to his lair of bros. Used it like it was as commonplace as a handshake and as equally unremarkable.

I hadn't even understood what was happening until it was mostly over. One second he'd asked me a question and the next he'd moved seamlessly to take the other man's arm in that punishing grip. Hard enough to make him *squeal*.

Yes, yes, the thrill of it was definitely winning. So much so that whatever small portion of me remained appalled was being shouted down in a filibuster of epic proportion by my entire reproductive system that was now intent upon having this man sire a brood of children. Shoving down my innate cavewoman response to link myself to the strongest hunter and procreate, I focused on his question.

"Yes," I replied. "I'm fine."

He smiled, and it was as dazzling as it had been earlier that day. Dimples winking on in all their glory, teeth gleaming in a nice, straight line of white enamel, and full lips curving in a way that skated right next to wicked without quite getting there. In another suit, this one a black so deep it bordered on obsidian, he looked every inch the debonair gentlemen. And there were a lot of inches of him.

In my heels, I stood six foot three and he was taller. Not much, but still. The number of times I'd had to look up, even by an inch, to meet a man's eyes I could count on one hand and have fingers left over. Thrilling, indeed.

"I'm glad to hear that," he said, his voice rich and deep. It now lacked the sharp edge from when he'd spoken to our erstwhile companion. "I . . . uh . . ." He rubbed the back of his neck. "I didn't mean to overstep, but I saw you from across the bar there and thought you might need . . . er, that is I wanted to make sure you *didn't* need any assistance."

I acknowledged the flutter of pride at this man noticing me from across the room. I also noted the way he walked back that I needed him to step in and took pride in that as well. Even if he thought I needed help, he'd recognized my handling of the situation and gave it the deference it deserved.

"Is that always how you offer assistance, by making grown men cry?"

"I hardly think he could be called a grown man by any reasonable standard."

"Oh, why is that?"

His smile was back, this time trending most assuredly toward wicked. "Because a grown man—a real grown man—wouldn't have required the lesson I taught him tonight. He would've learned it early and wouldn't need to be reminded."

*Well, that was fucking hot.* My cavewoman instincts roared back to life, demanding that I mate with this man right there on the bar to lock things down and make him my hunter. Ignoring her, I asked, "Chivalry is part of your DNA, then?"

He nodded. "My mother made sure of it."

"Are you some sort of newly minted Disney hero, here in Vegas for beta testing or something?"

He laughed. "What?"

I shrugged. "You dress like . . ." I waved a hand at his clearly expensive suit ". . . *that* while vanquishing trolls and extolling the lessons of chivalry bred into you by your mother. If you start drawing moral parallels for me, I'm out of here."

Another laugh. "No parallels, I promise. The last thing I want is for you to leave. Especially not before I learn your name. As I said, I didn't catch it at the airport."

A fizz of awareness worked its way through me in a pleasantly carbonated sensation, tickling its way along my nerve endings. "You didn't catch it because I didn't throw it your way," I replied, softening my response with a teasing grin.

He matched it with one of his own. "Really want to start off discussing what you threw at me in the airport?"

There was no stopping the flaming blush that stole over my cheeks at the reminder of my Astroglide sailing toward him. Pushing down my embarrassment, I put a hand on my hip and narrowed my gaze. "And here I thought you didn't want me to leave."

A deep chuckle rumbled out of him, and he held up a hand. "My apologies. Not exactly living up to my Prince Charming potential, am I?"

Electric blue eyes grew serious, and he seemed to get closer, even though he hadn't moved. It was as though the space between us shrank when I met his gaze.

"Well," I said, heady with confidence from the way he was looking at me. "If you don't want me to leave, what is it you want me to do?"

The fizzing feeling expanded until it felt like electricity had taken over my bloodstream. I could feel the snap, crackle and pop of it pulsing through me. If my base level instincts knew what electricity was, they would've been thrilled. Instead, they gestured excitedly toward him in rudimentary and extremely graphic sign language.

"The better question, I believe," he said, tucking his hands in the pockets of his slacks, "is what you want to do."

I leaned against the back of my barstool, mimicking his casual posture. "How can I know the answer to that question if I don't know my options?"

I could feel the weight of his gaze as it traveled over my face, outlining each of my features. Pulling a hand from his pocket, he rubbed a thumb over his bottom lip. "A woman like you should have every option she wants."

"A woman like me?" I laughed. "And what kind of woman is that?"

He stepped closer. Close enough to show interest, but not so close it felt overbearing. His hand dropped from his face to rest against the corner of the bar. I took note of the casually careful way he made sure not to cage me in. "The kind of woman who makes a certain kind of man hope she wants to join him for dinner."

"A certain kind of man, huh?" It was my turn to move closer, pushing away from the barstool and standing just outside his personal space. The fizz in my bloodstream was at an all-time high, his proximity generating a sparkling frenzy the excited hiss of which I could practically hear.

He nodded.

"Not the kind of man you chased off a few minutes ago?"

His mouth flattened and those thick brows carved down into a deep V. "I think we've established that wasn't a real man."

"If not him," I dipped my chin to cut him a look, working my mascaraed lashes to their full effect. "Then who?"

His hand tightened its grip on the bar, making me wonder what his forearms looked like under his suit jacket and dress shirt. "Then me," he said, and those two words brought the sparks in my bloodstream to a dazzlingly bright crescendo.

Was it a reaction to his rescue? Was I still riding the high of being in Vegas and starting this dream job? Was it the deliciously ice-cold glass of tequila I'd finished? Was it all three? I didn't know and didn't care. All I did know was that I was extremely attracted to this man in a way I very much enjoyed. Somehow—call it fate, kismet, blind luck, or whatever—Airport Guy had reappeared in my path tonight. I wasn't the kind of woman to question something like that. I was the kind of woman who embraced it.

## JAMIE

After she assured Andreas another place setting wasn't necessary—"Thanks so much, but I've already eaten"—my erstwhile airport buddy agreed to join me while I had dinner.

"What about a glass of wine?" I offered.

Twisting the bottle to see the label, she traced a green painted nail over the picture of the giant squid featured there. Looking to me, she asked, "Are you a fan of mythical sea creatures?"

"I'm a fan of reds," I said, which made her laugh.

Nodding at Andreas, she said, "A glass of this would be great, thanks." He hustled off to get her a glass, while she relaxed back into her chair. Her calf grazed mine in the process, but she didn't pull away. Just shifted a little, her knee brushing mine.

"Sorry," I said, moving back in my own seat to try to create more space. A failed effort on my part, since it resulted in my knee coming to rest between hers. I felt the delicate press of her thighs on either side of my leg, warm through the fabric of my slacks. Stifling the inclination to prolong the contact, I swiveled to my left.

"Sorry," I said again, lifting my glass to wet my suddenly dry throat.

She smiled and shook her head. "Don't worry about it, please. I've lived with these," she gestured generically beneath the table, "since I was about twelve. Believe me, I'm practically immune to my knees playing bumper cars with my dining companions."

Denying the sting delivered to my male pride by her alleged immunity to our legs constantly touching would've made me a liar. Especially since I was anything but immune to the sensation.

"Although," she added, "I will say this is the first time in a while I've had to maneuver around someone with quite so much length to them."

I almost choked on my sip of wine, setting the glass down on the table so hard its contents sloshed precariously near the rim. Andreas would've been disappointed in me. Clearing my throat with a rough sound, I blinked at her. She smiled back at me, a playful glint in her eyes that let me know she knew what she'd said and even more so how it sounded.

"Well, I . . ." I cleared my throat again. "I can't say I've ever apologized for my . . . length before."

She lifted a shoulder, the movement making her hair slide behind it. "Why would you? I can't imagine there've been many complaints."

Andreas set down my filet and filled the glass he'd brought for her, studiously ignoring our conversation like a seasoned Vegas pro.

Once he departed, I said, "No complaints that I'm aware of. At least, not until tonight."

Unbidden, a quote from the *Rakes* article popped into my head. *Jamie's relationships with women are more window dressing than reality.*

Pushing away the unwelcome intrusion, I refocused on my dinner companion. "Oh, I'm not complaining," she said, her smile morphing into a lopsided grin that pressed one corner of her mouth higher into her cheek while her mesmerizing eyes sparkled with mischief. "I'm just observing."

Her leg brushed the outside of mine in a long, slow slide that was unmistakably intentional.

"You know," I said, extending my leg toward her and enjoying the slight flare of her nostrils and twitch of her brows. *Immune my ass.* "I feel like we need to revisit something."

Her foot hooked around my calf. "Oh?" she asked, one brow quirking upward. "I'm satisfied with the direction we're heading. Why go back?"

My fork clattered against my plate as her foot teased the back of my calf. "Well," I said, trying to focus on words instead of the slow back-and-forth stroke of her foot. "Because normally when I'm heading in this direction, I at least know the name of the person I'm traveling with."

She laughed, her foot continuing its impersonation of the sexiest metronome in the history of time. "Do you normally come to the rescue of women through the use of another guy's pressure points?"

"Normally?" I shook my head, slicing off a piece of steak and chewing as I considered her question. "No, I think to be considered 'normal' something has to occur regularly."

"Okay. And when you're, as you said, headed in this direction, does that normally occur in Vegas?"

"Well, no," I admitted. "I should add that 'normal' in this instance shouldn't be interpreted as my traveling this direction regularly with multiple different people. I mean, I don't walk the road solitarily all the time or anything, either." I huffed out a breath at how off the rails I was getting. "What I'm trying to say is that I'm on this road with the appropriate amount of frequency both with a companion and by myself."

"Good to know," she said, her half grin hitching higher as her foot did the same on my leg. "But I think we can agree that nothing about tonight has been normal, right?"

"Yeah," I agreed. Concentration was becoming more difficult with each inch higher her foot climbed, but I did my best. I'd had a point here. I knew I'd had an initial point before I got bogged down in the whole traveling analogy. I felt the brush of her toes against the back of my knee and struggled mightily to remember what point I'd been trying to make.

*Her name, dipshit,* my subconscious helpfully reminded me. *You're trying to get her to tell you her name.*

"My point is that I'd really like to know your name. Hell, I'd love to hear about anything you feel like telling me," I said, pushing my steak to the side and reaching under the table to catch the back of her heel. The skin at her ankle was smooth and cool to the touch. My fingers twitched with the desire to move higher and find out if she was that cool and smooth all the way up her leg. But I held firm, waiting for her answer.

Her laugh was warm and rich as she shook her head. "*My* point," she said, lifting her foot and moving my hand farther up her leg, "is you don't need to know all of that for tonight to be what it's supposed to be."

The consistent refusal on her part to disclose anything personal snagged like a burr in my chest. Why was she so opposed to giving me her name? And why was I so determined to gather any crumb I could about this woman?

*Jamie's interest in women is like the Everglades—expansive, yet surprisingly shallow.*

That article was really fucking with my head tonight and, if I weren't careful, it could ruin what promised to be a spectacular evening. Determined to get back into the groove, I stroked a thumb against her calf and watched the hint of blue in her eyes gleam like a dark jewel as her lashes fluttered and her throat moved with a swallow. "And what is tonight supposed to be?" I asked.

"Anything but normal."

My mouth went dry, and my pulse roared in my ears at the thought of doing "anything but normal" with this woman. It held a primal, visceral appeal. But then so did knowing her name, which she'd somehow made more intimate than the tantalizing evening she was offering.

I swallowed, resting my free hand on the table. "That is a very appealing concept."

She leaned forward, trailing her fingers between mine. "It is, isn't it?"

"It'd sound even better if I knew your name."

She sighed, picking up her glass and taking a long swallow. "Today has been a great day for me." She eyed me. "Aside from tossing my Astroglide at your feet in the airport . . ." Her cheeks went a little pink and she grinned. "Kudos on not fully bringing that up yet, by the way."

"A gentleman never discusses lube before dessert," I said, returning her grin.

She laughed. "Anyway, it's been one of the better days of my life. Really, it's the start of some of the best, I think. Assuming everything pans out the way I hope it will. I'd like to take tonight and celebrate the start of these better days. And I'd like you to be a part of that celebration. But I don't want to pretend this is going to be anything more than what it is—a single night with a devastatingly sexy and achingly chivalrous man that fate saw fit to toss into my path twice in the same day. I want to take my . . ." She cocked her head and looked at me with a calculating expression before continuing, "We'll say six foot four welcome to Vegas gift, spend an incredible night with him doing all of the things you only do with someone you just met in Vegas and not have any expectations that it's anything more than that. Tonight has been awesome and will, hopefully, get even better. But it's tonight and that's it. Which means I don't need to know who you are, or why you're here or where you're going when you leave here. I know all I need to know about you right now, just like you do about me. There's no need to take that part of this any further than we have."

Where we'd taken it was exactly nowhere. All I knew was what I'd learned at the airport. She was in Vegas for a new job. Beyond that, the woman was a complete mystery. Her logic for keeping it that way was sound, sort of. Fewer complications and all that. I didn't like it, but could see where she was coming from. But I still couldn't let it go.

"What am I supposed to call you if I don't know your name?" I asked.

"That hasn't been a problem yet."

"I haven't been naked and inside you yet," I said, testing her commitment to a single night of just sex. "That makes a difference."

If her eyes had been hot before, they were now a blaze of blue flames surrounded by swirling smoke. She pulled her lower lip between her teeth with a wet sucking sound that transmitted directly to my dick.

"What do you normally call women in the middle of sex?" she asked, her voice husky.

"I thought we agreed this was anything but normal."

Her laugh was low and silky. "Touché. You're not going to let this go, are you?"

I shook my head, surprised by my own tenacity. "No, I don't think so."

"In that case, you can call me Ariel."

"I can call you that, or it's your name?"

"I'll answer to it."

Lust and frustration warred within me, and I couldn't figure out why. What did it matter if this woman didn't want to give me her name? She'd made it clear this was a one-night deal. Why was I pushing this? Why did it matter? Why was I making this into something bigger with this quest for her name? God knew I wasn't in a position to deal with anything more than what she was offering. Not with the Shattucks deal on tenterhooks back in Boston. One night with a girl who was giving me an obviously fake name was about all I could handle right now. I should shut up and accept that if she wanted me to call her Ariel, I should fucking call her Ariel and give her the night she wanted.

The night *I* wanted. Even as I told myself this, tried to convince myself it was the right thing to do . . . it didn't fit. Like a shirt that was slightly too small, shrugging into the idea felt wrong and uncomfortable. It tugged and caught in all the wrong places in my brain. Most notably on the quotes from that stupid fucking article that kept cropping up when least expected. And the way I'd started questioning whether there was any validity to how I'd been portrayed. And what I could do to change it.

It was the ultimate irony to be confronted with all my romantic shortcomings in that article only to have them be my best attributes in the pursuit of the living breathing fantasy of a woman in front of me. The moment I'd started wondering how to be a better man, I met a woman who wasn't the least bit interested in changing my ways. She wasn't even interested in *learning* my ways. She wanted the guy who only went skin deep, so who was I to question it? And what more could there be for us after tonight, anyway? I needed to embrace the now and accept what she was willing to give. My existential crisis could wait until I was back in Boston.

Because I could tell she wasn't going to cave. She'd decided this was as far as she'd bend on the name issue. I knew innately that if I pushed, she'd be gone. Fate or not, she'd drawn a line in the sand and wasn't going to let me cross it. I didn't want her to go. Didn't want my night with her to end.

"Okay, Ariel," I said, squeezing her calf. "I'm Ja—"

She held up a hand. "Nope, don't want to know."

I swallowed my protest and nodded. "Fair enough."

# chapter five

## CORAL

The way he'd pouted when I'd refused to give him my name or any other details about myself was adorable. It wasn't a description I'd expected to associate with him. Hot, sexy, smoldering. All of those easily leapt to mind at the sight of my dinner date. But the way his forehead wrinkled, and the corners of his lips turned down with disappointment at being told no—something I doubted he heard often from the fairer sex—had been downright precious. Or was it precocious? Maybe a little of both. Either way, I'd had to hide my smile to not give away how cute I thought it was.

As tempting as it was to give in to his doggedly determined quest, I'd learned my lesson on handing out personal details too early on. It never ended well. I wasn't famous by any stretch of the imagination. But, I did have a decent social media following coupled with a unique name. I mean, c'mon, a professional mermaid named Coral Triton? Easiest internet search EVER. With everything you could find out about a person on the internet, it was better for a single woman in my position to protect herself with a little anonymity.

And, while I didn't get the creeper vibe from smoking hot Airport Guy, it never hurt to be careful. Plus, it wasn't like this was going anywhere, so what did it matter if I gave him a fake name? We'd have our one night in Vegas and go our separate ways without any expectations, or opportunities for internet sleuthing on either of our parts.

With no expectations, you weren't left wondering if they'd call, or why they hadn't called, or what was wrong with you that kept them from calling. All questions I'd grown up hearing my mother ask her friends on the regular. Discussions that were often followed by an announcement that we were moving. Again.

"We're off to greener pastures, Coral," she'd say as she perfected her winged eyeliner in the mirror. "This place"—whatever place it was where she'd experienced her most recent heartbreak—"doesn't have anything left for us."

And, anyway, it wasn't like my professional life allowed much space for anything long term. I needed the freedom to pick up and go if an opportunity came up. Being tied down was not an option for me. At least, it hadn't been. Now, though, if things worked out with this new job, permanence instead of transitory would become a plausible option for me.

Maybe that was why I'd almost given in tonight. Almost succumbed to the what ifs that ran through my brain during our debate over his request for my name. What ifs I normally pushed aside the moment they entered the chat. What if he would be in Vegas for longer than a few days? What if the look on his face when he heard the name that obviously wasn't my real one came from genuine disappointment? From a legitimate, heartfelt desire to know me.

What stopped me, though, was the knowledge that men who looked like him, wore suits like his and who swooped in to save women from aspirating on the cologne of douchebags the world over were not residents of cities like Vegas. They came to places like this to close a deal, attend a conference, or just blow off steam for a few days before going back to their real lives. Their presence here was a transient state. Blink and you'll miss it. For men like him, Vegas, and all the places like it, was little more than a way station.

Which meant there would be little chance, even if I told him my name or some other detail, that I'd ever see him again. So, my innate sense of self-preservation rose up within me and quashed the unfamiliar desire to share more of myself with this guy and learn more about him.

I didn't need to think about what names started with "J," or whether the earlier disappointment I'd seen in his eyes was real. I needed to stay realistic myself and keep in mind not what was possible between us, but what was plausible. Plausible was safe because it was practical. It was plausible for me to take advantage of the fact that he was here now without considering what could happen after. It was plausible we'd have tonight, and that would be it. There'd be no exchange of names, numbers, or other personal details beyond our current sexual health status. He would be the perfect end to a great day. Nothing more.

Our waiter appeared with the check, and, with the hand not on my leg, my plausible partner took the smooth black booklet with a smile. "Thank you, Andreas," he said. "Everything was great."

He glanced at the barely touched steak on the table and frowned. "Are you sure? I could bring you something else, Mr. Sta—"

"No need," he said quickly, keeping Andreas from revealing his last name. "My appetite just shifted a bit, that's all." I felt the look he shot me like a physical caress and my breath caught in my throat with the impact of it. Tonight was going to be *fun*.

While he scribbled his signature and what I assumed was his room number on the check, I stroked my foot along the inside of his thigh, letting him know I appreciated his effort. His nostrils flared at the same time his fingers gripped the muscle of my calf.

"Can I get you anything else?" Andreas asked him, oblivious to the body language discussion the two of us were having.

He shook his head, hand relaxing on my calf. "No, I think we're good here, thank you."

With a slight bow, Andreas left, and we were alone once again.

"Is this the part when I ask if you want to get out of here?" He punctuated the question with a rippling stroke of his fingers. "Or is that too cliché?"

"Depends," I said, easing my foot forward and making him stiffen in his seat.

"On what?"

"On whether you're in a position to stand up right now."

His grin was all temptation and heat as his hand came to my heel and drew my foot the rest of the way up his thigh. "I don't know," he said. "What do you think?"

The heels I wore bared the arch of my foot, the curve of which he'd positioned against his lap in a way that let me know he was looking forward to the next phase of the evening as much as I was. Unless he'd stuffed a sleeve of poker chips down his pants, the night's potential had firmed up in a major way.

"I think," I said, angling my foot to put the slightest hint of pressure against his crotch, "that I want to get out of here."

The rumbling noise that came from somewhere deep within him made my inner thighs clench and my breathing speed up.

"To be clear," he said, brushing a thumb against my instep, "you want to get out of here with me."

He said "with me" in a low, decadent voice that rolled over me like a wave, making me shiver with anticipation. Even though it was a statement and not a question, I nodded, biting my lower lip and enjoying the way his eyes lasered in on my mouth. It was a hungry look. No, hungry wasn't right. Voracious was the only word that worked for that look. A look that said he could devour me in one gulp while still savoring the taste, and I felt it *everywhere*.

With a purposefully slow movement, I let my lip slide free and said, "Every last inch of you."

"Jesus fucking Christ," he swore softly and rubbed a hand over his face. "You're killing me, Ariel."

For the barest fraction of a second, a millisecond really, I hated that he didn't know my real name. But then he was moving, standing from his chair to make certain adjustments for polite company, and coming to help me from mine. And the moment passed. Replaced by the thrill of having him all to myself until morning.

We made our way out of the restaurant and into the casino, his hand at my lower back the whole time. The warm spread of his fingers just above the waistband of my shorts was like a prelude to the rest of the night. A hint of a touch holding the promise of so much more. It was sexy, the way he let his hand rest there, never dipping below to the curve of my ass, or sliding higher up my side. Just settled, confidently posses-sive, at the small of my back. Staking an unmistakable claim with that simple touch. I refused to examine why I liked it so much.

Plus, I couldn't think too much about it, because instead of steering me toward the queue of people at the elevator he directed us back toward the main lobby and the front doors.

"I thought you were staying at this hotel," I said, slowing my steps. His hand never left its place on my back, his thumb sweeping rhythmi-cally back and forth to the left of my spine in a slow arc. Again, a light touch, but it sent liquid heat sizzling through me, nonetheless. I glanced over at him, but his face was impassive.

"I am," he replied, still heading toward the main doors of the hotel.

"Then where are we going?"

"Given that we don't know each other's names and you've steadfastly avoided any and all of my attempts to wheedle anything personal out of you or even tell you my name, I can't ask if you trust me. Because, again, you know nothing about me by your own design."

"Okay," I said slowly, wondering what had happened to change the trajectory of the evening.

Jamie pulled me to a stop in front of the aquarium and his hand slid back to his side. "I know we both agreed what road we're on tonight. A road that will, hopefully, end with you gloriously naked and rumpled in my sheets."

My body pulsed at the image of being sweaty and tangled up in the sheets with him. Heat crept up my chest at the thought. "Hence my confusion as to why we are headed *outside*."

His grin was infectiously boyish, almost bashful. "We've got all night, gorgeous. And even if you won't give me any personal identifiers . . ."

I laughed and his grin spread as he continued. "Even if you won't give me anything too terribly personal, I'd like to spend a little more time learning what you're willing to share with me. Anything you're comfortable telling me, even if it's just your favorite color or the name of your dog in high school."

He shrugged, the bashful look returning. "There's just something about you, Ariel." His eyes rolled slightly at the moniker, and he shook his head. "Something about you that makes me want to know more. And not just why you carry quarts of Astroglide."

I laughed. "We haven't had dessert yet, so technically you can't bring that up."

"Then join me for dessert," he said, crooking his elbow out in invitation. "I promise we'll get to the destination we both want, but let's enjoy the journey a bit more first, okay?"

I hesitated, glancing from his offered arm to his earnest face. He was proposing a detour from the path of simple physical pleasure. One I'd made a point of avoiding after Doug. But I'd already had dinner with the guy, what harm could come from joining him for dessert? It wasn't like he'd proposed waterboarding me until I told him my life story.

I slipped my hand into his elbow, enjoying the feel of strong muscle beneath the finely woven fabric of his suit coat almost as much as the way his smile spread up to his eyes and made the skin next to them crinkle just a tad. "Lead the way."

# chapter six

## JAMIE

The moment we stepped out into the Vegas night air, I realized my mistake. In her shorts and tank, Ariel wasn't equipped to stroll down the Strip. It might be Vegas, but it was still February. I shrugged out of my suit jacket and draped it over her shoulders.

"Oh, you don't need to do th—"

"Yes, I do," I said, pulling the lapels closed to keep her from shrugging out of the jacket.

She wrinkled her nose, but stopped trying to wiggle out of it. "Won't you be cold?"

I laughed. "If I answer that question the way I usually do, I'm afraid I'm in danger of divulging some of that personal information you seem so allergic to."

Her answering laugh was as bright and vibrant as the rest of her. "Fair enough," she said and looped her arm through mine again. "So, where are we going?"

"Not far," I assured her. "Just over to Caesars. I'd say we could get a car, but . . ."

She glanced out at the traffic crawling by on the busy Strip. "Seems faster to walk."

I nodded. "If you're not too cold, that is."

She shook her head. "No, like you said without saying, I'm used to the cold."

We joined the crowds on the sidewalk to head over to Caesars. I enjoyed the feel of her next to me more than I had anything else in a long time. I wasn't sure what prompted me to suggest our dessert outing. It was obvious she was more interested in heading to my room than heading out. Something that held an equal appeal to me.

But something about her had stirred up some inner part of me that wouldn't just slink back into its corner. It was like her refusal to see me as anything more than a good time made me want to show her I could be. No, that wasn't exactly it. I wanted to know if I could be. If, faced with the chance at something more, I could be more. Which was ludicrous, since this was Vegas, not Boston and there was no way things between us would lead anywhere. The thought was laughable.

And yet, that pull to show her I could be more than a welcome gift remained lodged under my ribcage with an uncomfortable twinge. One that had me leading her to sample desserts and, hopefully, share a little bit more about herself instead of escorting her back to my room. What the hell was wrong with me?

"So," she said, bringing me out of my confusing swirl of thoughts as we dodged around a bachelorette party decked out in feather boas and drunkenly wielding penis straws. "What brings you to Vegas?"

I blinked, sure I'd misheard. "What?" I asked, moving her in front of me so we could navigate around a lively bachelor party trailing in the wake of the bachelorettes. I didn't miss the way several sets of male eyes shifted to Ariel's legs and subtly pulled her closer.

Oblivious to my possessive thoughts, she said, "I thought you wanted to do the small talk thing. I'm not great at it, but figured asking what brought you out here was a good place to start."

She looked at me sideways with the half grin I was starting to like a lot. "Nothing too specific, though. Just cocktail party conversation, okay? Keep that in mind when you're mapping out your twenty questions, or whatever other interrogation techniques you've got planned for dessert."

"You make this sound like an inquisition," I said, guiding her into the expansively gaudy lobby at Caesars. "All I want to do is extend our evening a bit. Think of it as delayed gratification."

"Mm-hmm," she responded noncommittally. "I don't need personal details to know you're a guy used to getting what he wants when he wants it and doesn't enjoy being told no."

"Who does?" I countered, steering her toward the dessert bar Jocelyn had told me about over Christmas.

"Yeah, but I can tell you're not used to hearing it, which makes it much more difficult for you to accept."

With a hand at her elbow, I tugged her to a stop, the scent of vanilla wafting out from the door of the little café. Blue-gray eyes looked expectantly at me from under a fan of inky black lashes. "Let me assure you," I said, needing her to understand I was serious. "When a woman says 'no,' I understand what that means."

Those eyes went soft with her smile, and she put a hand on my chest, her gaze almost level with mine. "That much was obvious in the way you interceded with that slug at the bar earlier tonight. But when a lady is less than forthcoming with personal details, you seem to have some difficulty with the concept."

"Is it so wrong for me to want to get to know you?" I heard the whine in my voice, hating the way it made me sound like a pouting child.

"Not wrong," she replied, toying with a button on my shirt. "Just . . . unexpected. I can't think of many guys who opt for dessert over sex."

I laughed. "It's dessert *before* sex. Big difference."

"Noted," she said, giggling. Tipping her head toward the restaurant, she added, "Speaking of dessert, are you going to actually let me have some, or just stand out here smelling it all night?"

"I'm not a monster," I said, placing a hand at the small of her back and leading her through the door. "And to answer your first small talk question, I'm in Vegas visiting my sister. She moved out here for work last year and this is the first chance I've had to visit."

"Older or younger?" she asked as we waited for the hostess to return to the podium.

"She's the baby," I said. "I'm the oldest." Glancing down at her, I asked, "Do you have any siblings?"

She shook her head. "No, it's just me." The way she said it struck me as sad. Not, I'm an only child, or it's just me and my parents. It sounded so much more solitary the way she said it and made me want to pull her close. Given she seemed fine with physical stuff, I gave in to the impulse and wrapped an arm around her shoulders, tucking her next to my side.

Glancing up at me, she gave me a puzzled look. Unable to explain my sudden need to hold her, I chose distraction instead. "You're here for work, too, right?"

Nodding, she said, "Yes, I start in a few days."

"And I'm guessing you won't tell me where."

She laughed. "You're finally catching on."

"What if I guess?" I asked, which only made her laugh harder.

"You can certainly try," she said.

"And you'll tell me if I'm right?"

"Maybe."

"Showgirl at the Cosmopolitan," I said instantly.

Her nose wrinkled and her lips twisted to one side as she considered something. "Do they even have showgirls at places other than the Flamingo these days?"

I shrugged. "I have no idea, but judging from your facial expression, my first guess was incorrect."

"No, I am not a showgirl at the Cosmopolitan," she confirmed, right as the hostess appeared.

"Sorry for the wait," she said, a little breathless. "We're a little short staffed tonight. Just the two of you?"

At our confirmation, she let us know it would be another few minutes before hustling away. When we were alone again, I said, "Newest celebrity chef whose specialty is a deconstructed crème brûlée."

She grinned and shook her head. "Sounds delicious, but no. I can actually make a delicious Spaghetti Bolognese, but crème brûlée—constructed and deconstructed—is way beyond my skill set." Blue-gray eyes cut sideways at me. "And if I were a celebrity, wouldn't you know who I was?"

I shrugged. "Not necessarily. I'm a thirty-nine-year-old guy with an MBA. Celebrities aren't exactly my specialty."

"An MBA, huh?" Cocking her head to the side, she gave me a once-over, as though just seeing me. "So, you're what, some sort of finance bro?"

"Ouch," I said, clutching at my chest.

"Ouch because I'm on target, or ouch because you're offended?"

"I'm offended you'd even have to ask if you're on target with that. Do I look like a finance bro?" I gestured down the front of my body. "Do you see a quilted vest embroidered with some company logo?" I turned in a dramatically slow circle. "Ray-Bans hanging from Croakies anywhere?" Holding out my sleeves for her inspection, I asked, "Monograms on my shirt cuffs? And have I once mentioned the word 'capital' or 'IPO'?"

Her giggle turned into a loud snort, which made her eyes go wide and she clapped a hand over her mouth. I snapped my fingers. "I've got it. You're auditioning for the live action Muppet Show as the role of Mis—"

Hands on hips, she cut me off with a narrow-eyed glare. "If you say Miss Piggy, I won't be held responsible for my actions." Glare aside, there was a hint of a smile on her lips.

I held up my own hands in surrender. "That was too far, my mistake."

"You can make it up to me with macarons," she said as the hostess reappeared to lead us to our table.

## CORAL

"You seem to have a special talent for finding the best table in a place," I said, taking my seat at the table for two tucked into a corner than not only gave us privacy, but also a view of the Atlantis Show through the plate glass window. Even dark, the staging for the show was impressive, with its nine-foot statues perched on Corinthian columns among massive fountains.

His grin was part pride and part self-deprecating, as if he couldn't decide whether he was ashamed of this skill or extremely proud of it. "I'm afraid I can't take credit for the table at the restaurant. That was more of a friends in high places situation. And this . . ." He spread his hands over our table. "This is me slipping a little cash to the hostess because I'm trying to impress a girl."

The flush that crept up my chest was as unexpected as his answer. Sure, it could've been a line. I certainly hadn't seen any exchange of cash between them. But even so, it was a damn good one because I hadn't blushed from a compliment in a long time. "Oh, you're good," I said.

He laughed, unfurling his lavender napkin across his lap, and picking up his light pink menu. The pale, frothy colors stood out starkly against the charcoal of his shirt and pitch-black of his suit pants. Watching me instead of looking at his menu, he said, "My wooing skills are a little rusty, so it's good to hear I haven't completely lost my touch."

"Now that, I find hard to believe," I said, looking at the cavalcade of dessert options spread across the high gloss pages of my own menu. If I hadn't glanced up, I would've missed the quick, but troubled dip of his brows. The movement was so brief I wondered if I'd imagined it. But still, I found myself asking, "Something wrong?"

He started to shake his head, but then pursed his lips and glanced away. His exhale was long and heavy. "Honestly?" he asked, looking back to me. "Tonight with you is the first thing that's gone right in the last week."

There was a swirling sensation in my chest, like a warm ocean current. Blue eyes met mine with an electric snap that ricocheted through me, lighting up every nerve ending like a pinball machine. Everything intensified, and suddenly the brush of the cushion at the back of my thighs felt like a caress. The silk lining of his jacket whispered against my skin and the intoxicatingly earthy scent of his cologne wrapped around me.

"I'm not sure whether to say I'm sorry to hear that, or thank you," I said, my voice coming out huskier than normal.

His laugh was a tad rueful. "Don't feel too bad for me. It's safe to say I should've seen it coming." The hand he pushed through his hair made the blond strands fall in an even sexier tumble than before.

Before I could ask anything else, our waiter appeared. "Good evening," he said, with a brief bow. "I'm Antonio and I'll be your server tonight. I'm happy to go over the menu and answer any questions you might have, but before I do, can I ask if there are any allergies?"

Grateful for the cue, if not necessarily the interruption, I said, "Thank you for asking. I've got celiac disease, so I'll need a rundown on the gluten-free options, please."

Another little bow from Antonio. "Very good, miss. Those options are on page four of your menu, but if you see something you like on any other page, the chef usually has a way to accommodate. I will also let the kitchen know to avoid any issue."

I smiled at his graciousness. "Thank you. I appreciate that."

"Of course," he said. "Sir?" He turned to my dessert date. "Did you have any dietary restrictions?"

He looked a little startled, blue eyes wide and brows slanted into a questioning arch. "Uh, no. No, I'm good with . . ." A broad hand waved over the menu. "Anything."

Once the waiter left and before I was asked, I gave my standard spiel. "I have celiac disease, which means if I eat gluten, my body starts attacking my small intestine. So, I always let the kitchen know."

His face fell. "And I took you to what is essentially a palace made of gluten."

I laughed at his comically droopy expression. "No, you didn't. They've got plenty of options for me, don't worry. And, even if not, it's not like you could've known. I'm the one who vetoed personal details."

He relaxed a little, full lips easing back into a grin. "True, although I think you're starting to cave on that a little."

I rolled my eyes, then looked back at my menu. "Ah, yes, the sexy revelation of my medical history. Learning how my body is at war with itself sometimes really heats up the evening, doesn't it?"

His pointer finger appeared at the top of my menu and angled it down. "Tell me more about it."

I blinked at his earnest expression, eyes lit with interest over an encouraging smile. "Seriously? You want to hear more about my body's failure to process anything that comes from wheat, rye or barley? I hardly think it's that interesting of a topic."

With a snort, he shook his head, eyes never leaving mine. "In case you haven't noticed, I've been begging for scraps of information about you all night. I'm not going to walk away now that you've volunteered something."

I laughed and ignored the little flutters in my chest at his seemingly genuine interest. I settled back in my chair, tracing designs on the pink suede seat with my fingertips. "Okay," I said. "What would you like to know?"

He considered the question, eyes drifting over my shoulder to the showcase of sugar housed in the display case to his left. His shoulders stiffened and worry creased his brow as his gaze bounced back to mine. "You said no wheat, rye or barley?"

I nodded, and he clutched his chest dramatically, seemingly crestfallen. "No beer?"

I laughed again. "No, no beer for me I'm afraid."

"That," he said, closing his eyes and biting his bottom lip with a sad shake of his head, "is a goddamn tragedy."

"It definitely makes things a bit complicated sometimes," I admitted. "Because it's not just that I can't eat it. If someone I'm with eats or drinks something with gluten in it and then we kiss, there's a risk of what my doctor calls cross contamination and what I refer to as 'being glutened' by accident."

No longer teasing, he shifted forward, one broad palm settling on the small table. "And what happens if you are?"

"Worst-case scenario? A trip to the hospital. Best case? Well, it's not polite conversation, but would make great content for a Farrelly brothers movie."

He laughed with me, then pushed a hand through his hair, and yes, it somehow got even sexier once more. "Being celiac sounds pretty rough," he said with a sympathetic frown.

I shrugged. "I've been diagnosed for so long it's second nature for me to ask the right questions and guard against the risk of exposure." I nodded at Antonio on his way back to our table. "But it's nice when others make an effort, so I feel like less of an inconvenience."

He blanched at my description, lips pulling down into a frown that darkened his eyes. "It's not like you chose this condition."

"Tell that to my mother," I said, and immediately wanted to claw the words back. They'd just slipped out in the rhythm of conversation. As easily uttered as a request for the gluten-free macarons. Because talking to him was easy. Too easy, as evidenced by my bringing up my mother. *Ugh!*

His eyebrow lifted in a tentatively curious arc. "Your mother isn't . . ."

I broke into his pause just as Antonio reached our table. "Nearly as interesting as the selection of macarons here. I could order a dozen and still have more flavors to sample!"

Antonio beamed down at me, unwittingly aiding my escape from the conversation. "I will happily bring you as many as you choose for as long as you'd like to stay," he promised, a grin pushing up the corners of his neatly trimmed mustache.

"Challenge accepted," I said, diving into the litany of flavors and avoiding the searching blue eyes across the table.

Just shy of too many macarons later, but only because my partner in sugary gluttony saved me from embarrassing myself by ordering a dozen more—along with a gluten-free strawberry shortcake—to-go, we found ourselves back at L'Atelier passing a throng of people at the guest elevator bank.

"Shouldn't we . . ." I gestured vaguely over at the elevators.

He shook his head, using the hand not carrying precious cargo of delicate French pastries, to point to an elevator at the far wall. "The ones for my floor are over here."

*A separate elevator to his floor? Who exactly was this guy?*

Feeling my gaze on him, he turned to face me, eyes inquisitive. "You good?"

"You mean other than feeling like a serving girl heading to the king's bedchamber? Yeah, I'm fine." And, all jokes aside, I was. I was better than fine, actually. And it was all because of him. After my slip about my mother, he hadn't pushed the subject. Hadn't even tried to broach it again. Instead, he'd kept things as light and airy as the macarons we'd devoured, devising a *get to know you* game that wouldn't reveal too much while providing enough insight to keep things interesting.

"We'll call it, 'Inquiring Minds Want to Know Just Enough, But Not Too Much,'" he'd said, after biting into a chocolate macaron.

"Name needs work, but I'll go with it," I agreed, sampling a blueberry lavender macaron that made my tastebuds dance.

Through his game, he'd learned *Splash* was my favorite movie.

At my naming it, he'd rubbed his chin, brows knitted in thought. "Is that the one from the eighties with Daryl Hannah and Tom Hanks? She shows up naked in New York, or something?"

"You would remember that part," I teased, and he laughed.

"Puberty is a helluva drug," he said, and I joined his laughter.

To my "what about you" question, he'd responded, amusingly enough, that his pick was *Spirited*, with Will Ferrell and Ryan Reynolds. "What can I say?" he'd asked, with an unapologetic grin. "I'm a sucker for the holiday season. And a *GQ* Santa suit."

Bonus fact, he also harbored a significant man crush on Ryan Reynolds. A revelation which led to my disclosing that would work perfectly, since I worshipped Blake Lively as a fashion icon and all-around amazing human.

"So, I get Ryan and you get Blake, huh?" he'd asked.

"Depends," I'd replied. "I could be tempted to switch if it meant I got to wear the *Deadpool* suit."

He'd aimed a finger gun at me. "Good call. Think she'd teach me how to walk with a cane like she did in *A Simple Favor*?"

"Bad news for you, man. *No one*, man or woman, could walk with a cane like Blake did in that movie." Touching the lapel of his suit jacket still draped around my shoulders, I'd added, "Although you and she do both seem to favor a well-tailored suit. I don't know that I've met many people who chose to dine alone all suited up."

Passing me a blackberry macaron, he'd said, "You can thank my Grandpa for my sartorial choices."

"Grandpa, huh? I'm intrigued."

"He was an intriguing guy," he'd replied. "Worked in finance his entire career and always dressed the part, even on weekends. I don't think he even owned a pair of jeans. The most casual he got was on Christmas mornings when he'd forgo his jacket and tie. Not the vest, though."

"Sounds very dapper."

He'd nodded, reaching for a strawberry macaron. "Oh yeah, no question there. He always used to tell me, 'you can never be overdressed, or overeducated.'"

"Oscar Wilde. Very nice."

He'd laughed. "Grandpa was a big believer that the clothes made the man and an even bigger believer in my being a man who made something of himself."

His having access to a private elevator in the swankiest new hotel in Vegas lent credence to the idea he'd taken his grandfather's advice on more than just attire. He laughed, the sound warm and rumbly, and it wrapped around me like a blanket fresh out of the dryer. "I don't know about the king's bedchamber, but it's a nice suite." After waving his key card in front of the elevator call panel, he tucked it into his pants pocket and stepped closer to me.

I shifted in my heels, my shoulder bumping the side of his chest. Glancing over at me, he slipped a hand under the hem of his jacket, fingers skimming across my back to curve around my hip, drawing me closer. The shift in posture dislodged his jacket from my shoulders, but I caught it before it tumbled to the ground.

"Close call," I said, handing it to him. He draped it over one arm and replaced his free hand on my hip, tucking me back in close. I leaned in to the solid warmth of his body next to mine.

Even with his fancy set of elevators reserved for Vegas royalty or whatever, we were not alone. Two other couples and a group of girls got on with us. With some shuffling adjustment, we claimed the back corner. I listened as the girls tipsily recounted their evening thus far and exulted over the concierge getting them a good table for the late performance at Magic Mike.

I could feel him at my back, broad and warm. Each inhale made his chest graze my shoulder blades in a soft brush of finely woven cloth. The anticipation buzzing through me grew, climbing along with the elevator as each of our fellow riders exited at their respective floors. It wasn't nerves or any sort of anxiety, but a conscious awareness and expectation of how the remainder of the night would go. A sense of delicious possibility.

As we continued our ascent into the Vegas skyline, it dawned on me that this guy was more than a well-made, well-filled-out suit. The upper levels of hotels like L'Atelier were reserved for VIPs. Those with money to burn who were eager to toss it onto the flames of the high stakes tables and laugh as it turned to ash. I remembered his quip about friends in high places and wondered briefly just who it was he knew at L'Atelier to score this sort of treatment.

When the last couple got off on their floor, the doors slid closed, and I angled my head back to look at him. "You some kind of high roller, or something?"

His smile was a twitch of his lips, almost as though my question amused him. "Something along those lines," he replied. "And I knew you were warming to the idea of getting to know me."

I rolled my eyes, but didn't deny it. The elevator dinged to announce our arrival on his floor, doors sliding silently open to reveal muted lighting and a plush carpeted hallway.

He extended his arm. "After you."

I stepped off the elevator, taking in the elegantly understated wallpaper and black-and-white pictures lining the walls. He came to stand beside me, and I arched a brow. "I mean, I hadn't planned to slum it tonight, but I guess I can suffer through this." I waved an arm at the lushly appointed space.

He laughed as I looped my arm through his. "I appreciate the sacrifice you're willing to make." His voice dropped a little when he added, "I'll do my best to make it up to you."

A shiver of excitement rippled down my back at his promise.

"I'll hold you to that," I said, letting him lead me down the hall.

At the end of it, he keyed us into a corner suite. I could see the dining room from the doorway. Because, yes, the man had a suite *with a dining room*. Not a dining nook, not a desk that doubled as a place to eat. A dining room, complete with a table and eight chairs.

Moving farther into the suite, I saw a kitchen and a beautiful living area with a deep and inviting sectional. The art in the hallway had been cool, but here it was even better. Although it paled to the view given by the glass walls of the suite. All of Vegas was laid out before me, lit up and gleaming.

"Yes, good evening," he said, and I turned to find him on the phone, leaning against the back of the sectional. "I need to order room service, please." He paused, then said, "Is that right? Well, please tell management their efforts are very much appreciated." Another pause, then, "A bottle of Veuve with two glasses, please." Another pause, then, "Very good, thank you."

After he hung up, his brows drew down contemplatively and his eyes wandered toward the ceiling.

"What?" I asked.

His gaze returned to me with a wry grin. "Just trying to remember what I ate and drank today. What should I do to make sure it's not an issue?"

Momentarily puzzled, I cocked my head. "Make sure what isn't an issue?"

"You said earlier that with your celiac, sometimes kissing can lead to unwanted complications." His smile was sweetly wicked. "I do plan to kiss you, and I want to make sure when I do, the only reaction you have is to want more."

I smiled, at once touched by his concern and titillated by his words. "Well, the recommendation is to brush with gluten-free toothpaste, mouthwash, and then floss just to make sure there's no trace of glu . . ." My words drifted off when he stood up and walked toward the door at the far edge of the room. "Where are you going?"

He glanced back at me. "First, to check my toothpaste to make sure it's gluten free. Then, if it is, to brush, gargle and floss. I'll be right back."

My mouth fell open at his response. Not that other guys had been total dicks about it. At least, not for the most part. But I couldn't recall someone being so willing to go the extra mile on the offhand chance there'd be a problem. Especially someone I'd just met. I knew the chances were small anything would go wrong based on the baked potato and steak he'd had at dinner, or the wine we'd shared. And everything at the dessert place had been gluten free. That would normally be enough for most people, who'd either assume everything would be fine or weren't that worried about what would happen if it wasn't.

That tickle in my brain came back. Would it be so bad to let this guy in a little more? As in the barest, tiniest bit by telling him my real name. It didn't mean anything would last beyond tonight. But maybe it could make tonight even better. Give this memory a little more of a glossy sheen than others. *Like it doesn't have one already?* Now that she'd been assured we were having sex with a strong hunter, my inner cavewoman had been replaced by an irritating smart-ass. I much preferred the lewd sign language to the snark.

I crossed to the window and looked down at the Strip, watching cars pass, lights pulse and flicker and electronic billboards advertise all the current Vegas hot spots. It was a bit surreal to be here, staring down at everything like a queen surveying her kingdom. Only, this wasn't my throne. It belonged to the guy currently in the bathroom, brushing his teeth. *But he invited you into it,* my subconscious piped up again. *What's the harm in giving him a little something in return? It's just your name, for goodness' sake, not some sort of state secret.*

"Hey," he said from behind me. I turned from the window to see him grinning at me from the doorway that must lead to the bedroom. "You didn't mention it, but I washed my face too. You know, just in case . . ." He shook his head. "Wow, I just realized that makes me sound like a super sloppy eater. Not what I was going for there. I just thought maybe it would ma—"

"Coral," I blurted, and he blinked in surprise.

"What?"

"My name," I explained, blushing a little. "It's Coral." For once, I was glad my mouth moved before my brain could catch up. It was out there now, for better or worse. Anonymity was gone, replaced by the connection of a name. I waited to regret it, to wish I'd held it back. But as I watched him process it, saw his eyes warm and lips turn up in a small, appreciative smile, the regret never came.

# chapter seven

## JAMIE

For a second, I just stared at her. At Coral. The name fit her. Beautiful, but with some hidden sharp edges. Relief, followed quickly by a surge of gratitude, flooded through me at learning her real name. That she'd judged me deserving of knowing it. That she'd seen something in me that made her seek out a deeper connection. It soothed a raw part of me. One that had chafed ever since the *Boston Commons* article.

Recovering, I said, "Coral."

She nodded, looking a little surprised she'd given me her real name. "That's me."

"So, do I tell you my name now?"

She mulled that over, brow wrinkled. "Turnabout's fair play, I guess. But first names only, okay?"

Her protests seemed almost rote now, as though she were reminding herself as much as cautioning me that there needed to remain some distance between us. It was obvious she'd already opened up more than she'd planned and was still figuring out how to feel about it. I needed to play it safe to make sure she didn't regret her decision. "Sure. Right. I'm Jamie, then."

"Nice to meet you, Jamie," she said with a smile.

The doorbell of the suite rang, and her shoulders jerked in surprise, eyes wide. "You have a doorbell?"

I laughed. "It would appear so. One second."

I let the room service waiter in with his cart.

"Good evening, sir. Would you like me to open the champagne?"

I shook my head. "No, thanks, I've got it."

"Very good, sir. Did you need anything else this evening?"

I shook my head and passed him a tip. "Thank you."

The door clicked shut behind him and I looked at Coral. "Thirsty?"

"Anyone who'd say no in the face of Veuve is not someone I'd want to spend much time around."

I laughed. "A lady with taste, I see."

She spread her arms wide and spun in a slow circle. "I mean, what was your first clue?"

"Am I included in that indication of your good taste?" I asked, pulling the bottle from the ice and unwrapping the foil from the top.

Her eyes narrowed. "You know good and well a guy who looks like you is every woman's taste."

My knowledge of women was proving to be suspect at the moment, but I still asked, "Who looks like me, huh?" I twisted the wire cage free from the cork. "And how exactly do I look?"

She rolled her eyes but came to stand closer. "Are you going to make me say it?"

"Say what?" I asked, twisting the cork so it released with a *pop!*

"Whee!" she said, and I couldn't hold back a laugh.

Coral grinned unabashedly back at me. "Sorry, but that sound deserves to be acknowledged for the celebration it is."

"I'll remember that," I said, pouring a glass and passing it to her. "But don't think I'm going to let you dodge my question." I poured my own glass and tapped it to hers. "Cheers."

"Cheers," she said, and took a drink. Swallowing, she lowered the glass and drummed the fingers of her other hand against it. "Why do you need me to describe you?"

I shrugged, taking a drink to mask my nerves at hearing her answer. "I'm interested to hear how you see me."

She sipped her champagne, then shot me a mischievous glance. "I'm in your hotel suite drinking champagne after playing footsie with you. Isn't it obvious how I see you?"

"Footsie?" I couldn't hold back a laugh at that. "Do people still say that?"

Coral lifted a brow and cocked a hip, but she smiled back at me. "How else would you describe dinner's under the table activities?"

"I guess there's no other word for it," I admitted, taking another drink. "But back to my original question."

"How do I see you?" She tapped her chin, tilting her glass this way and that as she considered the question. "Hmm, let me think."

Another wave of nerves crested in my gut while I waited for her to answer. It wasn't that I didn't know I was an attractive guy. I knew that much from looking in the mirror. It wasn't a secret. But I hadn't been lying when I said I wanted to hear how she saw me. Because I wasn't blind to how tonight could've been slotted right into the *Boston Commons* article as another example of my interest being limited to the superficial and short term. After all, it was what she wanted tonight to be. Had that been why she picked me? Because she could sense it, scent it on the air like some tell-tale philandering pheromone? The thought landed heavily, pressing down on me in weighty disappointment.

Oblivious to my inner turmoil, Coral said, "I could say that I see you as the cherry on my sundae." A smile played at the corners of her mouth. "But that's not accurate, because I always trash the cherry on any ice cream sundae. Don't like them at all." Her grin broke free. "Another fact for your game, I suppose. So, I can't use that analogy."

"I'm hoping that means I rank higher than a preserved, syrupy cherry?"

She nodded, her smile turning into a chuckle. "You do."

Her laugh lifted some of the weight, just the sound of it making me feel lighter. "It would probably mean more if I knew the entirety of the scale you were working with, though. If maraschino cherries are the bottom, we'll say, what's the top? A basket full of puppies who are already potty trained?"

"That's a good one," she said with an approving nod.

I tried my best to look humble. "I'm not foolish enough to think I'm even close to that."

"You're smarter than you look," she teased, nibbling on a strawberry room service had sent with the champagne. She chewed for a moment, then said, "Jamie, tonight I see you as the equivalent of the last slice of gluten-free pumpkin pie at Thanksgiving."

I blinked, unsure what I'd been expecting, but certain it hadn't been that. "This sounds promising."

She nodded, stepping closer to me as she took another sip of champagne. "It is."

"Tell me more."

"The last slice of pumpkin pie at Thanksgiving is a bit of a prize, wouldn't you agree?"

I nodded as she came closer, watching me with those blue-gray eyes. A memory flashed of a storm off the coast of Nantucket a few summers ago. Clouds had gathered, thick and heavy with rain, roiling across the sky. Lightning arced within the clouds, turning the gray into flashes of a deep, fathomless blue. I hadn't seen that color since, but I was staring into it now as I met Coral's heated gaze.

Her free hand came to my chest, her thumb stroking over the buttons of my shirt. She smiled, a lazy curving of her lips as she kept her eyes on mine. "It's something you want all for yourself," she said, fingers slipping lower.

"Something"—her thumbnail ticked against my shirt button, and I concentrated on breathing evenly—"you can only get once in a while."

Long lashes fluttered as her smile widened. "Something you simultaneously want to savor while devouring whole. But either way . . ."

She put her glass down on the table next to us and took one last step forward, the toes of her sandals almost touching the tips of my shoes. Coral's pause was heavy with seduction and thick with promises of what was to come. My hands itched to reach out for her, to touch her, to drag her against my chest and kiss her until she was breathless.

The high wedge of her sandals put her gorgeous eyes almost level with mine and her lips excruciatingly close. The smallest fraction of movement on my part would get me the contact I ached for. But I waited, needing to hear how her description would end.

When she spoke again, I felt the breath of her words against my lips. Her eyes dipped to my mouth as she said, "It's something you can't wait to taste."

I couldn't say with any degree of certainty which one of us moved first, only that she'd barely finished her sentence before our lips met. I felt the shape of the word "taste" on her lips as I kissed her. Coral made a sound, halfway between a sigh and a groan as her hands slid behind my head, fingers working into the hair at the nape of my neck. Her mouth was soft and eager under mine, and I couldn't stifle my own groan of approval at the feel of her.

My hands came to her waist, then slid around to her back, pulling her flush against me. The soft cotton of her shirt bunched under my fingers as I held her close. Coral's head tilted to the side, and at the teasing brush of my tongue at her bottom lip, she hummed and tightened her fingers in my hair. We pressed impossibly closer to one another as her lips parted and my tongue swept into the velvet luxury that was her mouth.

Her tongue met mine hungrily, challenging each stroke or lick with one of its own. Following when I withdrew, so she could taste me as well. The first brush of her tongue against my teeth sent sparks down my spine and I groaned into her mouth. I felt her smile as she continued her exploration, greedy for more.

My hands fisted in her shirt, and I tugged roughly at the fabric, pulling it free of the waistband of her shorts and shoving it hastily upward to bare her skin. It was as soft and silky as I'd first imagined it would be at the bar. Smooth and supple beneath my fingers as they teased along her sides, running a thumb beneath the satin band of her bra.

Coral broke our kiss with a catlike sound, not quite a purr, but something very close. Her eyes were heavy lidded when she looked at me, hands coming to the hem of her shirt and unceremoniously yanking it off over her head. She tossed it in the general direction of the couch, then grabbed my jaw and kissed me again.

It was hot and wanton, a needy press of her lips and desperate flicker of her tongue. My hands came to her breasts, still covered in the satin of her bra. She moaned into my mouth when I cupped the swell of them. Fumbling like a teenager, I found the front clasp of the bra and tugged. With a small *click*, it opened, and her breasts tumbled into my palms.

Lifting my lips from hers, I drew in a ragged breath as I watched myself thumb her tightly budded nipples. They were a dusky pink against the lighter skin of her breasts. Perfect and taut under the pads of my thumbs.

"Fucking hell, Coral," I whispered, taking one of the pink tips between my thumb and forefinger. Her body shuddered at the gentle pinch of my fingers and her hands came to the buttons of my shirt. Nimble fingers made quick work of them, and she pushed the shirt open.

"Off," she commanded, shoving it farther down my shoulders.

Reluctantly, I lifted my hands from her breasts to shrug out of my dress shirt and pull my undershirt over my head, tossing it behind me to join hers. Long, restless fingers splayed out over my torso as she looked at me.

"Fucking hell is right," she said, tracing the lines of my stomach and chest. "You're gorgeous."

I laughed, but preened, at her praise. "You'd know all about being gorgeous, sweetheart," I said, reaching for her once again. Her breasts pressed against my chest as we kissed, the skin-to-skin contact making both of us hiss in a breath. I needed to feel more of her, see more of her, *taste* more of her.

Pivoting, I shifted toward the dining table. Bending slightly, I cupped her ass and lifted her against me. She squeaked in surprise against my lips, but curled those devastating legs around my waist. The press of her center against my growing arousal was enough to elicit a whimpering groan from her. I heard the thud of her shoes behind me as she slipped them off. Nudging one of the chairs out of the way, I set her gently on the table. Her knees were bent, legs still wrapped loosely around me. Her heels hooked around the backs of my thighs.

I put a hand on either side of her hips and leaned further into the kiss, tilting her backward and taking control. Her knees pressed into my hips, and her heels dug into my hamstrings as she clutched my shoulders.

Drawing back, I pulled her bottom lip between my teeth with a soft nip before trailing kisses down the side of her jaw to just behind her ear. She shivered as I sucked the tender skin there, fingers curling around my wrists. I kissed my way down her neck and over her collarbone to the tops of her breasts. They were high and full, and I wanted to map their entire surface with my mouth and start all over when I was finished.

Coral tugged at my wrists. "Touch me," she implored on a whisper, arching her back.

I obeyed, cupping each of her breasts in my hands, working and teasing the curves of them. Stroking the underside of them, the valley between them, and the satiny rise of their upper swell.

"Jamie." She groaned, tugging at my wrists, trying to guide my fingers to her nipples.

"Don't rush me," I said with a grin, continuing to stroke her skin and enjoying her frustrated groan almost as much as the way her nipples pebbled even further. Her feet flexed, digging her heels into my legs with her frustration.

"You can take all the time you want," she huffed, eyes dark and threatening. "Once you get to my nipples."

I laughed. "Since you put it that way." I licked each thumb in turn and slid them over her nipples at the same time.

Coral's shoulders snapped back, and her breasts jiggled with the force of her movement. She moaned. "Oh, fuck, Jamie."

I repeated the motion, adding both forefingers this time and gripping her nipples in a slippery pinch. She cried out again, writhing on the table. At this point, I'd have bruises on my thighs from its edge, but I did not give a single shit.

"You like that, Coral?" I asked, enjoying her name on my tongue.

"Like," she panted, "doesn't even come close."

Bracing one hand just behind her hips, I leaned down, letting my breath drift over her skin. She shuddered and I exhaled again, blowing a stream of warm air down the slope of her breast to her nipple as I teased it gently. The sound of her cries was low and lush as she arched closer. Licking my fingers again, I did the same to her other breast, letting my mouth hover just over her skin and my breath tease down to where my fingers worked her nipple in a steady, tugging rhythm.

"Well," I said, speaking directly to her breast. "What about this?" I drew one nipple into my mouth, sliding it slowly past my lips and grazing it with my teeth in a testing bite. I soothed the sting of it with the flat of my tongue, then nibbled a bit harder.

"Yes." Coral hissed, her hand coming to the back of my head to keep me there. "Yes, oh, yes, I like that." Her nails scraped against my scalp as she held me in place.

I laughed against her skin, suckling harder and flicking her nipple with the tip of my tongue. I kept her other nipple trapped between my fingers, squeezing and releasing in time with the sucking pulls of my mouth.

Her head fell back, and she scooted forward, pressing herself as close to me as she could while she whispered pleasured syllables to the ceiling. My hips shifted forward of their own volition, and I could feel her heat through our clothes. Ignoring the driving need to push forward, I eased back. We had all night, and this was just the beginning.

I switched breasts and Coral shivered. She was so sensitive, so impatient for more that I wondered if she could come from this alone. If I could make her come from this.

## CORAL

I still had my shorts on, and I was on the verge of orgasm. Even with the layers of cotton and lace between us I could feel the hazy possibility of an orgasm forming. It wasn't a fully actualized thought or concept just yet, but it was there. Loitering in the background of my sexual consciousness like the Ghost of Orgasm Future—wispy, ill-defined, but definitely conceivable.

His oh-so-talented fingers seemed to be touching every single one of the hundreds of nerve endings that made up my nipples. Like he was mapping them for future expeditions. *This way to the erogenous zone, fellas! Follow the highlighted trail to make her mind turn inside out and forget her own name.*

And when he brought his mouth to my breast, I'd honestly seen stars. Or at least hot pops of light behind my eyelids. Hot pops of light that transmitted some sort of pleasure frequency directly to my core. Which pulsed hotly with every roll of his tongue, scrape of his teeth and pull of his soft, full lips. Each nip seemed to gather the threads of whatever sensation this was and draw them tighter, pulling and gathering them into a knot of throbbing need centered somewhere between my nipples and the innermost point of my sexuality.

My world shrank to the feel of him. The hot flutter of his tongue. The sharp rasp of his teeth. The erotic scrape of his stubble on my skin. The soothing brush of his lips after the fiery pinch of his fingers. His breath, warm and humid against my skin. The slight roughness of his palm where he cupped the undercurve of my breasts.

I closed my eyes and gave in to feeling all of it. Experiencing everything he was offering through his touch. His tongue traced slow looping circles around my tautly puckered flesh, each one drawing me closer and closer to the edge of something I'd never experienced. My body tightened all over. Hands clasping the back of Jamie's head, fingers twisting through his hair in what had to be a painful grip. But I couldn't stop, couldn't relax. Because if I loosened my grip, I would've flown off into some other dimension. My knees were tight at his hips. I could feel the leather of his belt and the softer fabric of his dress pants.

He drew my nipple back into his mouth and hummed. The vibration of it ricocheted through me and when he brought it between his teeth with yet one more nibbling, suckling pull, I cried out, bucking my hips as the orgasm took hold.

My core clenched around nothing, and I groaned at the unfamiliar sensation of warmth spiraling through my breasts. Each time Jamie's tongue or teeth touched my nipple, it sent the sensation twirling back through me in a volley of pleasure. Waves of that heat radiated through me, working their way into every joint, every muscle, every cell until I felt almost weightless. Tethered to the earth solely by Jamie's lips at my breast.

Sensing my immolation, he gentled his strokes, the sweep of his fingers almost reverent as soft kisses and tender strokes of his tongue replaced the biting sucks that had driven me over the edge into a nipple-gasm. He nuzzled the valley between my breasts, kissing his way up my chest to my neck. His lips moved under my jawline to my chin and finally to my lips where he gave me a long, slow kiss.

Lifting his head, he said, "That was . . ." he looked down at me with an expression akin to awe before shaking his head with a wicked grin. "That was, hands down, one of the hottest fucking things I've ever experienced."

His brow furrowed a little. "I mean, I'm not wrong about what just happened, am I? That is, I mean, you did . . ." His cheeks reddened slightly, and he cleared his throat. "You just came, right?"

His embarrassment at seeking confirmation was adorable. I smiled and looped my arms around his neck, my overly sensitive breasts tingling at the contact with his skin and sending a shiver down my back. "No, Jamie, that's not right."

The red tint on his cheeks went deep crimson, and he chuckled abashedly. "Right, well, sorry. I just tho—"

I gripped his chin in one hand and kissed him quickly. "It's not exactly right," I clarified, looking him in the eye. "*You* made me come. Your mouth, your tongue, your delightfully dexterous fingers and those naughty nipping teeth of yours are what made me come, Jamie. Which makes me wonder . . ." I drew a finger down his chest, over the ridges of his abdomen, and dipped it just under the waistband of his pants. I felt as much as heard his sharp inhale, and it was my turn to chuckle.

"If that's the kind of pleasure that comes with you rounding second base, what kind of fireworks can I expect when you slide into home?"

His eyes went dark, and his smile was every sinful Vegas thought rolled into one. His fingers curled around my wrist, and he tugged me forward, placing my hand on the flat of his stomach. "Now, Coral, why would you go straight to home plate when you've yet to experience third base?"

I thought of his mouth on my breasts, the lingering and lavish way he'd worked his tongue over them, the feel of his breath on my skin, the light touch of his fingers . . . and then I imagined the same attention being focused due south. A clenching desperation rolled through me at the thought. My mouth went dry in anticipation of the glory that would be oral sex with this man. It simply had to be. As in, it could not be bad because the universe would not allow for that to happen even if it required divine intervention from the goddess of female pleasure herself.

"I've never been one to take a shortcut," I said, which made him laugh.

"I can't recommend you starting now," he said with mock solemnity. "Especially when the scenic route is so much more fun."

My hands moved to the waistband of my shorts, but he stopped me, his large hand covering mine. "As much as I might enjoy making a four-course meal out of you right here on the dining room table, I have to imagine you'd much prefer eight hundred thread count to wood grain."

I blinked. "I'm sorry, did you say, 'eight hundred thread count'?"

Jamie's smile crinkled the corner of his eyes. "See for yourself, sweetheart."

Before I knew what was happening, he lifted me from the table and into the air, hands curving familiarly around my ass. Reflexively, my legs wrapped around his waist and my arms around his neck. The ease with which he maneuvered me into his arms was unexpected. At my height, it wasn't often I got lifted into the air like I was the size of Simone Biles or Olivia Dunne. And yet, he'd done it so easily it took my breath away.

Jamie kissed me, a quick and playful peck, before heading toward the door he'd disappeared through earlier. He stopped before reaching the sectional, though, and returned to the dining area.

"Forget something?" I asked with a laugh.

Shifting my body to the side, so one arm looped under my ass, he handed me the champagne bucket and picked up the to-go box of desserts. "For afterward," he said, shooting me that naughty grin I was starting to suspect was his trademark. "Or during, if you're into that."

# chapter eight

## JAMIE

Coral shifted against me, and the icy metal side of the champagne bucket pressed into the bare skin of my chest. I sucked in a breath, and she laughed softly.

"Sorry about that, but better your tits than mine."

"Oh, I don't know," I said, turning left into the master bedroom of the suite, thankful I'd remembered to stash the framed copy of the article in the closet when I'd brushed my teeth. "I think your tits and I could have a wonderful time with nothing more than an ice bucket and my imagination."

Her legs tightened at my waist, and she pressed closer to me, thankfully holding the ice bucket away from both of us. "Tell me more about this imagination of yours," she purred into my ear before nipping the lobe.

I swallowed a groan as I deposited the bakery box onto the nightstand. After taking the champagne bucket from her, I put it down as well. Her cold hands pressed against my chest when I centered her in my arms. Dropping my head, I pressed kisses from her shoulder to her collarbone and then trailed my lips up the line of her neck. She angled her head to allow me more access, arms twining around my neck.

Reaching her ear, I said, "I'd much rather show than tell, Coral." The words produced a shiver and goose bumps rose on her skin.

"You know what they say about actions and words," she said, arching her back and dragging her nipples against my chest.

After toeing off my shoes, I put one knee on the bed and reluctantly dropped one hand from her ass to support both our weight as I maneuvered us down to the mattress. Once we were in the middle of the bed, Coral's arms unwound from their loop around my neck, and I put a hand between her shoulder blades to ease her back onto the comforter.

Her legs still encircled my waist at a deliciously enticing angle, which felt even better when I lowered myself to my elbows to kiss her. She hummed against my mouth, her hands finding their way into my hair when I deepened the kiss. Her tongue met mine in a slow slide and the sounds she made, little hums and huffs of pleasure, drove me crazy. I wanted to hear more of them, different versions of them, louder variations of them. I wanted her calling out nonsense because she was lost to anything but the pleasure of my touch.

I felt her laugh and broke the kiss. She grinned up at my confused expression. "Did you just growl?"

"Did I just what?"

Her grin widened. "You did, you just growled while we were kissing."

"Only because you were purring," I said without thinking.

She drew a finger down my jawline. "I guess we bring out the animalistic side of one another."

"Sweetheart," I kissed the hollow of her throat, "you have no idea."

"Just one more thing for you to show me, then," Coral teased. Her legs slid down the sides of my thighs to the mattress. Flattening her feet, she pushed herself back into the pillows, tilting her head back and exposing the slender column of her neck.

Like the animal she'd turned me into, I lunged, letting my teeth scrape across the tendons of her throat with each kiss. I felt her hummed response as I made my way down the center of her chest. Palming her breasts, I dropped open-mouthed kisses along the crest of each breast, sucking at the tender flesh and making her squirm and clutch at the comforter. I stroked her nipples with the tips of my fingers, and she gasped, eyes going wide and locking onto mine.

When my strokes became teasing pinches, her gasps turned to groans, and she bit down on her bottom lip. Leaning down, I licked one straining peak and then the other.

"Oh my God," she moan-whined, her eyes hazy as she looked down at me. "How does that feel so fucking good? What are you, the freaking nipple whisperer?"

I laughed. "Not a title I've been granted before, but I'll take it."

Her lips twitched and her gaze narrowed. "Well, the girls have had their turn and, as enjoyable as it is, let's not forget your promise of a thrilling third base experience." She pushed her fingers into my hair and gave my head a playful shove south.

Grinning, I moved lower down her body and rocked back on my knees, resting my hands on my thighs and just looking at her. Taking in the rosy perfection that was every long-limbed inch of her. She didn't shy away from my perusal, made no attempt to cover up or shift my focus from her luxuriously half-naked form. Coral stretched slowly and settled her hands behind her head on the pillows with a "Show me what you've got" smirk on her face. Her comfort level with her own body was erotic as hell.

Lifting one foot, she placed it in the center of my chest. "Are you waiting for an engraved invitation, Jamie?"

I took her heel in my hand and shifted her foot to my shoulder, putting her calf within kissing distance. "You know what my first thought was when I saw you sitting at the bar?" I rubbed her calf with my thumb.

She lifted her eyes to a spot above the headboard, as though she were considering her answer. "Hm, let me think . . ." Meeting my eyes again, she said, "Of all the gin joints in all the towns in all the world, she walks into mine."

"Very funny, Bogie."

Laughing, she corrected me. "Pretty sure I'm Ingrid Bergman in this scenario."

"Either way, I did not mentally quote *Casablanca*," I replied, while silently admitting to myself it would've been a lot cooler thing to say.

"Okay," she frowned in thought, then grinned. "You complete me?"

I groaned while she laughed harder. "I guess," I said, pinching the inside of her thigh and making her squeal, "I should be glad you didn't pick some other *Jerry Maguire* quote."

"'Show me the money' is a lot more Vegas than 'you complete me,'" she said, still laughing. I maintained a stern face for as long as possible before joining her laughter.

"Okay, okay, okay," she panted, trying to stop her runaway giggles. Clearing her throat, she settled her mouth in a serious line that only twitched a little. Humor still lit her eyes when she asked, "What was your first thought when you saw me sitting at the bar?"

I lifted her foot and pressed my lips right above the inside of her ankle. "I wondered precisely . . ." Another kiss to the curve of her calf. "How long . . ." My lips brushed the inside of her knee, and I felt the muscles of her leg contract and release. Her eyes held no trace of humor now. Just heat.

"How long what?" she asked, tracing a finger between her breasts.

"How long it would take . . ." Bending slightly, I reached mid-thigh and gave the supple skin there an open-mouthed kiss. Coral's knee flexed around my shoulder.

"For what?"

I lowered myself down onto my stomach, my lips hovering at her inner thigh just below the hem of shorts. I stared up her body, over the slope of her stomach and the fucking exquisite curves of her breasts, and into those swirling storm cloud eyes.

"I wondered, Coral, precisely how long it would take for me to kiss my way from your ankle all the way up these legs." I ran my thumb beneath the hem of her shorts and her breath caught. "These lavishly long legs, Coral. They were one thing at the airport in jeans, but in these shorts." I shook my head. "They're fucking lethal, sweetheart. You damn near killed me."

"A lady isn't responsible for a man's reaction to her outfit," she said, bending her knee to rest her foot at the small of my back.

"Of course not," I said, inching my hand higher on her leg until my thumb disappeared under the hem of her shorts. Her skin was warm and soft to the touch. "I'm just letting you know, in case you're interested, that seeing you in that bar tonight while wearing these shorts was enough to bring me to my knees."

"Funny, I didn't notice you kneeling before me," she teased.

"A problem easily remedied," I said.

"What do you me—EEP!"

Her question ended on a shriek when I slid one arm under her lower back and swung my legs sideways off the edge of the bed. The swivel slid her body perpendicular to the mattress and knocked off a half dozen pillows. My knees landed on the carpet next to the bed and hers came to either side of my ribcage.

Flustered, she pushed up onto her elbows, brushing hair out of her eyes. "What in the world?"

I smiled up at her, resting my hands on her bare thighs. "You wanted me on my knees, sweetheart, so here I am."

# CORAL

*Holy shit, holy shit, holy S-H-I-T!*

I stared down at the man ensconced between my knees. No, scratch that. The man who'd pulled some sort of ninja sex move to land on his knees while staying between mine. That shit didn't happen in real life and when it happened in a movie, it took a director, an intimacy coordinator and three or four takes to get it right.

And yet there he was, shooting me a self-satisfied grin from his position kneeling before me. With his tousled blond hair and big hands spanning the tops of my thighs. His touch registered about a millisecond after his smile, the broad expanse of his palms hot against my skin. That same heat spread through the thick lines of his fingers curving around the outside of my thighs, while his thumbs swept in scorching arcs just below the inseam of my shorts.

"Better?" he asked, yanking my attention away from the five-alarm fire currently making its way up my thighs from where his hands rested. His *big* hands.

With a smile I pushed my fingers through his hair, nails grazing his scalp until I could interlace my hands at the back of his neck. "Better than having you half naked and on top of me?" I lifted a shoulder in a shrug I hoped was casual and didn't look like I was a marionette on a string. "I guess it depends on what you plan to do now that you're down there."

"Well, as much as I've grown to love them, for me to do what I want to do . . ." Jamie reached up and tugged on my shorts. "These have got to go."

"I thought you'd never ask," I said, reaching for the zipper of my shorts.

He brushed my hands away. "Please, allow me."

To be clear, this entire night had been hot. So hot. So sexy. So . . . fantasy Vegas. But when his fingers brushed my stomach, then dipped just inside my waistband to unhook the tiny button, it was like a match touching the fuse. Sparks of desire shot out from the downward slide of the zipper in a blazing trail of lust all the way to my core.

There was something so intimate about watching him undress me. How the tab of the zipper looked so small between his fingers. The way he watched the fabric open inch by inch until it hung open in a loose V, exposing the thin fabric of my G-string. Blue eyes came to mine.

"Lift up for me, sweetheart," he said, his voice a little rougher than it had been.

I obliged and shifted my hips up, allowing him to slide the shorts down my legs and off. I was naked except for the little black panties I wore, and Jamie took his time in an appreciative survey of my near nudity. Blue eyes wandered over me in a slow cataloging of what seemed like each slope and curve before him. The way he drank me in made the heat in my core unfurl outward in a slow, incendiary burn.

I reached for him, desperate for more. I pulled him toward me, and he came with an equal desperation, our lips meeting in a searing kiss. He groaned into my mouth as his tongue slid inside. Strong thighs pressed into the mattress between my legs when he cupped my face in his hands and angled my chin up to deepen the kiss. His kiss was greedy and bold, an impatient claiming of my mouth. I clung to his shoulders and let him take and plunder with lips, teeth and tongue.

One hand trailed down to cup my breast, his broad thumb ghosting over my nipple. I moaned and felt him smile against my lips.

"You're so sensitive," he whispered, nipping at my lower lip, and continuing the teasing stroke of my breast.

"You're such a tease," I countered, rolling my hips against him.

He chuckled darkly. "Lie back, Coral," he murmured, putting one knee between mine and his free hand on my back. I obeyed, letting him lower me to the bed, pressing his chest to mine as he kissed me. It was more leisurely now, lazy strokes of his tongue against mine. When he withdrew, I was dizzy with lust.

He moved lower, kissing his way down my body, nuzzling the curve of each breast and sucking at the skin of my abdomen. I rose up on my elbows to watch him tug playfully at the waistband of my panties with his teeth before hooking his thumbs underneath it and pulling them down.

Again, I arched my hips to assist the slide of them down my legs and then I was bare to him. Broad shoulders pushed my knees wide, and he rested his hands once more on the tops of my thighs. He looked hungrily at my center and licked his lips. Flicking his gaze up to mine he gave me a wolfish smile before grazing me with his thumb.

Hips jerking eagerly, I gasped at the fleeting touch, already yearning for more. He grinned and lifted his thumb to his mouth, sliding it between his lips. A growl of approval rumbled from his chest. "So sweet, Coral. Just like I knew you would be."

Under the weight of his heated gaze, the moment suddenly felt too intimate. The look he gave me was too knowing, like he could see into the deepest part of me. Like my body wasn't the only thing laid bare for him. It began to feel too much like the start of something. Or maybe the culmination of something that started at the airport this morning and only blossomed from there. Something I wasn't ready to even put a name to, much less experience.

I blinked and swallowed hard. *Get back on your game, girl. He's just another guy.*

My oh-so-helpful inner voice piped up. *Yeah, a guy you've already broken the rules for in so many ways.*

I grappled for control of my careening thoughts, struggling to reconcile them into some semblance of order. This wasn't anything more than what it had started out to be. Regardless of the interlude of dinner and dessert, we'd still ended up here in his room for the final act of this one-night performance. Nothing had changed that, and nothing would change from here.

# chapter nine

## JAMIE

The barest taste of Coral was electrifying and left me eager for more. I wanted to bury my face between her thighs until her orgasm covered my tongue and then go back for seconds, even thirds if she'd let me. Need pulsed through me with a drugging intensity so strong it took every ounce of self-control not to surge forward and devour her.

The light brush of her fingers over my bare shoulder made me glance up the long line of her body to meet her eyes. Whereas before they'd been hooded with lust, now there was something in the smoky swirl of her gaze that made me pause. I couldn't pinpoint what it was, only that it seemed off.

"Still with me, gorgeous?" I asked, keeping resolutely still between her knees, even though it killed me not to touch her. She'd been right there with me seconds ago, so I wasn't sure what had happened.

She blinked and whatever I'd seen—uncertainty, maybe?—in her eyes before was gone. Replaced by a hazy look of seduction. Her lips curled into a come-hither smile, and she sat up. Slender fingers tunneled into my hair, the scratch of her nails over my scalp raising goose bumps on my skin. With a light tug, she tilted my head up and inched forward, her thighs sliding against my ribs. She was close enough for me to feel the heat of her sex a few scant inches from my chest. I drew in a ragged breath, which made her smile widen.

"Most definitely," she said, giving my sides a squeeze. "But there's one little problem."

"Oh?" I asked, running my hands over the tops of her thighs to settle at the naked curve of her hip. I grinned at her. "Worried I really am sloppy when I eat?"

With a laugh and a shake of her head, Coral said, "Nothing I've seen tonight would lead me to believe that." She dragged one foot up the back of my trousers. "It's only that I think you're a bit overdressed for this party."

I kissed her thigh and felt the muscle tense under my lips with the slight press of her knees into my sides. Looking up at her, I ran my tongue over my bottom lip and watched her eyes heat.

"A problem easily solved," I said, easing backward and letting my hands slide down her legs. I didn't miss the shiver that worked its way over her body at my touch. I'd been hard since we kissed in the living room and was now aching with the need to have her, to cover her body with mine, part those gorgeous thighs and slide into the hot, wet heat of her.

Shifting to stand, I stared down at her as I undid my belt buckle, sliding the leather through the loops with a sharp snap. Her eyes widened at the sound, pupils dilating and irises going impossibly darker. Coral bit down on her lower lip with an appreciative hum as her hands twisted in the comforter.

I tossed the belt aside and undid the fly of my pants, watching her watch me pull the zipper down. I let the slacks hang at my hips for a moment before shoving them all the way off. Coral's eyes went straight to the bulge in my boxer briefs, those straight white teeth sinking deeper into her full bottom lip.

"Enjoying the view?" I asked, unable to keep from smirking at her as I stepped out of my pants.

She glanced down with a throaty giggle. "It's the dress socks that are really doing it for me," she teased, eyes moving to my calves still covered by black socks.

"Kinky," I said, pulling off the offending footwear. "I like it."

Coral focused in on my dick once more. "So do I, Jamie."

It twitched in response to her gaze, and she grinned, meeting my eyes. Hers were more focused now as they wandered leisurely away from my crotch and up the planes of my stomach to my chest. When they locked with mine, the sharp hunger that matched my own had me lunging forward to regain my place between her thighs. My mouth watered at the thought of her taste.

She surprised me by sliding backward on the bed. "Come here," she said, beckoning me with a ripple of her fingers.

With only the briefest hesitation, I obeyed, coming off my knees to join her on the bed. Cupping my face in her hands, she drew me up her body and I braced myself over her on my elbows. Silky strands of hair brushed my fingertips as my hands came to either side of her head.

"Coral, don't you want . . ." My voice drifted off as her nails trailed down my ribs, the light scratch of them making me groan. She paused at my waist, her hands notched at my hips and her thumbs teased the sloped V of muscle at the waistband of my briefs.

"This," she stroked it reverently, and I swallowed a curse at the feel of her fingers feathering along my lower abdomen. It was divine torture of the highest order. And all I wanted was for her to venture just a bit lower.

"This," she repeated, looking up at me with a devilish gleam in her eyes, "is not the body of a man who eats strawberry shortcake on the regular." Her mouth spread in a naughty grin. "And on behalf of Adonis fans worldwide, let me say that I acknowledge and appreciate your sacrifice."

I laughed. "Adonis?"

Her index fingers slid down the line of my abs to dip just inside my briefs and I sucked in a breath. Without coming anywhere close to where I wanted her fingers, they withdrew and moved back up the line of muscle that was now quivering at her touch. "This," she repeated the motion, and I fought to maintain control, "is called the Adonis belt. Seems fitting, doesn't it? Him being the god of fertility and all." A red brow quirked at my tensed jawline, her fingers still in motion along my waist. "We can always call them something else, if you prefer. What do you call them?"

Her teasing caress was short-circuiting my brain. Distracting me from her artful dodge of my attempt to go down on her. All of the blood in my body was headed straight for my dick, thanks to her trailing fingers. I concentrated on what she'd asked me, trying to formulate an answer. "Abs?" I managed to choke out.

Coral shook her head, that sultry mouth of hers turning down in a pout that made me want to kiss her for the next month. "Nope, nowhere near descriptive or appreciative enough." Her eyes went the color of molten steel. "And these,"—she flattened her palms against my stomach, the tips of her fingers centimeters from my straining erection,—"deserve to be appreciated."

Her left hand shifted, the end of her middle finger brushing against the crown of my cock in a touch so light I wondered if it really happened. "Of course," she said, her hand sliding still lower, fingertips delving into my briefs to wrap around me in a sensual squeeze that left no question of her touch, "tonight I plan on appreciating every last inch of you."

I groaned and rocked into her hand like an overeager teen. "Fuck, Coral."

Her laugh was sultry as she stroked me with one hand. "Yes, Jamie, I believe that is the agreed-upon plan."

One touch from this woman and I was already primed and ready. I drew in a steadying breath and forced myself not to thrust once more into her palm. Her warm, soft palm that was currently holding my cock. *Focus, for fuck's sake, man!*

Supporting myself on one hand, I used the other to hold her wrist still. The grin she shot me told me she knew exactly what she was doing. "As good as that feels, sweetheart," I said, breathing deeply, "I think it's time we put that agreed-upon plan in motion."

Her thumb dragged over the head of my cock, swiping at the bead of precum and rubbing it back and forth. I growled and tugged her hand away before the next swipe of her thumb. Pushing myself off the bed, I pointed at the pillows lining the headboard. "Get comfortable, Coral. You're going to be there a while."

Rolling onto all fours and damn near giving me a heart attack at the sight of her naked backside, she sidled her way up to where I'd pointed. She knew what her slow, swaying crawl up the bedclothes looked like and there was no way she didn't also know what it was doing to me to watch. Time to take back the control I'd had earlier. The control she'd enjoyed even as she begged me for more.

"Feel free to stay in that position if you want, sweetheart," I said, yanking open the drawer of the nightstand to retrieve a condom. "I can make that work just as well as what I had in mind."

She shot me a look over her shoulder that was all heated defiance. "And here I thought we'd try both before it was all said and done."

I tossed a strip of condoms onto the bed next to her knee. "The only way we're stopping at 'both,' Coral, is if you say we have to. Now be a good girl and pick your first position." Even if oral sex wasn't something she wanted, I had plenty of other tricks up my sleeve and I planned to use as many as she'd let me.

From my position at the side of the bed, even with her still on her hands and knees, I could see her nipples cinch into tight buds at my demand. The goose bumps rippling over her skin didn't escape my attention either. Nor did her sharp intake of breath or the way her fingers curled into the comforter as her back arched. Her body telegraphed its pleasure in my taking control.

A fact further confirmed when she shifted backward, widened her knees and settled on her elbows with her ass high in the air. Blood roared in my ears at the sight of her. At the supple curve of her ass and the subtle sway of her breasts with each shaky breath she took. Coral turned her head to look at me with those thundercloud eyes. "Your move, hotshot."

I shoved my underwear down my legs and basked briefly in the flutter of her lashes and the pink swipe of her tongue across her lips at the sight of my dick. I gave it a stroke and she swallowed, then sucked her lower lip between her teeth before looking at my face.

"Still think you only want 'both'?" I asked.

Coral shook her head in a slow, determined motion. Red tendrils of hair slid over her shoulder blades. "I think," she said, her voice a low, husky purr, "that I want all you have to give me."

Olympic broad jumpers would've been impressed with the way I launched myself onto the bed. Coral only giggled at my impatience. On my knees behind her, I reveled in the sight of her. With both hands, I stroked up her strong thighs to her lushly rounded ass and back down again. Coral rocked back into my touch, and I bit back a groan at the view of her center. Glistening pink folds begged for my cock and in my haste I fumbled the strip of condoms.

Finally, I separated one and sheathed myself. Holding my dick with one hand, I placed the other on the curve of one delectable ass cheek. I traced a thumb through her folds, and she shuddered, once again pushing back into my touch, seeking more of it. I wanted to surge forward and bury myself to the hilt, but I held back. I teased her entrance, outlining the lips of her sex with my thumb, but not giving her the penetration she wanted.

On her next backward push, I slapped the back of her thigh, making her squeal. "You chose the position, sweetheart," I chastised. "But I'm choosing the pace."

Her moan was stifled by the pillow, and she gave another testing push-back, which was rewarded by a slap to her other thigh. Another moan and her hips tilted higher. A full body shiver worked its way through her, and I ran a hand down her back to soothe her. My fingers slid down her spine and over the line between her cheeks until they reached the full, swollen lips of her sex. The noise she made at the light touch was almost keening, and it made me smile in triumph.

"That's a good girl," I said, slipping two fingers inside the hot wet heat of her. "You're so wet, sweetheart. So eager. So needy for my touch."

I could feel the tension in her body, her trying to hold still as I pushed my fingers deeper into her, stroking and stretching her inner walls. She lifted her head from the pillow and gasped as I hit a particularly sensitive spot. Her hips bucked reflexively to chase the sensation. When I only increased the pressure instead of backing off, Coral moaned and rocked her hips back into my hand.

I kept my other hand circled around the base of my cock as she rode my fingers. Her movements became jerky, and I felt her walls clamping down around my fingers, sucking me deeper.

"Not just yet, gorgeous," I said, pulling my hand back to tease at her outer lips once more.

Coral gave a broken cry of disappointment that changed to an eager moan when she felt the tip of my cock take the place of my fingers.

"That's better, isn't it, my greedy girl?"

"It will be," she rasped, "once you're all the way inside me instead of being a fucking cock tease."

I circled her entrance but didn't press forward. "I don't think that's a thing."

"You have a cock," she said, letting out a small groan as I gave her just the head. "And you're teasing me with it," she panted when I held still. "What else would you call it?"

"Want to go back to just my fingers?" I asked, making a move to withdraw from her.

She countered by pushing back and my dick slid deeper.

"Do you?" Coral asked, and I heard the triumph in the question. She knew there was no way I was pulling out now that I'd felt the hot clench of her around my cock.

I groaned at the feel of her, even through the condom. Liquid heat encircled me, at once drawing me in and resisting my presence. I felt her breathe and her muscles relax as she adjusted to me. "No fucking way," I said, gripping her hips and pushing forward, inch by inch, in a slow, deliberate slide until my own were pressed against her ass.

I held myself there, breathing heavily and giving each of us a second longer to acclimate to the feel of each other. Her inner walls gradually relaxed to the point I thought I could move without hurting her. "You good, Coral?"

"I'll be better once you're moving," she said, emphasizing her point with a roll of her hips that made us both groan.

"As you wish," I said, leaning over to cup her breasts. They were full and heavy in my palms, and I kneaded them as I began to move in slow, deep thrusts. Spreading my fingers, I trapped her nipples between two knuckles and pinched as I thrust into her. Coral's head came back with a throaty cry, and she redoubled the roll of her hips against mine. The deeper I went, or harder I tugged on the taut tips of her breasts, the louder

Coral moaned. The sound of it reverberated through my brain and down my spine, making me desperate to hear it again and again.

"Jesus, baby." I grunted, glancing down to watch my cock move in and out of her. "You're fucking perfect. Every goddamn inch of you is fucking perfect."

"Jamie," Coral cried. Her hands slid from under the pillow to brace against the headboard. My next thrust went deeper than I'd imagined, and a groan tore out of my throat. My spine tingled and my balls tightened, signaling the approach of an orgasm. I wanted to see her when I came, to look into those gorgeous fucking eyes of hers and watch her come apart. Which meant I needed to get her there first and then again with me.

Releasing one of her breasts, my hand came to her clit, stroking the swollen bundle and making her moan so hard I felt it from inside her. "Oh, God, Jamie. Yes, fuck. Right there, baby. Yes, that spot . . . that . . . spot . . ."

Her words drifted off as her body tensed, her back arching, and I heard the scrabble of her nails at the headboard. She was close. I could feel her tightening around me. I rolled my hips forward, pressing deeper and holding as I pinched her nipple and strummed her clit.

"I know you're close, baby. I can feel it in the way you're sucking me in so deep. You like being full, don't you baby? So full of my cock while I'm playing with your clit?"

Coral moaned and bucked against me. I held still and let her use me, fucking back against my cock as I squeezed and toyed with her nipple.

"Take what you need, baby," I encouraged her, increasing the pace of my fingers between her legs. "Take it, Coral, take it all."

The first ripple of her orgasm clamped around my dick, and I groaned right along with her. "That's a good girl," I praised her as she rode out her climax with throaty moans and whimpers, slightly muffled by the pillows beneath her. The throbs and pulses of her body slowed, as she collapsed forward, her breast sliding from my hand.

I withdrew from her body, still hard as a rock and with the tingling ache of a building orgasm still in full effect. Looping one arm under her belly, I flipped her onto her back. Coral stared up at me with a dazed, sated expression. Hooking one arm under her knee, I pulled her back toward me.

"That was one," I said, bending to kiss the tips of her breasts. "Now we're going for 'both.'" I grinned down at her. "Which, for you, sweetheart, translates to three on the evening."

"Oh, God, Jamie," she said, her voice a heady whisper. Her hips jerked as I stroked her swollen clit with my cock. "Oh, God," she said again as I shifted lower and pressed inside her once again.

There was no resistance, as her body had already grown used to mine. There was only acceptance and the fluttering sensation of her orgasmic aftershocks working their way around my shaft. The feeling was so erotic I groaned and pushed deeper. Coral's inner muscles pulsed against me, and she moaned, tilting her hips to let me slide all the way in.

Reaching behind her, I grabbed a pillow and pushed it under her hips. Coral's throaty murmur and the way she gripped my shoulders let me know the change in angle was enough to let me hit the spot within her I'd brushed with my fingers earlier. With a gentle hand, I drew her leg up and around my hip. I lowered myself over her until we were chest to chest.

I kissed her as I began to move in hard, quick thrusts. Her hands came to my hair and her tongue tangled with mine. Our kisses were hot and frantic, interspersed with carnal sounds and feral grunts of pleasure.

"Jamie," Coral whispered against my lips. "I'm . . . I think I'm . . ."

"Tell me what you need, baby." I was so close to coming that I wasn't sure how much longer I could stave off my orgasm. I wanted to. Wanted her to fall one more time before I gave in.

"I . . . I need," her words were a choked rasp as she wound her legs around mine and tilted her pelvis, seeking the friction she needed. "There," she gasped, nails digging into my shoulders. "Right there, Jamie. Oh, God, yes!"

I pumped faster. Quick jerks of my hips, over and over until I felt her stiffen then relax with a final cry as her release took her under. One, two, three more thrusts and I followed.

"Coral!" I threw my head back on a guttural groan as my body went on autopilot, pummeling into her with the thundering force of an orgasm held off for too long. Tiny fractures of lights burst behind my eyelids and my pulse thrummed like molten energy through me.

I couldn't say if it went on for seconds, minutes, or unrealistic hours. Only that afterward I was spent, my body felt wrung out and used up. A strong gust of wind could've blown me off the bed in that moment. It was all I could do not to crash down on top of Coral. My arms trembled with the effort of holding myself up and not crushing her.

She blinked up at me, a slow, satisfied smile curving her beautiful mouth. Shifting my weight to one elbow, I traced the lines of her face with one finger.

"Hi," I said, grinning like an idiot.

"Hi there, Adonis," she teased, her hand coming up to cup my cheek. Lifting her head, she pressed a kiss to my lips. I returned the kiss, enjoying the softness of her lips against mine. The softness of all of her against all of me. I could've stayed there the rest of the night, exchanging subtle touches and kisses with her.

I kissed the tip of her nose. "Don't move," I ordered and rose off the bed to dispose of the condom.

# CORAL

Jamie padded into the bathroom bare ass naked. I managed to lift my head to check out his ass, appreciated the view for approximately one point six seconds, and then collapsed back onto the mattress.

Staring up at the tastefully ornate light fixture above the bed, I bit back a laugh. There was little chance of me moving after he'd officially banged my brains out. I was impressed he could still move with such agility. If I'd tried to get out of bed, I had no doubt my legs would've collapsed beneath me, and I would've face planted the minute my feet hit the floor.

My body was stretched and tender in a supremely well-fucked manner. Muscles I didn't know I had ached like they'd just been used to run a marathon, or wind sprints at the very least. Even my skin was tired. The man had wrung every ounce of energy from every part of me. And it felt amazing. At least it would feel amazing after a nap and infusion of electrolytes.

Turning my head, I eyed the lilac colored bakery box on the nightstand next to the bottle of champagne. It might not have the same refueling capacity as a power bar and some Gatorade, but it called to me, nonetheless.

The faucet shut off, signaling Jamie's imminent return. Maybe he'd just drop morsels of dessert into my open mouth, so I didn't have to leave the increasingly comfortable Coral-shaped indention I imagined we'd made in the mattress. The champagne would be trickier with the whole fizzy aspect, but I was sure we could work something out that wouldn't involve me moving.

His low laugh interrupted my planning. With effort, I lifted my head again to look at him standing in the doorway of the bathroom. "What's so funny?" I asked.

He was still gloriously naked, so there was nothing amusing about the view I had. The man was a vision. A true feast for the eyes with his sex-mussed hair, bedroom eyes, megawatt smile, and all of that was above the neck! Below the neck, the man was obscenely fit. Broad shoulders and chest, tapering down to the aforementioned Adonis belt and his *thighs*! Good God, he could've cracked walnuts with those things. Maybe even coconuts, although that was probably the sex endorphins messing with my mind. Either way, I'd have watched him try.

"I've never seen someone try to move food closer with their mind," he said, still chuckling.

"Well, I've never been rendered immobile by orgasms before, so it looks like both of us are experiencing a couple of firsts tonight."

Jamie lifted one brow, his grin turning smug. "Rendered immobile, huh?"

I flapped a hand down my body. "What else would you call the state I'm in right now?"

Blue eyes flashed darkly as they raked over my still naked form. I held up a hand to stop his perusal and the chain of thought I knew accompanied it. "Nope, no, nuh-uh. Not until you feed me some of that cake and funnel champagne down my throat. Then we can discuss the possibility of round two."

Jamie laughed and strolled toward the bed, stooping down to grab his boxer briefs from the floor and step into them. The thin black cotton molded to his form and lived up to the name "brief." Rather than slide into bed on the other side, he crawled over me, pausing halfway to kiss me. My body hummed in response, and I was happy to have it show signs of resuscitation.

Kneeling on the side of the bed closest to the food, he started arranging the ridiculous number of pillows in some sort of U-shaped throne. Once he was satisfied with the fluffy structure, he pulled the covers down and shifted on his knees to regard my still prone form. With a grin, he slid one arm under my shoulders and the other under the backs of my thighs before lifting me against his chest.

All night, I'd enjoyed the way he made me feel delicate. I'd been a five-foot-eight high school freshman and four years later graduated an inch shy of six feet. And my height had never been described as anything close to "willowy." I was tall and strong with muscular shoulders and arms I'd used in swimming my whole life. I hadn't been small enough for most men to cradle in their arms since I'd been old enough to know it would have any appeal.

But Jamie lifted me easily and tucked me snugly against his bare chest. The hum I felt when he'd kissed me became more insistent the tighter he held me. The backs of my thighs tingled where they rested on his forearm, and my breast didn't miss the fact his hand was mere inches away.

"Kneeling seems to be a thing with you," I said, my hand resting on the center of his chest. His skin was warm to the touch.

His laugh ruffled my hair. "You bring it out in me, sweetheart." I felt his stomach muscles bunch and contract and his biceps bulge when he lifted me higher to allow himself to settle against the pillows. Rolling his shoulders, he burrowed backward in a move so childlike I had to laugh.

"Are you mocking my pillow lair?" he asked with a teasing glare.

"How could I mock something as serious as a pillow lair? I'm not some bottom-dwelling cretin," I assured him.

"Good, because I'd hate for you to miss out on its benefits," he cautioned.

I tilted my head back to give him a questioning look. "Benefits?"

His answer was to nod and lower me in his arms, using his grip on my legs to shift me into a position parallel with his against the headboard. Long legs dusted with blond hair extended on either side of mine and he pulled my ass flush with his groin, guiding my shoulders back to rest against his chest. Leaning us both forward, he pulled the covers up to just beneath my breasts.

It was cozy, tucked into bed with him like this. More than cozy, in fact. With Jamie surrounding me on all sides, an innate sense of security welled up within me. A feeling of being cherished and protected from everything there in the fortress of goose down and solidly built male perfection. I tried to shake it off, telling myself I was reading way too much into whatever this was. But, despite my best efforts, the feeling settled deep within me, embedding itself into my psyche with an unnerving sort of permanence.

"So many benefits," Jamie said, tucking me closer and brushing my hair to the side. "The first benefit," he said, nuzzling into my neck and kissing my bare shoulder.

"I'm beginning to see the perks," I said, cocooned in his full body embrace and surrendering to the security of it. I'd have plenty of time to cram down any feelings later. Now, I was just going to enjoy it.

Jamie reached over to the nightstand to retrieve the box of goodies, setting it on my now sheet covered lap. Picking up the fork, he neatly carved off a bite of shortcake and held it to my lips. "Benefit number two," he said.

I opened my mouth to accept the bite. Tartly sweet strawberry and rich vanilla coated my tongue, and I groaned. "The picture is becoming clearer by the minute," I said around my mouthful of delicious baked goods.

He laughed, cutting his own sizable bite and shoveling it into his mouth with an appreciative grumble.

I swallowed. "Just two benefits, then?"

Jamie held up a hand as he chewed and swallowed. "Oh, ye of little faith." He lifted the champagne bottle from the bucket on the table and put it to his lips to take a swallow, then pass it to me. "Benefit number three."

Laughing, I took the bottle and wiped the side of it with the comforter. The cool bubbles danced down my throat with my first sip. The innocent fun of dessert in a pillow fort while swigging champagne from the bottle was a one hundred and eighty degree turn from hot, sweaty sexcapades. But I found myself enjoying it just as much.

Jamie grabbed the remote from the nightstand and flicked on the massive TV on the opposite wall. He scrolled over to the Netflix app and pulled up a rom-com set at a wedding in Australia. "Last but not least," he said, replacing the remote, "benefit number four."

I pinched his arm, and he yelped. "What was that for?"

"Just confirming that you are in fact real," I said, forking up another bite of shortcake.

"Don't you normally pinch yourself to make sure you aren't dreaming?" he asked, fingers gliding over the underside of my breast in a gentle pinch.

Ignoring the way my body thrummed in response, I said, "I'm going to need at least another half an hour and several more bites of cake before I'm ready for round two."

I felt his laugh behind me as his lips brushed my ear. "I can work with that, gorgeous."

As the couple on screen stumbled through their meet cute, I looked back at Jamie. "Hey, Jamie?"

"Hm?" he responded, glancing down at me.

"Tonight was . . ." I bit my lip, trying to figure out how to tell him what I was thinking without making it seem like this was something more than what it was.

He shifted behind me, so our faces were almost aligned. "Tonight was . . .?" I heard the question in his tone.

"Tonight was everything I needed it to be," I said. "Mixed in with little of what I didn't even know I wanted."

Jamie smiled and tucked a strand of hair behind my ear. "I stand by what I said over macarons, Coral."

"That you want to look as cool as Blake in a suit and tie?"

His smile pushed higher, making his eyes crinkle at the corners. "That too, obviously. But I'm talking about you being the best part of my week."

"I thought you said I was the first thing that had gone right for you in a week," I said, resting my head on his shoulder. I could get used to the way he looked at me. The way his eyes went soft, and his smile turned sweeter. The way it felt to be in his arms, cradled like something precious and valued.

"You were paying attention," he countered with a low chuckle. "The truth is, Coral, it's been a lot longer than a week since I've experienced anything close to being with you."

The same sensation I experienced at seeing him on his knees earlier flooded through me. The entire too muchness of the evening threatened to overwhelm me. But something about the way Jamie looked at me kept it at bay, lurking in the shadows but not stepping into the light to ruin the moment like it had before.

Morning would come soon enough, but until then, I decided to sink into the evening and revel in all of it while I still could. So, I smiled up at him, kissed his chin and said, "Something tells me you're a pretty singular experience yourself, Jamie." And when he smiled and tucked me closer to continue watching the movie, it no longer felt like too much. Instead, it felt more like I'd never get enough.

# chapter ten

## JAMIE

The room was dark when I woke up, which wasn't a surprise given the blackout curtains in the bedroom. I reached for Coral, but found cold, empty sheets instead. My hand stretched across the ludicrously sized mattress, convinced if I reached far enough, I'd connect with the silk of her skin. But high-quality cotton was the only thing beneath my fingers. Cotton that had long ago relinquished her body heat.

Groggily, I sat up and flipped on the bedside lamp. It bathed the bed in a hazy glow of light that confirmed I was its only occupant. The door to the en suite bathroom was open, and the room was dark.

"Coral?" Her name was met with silence. Maybe she was in the kitchen and couldn't hear me. I snatched my phone from where it was charging on the nightstand to check the time: 5:16 a.m. I set it back down with a thunk, almost knocking off the now empty champagne bottle. I'd sucked the last of it out of her belly button just hours before. The memory made my cock twitch.

Swinging my legs from beneath the covers to the floor, something crinkled under my foot. Lifting it, I saw it was a condom wrapper. One of several littering the carpet at my feet. I shoved a hand through my hair and stood. I grabbed my underwear off the footstool of the chair by the bed and pulled them on before heading to the kitchen.

"Coral?" I called again. And again, her name was met with silence. The living room was dark, as was the rest of the suite. I flipped on lights in the asinine hope she'd be sitting on the couch in the dark. Spoiler alert—she wasn't. Nor was she in the kitchen. I knocked on the door to the half bath, then opened it when there was no response. Empty.

Had she gone to get coffee? I scrubbed my hands down my face. *Get a grip, you idiot,* I chastised myself. It was just after five in the morning, and we'd only unwound ourselves from each other around three. Why would she leave my bed to get coffee a mere two hours later? That made zero sense, and yet part of me still clung stupidly to the chance she'd come bursting through the door with coffee and a smile any second.

It was on my second scan of the room that I saw it. A folded paper square with a big letter "J" scrawled on the front sitting in the middle of the dining table. Relief coursed through me. She'd left me a note to explain her absence and say when she'd be back.

In my haste to grab the note, I stubbed my toe on the leg of one the dining chairs.

"Fuck." I grabbed the edge of the table as my toe throbbed. Jerking the note off the table, I unfolded it and began to read.

*Jamie,*

*Last night was . . . well, you know what last night was because you were with me. It was everything I wanted for my first night in Vegas. You were amazing. Thanks for everything.*
*C*

*What the fuck?* I had to be sleep-deprived and reading this wrong. I shook my head to clear out the cobwebs and re-read the note, certain that on a second read it would say something that made sense. Something like, *Hey, needed a pick me up, be right back for yet another round of the best sex known to mankind.*

But that's not what I read. Instead, it said the same fucking thing it had the first time I'd read it and remained the same fucking words on the third read. *Thanks for everything? You were amazing?* I wasn't a fucking VRBO host, for Christ's sake! I was the guy who'd explored every inch . . . no, every freaking *millimeter* of her body last night. And she left me a note that read like a *Yelp!* review?

I thought back to what she'd said while we watched a movie. *Tonight was everything I needed it to be.* A similar sentiment to what she'd written, but one that seemed different last night. More personal than the stark black words on the page in my hand. Maybe I'd read too much into it, though. I'd been so in my head about that article. Maybe I'd fabricated some deeper connection with Coral because I wanted to prove—at least to myself—that I could forge that sort of connection.

I almost crumpled the paper into a ball. Almost. But something kept me from closing my fist around it. I dropped the note onto the table and slumped into the chair that had tried to sever my toe, struggling to wrap my head around her being gone. Had she promised anything other than last night? No, she had not. Instead, she'd made it clear we only had one night together. But did she have to slink out in the pre-dawn hours of the morning?

I'd drifted off with thoughts of sharing breakfast with her. Maybe even asking her to dinner. I'd thought, obviously incorrectly, that she'd warmed to the idea of more than a single evening. She'd given me her real name, shared more than a few things about herself. Things that weren't earth shattering by any means, but revealed more than what I assumed she normally shared. But it seemed I was the only one who'd suffered any illusions about last night.

My hand rasped against early morning stubble when I rubbed my jaw. Coral had made no secret of her complete *dis*interest in any sort of plan beyond the one she had for last night. But then we'd spent the night together, and it had been . . . I refused to use the word amazing. In fact, I had a sneaking suspicion that word would be tainted for me for some time to come. Amazing. I snorted and scratched at my stubble again, flicking her note with my finger and making it spin in a wonky circle.

I knew I was pouting like a toddler. Hell, I was close to a full-blown tantrum. As though she were a toy that had been taken away, instead of a woman capable of leaving when it suited her. The problem was, it didn't suit me. At all. Because I wanted more of last night. And not just the sex. I wanted more of . . . her. More of us. More of all of it.

Coral was . . . shit, she was exhilarating. The woman radiated a certain willful energy that was magnetic. Plus, she was funny and brashly confident, so secure in herself and unafraid to take what she wanted. At least, that was my read on her from the hours we'd spent together. And after those hours, I wanted more time with her. To get to know her. Pull more of the little details from her that would give me the whole picture.

But now, with the light of early morning peeking around the thick curtains to cast the suite in a gray pallor, I had to face facts. My eyes dropped to the note with a frown. It was hard evidence she obviously did not share my feelings. Evidence I needed to put last night in the rearview and stop moping about like a heartsick teenager. She'd given me the night she'd promised, and I needed to accept that and get over it. Hell, I should be grateful for it, considering everything else on my plate at that point.

Gratitude was the right approach, not the nagging concern that I'd proven myself to be exactly the person that goddamn article said I was.

That by agreeing to Coral's request for one night, I'd shown her my true colors, and she'd bailed without a backward glance. That she didn't believe I was capable of more. That maybe, deep down, I wasn't.

"Fuck," I said to the empty room. I was getting too in my head over this. Her leaving had nothing to do with my past. She'd set the ground rules before knowing anything about me. I needed to let this go and get some sleep.

I picked up the note and stood, walking into the kitchen of the suite. I'd just trash the note and go back to bed. Pulling out the trash drawer, I let the paper float down to the bottom of the wastebasket and closed the drawer. With a jaw cracking yawn, I headed back to the bedroom. Sleep would restore my proper perspective. Well-rested me would see Coral's amicable, if somewhat dismissive, departure as the proper ending to last night. A nice, neat ending with no muss or fuss.

# CORAL

"Ms. Triton?"

The sound of my name pulled me from a memory of Jamie's arms winding around me the night before. One of many that had been playing through my mind since I'd slipped from his room just before five that morning. He'd looked positively sinful with the sheets tangled around his waist and face relaxed into a deep sleep, long lashes dusting his cheekbones. Adonis at rest before waking to wreak havoc on mere mortal women. The temptation to stay had been so strong, I'd almost given in. Almost crawled back into bed and tucked myself against him. Thank goodness this morning's meeting with Jocelyn saved me from myself.

I couldn't just leave, though, so I'd left a note. A hastily scribbled, half-thought-out paragraph that didn't convey most of what I wanted to say. For a brief, sleep-deprived and overly sexed moment, I'd considered leaving him my number, or suggesting we could meet up. But I'd quashed that as soon as I'd thought it. Jamie had been unexpected in all the best ways, but that didn't mean I needed to deviate from my initial plan. I'd wanted a perfect welcome to Vegas, and he'd given it to me. Best to leave it at that and savor the memory. A memory that had been on repeat in my brain since the door to his suite clicked shut behind me.

Now wasn't the time for that, though. I looked up at the smiling woman standing in the doorway across from the leather couch I was sitting on. "Yes," I said, rising and slinging my bag onto my shoulder.

She held out a hand for me to shake. "I'm Meredith, Ms. Standard's assistant. She's ready for you."

"Great," I said, putting on a confident smile. I wasn't exactly nervous to see Jocelyn in person. After all, she'd been the one to contact me about the job. A job I already *had*, so this wasn't an interview. Just an . . . informal hello, like she'd said in her note. But the little flip my stomach gave confirmed I wasn't completely relaxed about it either.

My phone chimed from within my purse, and I hurriedly searched for it to set it to silent. A brief glance at the screen showed it was a text from my mother, once again asking when I could come home to meet her new man. No inquiry about my job, or how I was settling in. Not that I expected anything of the sort from her now that there was a new Mr. Right within reach. She'd have a one-track mind until he joined the battalion of Mr. Wrongs that came before him. I'd deal with her later.

I followed Meredith down a hallway lined with art that rivaled what I'd seen last night with Jamie. The flip in my stomach intensified at the thought of him, but I shoved that away and focused on the reason I was here. First impressions were important and, regardless of whether I had the job or not, I wasn't going to blow mine with Jocelyn by not having my head fully in the game.

Meredith stopped in front of an already open door, rapping once on the doorframe. "Jocelyn, I've got Ms. Triton for you."

"Very good, Meredith, thank you." Jocelyn's voice floated out into the hallway as Meredith stepped back and gestured for me to go in.

Obeying, I crossed into a powerfully feminine space. The walls were a deep wine red, which provided a rich contrast to the ivory couch and chair angled around a low glass-topped table. The base of it appeared to be made from pieces of gnarled wood.

"They're grapevines."

The comment pulled my eyes from the table and over to the woman rising from behind her desk on the far side of the room. Jocelyn's smile was wide, and her blue eyes were welcoming. She almost looked familiar, which made no sense. We'd spoken on the phone, but I'd never seen her before. I brushed off the strangeness of that feeling and accepted her outstretched hand.

She nodded again toward the table. "The base. It's made of old grapevines from one of my favorite vineyards in Napa."

"Oh," I said. "That's very cool."

Jocelyn released my hand with a laugh. "My brother would say it's pretentious, but then he's the expert on pretension, so I guess he'd know."

I joined her laughter, liking her already.

She waved a hand at the couch. "Please, have a seat. And thanks for coming in on a Sunday. Weekends are often our busiest times, so Sunday is usually a full workday for me. Would you like anything to drink?"

I shook my head. "No, I'm fine, thanks. And believe me, I'm used to a different sort of schedule."

Jocelyn took a seat across from me, brushing her long blond hair back over her shoulder. Reclining back in her seat, she crossed her legs, giving me a great look at her leopard print heels.

"Love the shoes," I said.

She glanced down and grinned. "Thanks. One of the perks of working in Vegas. Leopard print really is considered a neutral out here." Twisting her wrist, she looked down at her watch. "We're just waiting on Xavier before we get started, but in the meantime, tell me how you like your room. Is there anything else you need? Anything we're lacking?"

"I don't know anyone that would categorize my room as lacking anything," I said with a smile. "It's perfect, thank you." My heart sped up at the thought of meeting Xavier Raulston. Although I knew he would be involved in the show, I hadn't realized he'd be here this morning. His being a part of what Jocelyn was doing at L'Atelier was a huge reason I'd jumped at the chance to be a part of it. The man was a freaking legend in the merpeople realm. A true master underwater and how I knew Jocelyn was wholly serious about making this show the best. Xavier wouldn't have agreed to be involved if it were anything less than spectacular.

"I'm glad to hear it. Please let me know, though, if you need anything else."

A knock sounded at the door before I could reply. Both of us turned at the sound and I was dumbstruck at the sight of Xavier standing there grinning at us. A little squeak of excitement slipped out before I could stop it. I tried my best to cover it by clearing my throat.

Jocelyn returned his smile, rising to greet him warmly. "Xavier," she said. "I'm so glad you could join us today."

He pushed off the doorframe and entered the office. Ripped jeans encased muscular legs, and a worn leather vest showcased a wealth of mocha colored skin and the lion's head tattoo on his right pectoral. A nose ring glinted from his left nostril and sunglasses held back his long dreadlocks.

"Hey, Joss," he said, using her handshake to pull her into a hug. Her much smaller frame almost disappeared in his embrace. His voice was deep, the baritone sound of it plusher than the velvet couch I was sitting on. Releasing Jocelyn, he looked at me, a wide smile on his handsome face. "This must be the mermaid I've heard so much about."

He held out a hand. "Xavier Raulston, nice to meet you."

I blinked stupidly at his hand for a few seconds before recovering and standing up. My hand shot out to shake his. "You're Xavier Raulston," I said, like an idiot.

He grinned and nodded, dreads swaying against his bare shoulders. "I am. And you're Coral Triton."

Belatedly, I realized I was still pumping our clasped hands like I expected water to spout from somewhere. "Sorry," I said, releasing his hand. "It's just that you're Xavier Raulston."

Xavier laughed. "Seems like that means a lot more to you than it does to me, Coral."

"Sorry," I apologized again. "I'm trying not to fangirl, but I don't think I'm doing a great job of it."

He waved off my flustered apology, the heavy silver ring on his middle finger flashing in the sunlight. "I'm a fan of yours too," he said, taking a seat in the chair opposite Jocelyn.

"Me?" The incredulity in my voice probably wasn't killing it for the whole first impression thing, but I couldn't help it. The idea that a guy who'd grown famous from his videos swimming with sharks—famous to the point he'd been selected by at least two uber-successful singers to star in their latest music videos—would even know who I was, much less be a fan, blew my mind. Rumor had it that one of those singers had commissioned a custom-made tank for Xavier to use as a part of her next world tour.

He nodded, leaning forward to rest his elbows on his knees. The jumble of necklaces he wore swung forward in a tinkle of sound. "Jocelyn sent me some of your clips when she broached the idea of the live mermaid show. Pretty impressive stuff, especially that one from Rainbow Springs."

"Thank you," I said, unable to keep the awestruck tone out of my voice. Xavier Raulston liked my work! I could die now, and they could write it on my tombstone.

"Xavier encouraged me to reach out to you, Coral," Jocelyn said. "Your videos caught my eye, of course, but when I forwarded them to Xavier, he was as excited by your talent as I was."

Pride suffused through me, filling me like a hot-air balloon. Few things felt as good as someone complimenting my work. Work that had once seemed like a pipe dream and was now on the precipice of true fulfillment.

"It's true," Xavier said. "This is going to be one hell of a project to get things up and running, so we need the best and brightest working on it. Which is why I wholeheartedly agreed with Joss when she mentioned bringing you on board."

Jocelyn nodded. "I think you and Xavier are the perfect team to get our mermaid pod off the . . ." She looked over at Xavier. "Is it right to say 'ground'? I feel like there should be some under the sea term to use instead."

Xavier laughed and relaxed back in his seat. "Don't worry, Joss, you'll get a handle on mermaid culture soon enough." He smirked at her. "Who knows, maybe you'll even develop your own mersona and join us in the tank."

Jocelyn laughed. "I think that is best left to the professionals." She shot me a sly look. "Although, I have to say, those tails you have are tempting. They're so gorgeous!"

I smiled, still riding the high of their praise, then pointed at the blank wall behind her desk. "You could get one, you know. They make great wall-hangings even if you don't wear them. Cam, the mermaid I suggested join the team once she's wrapped in Florida, has all of her tail racks at home arranged like an art gallery." Then what Xavier said finally sank in and my head whipped around to look at him. "Wait, did you say join 'us' in the tank?"

He grinned back at me. "What, you didn't think you were going to have all the fun, did you?"

"You're going to swim in the show?" I'd assumed he would be too busy to swim, that he'd be involved in planning and choreography, but the idea we'd swim together was enough to make my brain fizzle out.

"If you'll have me," he teased.

My mouth fell open, and I gaped at him.

Laughing, he said, "You already have the job, Coral. No need to impersonate Flounder to try and get brownie points with me."

Jocelyn laughed. "Yes, Xavier has graciously agreed to be a part of our show when it opens and before he goes on tour later in the year."

My brows shot up. "So it's true? You're going on tour with Rhi—"

He mimed locking his lips before I could finish. "I'm afraid I'm not at liberty to say. That's all being kept under wraps for now, as you might imagine." Xavier grinned. "But in the interim, I get to be your mertender and maybe spend a little time in the tank with you. If that's all right."

"I'm sorry," Jocelyn's brows drew down with confusion. "Did you say 'mertender'?"

Xavier and I laughed at her puzzled expression. "Sorry," he said. "Didn't mean to lapse into our particular vernacular there. A mertender helps the performers in and out of the tank, monitors the air hoses and our finned friends to make sure everything stays friendly under the sea."

"I'll have to remember that," Jocelyn said.

Another knock sounded at the door and Meredith poked her head in. "I'm sorry to interrupt, Ms. Standard, but your brother's here. He says he has an appointment, but I have you blocked through lunch."

Jocelyn rolled her eyes, checking her watch with a sigh. "*He's* my lunch appointment, for which he's arrived early." She grimaced at me. "Do you have older brothers?"

I shook my head, and she sighed. "Want to take mine off my hands? I'll give you a good deal on him."

I laughed. "Something tells me I might regret accepting that offer."

Xavier rose from his seat. "Why don't I take Coral down to see the tank? I'd planned to once we were through anyway. That should free you up to meet your brother."

Jocelyn frowned, obviously perturbed her brother's early arrival disrupted her schedule. "I hate to cut this short," she said.

I stood up, unable to disguise my excitement at seeing the tank. "Don't worry about it. I've been dying for a closer look at the tank since I got here."

My reassurance erased Jocelyn's frown. "I saw your post about it yesterday," she said. "And that you tagged the hotel in it." She gave me an approving smile and rose to her feet, smoothing the front of her fitted black sheath dress.

Holding out her hand for another shake, she said, "It was so nice to finally meet you in person, Coral. I'm so happy you're part of the team."

"Likewise," I said, taking her hand in mine. "And good luck with your brother. He sounds like a real handful."

# chapter eleven

## JAMIE

"You can follow me back, Mr. Standard," Meredith said.

I turned from the shimmering Vegas skyline outside the window to find her waiting for me. "How many times do I have to tell you, Meredith? Mr. Standard is my father and even he isn't that formal. Call me Jamie, please."

She smiled and said, "If you'll follow me."

Obediently, I trundled along behind her. Feminine laughter wafted down the hall and I froze. Meredith noticed my lack of progress and paused to look back. "Mr. Standard?"

I blinked, ears straining to catch another hint of the rich, husky laughter. The familiar sound of it triggering a memory of Coral laughing up at me, her red hair splayed across my pillow as she held the sheet against her chest. I spun around in a slow circle, fully aware I looked insane. And maybe I was going crazy. Maybe I'd imagined the sound of her laugh.

"Mr. Standard?" Meredith asked again, now sounding legitimately concerned.

"Did you hear that?" I asked her.

She frowned. "Did I hear . . . what?"

"That la—" I cut the words off with a regretful shake of my head. No need to give voice to my absurd delusion. "Nothing, sorry."

Meredith cocked a brow at me. "Are you all right, sir?"

"Yes," I said, giving her a forced smile. "Just didn't get much sleep last night. I'm a still a little punchy, I guess."

She nodded slowly, not buying my excuse for a minute, but too professional to comment on it. Two sharp raps on the doorframe to my sister's office announced our arrival. "Your brother Jamie, Jocelyn."

"Thank you, Meredith," Jocelyn said. She was standing by the side-board to the left of her desk, pouring a glass of water. Setting down the pitcher, she turned to look at me, inventorying my appearance.

"Congratulations, brother dear," she said.

I raised a brow. "On what?"

"On managing to look like hell in a three-thousand-dollar suit. That takes real skill."

"Thanks so much," I replied flatly. "You'll understand if that opinion doesn't hold much weight coming from a woman wearing cheetahs on her feet."

"They're leopard print, you caveman. And they're couture," she snapped without any real bite. "You're still the only man I know who vacations in a suit. Grandpa would be proud." She spread her arms wide and grinned at me. "Now get your ass over here and give me a hug."

I returned her smile and crossed to her, enveloping her in a hug. "I've missed you, sis," I said, giving her one last squeeze before letting go.

"I don't see how you've had the time," she said, rounding the corner of her desk and opening a drawer. After withdrawing a copy of *Boston Commons*, she tossed it onto the polished wood surface.

I glanced down at the paper and swore. "How many copies of this did you buy? And why do you even get this rag?"

She smirked at me. "How else would I keep up with my big brother's escapades?"

"So, we're just launching right into it? No warmup at all?"

Jocelyn shrugged. "I figure the quicker we get it out of the way, the better you'll feel." She leaned a hip against her desk. "And I'm guessing you're at least somewhat anxious to spill the beans, otherwise you wouldn't have shown up a half hour early and forced me to cut my meeting short."

I winced. "Shit, Joss, I'm sorry. I didn't even think about that. I just . . . Well, shit." I'd thought of little other than Coral all morning, which had been driving me up the wall. Anxious for any sort of distraction, I'd selfishly shown up early and disrupted her day.

She smiled and patted my arm. "It's fine. They had some other things to attend to, so it worked out." Cocking her head, she surveyed me. "Thank God I sent them down the back elevator, so they didn't have to see your pitiful countenance. They would've thought we had a death in the family or something."

For a second, the laughter I'd thought I imagined popped in my mind. Had Coral been my sister's meeting? I dismissed the thought as soon as it formed. I was being ridiculous, trying to catch glimpses of her everywhere. I pushed all thoughts of her firmly to the side and focused on Jocelyn. "Your flattery is doing wonders for me, sis."

Going back behind her desk, she opened a different drawer and removed a bright red purse. "I'll make it up to you with lunch. C'mon, let's get some food in you and you can tell me all about being one of the Boston Bad Boys of Business."

"Ms. Standard," the maître d' cried. "How lovely to see you again."

"Likewise, Jean Paul," Jocelyn said, accepting the diminutive man's air kisses on each cheek. "I know we don't have a reservation, but I was hoping . . ."

He slashed a hand through the air. "You insult me with your 'hoping,'" he chastised. "As if there would ever be a time when I would not have a table for you."

"I'm never one to presume," she insisted, following as he led us to a table in the back corner. One with a *Reserved* placard.

"Bullshit," I whispered right next to her ear, which earned me an elbow to the gut.

Jean Paul whipped off the placard and placed our menus on the table with a flourish. Snapping his fingers, he signaled a waiter, who hustled over. "This is Eric, he is one of our best and will get you anything you need."

"Thanks so much, Jean Paul," Jocelyn said sweetly. "Eric, we'll start with some ice water, please."

Once both her admirers departed, I asked, "Do I even want to know why they treat you like the Queen of Sheba?"

She shrugged, picking up a menu. "Jean Paul's daughter got married last year. They had a pipe burst in the kitchen the night of the rehearsal dinner. I set them up in one of our restaurants."

"Pays to have friends in high places," I teased, reviewing my own menu.

Jocelyn snorted. "My older brother once told me that business was all about cultivating relationships. I paid attention."

"He sounds like a smart guy."

She lifted her eyes from the menu. "I thought he was. Then I read the Boston paper." Her eyes glittered with amusement. "Turns out he's not smart enough to walk away from a gossip columnist hell bent on splashing details of his love life—or should I say sex life—all over the glossy pages of a snooty women's magazine. Thank God Mom is on one of her jaunts to Dublin visiting Aunt Jessica. You know she has a subscription to that rag."

I winced. "Hard copy instead of online, thank goodness. I'm just waiting until someone sends her a link to it. Is it wrong to hope the internet goes down in the entirety of Ireland?"

She frowned at me over her menu. "What I can't seem to fathom is how you've managed to develop any property in the last year or so. If that article is to be believed, you've been too busy seducing half of Boston to get any work done. And yet all of those ladies seem to think the only thing you'll ever be wedded to is your beloved business."

One elegant brow rose in challenge when I didn't say anything. "I know you haven't been serious with anyone since college. And you've resisted all of Mom's efforts to find your one true love."

When I opened my mouth to respond, she held up a hand. "I'm not advocating you finally let her matchmake. I'm just asking whether maybe this article shouldn't be a wake-up call for you. I mean, sure, having your own sustainable development empire at thirty-nine is awesome. But what is an emperor without his empress? Or other co-emperor, if that's your thing." She grinned. "Although I'm sure if you'd dabbled in a little same sex fun, I would've already read about it."

I scrubbed both hands down my face with a groan. Leave it to my baby sister to strike right to the heart of things in a surgical slice. Yes, I was dedicated to making Standard Development a success. That was the end goal. The only goal, really. A goal I wanted to achieve with a ferocity and single-minded focus that left little room for anything—or anyone—else in my life.

But I was still a heterosexual man, not a celibate monk. I *liked* women. Almost everything about them, in fact. The way they looked, the way they thought, the way they always seemed to smell good. Women were one of the most enjoyable things about being a man.

Which is really where it seemed my problem started. Because I enjoyed the company of women, a lot of women. A lot of different women. But I'd never made any promises or lied about my intentions. I was always clear that I wasn't looking for a relationship. That demands on my time wouldn't allow for that right now.

Except Gideon had the same demands on his time and he'd found a way to make things work with his fiancée, Everest. Granted, she'd sort of fallen into his lap during a development deal down in North Carolina, but he'd still had to work damn hard to convince her to give him a shot. He'd upended his life for her, leaving Boston and moving to Mimosa to open a satellite office of Standard. And he'd never been happier.

"Well," Jocelyn flipped out her napkin, no longer interested in waiting for me to respond. "Having read the article myself, let me give you my take on the Jameson Standard story."

"Do I have a choice?"

"None whatsoever, I'm afraid."

"All right then," I said, pushing back into the worn leather of the booth and bracing for impact. "Hit me with it, then."

"The good news is that it wasn't as bad for you as some of the others mentioned in the article. Talk about your toxic bachelors." She shuddered a little and I laughed, the sound as dry and brittle as the turn of a pepper grinder.

"I'm not sure my being one step above toxic is anything to brag about."

"Oh, definitely not, Jamie. But it shows you can be salvaged."

Before I could respond, Eric returned with our waters. "Did you need a little more time with the menus?"

"I don't believe so," Jocelyn answered for both of us. "But my brother here will need something stronger than water." She looked at me. "Will beer work, or do we need to go straight to the heavy stuff?"

An image of Coral flashed unbidden in my mind. "I'll pass on the beer," I said. "But I won't turn down a dirty martini."

"Very good, sir. Anything for you, Ms. Standard?"

"I can't very well let you drink alone," she said to me and to Eric, "Make it two. We'll start with the calamari, then two of the branzino specials."

When we were alone once more, Jocelyn continued as though she hadn't been interrupted. "What I find most interesting is that the actual quotes about you weren't that bad. If anything, I got the impression you were straightforward with most of the women mentioned in the article. Some even seemed like they still had a certain fondness for you. Especially the one who said . . ." She paused to tap a finger to her lips. "Oh, what was it she said? It was quite a catchy phrase."

Pulling out her phone, she tapped the screen, then scrolled for a second. Her fingers snapped in a sharp crack before reading, "'*Dating Jamie is the equivalent of a luxury short-term vacation rental—thoroughly enjoyable for a limited time with zero option to extend your stay because it's already fully booked.*'"

"Do you have the damn thing bookmarked?" I asked, aghast. "And also, how does that quote connote any sort of fondness for me?"

Jocelyn shrugged a shoulder. "Question one: How else could I reliably rag on you about it without immediate access to the source material? Question two: She called you a luxury rental instead of a motel that rents by the hour."

I laughed. "Somehow, I'm not sure that quip was meant to be a compliment, but I appreciate you seeing it that way."

"My point is that while the reporter tried her best to lump you in with the more despicable subjects, it was more of a guilt by proximity than any real condemnation of you as a man. Because she couldn't find someone to comment on anything worse than your dedication to your work. Sure, she shaded all of it with her own view of your 'fear of commitment,' but to me at least it rang a little hollow. I mean, I am biased, but the whole thing read less carefree playboy and more workaholic bachelor. If anything, it spoke of the collective female disappointment that,"—she consulted her phone again,—"'there will always be a third person in the relationship. His work.'"

Taking a sip of water, she continued, "I'm honestly surprised your segment of the article wasn't a casualty of editing. There certainly didn't seem to be a dearth of material on the other subjects of her poison pen that would've been much more salacious than 'He works too much and doesn't see me as wife material.'" Her smile widened. "But then they wouldn't have been able to use the pictures of you."

I groaned. The article was bad enough on its own, but the pictures they used made me seem like some meathead jock. Even worse was the knowledge I'd been duped into posing for them, albeit unknowingly. I'd signed a generic photography consent form, which allowed them to use photos of me in the article. What they now claimed was that consent covered the cell phone pictures someone had taken of me while I was working out. For what seemed like the hundredth time, I mentally kicked myself for not heeding Davidson's warning.

"The timing on this whole thing couldn't be worse," I grumbled, right as Eric arrived with our drinks, and I took a grateful sip of the sharply icy martini. Pulling off one of the three olives, I popped it in my mouth and chewed. Jocelyn sipped her drink, waiting for me to elaborate.

"You know about the Union Square project I've wanted to build in Somerville, ever since they announced the new Green Line station there."

She nodded. "I remember you and Dad talking about how Somerville property is a hot commodity right now," Jocelyn said.

I nodded. "Which is why we've been making plans for a new high-rise off of Prospect Street, right next to the new station. There's also been discussion of rehabbing some of the older buildings to attract higher end commercial tenants."

"Seems like a no-brainer."

"That was my view, which is why I devoted the better part of the last year to working on it."

"Much to the chagrin of the ladies of Boston," Jocelyn teased, and I resisted the urge to throw an olive at her.

"Anyway," I continued. "Gabriel Shattucks owns the land next to the new train station. Land we need for the project to even have a chance of getting off the ground."

At the mention of Shattucks, her eyes went round with recognition. Jocelyn might be a Vegas resident now, but she'd been born and raised in Boston just like I had.

"Shit," she said, her lips drawing down into a deep frown.

"Exactly," I agreed, finishing my drink with a large swallow. "I'm pretty sure the man still has cold roast beef every Monday."

"The original cold roast Boston family," Jocelyn said with a dry laugh. "Never met a penny they couldn't pinch, an Irishman they could stand or press they enjoyed."

"The press part is the focus here," I slumped back against the booth. "It's also why I've stepped away from the deal right now. If Shattucks has gotten a whiff of this thing, I don't want my involvement to be an impediment to the deal."

"But it's your deal," Jocelyn said, affronted on my behalf. "You shouldn't have to skulk away and hide, especially when you haven't done anything wrong. It's not like you asked to be objectified here."

Eric appeared with a fresh martini for me along with our appetizer. "I didn't order that." I pointed to the martini.

He lifted a shoulder. "You looked like you could use another."

"Who am I to argue," I said, trading my empty glass for a full one. To Jocelyn I said, "I have to put the company first here. I can't let my wounded pride get in the way. And if that means I need to step aside and let Gideon and Davidson take the lead, then that's what I'll do." I forced a grin I didn't wholly feel. "Plus, it frees me up to spend quality time with my baby sister. What's better than that?"

## CORAL

"I think I'm in love."

From beside me on the platform at the top of the tank, Xavier laughed. "It is a thing of beauty."

I stared down into 150,000 gallons of saltwater perfection. From this angle, I couldn't see many of the fish that occupied the water, just flashes of color here and there moving between elaborate coral and stone formations rising from the tank floor. It was colossal and beautiful, and I couldn't wait to go for a swim.

"Would you think less of me if I told you it's taking everything in me not to dive in right now?"

Xavier grinned. "Only if you do me the same courtesy." He clapped his hands together. "But first things first, let me give you the lay of the land."

Dragging my eyes away from the tank, I met his serious gaze. "I know you're no newbie, but I'm not taking any chances. Over the next six months, you and I are going to put together one helluva show, which means I don't need anything to happen to you before we even get started.

So, I'm going to go over the basics, just as a reminder to both of us not to get too cocky."

"Says the man who swims with sharks on a regular basis," I joked. "Cocky comes with the territory where you're concerned, I think."

He shook his head, long dreads swaying with the movement. "Confident, but not cocky. Confidence results in gigs booked, cocky leaves you open to disaster."

I wanted to kick myself for sounding so flippant. Despite how badly my six-year-old heart wanted it to be, human beings weren't designed to live in the ocean. What Xavier and I did for a living presented many physical challenges that shouldn't be taken lightly. And that was before you got to the part where we swam with live animals. I couldn't afford for Xavier to think I wasn't taking all of this seriously.

Appropriately chastened, I nodded. "You're right, of course."

Xavier bumped my shoulder with his. "We're in this together, Coral, which means we take care of each other. Now, let's chat about water temperature in the tank. I know, based on your videos, you've done some aquarium swims before, right?"

"A few," I confirmed. "But nothing on this scale and not since last fall." Most of the work I'd done recently was more in line with what Cam was doing in Miami—commercial or promotional shoots. Posing for pictures in a tank where the fish would be added later by someone's art department couldn't compare to swimming with live mantas.

"Okay, then, refresher course. The water is between seventy-six and seventy-eight degrees, which is ideal for those animals that live in salt-water, but as you know, not the perfect temperature for those of us who do not. Swims in this tank are designed to drum up interest in the show we're creating, not give you hypothermia. Which means they will be time limited." He held my eyes with a stern look. "A time limit that will be strictly enforced."

I nodded. "I understand." As excited as I was about the opportunity, I knew the associated risks with overexposure. I'd dodged them this far and wasn't eager to experience them.

"We've got several species of fish in this tank. Stay away from the puffer fish. He's a temperamental little shit. The manta is as gentle a giant as there ever was, but as usual, you'll need to stay out of his way."

"Got it," I said, positively twitching with the need to get in the water.

"Once you're used to the water and all of its inhabitants, we'll work through some routines. Nothing too elaborate. We'll save all the good stuff for the real thing, but let you showcase enough to stoke a real interest in what we're doing here."

"Sounds perfect," I said, nodding so hard I resembled a bobblehead doll. Xavier grinned at me, his warm brown eyes lit with laughter. "If I said the only way you could get into the tank was by dressing as an avocado, would you nod and say 'Perfect'?"

I laughed, unashamed of my enthusiasm. "Probably."

"Then I guess we'll see what you've got at two o'clock tomorrow afternoon." Xavier grinned at me as I bounced up onto my toes at the news I'd be getting in the tank.

"For real? Without any sort of practice run?"

He waved a hand through the air. "I've watched your film, girl. You're ready for this, I have no doubt. And I'll be here to yank you out if, for some unimaginable reason, I'm incorrect in my assessment of you as a mermaid. So, yes, I am very much for real. You're swimming tomorrow afternoon."

I threw my arms around his neck and squealed with delight. I'd start swimming the dream tomorrow and I couldn't wait.

# chapter twelve

## JAMIE

The next afternoon, following lunch with a buddy from my MBA program, I swerved around a crowd of young women dressed in an interesting array of cutoffs, shredded shirts and shockingly pink cowboy hats. They clamored around the concierge desk at L'Atelier.

"We're here for the VIP meet and greet with Chappell Roan," their ringleader said, bouncing in her rhinestone emblazoned boots. Her entourage joined her excitement in an exuberantly enthusiastic display of support, punctuated by squeals of pure joy. *Ah, Vegas.*

I headed across the lobby to the elevator, noting the aquarium to my right. Tropical fish darted here and there in vibrant flashes of color. A familiar shimmer of scarlet caught my eye and my steps faltered. Turning to face the enormous wall of plexiglass I searched once more for the ripple of red. When I found it, my feet stopped moving and implanted themselves into the elegant marble surface of the lobby floor. I blinked, certain I was suffering some form of delusion, because what I was seeing made little to no sense.

Red hair undulated slowly in coppery waves around an elegantly shaped face with wide-set eyes. Eyes that even underwater and semi-distorted by the glass were an arresting swirl of blue-gray. Squeezing my own eyes shut, I rubbed the heels of my hands over the closed lids and reopened them, expecting my vision to clear and for her to disappear once more. Only that wasn't what happened when my eyes blinked open. Coral was still there. Or at least someone I thought was Coral was still there. Except the person I saw wasn't a person at all. Because she had a tail. As in from just below her navel, shimmering blue-green scales tapered down to fan out into a giant filigreed fin.

I had to be hallucinating. That was the only reasonable explanation for me discovering the woman with whom I'd spent an incredible night was a mermaid. I stepped closer, propelled by an instinctual curiosity to prove whether what I was seeing was real. The longer I looked, the more I expected something to shift in my vision. For the water to grow either murkier or clearer and the woman I saw swimming with a graceful flick of her *tail* to transform into something that made logical sense.

But she didn't. The closer I got, the more in focus she became and the more undeniable it was that the mermaid flitting around with tropical fish like she was one of them was the same woman who'd shared my bed two nights earlier. Somehow, some way, with some sort of Vegas magic sprinkled over our encounter, I'd slept with a mermaid.

I couldn't look away from her. I was transfixed, honest to God rooted to the spot I'd reached less than a foot from the curve of the aquarium. On its own accord, my hand reached toward the glass, wanting to touch her. To confirm she was real and not some gossamer figment of a memory.

Coral caught the movement and smiled, a brilliant flash of teeth and smooth curve of red lips. She swam closer, the delicate filigree of her tail undulating behind her. Her own hand came to the glass, and she beckoned me closer. Like so many doomed sailors before me, I followed the siren's call, placing my hand against hers, our palms touching yet separated by the thickly reinforced glass.

She was even more beautiful than she'd been the night we met, as though her being in the water heightened everything about her, from the auburn sheen of her hair to the radiance of her smile and the long lines of her body. My fingers tensed against the glass as Coral pushed off in a smooth arcing circle. The grace with which she moved was so fluid and nimble, it was almost as though she flowed with the water. Like it was a part of her. She curved and rolled, floating through the water with firm, yet elegant flutters of her tail. *Her tail, for fuck's sake.*

This was pure insanity, but I kept following her around the tank like some sort of awestruck child until she spiraled upward with sure strokes of lithe arms and flicks of shimmering tail. She was heading to the top of the tank. Surfacing for air, no doubt, because despite how at home she looked in the water, the woman did not have gills anywhere on her body. And I'd know, since I'd mapped every inch of it in the night we spent together. And had revisited the memory of it too many times to count.

Coral disappeared behind a strategically placed grouping of large rocks. That had to be there to shield the . . . I chuckled in disbelief . . . to shield the *mermaid* getting out of the water spoiling the illusion. But if she were getting out of the tank . . . my mind started clicking faster. If she were getting out of the tank, that meant she would be somewhere in this hotel.

No, wait, it was better than that. My head cleared more quickly, now that the shock of seeing Coral was wearing off. Her job, the one she'd just started, was in this hotel. Albeit as a mermaid, which was extremely bizarre to me, but it was *here.* Which meant Coral would be here each day of my planned two-week visit. She hadn't slipped away from me with a generic note.

I'd rescued the generic note from the trash yesterday and tucked it into my jacket pocket that morning for reasons I still hadn't fully processed. I patted that pocket, feeling the crisp edge of the note. Taking several steps back, I surveyed the tank in front of me. The thing was enormous, which was saying something in Vegas. I scanned over the rugged rock exterior along its edge and my eyes snagged on a door recessed behind two stone pillars on the far side of it. It could lead to nowhere but the inner workings of the aquarium. And whatever Coral used to get in and out of it.

I made it almost to the rocky alcove housing the door before stopping to take stock of my actions. What the fuck was I doing? I couldn't go accost this woman at work, for God's sake, regardless of the way she'd smiled and beckoned me closer. She probably hadn't even recognized me, given she was immersed in saltwater and behind inches thick plexiglass. A much more logical conclusion was that she'd simply reacted to some blurry blob reaching out. And even if she had known it was me, who was I to barge into her job and demand to know . . . what? Why she'd done exactly what she'd outlined she would? Why I thought I deserved more than she was willing to give?

And then something else occurred to me. Coral worked as a performer at L'Atelier. Which, as Jocelyn had explained when she'd taken the position as executive manager of hospitality here, meant that my baby sister was Coral's boss. *Fuck.* Coral worked for my sister. Which meant, aside from the obvious problem of being the boss's brother, the door I'd been charging toward seconds earlier would no doubt be locked up tight. There was no way Jocelyn would leave some unlocked or unwatched door available for any nutjob to stroll through and find her employees. Nor would she take kindly to her older and slightly idiotic brother attempting something similar. An overwhelming gratitude for Coral's safety rocketed through me even as disappointment chased behind it at my own inability to see her again.

With a sigh and one last glance at the door, I turned for the elevators. I needed to get my head on straight. I did *not* need to be traipsing along after a woman performing as a mermaid. A mermaid whose boss was my baby sister. A mermaid who'd made it clear she had no interest in anything beyond that single night we'd spent together. Coral was off-limits, that was certain.

"Off-limits," I muttered to myself, even as my fingers found their way back to the outline of the note in my breast pocket.

## CORAL

Surfacing from the water, I blinked rapidly to clear my vision. Xavier grinned down at me from the platform, offering a hand to help me up onto the ledge. I took it and levered myself upward, landing with a less than elegant *thump*. He handed me a warm bath towel, and I wrapped myself in it with a contented sigh.

Xavier passed me the bottle of eye gels and I took them gratefully, squeezing several cooling drops into each eye. "Someone is in their happy place," he said with a knowing grin.

I smiled and wiggled my tail, small ripples shooting out from where my monofin remained below the surface of the water. "You got that right." I handed the bottle of drops back to Xavier.

"I popped out into the lobby for a bit during your swim. You're as advertised," he said. "Very smooth lines and clean turns."

The satisfied approval in his voice made me want to jump back in and swim a victory lap. I settled for saying, "And I avoided the puffer fish as instructed."

He laughed again. "That you did." He cocked his head at me. "How was the vision in the tank?"

I pointed at the drops he held. "The vision? Like it always is in saltwater—blurry and burny. Why?"

One shoulder lifted in a shrug so cool it should be illegal. "While I was out there, I saw you interact with some guy, that's all. Joker was wearing a freaking suit. He watched you like he knew you, so I wondered if he were a friend of yours."

The fizzy feeling in my stomach doubled as I thought back to the hazy figure I'd glimpsed from the tank. He'd reached out a hand, and I responded as I usually did, with a brief touch to the glass followed by an arching swim away. Seeing anything in saltwater, no matter how clear, is difficult enough within the tank. Anything outside of it is distortion on a whole other level. Being able to discern much more than movement and shapes with shadowy faces is nearly impossible. And yet, for a moment, I'd thought maybe . . .

I shook that thought away as soon as it swam into my mind. Jamie was nothing more than a memory. A very sexy memory, but a memory just the same. I needed to remember that. No need to ruin it with thoughts of what-if now. Better to accept it for what it was and move on. Which would've been a lot easier if I'd stuck to my plan of a superficial night of anonymity and didn't have a name to give to the what-if. Or knew about the way he idolized his grandpa.

With a smile at Xavier, I said, "I just got here, how would I know anyone?"

He returned my smile. "Well, the crowd enjoyed it. Based on the number of phones trained on you, that interaction should give us some good traction on social media. Not too bad for your first swim."

"The first of many, I hope," I said.

Xavier nodded. "Oh, I think you can count on that, given the reaction from today's crowd. And that was without much publicity. Just wait until Jocelyn jump-starts the PR for this in the next few months. You'll be seeing more people than the slot machines."

"Let's not get ahead of ourselves," I cautioned him, even as the fizzy feeling expanded exponentially in my chest. And helped push thoughts of Jamie and his wicked smile out of my head, or at least to the back of my mind.

This job was a dream come true for me. I'd expected it was going to be unreal and known it would be fabulous, but whatever expectations I had were nothing compared to the real thing. It was the single most exhilarating experience of my professional mermaid career. This wasn't swimming in some cube at a rich guy's birthday, or sweating my ass off encased in a silicone tail on the side of a cruise ship pool. And it damn sure wasn't wrestling off my tail behind a portable tank hidden only by not-so-artfully draped beach towels. This was the real freaking deal, and it was happening to me.

Xavier kneeled next to me and rubbed my upper arms through the towel. "How are you feeling?"

"I'm good," I assured him.

His lips drew down into a critical frown as he squinted at me. "Not too cold?"

I shook my head. "No, I promise, I'm good."

The frown disappeared, and he nodded. "Okay, then, how about working through some figure eights and maybe a few torpedoes, so you can get a better sense of how those moves feel in the tank?"

I grinned. "I thought you'd never ask."

"Same time limit as last time," he warned me. "I'll flash the conch beacon light when you've got a minute remaining."

In a true moment of ingenuity, the folks at L'Atelier installed a row of lights along the bottom of the tank that were hidden from view from the outside but fully visible to performers within it.

I gave him a thumbs up. "You got it, Bossman."

Xavier rolled his eyes, but held out a hand to help me ease back down into the tank.

Once I was submerged, the familiar calming sensation I always experienced underwater spread through my limbs. Sliding into the silence of the saltwater, my body slowly adjusted to its chill. I let myself settle into becoming a mermaid, noting how the water supported me, that the fish paid little mind to my presence and the way the quiet surrounding me soothed my very soul.

*He watched you like he knew you.* Xavier's words rolled through my brain, and I mentally shook myself. Given the size of not just L'Atelier, but Vegas in general, the odds of Jamie strolling through the lobby at the exact moment of my first show were infinitesimal. Who knew if he was even still at the hotel. And even if he were, so what? We'd had our night together, and that was that. End of story.

Angling downward, I used a few dolphin kicks of my tail to gain momentum toward the sandy bottom, making sure to avoid the school of parrotfish to my left. The rolling motion of my tail-covered legs mimicked the up and down propulsion used by dolphins. Once I was close to the floor, I turned to face the lobby. Blurry though they were, I could tell there were still a fair number of people watching.

Continuing my swim sideways, I pointed one arm in front of me and rolled through a horizontal spin, careful to keep the lines of my body loose and allow the water to guide me through the twirling loops. Torpedoes were one of my favorite moves, because they let me use the entire length of the space. My timing was perfect, since the large manta ray chose that moment to swim above me like we'd choreographed it. It would make a beautiful photo and I hoped one of the ever present smartphones captured it.

Reaching the side of the tank, I arched back into the first curve of a figure eight, then twisted onto my belly to finish out the other side of it. It was more of an infinity symbol than an eight, but I liked that thought better anyway. Coming out of the symbol, I twirled my way up to the surface for a breath before diving down to work my way back across the tank in a zigzag formation. It was a good break from the horizontal movement and let me use the vertical space of the tank with dives and plunges in the pattern of a slow heartbeat. Unlike the frenzied rhythm mine had picked up when Xavier asked about the guy in the suit.

All too soon, the lights at the bottom of the tank flashed, giving me my one-minute warning. I swam to the front of the tank and blew a few bubble kisses to the people lining the perimeter, touching my fingers to my lips, and exhaling a long stream of bubbles into my palms as I extended my hands. Kids loved it, but it worked on adults too. With a final backward spin, I returned to the platform. The regret I felt leaving the water was normal and had nothing to do with any sort of disappointment at the lack of any blurry suited spectators this time around.

# chapter thirteen

## JAMIE

Coral surfaced from the crystal blue water a few feet away from the rock I sat on. She smiled, letting the gentle rush of the waves bring her closer to me. As she swam languidly through the water, long red hair trailed over her breasts, letting just enough skin peek through to reveal she was topless.

Before I could say anything, she dove into a wave. Her tail flashed a brilliant blue-green in the sunlight before it too went under.

"No, wait!" I called to the empty air, searching for any sign of her.

A wave crested against the rock in a spray of sea-foam and Coral burst out of the water with it. With an easy twist of her body, she landed next to me, close enough for me to see droplets of water glittering on her lashes. She smiled, and it turned her eyes a blue so deep it was almost navy. I leaned closer, eyes dropping to the sweet curve of her mouth. Coral mirrored my movement, tilting her head to the side and lifting her lips to invite my kiss. I reached for her, then, cupping her jaw in my hand and lowering my mouth to hers.

A loud shriek startled both of us and I pulled back to see where the noise was coming from. A mangy seagull swooped down, barely missing the top of my head, and continuing to make that god-awful racket. Sounds came out of the idiotic bird that weren't found in nature. Sharp, electronic shrills that sounded vaguely familiar. The gull circled back toward us, dipping low and heading straight for me, still emitting that piercing yowl.

I tried to lift my arm to block his kamikaze approach, but couldn't move. Something was wrapped around my arm. I struggled against it as the bird neared my face, panic setting in when I couldn't free myself. I looked over at Coral, only to see her slipping back into the water with a regretful smile.

On a strangled cry, I reached for her, sliding across the wet face of the rock until I tumbled off into the waves. Seaweed wrapped itself around me and I flailed against it. Except . . . the seaweed wasn't wet. *I* wasn't wet. I opened my eyes, expecting murky seawater. What I saw was the darkened interior of my hotel room. Lifting my head and looking down, I saw the "seaweed" was a tangle of bedsheets around my arms and legs.

I dropped my head back to the pillow. A dream, that was all. A very vivid dream, but a dream, nonetheless. Extricating an arm from the tourniquet of bedclothes I'd made with all of my thrashing around, I scrubbed a hand over my face to clear away the last few remnants of it. With the exception of Coral swimming topless. That one I had no desire to eliminate.

"Freaking seagull," I muttered, pissed the bird had ruined my imaginary almost kiss with dream Coral.

On cue, the horrible squawk sounded again, and I jumped. But now I knew why the stupid bird's call sounded so familiar. Because it was my ringtone. My cell bleated the noise again from the nightstand and I swore, swiping it off the table and glancing at the screen.

The Standard Development logo flashed beneath Davidson's name, and I groaned. Sliding my thumb across the screen, I accepted the call.

"What in the actual fuck are you doing calling me at . . ." I pulled the phone from my ear and checked the time. "Six in the goddamn morning?"

"And good morning to you too," Davidson replied, completely mellow in the face of my irritation. "As to your question, I'm calling you at six in the goddamn morning because I'm curious as to which part of my request from the other day you failed to understand."

Shifting, I propped another pillow behind me and leaned back into it. "It's too early for riddles, Davidson. What are you talking about? And why did we need to talk about it this early?"

"I take it you haven't seen it yet?"

Dread curdled my stomach. The last "it" in question had been the article in *Boston Commons* magazine. I swallowed. "Seen what?"

Davidson's long exhalation did little to calm my nerves. "Seen. What?" I bit out.

"As you may recall," he said, launching into his erudite general counsel voice that grated on my nerves, "I asked you to keep a low profile out there. Ring a bell?"

Anger started to bubble along with the dread in my gut. "I'm not an imbecile, Davidson, so there's no need to talk to me like one."

"Ah, so you do remember then?" he asked, unfazed by my tone. "Good. Then maybe you can explain to me how you becoming an overnight internet sensation fits within keeping a low profile?"

Anxiety joined my anger and dread, making it a real party as my gut churned in an acidic roil. "I have no idea what you're talking about."

"No?" Davidson asked. "Well, what if I asked it this way? What the fuck are you doing following around a . . ." His pause was punctuated by a muffled snort of laughter before he recovered and continued. "Following around a *mermaid*?"

I surged forward, gripping the phone hard enough it squeaked. Coral. How did he know about Coral? More than that, how did he know she was a mermaid? Cautiously, I asked, "A mermaid?"

This time, the snort was not muffled. "Do not try that shit with me, Jamie. There's no way you've forgotten a fucking mermaid." He blew out a breath and I could picture him straightening his tie. "Since you seem a little slow on the uptake this morning . . . or you're just trying to feel out how much I know before confessing . . . I'll spell it out for you, so you can return the favor and tell me what the hell is going on. There is a video. Of you. And a mermaid. In this video, you're standing in front of what I assume is an aquarium. A very large aquarium. And you're staring at this redheaded—and I cannot believe I'm saying this in an actual conversation right now—*mermaid*. Staring as in you're transfixed by this . . . merperson, and then . . ." Davidson couldn't hold back a wry chuckle. "Then, this is the part that's my favorite. You reach out your hand to touch the glass. She does the same before flitting away. It's like some bizarre underwater *E.T.* touch. There are even people who've blended it with the steamy handprint scene from *Titanic* to make a wholly separate meme, not to mention the thousands of *Little Mermaid* references now, ah, floating out there."

I sank back against the pillows. The moment I'd seen her yesterday was now all over the internet. I stifled a groan as I remembered the pathetic way I'd reached for her. This was not good. Especially with the *Boston Commons* article still gaining clicks by the day. This was not the sort of publicity we needed right now.

Davidson was still talking. "As far as I can tell, though, they haven't connected . . ." He gave another snort of laughter, the sound of which I was really starting to hate. Clearing his throat, he went on, "Sorry, they haven't connected 'blond Prince Eric' to the 'Boston Bad Boy of Business,' so that's a positive, I suppose."

"What do you think the chances are it stays that way?" I asked, daring to hope it was at least a possibility.

"As with anything on the internet, there's always a chance something could come along in the next millisecond and push you to yesterday's news. Unfortunately, my prayers for the livestreamed birth of albino Pygmy hippopotamus twins have yet to be answered. For right now, though, no one knows it's you. You're just . . ." Another clearing of his throat. "The 'suited-up brunch daddy thirsting after Ariel.'"

"Brunch daddy?" I asked, totally out of my depth.

"Don't ask me," Davidson said. "There are some things I'm perfectly fine not knowing."

Before my brain could tumble down the rabbit hole of possibilities behind the meaning of "brunch daddy," Davidson continued. "Jamie, be straight with me here. Are you somehow involved with this . . . mermaid? Because if you are . . ." He sighed. "If you are, might I advise the use of a bit more discretion than openly mooning over her in a hotel lobby in front of photo happy tourists with too much time on their hands?"

"We aren't . . ." I didn't finish my sentence. The truth was that aside from a single night with Coral—a single phenomenal night—we weren't involved. She'd seen to that with her pre-dawn departure from my room. But even knowing that, I couldn't bring myself to vocalize it.

"You aren't what, Jamie?" Davidson prompted. "Because, based on what I saw, you're definitely something for this woman. I'm only trying to figure out what, so I know the level of damage control I need to be doing on this."

"I met her at the airport," I hedged.

"The airport," Davidson repeated. "Swam right up to you in baggage claim, did she?"

"Something like that," I said, smiling at the memory of the Astroglide. "We met at the airport and then bumped into each other in the hotel later."

"Let me guess, the rooftop pool?"

"It was on dry land, you asshat. We had dinner together."

"And?

"And what?"

Davidson's sigh was more like a sharp gust of a very cold wind. "You know damn well what, Jamie. The absolute last thing I want to do is get the down and dirty on your sex life. I don't care if you slept with her. I care that by sleeping with her you managed to become the internet's latest clickbait. The situation with that stuffed shirt Shattucks is tenuous at best. He's an insufferable jackass, but he's an insufferable jackass that owns property we need for Union Square to get off the ground. Remember Union Square, Jamie? The project you came up with and spent the better part of the last year working on."

"Again," I said, feeling my temper flare back to life, "I'm not a fucking moron, Davidson."

"No? Well, you could've fooled me. Because only a Grade-A moron would get caught fawning over a goddamn mermaid in Vegas in the middle of trying to convince one of the most uptight pricks ever to punch a conservative ballot that he should sell to us. For fuck's sake, Jamie!"

Davidson's uncharacteristic burst of frustration roared loudly through the phone, dousing the heat of my anger with a wave of guilt. I'd pushed them to do the Union Square project. I'd extolled the virtues of it and insisted dealing with Shattucks wouldn't be an issue. And when it was finally crunch time, when the deal was within our grasp . . . I'd appeared shirtless in a magazine and was now an internet meme.

"Shit," I said, and Davidson barked out a laugh.

"Shit, indeed," he responded. I heard him exhale slowly, regaining his composure. "Just tell me this isn't going to be any more of an issue, Jamie. If you like the woman, fine, like the woman. If you want to sleep with her, also fine. Not that you need my permission. But just make sure you do it when she's not floating in an aquarium wearing a tail, okay? And if you can do it away from the prying eyes of your adoring public, that would be even better."

"I don't think you'll have to worry about any of that," I said. "I don't even know her last name. And she's made it clear she has little interest in . . ." I stopped, clearing my throat. "Let's just say she's made clear her lack of interest in any further contact. Plus, she works for my sister, so that's a problem unique unto itself."

There was a pause, then Davidson chuckled. "If I know Jocelyn, that problem is more insurmountable than Shattucks's aversion to anything . . ." His voice changed to a crusty Brahmin accent. "To anything common and low-born."

"Careful, Davey," I teased. "You're starting to sound like you'd fit right in with Shattucks and his elitest cronies."

Davidson laughed. "They'd throw my Irish ass out with the trash and not think twice about it." In the background, I heard the ring of his desk phone. "Look," he said, "that's Avis letting me know my nine thirty is here. Just promise me things will be low-key out there from now on, man. We can't afford any more distractions."

"Absolutely," I assured him. "Nothing but bass or baritone from here on out, you've got my word on that."

# chapter fourteen

## CORAL

Tuesday morning, I popped my knuckles against my breastbone and watched the elevator climb to the floor that housed Jocelyn's office, all the while fighting off the overwhelming sensation of being called to the principal's office. I'd woken up to a text from Jocelyn asking me to come to her office at ten instead of our planned meeting at two.

It was only a request for an earlier time. Very informal and nonthreatening, so I had no reason to be nervous. Nothing about it should've put me on edge. Plus, Xavier was so happy with my first swim yesterday. And yet my stomach knotted as I exited the elevator.

Meredith was waiting for me when I stepped off the elevator, a stack of files in her hands. "Good morning," she said brightly, which I took as a hopeful sign my anxiety was unwarranted. "You can go on back, Jocelyn is expecting you."

I smiled my thanks and headed back to Jocelyn's office, rapping lightly on the doorframe to announce myself before stepping inside. "Coral," she said with a friendly smile as she rose from behind her desk. My stomach relaxed slightly, now only double instead of triple knotted.

"I'm so glad you could join us this morning. Please, have a seat." She indicated the couch I'd perched on at our first meeting.

All I could focus on was the "us" part of her sentence. Who exactly was "us"?

I sat obediently, trying my best to mask my nerves. I must've done a crappy job, because Jocelyn's smile dimmed a bit, and she touched my arm in concern. "Coral, are you all right?"

I managed a weak laugh. "Sure, I'm good. I just . . ." I looked into her worried blue gaze and decided to be honest. "I guess I'm a little worried there was some problem with my performance yesterday." The sentence ended more as a question than a statement, and Jocelyn's eyes went wide.

"A problem? Whyever would you think that?"

"Uh, well, I . . ." I tugged on the ends of my hair, realized the nervous fidget for what it was and stopped. Clearing my throat, I held her gaze, seeing only genuine concern reflecting back at me. "In my line of work, getting called into a meeting with the boss right after a performance doesn't bode well for the future of the gig."

Her hand on my arm tightened in a reassuring squeeze. "Oh, Coral, I'm so sorry to have worried you. No, there was nothing wrong with your performance. In fact, it's quite the opposite."

"It is?" I asked, feeling the last clenched part of me relax.

She nodded. "Yes, the initial response has been overwhelmingly positive. In fact, there's a . . ." Jocelyn stopped talking. "Well, I don't want to have the meeting before the meeting. We're just waiting on my brother to join us."

"Your . . . brother?" If I'd been nervous before, now I was just confused.

Jocelyn smiled. "Yes, he should be here any min—"

Two loud raps sounded on the doorframe. "Honestly, Joss, I'm not used to being summoned like some sort of . . ."

The speaker's words tapered off as my heart climbed into my throat, choking off my ability to breathe or speak. The tension that had left my body moments before instantly returned with bone crushing force, pushing a squeaky sound out of me. Electric blue eyes locked on mine and time ceased to exist. I wanted to blink but couldn't. I wanted to pinch myself to wake up from what had to be a dream. Or even a nightmare in some ways.

Because standing in front of me and looking every bit as handsome as he had Saturday night was Jamie. Jamie who'd just referred to Jocelyn as "Joss" in a tone so familiar it could only mean one thing. A tiny sliver of me hoped I was wrong. That what had to be could not actually be.

That sliver shattered when Jocelyn said, "Well, don't just stand there like some starstruck oaf, Jamie. Come in and join us." Turning to me, she said, "Coral, this oddly wooden man is my older brother, Jamie. I promise, he's not normally this weird."

I knew I needed to say something in response, other than the odd dolphin-like noise that slipped out before. Give some indication I'd heard and understood her words. But I couldn't. I was frozen to the spot, willing the sumptuous couch to swallow me into its velvety depths.

Jocelyn was either unaware of my turning into a block of ice, or too polite to say anything, because she kept talking. "Jamie, this is Coral Triton. She's a new addition to our crew here." Her smile turned sly. "You might not recognize her, though, without her fins."

Jamie recovered from his stupefied existence first and resumed his entrance into the room. Maintaining eye contact with me, he held out a hand. "Ms. Triton."

I took it, registering the smooth warmth of his palm. And the tingle that came with his touch. I managed to nod. With one last glance at me, he released my hand and cleared his throat.

"Sorry, Joss, but I'm a little at a loss as to what I'm doing here."

She rolled her eyes at him and whipped out her phone. After typing for a moment, she flipped the screen to face Jamie. "Are you telling me this isn't you in the video?" He frowned and took the phone from her.

The mention of a video jolted me out of my cryogenic state. For a split second, I pictured a hidden camera in Jamie's hotel suite, capturing everything we'd done. My face flamed even as my blood went cold at the thought. "Video?" My voice was still more sea mammal pitch than human, but it was enough to garner Jocelyn's attention.

She looked at me. "You haven't seen it, either?"

I forced a swallow down my arid throat and shook my head, eyes going to Jamie, who was scowling down at Jocelyn's phone. For whatever reason, that made me feel better. Surely, he would've reacted more strongly to some sort of secret sex tape. As it was, he looked more irritated than furious, so that was good. Wasn't it?

Jocelyn plucked the phone from Jamie's hand and gave it to me. I clicked "watch again" and a video titled "Prince Eric and Ariel in Vegas" started to play. L'Atelier's lobby was unmistakable, as was the aquarium. Within seconds, I swam into frame just as Jamie came into view opposite me. On screen, he reached out a hand and I reached back.

*It had been him yesterday!* The tingle I'd felt from our handshake came back with a vengeance, along with a sudden rush of pleasure at the thought of him seeing me perform. I squashed it quickly and risked a look at him to find his mouth set in a firm line and arms crossed against his chest.

My gaze dipped back to the video, and I watched him follow me when I swam away. His long strides propelled him down the length of the tank like a panther in a bespoke suit. When he turned, his face came into view and the look on it was . . . pure predator, all heat and want and . . . nope, nope, nope. No thinking those thoughts while sitting next to his sister—*my boss.*

I peeked back up at live action Jamie to find him still scowling fiercely, the effect of which should've been considerably less thrilling. However, stern Jamie had his own animalistic allure. *Again, Coral, no! Nope, no, unh-unh, no way. Shut those thoughts down.*

Before my brain could reach full meltdown status, Meredith appeared with a cart holding a tray of assorted pastries and fruit, along with a coffee service. Jocelyn smiled at her assistant. "Thanks so much, Meredith."

To me, Jocelyn said, "You have to try one of these pumpkin muffins. They are so go—"

"She can't," Jamie's voice sliced in sharply.

Jocelyn whipped around to glare at him, her scowl every bit as intense as the one he was wearing. "Excuse me?" she asked, the two words deadly cold, almost glacial. She rose from her seat next to me, hands on hips and chin jutting out in challenge. "I know you did not just bark at me in my own office, and I also know there's no way any brother of mine would ever attempt to limit the carbohydrate intake of any female in my presence and expect to live to tell the tale."

The tops of Jamie's ears colored as he glanced at me, which was completely adorable. Another totally inappropriate thought about my boss's brother. This had to be the single most bizarre experience I'd ever had. And, as a woman who made her living as a mermaid, that was really saying something.

"Jocelyn," Jamie said, running a hand through his hair and heaving a sigh. "That isn't what I meant at all."

"No?" she asked, challenge in her voice. "Then what did you mean by saying Coral couldn't have one of the most delicious forms of pumpkin known to man?" Before he could answer, she plucked a muffin off the tray, placed it on a napkin, and held it out to me. "Do not listen to my idiotic brother. If you want a muffin, you can absolutely have one."

I hesitated, staring at the perfectly domed golden offering she waggled in front of me. "I appreciate it but unless it's gluten free, I'm afraid I ca—" I swallowed the word "can't," too aware of how suspicious Jamie's interjection already was without matching his language so exactly. "I'm afraid I'll have to pass."

Jocelyn was no dummy. Her eyes narrowed in thought as she withdrew her hand and placed the muffin back on the tray with a little *plop!* She resumed her seat next to me and fixed Jamie with a pointed look. Silence stretched, and I quelled the urge to fidget or fill it. My babbling out some half-cocked explanation would not help the situation.

Finally, Jocelyn asked, "Care to explain how you knew Coral couldn't eat the muffin, big brother?"

To his credit, Jamie didn't flinch or wilt under her imperious blue gaze. It was amazing how she looked down her nose at him while he loomed above her. Moving to the chair across from us, he sat, adjusting his cuffs and smoothing his trousers. If the prior silence had been uncomfortable, this one was enough to make me want to crawl behind the couch until they were finished glaring at each other.

Could I jump in and offer some sort of explanation short of, "The night I got to Vegas, your brother took me to heights of sexual abandon I'd never experienced"? Absolutely I could. Did I have any clue what that could be? I absolutely did not, so I stayed silent and willed Jamie to come up with something believable.

"I knew," he said, returning her frosty stare with one of his own. "Because I had the pleasure of meeting Coral the night I got Vegas. We had dinner."

*And sex!* I pulled my lips between my teeth to hold in the words. *Don't forget the sex!* I could feel a hysterical giggle working up my throat and clamped my lips tighter together to prevent its escape.

Jocelyn looked at Jamie for a long moment. "Dinner," she said, her tone rife with disbelief.

"Dinner," Jamie confirmed, his tone as certain as hers was skeptical.

Jocelyn looked over at me, as though seeking corroboration of Jamie's explanation. I nodded and parroted the single word. "Dinner."

Except when I said it, it sounded like I was Eliza Doolittle practicing for Henry Higgins, with nowhere near the certainty Jamie managed to inject into the word. Which made the dazzling smile that spread over Jocelyn's face that much more confusing.

"Well, that certainly makes things easier," she said.

"It does?" I asked at the same time Jamie asked, "Makes *what* easier?"

Jocelyn waved her phone in the air like it was the Olympic torch and she'd won all golds. "This video has garnered much more interest than we expected to have this early on." She looked at me. "Not that we weren't expecting your swims to do well, but this"—another triumphant wave of her phone—"jump-started things for us in a major way." Her gaze moved to Jamie, who no longer looked as comfortable in his seat.

Her eyes softened. "A way we'd like to capitalize on before something else takes its place."

"Capitalize how?" he asked, trepidation in his tone.

"Well," Jocelyn drew out the word. "Even though we're about six months away from opening the show, as I said, we still want to take advantage of any free publicity that's out there. And upper management has made a lot of suggestions already." Blue eyes bounced from me to Jamie. "Some of which are out of the question, since I would never put an employee in that sort of situation."

"What sort of situation?" I asked, curious.

"The situation where your boss asks you to date her brother," Jocelyn said with a laugh.

"What?" I rasped out, heat searing my cheeks as I glanced over at Jamie. Our eyes held for the briefest of seconds before ricocheting away from each other. Prolonged eye contact with this man was not something I could handle right then.

Jocelyn waved a hand. "Not to worry, Coral. You need to know that I protect my employees from nonsense that is an obvious violation of Title IX, not to mention demeaning and sexist. But . . ." Her pause hung in the air with an expectant weight to it, like the next thing she said had the power to flatten me.

"But?" I asked, resisting the urge to pop my knuckles to release a milligram of the tension I'd felt since Jamie walked in.

"But I think there is a way for us all to benefit from this unexpected bout of free publicity the two of you generated yesterday."

Jocelyn's grin unfurled slowly as she glanced back and forth between us. I might not know her well, but I knew that look. That self-satisfied look of a cat who got the cream meant she had something up her sleeve and was about to spring it on us.

"Enough with the theatrics, Joss," Jamie said, his voice bordering on harsh. "You've obviously got something in mind, so you might as well get on with it."

Her pert nose wrinkled and for a second, I thought she was going to stick her tongue out at him. Instead, she turned to me and said, "My brother has a bit of a PR problem right now."

Jamie made a choking sound while I said, "PR problem?"

Ignoring Jamie, Jocelyn nodded. "Yes, he's found himself the subject of a less than flattering article written by a modern-day Lady Whistledown and rife with quotes from what appears to be every woman he's slept with in the last decade. All of them touting his prowess while simultaneously bemoaning his lack of interest in settling down."

"Jocelyn!" Jamie said her name like the crack of a whip, but she was unfazed. There was obviously something here I wasn't privy to, and that Jamie wasn't keen about looping me in on.

"What?" she asked calmly. "It's the number one internet hit under a search of your name right now, so it's not a secret."

Jamie made a noise in his throat that was part growl and if he'd opened his mouth may have been closer to a howl. "That doesn't mean I'm ready for you to . . ." He threw a glance at me but didn't hold it, the slightest hint of pink darkening those perfect cheekbones. "It's not something I'm ready to discuss, Jocelyn."

Especially not with the latest woman in what was apparently quite the list of conquests. He didn't need to say the words for me to hear them loud and clear. He shifted in his seat, tugging at his cuffs and looking anywhere but at me.

Based on the night we'd spent together, Jamie was obviously well versed in the art of seduction. To think there had been no one before me would have been laughable. And it wasn't like I was some blushing virgin either. So, there was no pang of jealousy for the reality of those other women. Instead, his embarrassment struck a tender chord in my chest.

I hadn't read whatever article Jocelyn was talking about, but I had a good idea of the sort of clickbait it seemed to be, and it pissed me off on his behalf. I'd volunteered for the Wild West show that was social media—clicks, likes and swipes all increased my ability to book new jobs. This job at L'Atelier the best and most lucrative example of that thus far. If it weren't for my presence on socials, I wouldn't be here.

But for someone who wasn't a willing participant, being blindsided by your life being splashed across the pages of a magazine would rock anyone's world. And for a guy like Jamie, a guy who at least in my experience was someone who respected women, to be included in what sounded like a real hit piece would bear double the sting.

"I'm sorry," I said, and he whipped around to look at me.

"What?" he asked, face going a little slack with surprise.

"I'm sorry that happened to you," I said, and I meant it.

A beat passed, then his mouth quirked into a half smile. "Thank you," he said.

"I'm glad to hear you say that, Coral," Jocelyn said, interrupting the moment. "Because I think you're just the one to help him with it."

"Me?" I asked, my turn for a shocked expression. "How on earth can I do that?"

"By showing the world at large my big brother is capable of falling in love."

# chapter fifteen

## JAMIE

WHAT?" Coral's shriek echoed my own shout as we both stared wide-eyed at my sister who'd apparently lost her freaking mind. A fact underlined and emphasized by the way she cackled at our reaction.

"Oh wow," Jocelyn pressed a hand to her stomach as she continued to laugh. "You two should see your faces." She dragged in a breath and worked to stop laughing, waving a hand in front of her face.

"Okay," she said. "Okay, sorry. But that . . ." she pointed between us. "That was hilarious. You both looked like you'd swallowed your tongues."

"Um," Coral wiped her palms down her jean-clad legs, a wry smile teasing across her lips. "About that whole Title IX concern . . ."

Jocelyn almost dissolved again into giggles, but reined it in at the last minute. "Don't worry, Coral, I don't mean actually fall in love with you. Because you aren't actually going to date. You're going to fake it for the publicity!"

Yep, she'd officially lost it. The last thing I needed right now, as she well knew, was any more media focus on my love life while the deal with Shattucks hung in the balance.

I glanced at Coral, who still looked a little shellshocked. "As you may recall, Joss," I said slowly. "Publicity is something I can ill-afford at the moment."

"Au contraire, mon frere," she countered, pushing herself off the couch and crossing to her desk.

Again, I looked at Coral, who arched a brow at me. Her look transmitting the question, *Could this be any more weird?* God, how I wished we were alone right now. Both because my sister was spouting insane things about me falling in love with a mermaid and because . . . well, fuck, because I couldn't be in the same room with Coral without wanting to touch her. And with my baby sister as a chaperone, that wasn't going to happen.

Jocelyn returned and slapped a stack of printed pages into my lap. Looking at her instead of the printout, I asked, "What's this?"

"That," she pointed at what I now saw was a newspaper article, "is the feature piece the Boston Globe ran on Mr. and Mrs. Gabriel Shattucks's fortieth wedding anniversary last year."

I looked down and sure enough, there were Shattucks and his wife staring back at me dressed in formal evening wear and smiling broadly from the foyer of what I assumed was their brownstone back in Boston. I'd never seen this before, which was odd considering the legwork we'd done on Shattucks. But then, our focus hadn't been on the life and style sections of the news.

Raising my eyes to my sister once again, I asked, "What the hell does this have to do with anything?"

Jocelyn snatched the pages from my lap and waved them in the air. "Everything," she cried. Sitting down beside Coral once more, she continued, "After our lunch the other day, I did some research on your pal Shattucks. As you might expect, there isn't much information out there on a guy who is as press averse as he is. A lot about his business dealings and the like, but not much else. Until I came across this." She flapped the pages at me. "A whole spread focused solely on how much he loves his wife and their great romance."

Before I could ask once more what that had to do with Coral and me, Coral beat me to it.

"Sorry," she said, sounding genuinely contrite at the interruption. "But could one of you clue me in on what some old guy and his wife have to do with an article about Jamie's . . . social life?" I appreciated her diplomatic choice of words.

Rather than let Jocelyn take us on another tangent, I said, "I'm in the middle of a real estate deal right now. One that involves Gabriel Shattucks—the old guy. I won't bore you with the details, but property he owns is pivotal to the success of the project. We've either got to convince him to sell to us, or partner with us in the development."

"And he's not into either one?" Coral asked, brow furrowing.

"Let's just say the article Jocelyn mentioned didn't do me many favors with the guy. He's old school, very crusty Old Boston."

"So, he's a pilgrim?" Coral asked, lips twitching.

"If by pilgrim you mean a bit Puritanical, then yeah," I responded.

"Which means," Jocelyn interjected, "that Jamie being cast as some ne'er-do-well heartbreaking playboy doesn't advance the ball here."

"I thought you said I didn't come off that badly in the article," I protested.

"You being a part of it is bad enough," Jocelyn said. "And 'not that bad' isn't exactly what we want here either, is it?"

"What 'we' want?" I asked. "I'm sorry, when did you join the board of Standard Development?"

"Oh please," she scoffed. "You three nitwits would be lucky to have me. If you did, the article wouldn't have been an issue, because I wouldn't have let you do it."

It was an undebatable point because she was right.

"Circling back to the issue at hand," Coral said. "How do I fit into this?"

"Perfectly," Jocelyn said. "The article is already out there, and we can't unring that bell. What we *can* do, at the very least is distract from it and, if this works like I think it could, prove Jamie isn't the asshat Abigail Johnson wants people to believe he is."

"Who?" Coral asked.

"The reporter who wrote the article," I said.

She shook her head and turned to Jocelyn. "Sorry, I'm still not following how I can help with that."

"By taking the buzz generated by the video of the two of you and using it to rehab Jamie's image while simultaneously promoting you and L'Atelier's upcoming mermaid extravaganza!" Jocelyn almost vibrated with excitement at her idea.

"We can pitch it as a sort of kismet thing. That Jamie knew who you were because he'd seen one of your videos, or whatever. Then, he just happened to be planning a trip out here that coincided with your arrival and *whammo!* You two hit it off like gangbusters."

She reached out and touched Coral's arm. "Your followers will eat it up, right?"

"Sure, but I don—"

Jocelyn spoke over Coral in her excitement. "And you know who else seems to enjoy a good love story?" She shot me a pointed look and picked up the sheaf of papers again. "Gabriel Shattucks. Claims it was love at first sight when he met his wife and just got better from there."

"And you think that by what? Concocting some whirlwind love story between Coral and me will get him on board?"

"If not get him on board, at least prove he shouldn't put too much stock in gossip rags when making judgments about his potential business partners. Show him, and anyone else who read that stupid article, you aren't that guy. Or if you were, now that you've met the right woman all bets are off. He'll buy it because it's a modern-day version of his own story."

"Except this one has a mermaid instead of some debutante in it," Coral said. "How exactly is that going to go over in this scenario? I can't imagine this guy,"—she gestured to the picture of Shattucks,—"will be too thrilled with that aspect."

"And I'm only here two weeks, Joss," I said, pointing out what I felt was one of many rather obvious flaws in her plan. "Who's going to believe such a whirlwind romance? And what happens at the end of it? When he asks six months from now, 'How's that mermaid of yours doing?'"

"First, don't sell yourself short, Coral," Jocelyn said, and I mentally kicked myself for not offering reassurance to her first. "You're a beautiful, talented woman. A woman it's not hard to believe Jamie, or any other man, would fall for. And that's the selling point here."

She turned to me. "You're down to the real crunch time on this thing, right? You'll need Shattucks on board ASAP, which means six months from now won't matter because he'll have already signed on the dotted line. Hell, you can tell him Coral broke your poor little heart and that you're still pining for her at that point. What does it matter, so long as in the short term it gets you what you want and provides oodles of easy publicity for Coral and me in the build up to our first show? It's a win-win, Jamie."

I glanced over at Coral, who was chewing her lower lip and apparently considering this cockamamie idea. Fake dating to repair my reputation and get publicity for her show? A show I didn't truly understand, but was something big for both her and my sister. This was nuts, wasn't it?

Except . . . now that the initial shock of Jocelyn's proposal had worn off, I started to see definite advantages to it. First and foremost was the obvious opportunity to spend more time with Coral while I was in town. A wholly appealing prospect. And maybe Jocelyn was right and this reputation rehab via social media would help take the attention off that stupid article. Re-frame things for me in a way that wouldn't ruin the Union Square project. I could have the girl and the deal if it all worked how she'd framed it.

Only, I wouldn't really have the girl because we'd be faking it. Wouldn't we? I mean, that was how Jocelyn couched things, but after what Coral and I had already shared . . . how fake could things be?

I pushed a hand through my hair. "I don't know, Joss. This all sounds . . ."

"Like the plot to a rom-com?" Coral piped up.

I laughed. "That's one way to phrase it."

Jocelyn smiled at each of us. "It's just an idea, okay? An idea I happen to think will work wonders for all involved, but still just an idea. Tell you what? Why don't the two of you head down to Champagne Campaign and have brunch on me to talk about it? Feel out the idea and I'm sure you'll see there's merit to it."

## CORAL

I felt a little like Dorothy in the *Wizard of Oz*, as though a giant tornado had just picked me up, shaken my entire life upside down and then deposited me into some parallel universe. One in which I was sitting across from my boss's older brother about to discuss a fake dating scheme. Her brother who happened to be the same man I'd already spent an unbelievable night with and couldn't stop thinking about.

"So," Jamie said, drumming his fingers on the table. "This is . . ."

"I think the word you're looking for is 'awkward.' Although that seems wholly inadequate to describe our situation."

He laughed, activating the crinkles at the corners of his eyes. "You were honestly the last person I expected to see in Jocelyn's office this morning, that's for sure."

"I would have been less surprised if Ryan Reynolds walked in," I agreed.

"But what if Blake had been with him?"

"Obviously, I would have just expired on the spot."

His answering nod was solemn. "The only correct response."

"And that brings us back to how we're going to respond to Jocelyn," I said, taking a sip of water.

Jamie blew out a breath and sat back. "What do you think about it?"

I laughed. "In general? I think it's a little insane, don't you?"

"Which part?" he asked. "The fake dating part? Or her belief that Shattucks is going to be wooed by a love story?"

"Well, you'd know the answer to the last one better than I would, so I guess I'm referring to the fake dating part."

"Dating me sounds insane?" he asked, his half smile letting me know he was teasing.

I shook my head, ignoring the flutter in my chest. "*Fake* dating anyone sounds insane."

"But could it actually work?"

I eased back into the booth, considering it from my end of the spectrum. From a publicity perspective, it was a solid idea. Jocelyn was right in thinking it would generate a lot of early interest in the show. Something we could build off in the coming months as we got things up and running. It would also generate a lot of interest in me specifically. Which was not underrated. Social media opened doors for performers unlike anything else. If this thing took off, there'd be a decent chance I could get some sponsored product posts on my own page. Or even requests for special appearances. More eyeballs on what I was doing translated into job security.

"It's honestly a no-brainer from my side," I said. "Jocelyn's idea that my followers will be into a romance angle is spot on. And, if we highlight the hotel in whatever I post and then the hotel reposts it . . . even in just the two weeks we're talking about it could provide a good publicity push. It's not like social media has a long shelf life. That video of us is trending, but that won't last. So, yeah, the time to take advantage of it is now. Ride the wave of it for a few weeks to generate as much buzz as possible."

Jamie nodded and twisted his coffee mug around. "You seem pretty well-versed in this stuff."

I smiled. "Comes with the territory, I'm afraid. Doing what I do you have to b—"

"What is it exactly that you do?" he asked. "Maybe a better question is what are you doing here at L'Atelier with Jocelyn? What is this new show she keeps talking about?"

"Guess my personal details rule is out the window now, huh?"

Jamie chuckled. "It's safe to say that ship has sailed, gorgeous."

"Seems that way. The answer to your question is Jocelyn saw some of my videos on Instagram and a few other apps or sites and reached out to me about her idea for a live action mermaid show here in Vegas."

"Videos of you . . . as a mermaid?"

I nodded, and he looked perplexed. "What?" I asked.

He shook his head with a wry grin. "I guess I just never realized that was a thing."

"Oh, it's a thing," I assured him. "A thing that got me all the way to Vegas to help create a one-of-a-kind live show."

"Will it be in the lobby tank like you were yesterday?"

I shook my head. "That's a part of it, but more of a preview of the real thing. What she's got planned is a renovation of a portion of the theater space to use a large mobile tank. Think Cirque du Soleil but less acrobatics and more mermaids."

"I don't think my brain is capable of that," Jamie said with a grin.

"Good thing Jocelyn hired me instead of you then," I teased. "What we're designing will involve multiple merfolk performing in and out of the water."

"Merfolk?" he asked, brows raised.

"You gotta get with the lingo if you're going to have people believing you've got a mermaid girlfriend," I teased.

"Does this mean I need to re-watch *The Little Mermaid*?"

"Animated or live action?"

Jamie's brow furrowed. "You mean there's more than one?"

I laughed. "Oh man, do you have a lot to learn."

He smiled. "Certainly seems that way. But let's start with the basics. There's more to Coral Triton than being a professional mermaid. Tell me about you."

I shifted in my seat. "There isn't much else to tell."

Jamie shot me a disbelieving look. "I doubt that. For starters, you know I'm from Boston. What about you?"

I shrugged. "I'm one of those people who don't really have a hometown. My mom and I moved a lot when I was a kid. And you already know I don't have any siblings."

"You two must be close, then," he said, smiling warmly.

I swallowed and forced a smile. "Not exactly. Me coming out to Vegas has put us in the closest proximity we've been in for a while."

"Your mom lives in Vegas? She must be excited you're here, then." His optimism about my mother was sweet, if wholly misplaced. I thought about her nagging me to come home for dinner to meet her latest version of Mr. Right.

"In a manner of speaking, I guess," I hedged. "And no, she doesn't live *in* Vegas. Her house is about an hour or so away."

"I'm sure she's happy to have you this close," he said. "My parents were brokenheartedly proud of Jocelyn when she moved across the country from them."

"But their pride and joy first born stayed close to home?" I teased, glad to segue off the topic of my mother.

He grinned. "I am the apple of their eye. At least I will be until they get back from touring distilleries in Ireland to my current notoriety back home." His grin wavered a little, and it tugged at my heartstrings to see his concern over his parents' reaction to the article. "This is the one time I'm glad they're so resistant to joining the digital age and still have flip phones."

I reached out and covered his hand with mine. "Well, hopefully Jocelyn's plan will work the wonders she thinks it will, and they'll never be the wiser."

"Let's hope," Jamie said, glancing down at my hand on his. "Speaking of her plan . . . before that gets rolling, shouldn't we talk about the other night?"

"You mean we're not just going to pretend it never happened?"

"I don't think I could, even if I wanted to," he said, blue eyes going hot. "Which I don't." His brows came down in a stern "V" and he added, "But I'd love to forget waking up alone and realizing you'd snuck out on me."

I winced a little at his characterization. "I didn't sneak out. I left. After writing you a note."

"You mean this?" He pulled a folded square of paper from his suit jacket, opened it and put it on the table between us.

Surprise reverberated through me at the sight of it. "Uh . . ." I swallowed. "Why do you have that with you?"

"What?" He seemed caught off guard by my question.

I pointed down at my handwriting scrawled across the hotel stationary. "Why are you carrying that around?"

Jamie tugged at his lapels, then straightened, broad shoulders pressing back and down. "I have it because I . . ." He shifted slightly, squirming in his seat like a kid who knew he was in trouble. "That is, I kept it because I thought . . ." He cleared his throat, trying again. "I have it with me because . . ." The third time was not the charm, because he failed to finish the thought once more. Full lips pulled down into a thin line and he narrowed his eyes.

"Why I still have it isn't the question. The question is why you left it in the first place. Why you felt you needed to sneak out."

It was my turn to squirm a little. "I didn't sneak out. I left. Just like we both expected me to."

"No." The word was sharp and final. Jamie shook his head. "I had no expectation that you'd leave without a word."

I pointed at the note. "There's more than one word there, Jamie." I didn't mention that there had been a lot more words I'd considered writing. What was the point?

"Don't," he said, the single word a warning.

"Don't what?" I asked peevishly.

"Don't try and make the night we had seem small."

"I'm not trying to do that." That was precisely what I was trying to do. What I'd been trying to do since leaving him in the pre-dawn hours two days ago. Because if I made it small enough, I could pack it away and not linger on it. Not make it seem like more than it was. Like something other than a one-night stand. And if I kept trying, maybe I'd eventually succeed.

"No?" Jamie lifted a single brow, his entire posture radiating the skepticism I saw in his eyes. "Are you sure about that? Because that's what this"—he flicked the note with his index finger—"tried to do."

I swallowed roughly, feeling heat creep up my neck. "Jamie," I said, then stopped, because I wasn't sure what to say. There was no way I could tell him what I really thought. Even with a few days' distance, it was too much, too big, too overwhelming for me to even try to put into words. But I had to say something.

"I just don't want to make that night into something bigger than it was," I said, and knew it was the wrong thing to say as soon as it left my mouth. Why had I even said that? It wasn't how I felt at all.

Jamie frowned, a deep crease working its way across his brow line. "And what was it to you, Coral? Because to me it was fucking electric. *You* were electric. And then you were just gone, and I want to know why."

I opened my mouth, but he kept talking, leaning forward as he did. "And don't give me more of that trite bullshit about 'just one night' or whatever other nonsense you've got at the ready. I've heard enough of that from you already. So, how about you tell me the truth this time?"

"The truth, Jamie," I said, my own temper flaring in the face of his lecture. "Is that we had a great night together, but for God's sake, it wasn't like it could go anywhere. So, I left before it got awkward or weird. I left so we could remember it for the fun it was and go our separate ways without an uncomfortable morning after. No promises or expectations, just a good time. Something, based on the press you've apparently been getting, you're well-versed in, so I don't see why it's so hard for you to understand. Maybe because this time the shoe's on the other foot?"

We were practically nose-to-nose over the table, each of us rage breathing and wild-eyed. Jamie's blue eyes were hot with anger and his jaw was tight, the muscle at its corner bulging as he gritted his teeth.

"That was a low blow, Coral," he said, or really growled.

"Yeah, well, so was you trying to mansplain my own feelings to me," I shot back. Even though it was a decent recap of what I was feeling. The point still needed to be made.

"I did not," he said, affronted.

"Uh, yeah, you did. And this little tête-à-tête we're having right now? One of the multiple reasons I was right to just leave a note."

His mouth pinched downward, and he narrowed his eyes. "Why, because I call you on your bullshit and you can't take it?"

"Oh, I can take anything you care to dish out, sweetheart," I snapped.

The unintended innuendo in my retort echoed around us like a gunshot. His eyes dipped to my mouth, and I bit my lip, suddenly all too aware of his proximity. Of the scent of his cologne and the flecks of navy in his irises. The sound of his ragged breathing triggered a memory of the way it felt against my neck. Jamie licked his lips, eyes still locked onto my mouth. The world narrowed to the two of us, inches apart, half mad and half turned-on.

Until someone cleared their throat and we both looked toward the sound. The waiter stood there hesitantly, holding the check. "I'll just leave this here," he said and scurried away.

Jamie eased back into his seat and blew out a breath. Unclenching my hands, I settled back into my own seat. We avoided eye contact. Jamie slid the check over, filled it out and signed. The silence between us stretched into taffy-like proportions, sticky, unyielding, and thick.

Jamie broke it. "I'll have to talk to my partners about Jocelyn's idea before I can commit to it."

Wait, what? He still thought this was a good plan after . . . whatever had just happened?

"Okay," I said slowly.

"Assuming they're good with it, I'll let her know and we'll go from there, I guess."

"Okay," I said again, unable to come up with anything else.

He stood up and finally looked at me. Reaching into his jacket, he pulled out a slim card case. Opening it, he removed a business card and handed it to me. "My cell number."

I took the crisp white card from him. "Thanks."

Jamie nodded and rapped the table with his knuckles. "Well, I guess I—"

"Hang on," I said, snatching up the note that had so offended him. Using the server's pen, I scrawled my number on the bottom of it. "Here's mine, you know, just in case you get the green light for this." I held the paper out to him.

Taking it from me, he glanced at the number, his lips toying with the idea of a smile as he re-folded it along the creases and tucked it into his pocket.

"Care to share the joke?" I asked.

The smile broke free then, curving that sinful mouth and showcasing even, white teeth. "I just figured out why I kept your note."

I cocked a brow, giving him a half smile of my own. "Oh? And why is that?"

"So, you could finish it."

# chapter sixteen

**J**amie: *I got the go ahead from the guys to participate in this PR scheme of yours.*

Jocelyn: *If by "scheme" you mean carefully orchestrated plan to resurrect your reputation as a full believer in love and rescue your deal that is dangling by a thread, then I would hope so.*

Jamie: *You're a little too proud of yourself, Sis. I'm still not convinced this is going to work.*

Jocelyn: *Look at it this way, even if it doesn't it will buy you more time with Coral.*

Jamie: *What's that supposed to mean?*

Jocelyn: *I'm not going to answer that, because doing so would imply you'd actually asked it. Which would further imply you think I am that stupid. Or blind.*

Jamie: *You've lost me.*

Jocelyn: *No, I haven't. You know what I'm talking about because you're not that stupid, either. Most of the time. I'll let Coral know you're on board.*

Jamie: *I can do that.*

Jocelyn: *Like I said, not lost in the slightest.*

# JAMIE

I paced the living room of my suite like a high schooler about to ask his crush to prom. Which was ridiculous, seeing as how I'd already had the privilege of a night with Coral. What was left to be nervous about? All I had to do was send her a text letting her know Davidson and Gideon had given me the green light for Jocelyn's idea.

It was more of a yellow caution than a full green light, based on Davidson asking, "You want to do what?" before popping two Advil on the Zoom call. But, after I'd laid out what Jocelyn had planned, both he and Gideon agreed there was some logic to the idea. Even if it went directly against the "lie low" plan Davidson had initially advocated.

"Jocelyn didn't get where she is by accident," he said. "She knows her shit. And God knows she's more savvy in social media than any of the three of us. If she's confident in this, who am I to second guess her?"

"It worked in *Easy A*," Gideon chimed in with a laugh. "And Emma Stone is never wrong." He frowned. "Except for *Aloha*. That was a bad move."

"Your obsession with rom-coms was bad enough before you got engaged," I said. "Now you're a total lost cause," I said, and he laughed.

"This coming from a man desperate for a fake romance with a mermaid to salvage his reputation?" Gideon grinned at me from his square in the Zoom call. "You're basically starring in one right now, my friend."

Which would explain why I was acting like the star of a teen comedy, sweating over that first call to the female lead. I was a year from forty, for fuck's sake. I needed to stop acting like a child and just . . .

My phone buzzed in my hand. Looking down, I saw a notification bubble with "Coral Text Message" in it. Swiping up too fast, I turned on the phone's flashlight instead of opening the text. With a muttered curse, I tried again.

Coral: *Sorry I brought up the article yesterday. You were right, that was a low blow. Even if you don't get board signoff or whatever on Jocelyn's plan, I feel like I owe you an apology. So, I'm sorry. It was a shitty thing to say.*

I stared down at her text. Read it a second, then a third time. A spontaneous apology wasn't something I was used to. Normally, when people fucked up, they weren't keen on owning up to it. But here was Coral, apologizing without any prompting. It was so . . . adult and responsible. How the fuck was I supposed to respond to it?

*Like a responsible adult, you idiot*, I chided myself. I needed to think before starting to type. No sense in letting those damn three little bubbles give away the fact I was struggling to form an appropriate response. But I couldn't wait too long and have her thinking I'd just left her on "read" without answering. Shit, technology made this so much more complicated.

Jamie: *Thanks. You were just giving it back to me in equal measure. I shouldn't have acted like such a dick about you leaving.*

Bubbles appeared and danced for a while.

Coral: *Now that we're not so blindsided by this whole scenario, should we meet for a drink? Maybe talk about a few things before meeting with Jocelyn?*

Intrigued, I wondered what she would want to talk about separately from Jocelyn. Only one way to find out.

Jamie: *Sure, sounds like a great idea. Lobby bar?*

Coral: *Works for me. I'll be tied up until 4, but could meet you around 5 if that works?*

Jamie: *Looking forward to it.*

Coral was already seated at a high-top table when I got to the bar. A glance at my watch said I wasn't late, she was early. Dressed in black jeans with a slight flare and a fitted green top, she wore little makeup, and her hair was the riot of curls I'd seen at the airport.

Spotting me, she gave a little wave and smiled as I approached. When I reached the table, I was unsure of the protocol. Would we hug, shake hands, fist bump? Coral answered my quandary by slipping off her chair and giving me a brief side hug in greeting. Without her heels, the top of her head came just above my chin. She smelled like the beach, a mix of salt spray, coconut and fresh air.

"Thanks for coming," she said, retaking her seat.

"Thanks for the invitation," I replied, then hated how stilted it sounded.

Coral nodded. "I just thought we should take a second and talk through a few things before talking to Jocelyn. I get the feeling once she has an idea, she sort of steamrolls along with it. So, I didn't want us to get flattened in the process."

I laughed at her apt description of my sister. "You've got good instincts," I said. "But you should know that if you're uncomfortable with this idea of hers, you can tell her without any blowback. She's not like that."

Coral nodded again. "Yeah, that's what I thought, but it's still good to hear. I'm not, though. Uncomfortable with this. After thinking about it more last night, I think Jocelyn's really on to something. For you, for me, and for the show."

Relief swamped me that she wasn't bailing. "Glad to hear it," I said.

"All that being said, though . . . " Coral smiled at me. "I do think, given our . . . brief history that we need a few ground rules to make sure things don't get any murkier than they already are."

Trepidation replaced relief in a slow trickle. "Okay," I said. "Sounds like you've given it quite a bit of thought."

The waitress appeared before Coral could answer and we ordered— paloma for her and a bourbon neat for me. Once she was gone, I said, "You were saying something about ground rules?"

Coral looked at me directly, the blue-gray of her irises shining with intensity. "Jamie, this job is a dream come true for me. I know it's hard for someone like you to understand, but I've be—"

I had to interrupt. "Someone like me? What does that mean?"

Her smile was quick and brightened her eyes a little. One hand lifted in an up and down sweep aimed at me. "Someone like you. The quintessential businessman with his fancy suits—even on vacation—and some sort of job behind a huge desk and a cadre of minions to do his bidding. Someone who lives in his crisp, efficient black-and-white world with its spreadsheets and bottom lines."

"I happen to like dressing well," I said, tugging protectively at the lapels of my jacket. My grandfather hadn't been wrong about the clothes making the man. People sat up and took notice when you walked in a room wearing a suit. Much more so than if you strolled in wearing jeans. Suits instilled confidence that denim couldn't, which was why I owned more of one than the other.

Coral's laugh was as musical as I remembered from our first night together. "I can tell. But I can also tell, just by the look on your face when we talked yesterday, that my career . . ." She shook her head. "No, my entire life is difficult for you to comprehend. And, to be fair, my being a professional mermaid is hard for most people to wrap their heads around as a real job."

Her gaze regained its intensity. "But it is a real job and one I've worked hard at for over a decade. And I've come a long way from posing at kids' birthday parties, Jamie. What Jocelyn is offering me here is a huge chance."

"I underst—"

"No," she cut me off. "You don't. You can't, because you have no perspective. I'm a professional mermaid trying to forge a career. A career that has a shelf life just like a lot of other jobs in the entertainment business. At thirty-two, I'm a veteran who needs to start thinking about the next phase of my career. One that's not dependent on me being in the tank but directing others who are. Crafting and choreographing a show the size and quality of what Jocelyn wants to do here is a major stepping-stone for me to reach that next level. And starring in it as well lets me capitalize on the other facet of my career while I still can. I can build a brand here with L'Atelier that will provide a sense of stability I've never had. Ever. And I'm not going to jeopardize that for anything." She gave me a pointed look. "Or anyone."

"Wait," I said, confused. "I thought you said you were good with what Jocelyn proposed."

"I am," Coral said. "But I want us to be clear from the start that what happened before you were you and I was me cannot happen again."

"I've always been me, so I'm afraid I don't follow."

She scowled at me. "Before I knew you were you. When we had that perfect, first-name basis night together. That cannot happen again."

The waitress appeared with our drinks and a bowl of some sort of snack mix, then left us alone again.

"Of course not," I said, picking up the line of conversation and trying not to grin like an idiot because she'd called our night together perfect. "Because now I know your whole name."

Coral huffed out a frustrated laugh. "You know what I mean, Jamie. That night was . . ."

I leaned in, eager to hear her additional descriptions of it. I was destined for disappointment.

Reading my face, she smirked and waved a hand. "We both know what that night was. We also know it can't happen again."

"I . . ." I let the syllable stretch. "I'm not sure I knew that until you said it."

Which was true. After seeing her again, I wasn't sure how she felt about things between us. Whether she'd be willing to take things beyond the fake dating scenario. I'd been so stunned to see her again and then doubly so by Jocelyn's suggestion that I hadn't been able to sort out my own thoughts about it until much later. But I had. And those thoughts were if I had a chance to be with Coral again I'd lunge for it with both hands. I'd meant it when I told her our night together had been electric and I wanted more of it. More of her. But she didn't seem to share that sentiment.

She rolled her eyes. "You cannot be serious."

"I'm very serious," I said.

"Your sister is my boss," she said, as if that were reason enough in and of itself.

"My sister is the one who suggested the romance angle," I countered.

"The *fake* romance angle," she parried. "I'm finally where I want to be, and I'm not going to risk it all on a fling with some guy."

Ignoring the "some guy" remark, I said, "What if there were no risk?"

Coral's brows drew together, and she twisted her glass on its coaster. "How could there not be?"

"First, despite all appearances to the contrary, my sister isn't going to stick her nose into my private life uninvited. Her interest here is in helping me out of a tough spot, not in the nitty-gritty details of my sex life. And, even if she were prone to meddling like that, it would be me, not you, who'd be in danger of facing her wrath. Trust me when I say Jocelyn has your back, Coral. Absent you being caught burying my body, she would one hundred percent lay the blame for anything at my feet, not yours. So, you don't need to worry about the sister angle."

She still looked skeptical, so I continued.

"Second, as you know, I'm only here for two weeks, of which only about ten days are left. Assuming Jocelyn's plan works and my exile from Boston isn't extended." I gave her my best smile, head tilted, teeth evenly displayed, lips pushed up just enough at the corners to produce the fine lines at my eyes but not make them squinty. This smile closed deals of every variety. "How much trouble could we possibly get into in ten days?"

Coral's lips pressed into a flat line. "How often do you practice that smile?"

Said smile faltered a little. "What?"

"That smile." She pointed at my face. "That pasted on baring of teeth that I'm sure works just fine unless someone's seen the real thing. How often do you practice it?"

"I don't . . ." I cleared my throat, smoothed out my features. "I don't know what you're talking about."

Coral's lips twitched, then spread into a wide smile of their own. "Oh, yes, you do. You've just never had someone call you out on it. And you *absolutely* practice that smile. What I don't know is why you bother, when the real one is so much better?"

I felt a real one tugging at the corners of my mouth. "Is that so?"

She blushed, caught in her own compliment of me. "You don't need me to tell you that you have a nice smile, Jamie."

I let the genuine smile break free. "Need? No, I don't need it. But I do want it. Almost desperately."

Lifting her drink, she hid her own smile behind her glass as she took a sip. I used the pause to circle back to my earlier sales pitch.

"I've covered the sister angle and my limited tenure here, so that leaves me with the final, possibly most important point."

"Which is?"

"As much as I hated the article itself," I said, swirling my drink. "I can't deny the underlying theme isn't that far off the mark."

Coral's smile dropped. "Underlying theme?"

I nodded and glanced away, gathering my thoughts. "The main complaint about me seems to be that I'm too focused on my work. That it comes before everything else." I looked back at Coral. "Interestingly enough, I think that might actually be an advantage for me with you."

"Oh?" she asked, leaning forward. "How do you figure that?"

"You just said that you weren't willing to risk your dream job on a 'fling with some guy,'" I said, and she managed to look a little contrite over the "some guy" remark.

"What others see as a drawback—my focus on work—would be something you see as a positive. Neither of us is looking for any sort of long-term commitment other than to our work, but we obviously enjoyed each other's company. Why not continue in that vein while I'm here? No promises or expectations beyond that."

I didn't mention Jocelyn's suggestion it was time for a shift in my priorities, or that her suggestion resonated with thoughts I'd already had circulating in my head. Coral wouldn't be interested in that, because she wasn't interested in a real relationship. That much was clear. Plus, she was starting a life here in Vegas and I was deeply rooted in Boston. What would be the point?

She twisted her glass on its coaster as she considered my proposition. "Fake the love angle for the cameras but enjoy certain other . . . benefits behind closed doors?"

"There's a reason the chemistry in *Mr. and Mrs. Smith* was so good," I said.

"Because Brad and Angie were screwing behind the scenes?" she asked.

I shrugged. "I was thinking more along the lines of the fake marriage/real sex plot of the new Donald Glover show, but you make a good point, too."

She chewed her lip, but didn't say no, so I kept talking.

"You came to this meeting with an agenda," I said. "I've offered up one of my own. You need time to consider my counterproposal. There's no pressure. We can just fake it, if that's what you want." It might kill me to do it, but I would if that was her decision.

There was a long pause before Coral said, "This is not how I expected today to go."

"Coral, I think it's safe to say that since you first tossed your Astroglide to me, our entire relationship has centered around the unexpected."

She laughed. "Fair point." Taking another long drink, she said, "I'll consider it, okay? That's all I'm willing to concede."

My heart started beating in a desperate gallop I was surprised she couldn't hear from across the table. *Relax,* I chastised myself. *She only said she'd consider it, not that she agreed.*

"That's all I can ask," I said aloud, proud my voice stayed even and didn't crack like a teenager.

"You got Jocelyn's text about the photographer tomorrow morning?"

I nodded. "Ten a.m. at the tank."

"See you there, Jamie," she said and slipped off her stool and out of the bar.

# CORAL

"How are you already internet famous?" Cam asked with a laugh as we FaceTimed the next morning. "No," she said, her dark curls bouncing on my screen. "Let me rephrase that. How are you already internet famous with some smoking hot dude? You haven't even been there a full week."

I laughed and touched up my waterproof eyeliner in the mirror, glancing down at my phone when she groaned. "You of all people should know better than to leave me to my own devices in Las Vegas."

"Have you read some of the comments on this video?" Her laughter ended with a judgmental hum. "Some people are well and truly perverse."

"All these years as a professional mermaid and you're only now figuring out merverts are everywhere, especially the internet?"

She clucked her tongue. "These aren't just from mermaid-freaks, honey. Some of these women are *thirsty* for your scene partner, you hear me?"

"Oh, I've seen it," I said, while I thought, *They weren't the only ones.* Jamie's proposal ran through my mind all night and was the first thing I thought of this morning. It was so tempting to take him up on his idea of a no-strings fling. But I wasn't completely sold on his claim there would be no risk involved. It couldn't be as easy and carefree as he'd made it sound.

Cam's finger stabbed the screen, and I knew she was pulling up the video and its accompanying comment board. "This one is my favorite, though," she said, clearing her throat. "Sebastian4Eva says, 'I have it on good authority it is always hotta unda de watta.' And then DynamicDiva replies with '@sebastian4eva I mean, it IS better down where it's wetter . . .'" Her burst of laughter threatened the integrity of my phone speaker with its intensity.

I giggled. "I can't fault them, though. These comments pretty much write themselves, thanks to the movie and the remake."

"What I want to know," Cam asked with a sly grin, "is whether this guy has been down where it's wetter."

"Cam!" I barely avoided stabbing myself in the eyeball with my liner.

"What?" she asked. "I've seen the video, babe. This dude is looking at you like he knows exactly what you look like under those strategically placed seashells and wants to show you much more fun ways to use that Astroglide."

"Don't tell me you believe everything you see on the internet," I said, trying to buy time by pretending to concentrate on my makeup. I hadn't told Cam about Jamie. That is, I hadn't told her that the guy in the now viral video was the same guy from my first night in Vegas. Because I'd obviously told her about my night with Jamie as soon as possible. I hadn't had the opportunity to fill her in on what transpired since. With our varying schedules plus the time difference, we kept missing each other.

But she wasn't the only one who'd put in some quality time on the internet. Only mine had been spent researching Jameson Standard. How could I not, after his indecently enticing proposal? I needed to know who I was dealing with here. And . . . oh boy. He was a force to be reckoned with. The man had already built an empire at the ripe old age of thirty-nine. He and his two partners, Davidson Brooks and Gideon West, had developments all over the Northeast and recently started a satellite branch of their offices in some place called Mimosa, North Carolina. There was no shortage of pictures of him looking debonair at various dinners, ribbon cuttings, and other hoity-toity parties. Always with a glamorous female accessory on his arm, but seldom the same one.

Of course, the *Boston Commons* article came up in the search, but I didn't click the link. Based on how embarrassed he'd been about it yesterday, it felt like I'd be betraying him in some way if I read it. So, I closed out of my browser before temptation could get the best of me.

"Girl, please," Cam said. "Who do you think I am? Of course I don't believe all that nonsense. Which is why I'm asking you to tell me the real story." She paused and I could hear the speculation in the silence. "Something happened with this guy. I don't need Dirty Disney comments to know that."

I did not have time to get into all of it now. I was due at the tank in twenty minutes. "It's . . . complicated," I said. "But I promise I'll give you the lowdown soon, okay? I've gotta go, though, so I'm not late."

"I'll hold you to it," she said, and we hung up.

Lucas, the photographer Jocelyn hired in her publicity whirlwind yesterday, lounged outside the exterior door of the tank.

At my approach, he glanced down at my tailbag and then hefted his own camera bag. "You might have me beat."

I laughed. "Looks that way."

The recessed door that led behind the aquarium itself and up to the tank platform opened to reveal Xavier. "There's my sea sister," he said with a wink.

"Hey, Xavier," I replied. "Have you met Lucas?"

The two men exchanged hellos as we made our way up the metal staircase to the wide metal shelf that spanned the entire back of the tank's top. It was our landing pad of sorts, but was mainly designed as an operating platform for the caretakers of the tank's full-time inhabitants. Its gridded surface extended from the rear of the tank all the way out into its center, with retractable ladders and platforms to allow access to the water.

I scanned the staging area but didn't see Jamie. According to Jocelyn, he would be worked into today's shots in some way. I didn't have total clarity on what she was thinking, but her bright-eyed optimism that it would "be total merfection" made me laugh. She was trying her best to immerse herself in mermaid culture.

Lucas split off from us to get set up, and Xavier turned to me. "Seems like you've made quite the splash."

I groaned at his mermaid dad joke, and he laughed. "I wish I could say I was sorry for that, but I'm honestly not." He looked over his shoulder to where Lucas was fussing with his camera. "I'm going to go make sure he's good. Just give me a shout if you need some help getting into your tail, okay?"

"You got it," I said, and he headed across the room.

I stepped onto the platform and headed to the edge of the water. Grabbing my oversize beach towel from my bag, I spread it along the lip of the platform. Carefully, I extracted my tail and unfurled it on top of the towel. I concentrated on setting everything up to keep the nerves bouncing under my skin from completely taking over. Jamie would be joining me this morning in some form or another, so we could start painting the fantasy of our mermaid love story. *Only it won't have to be all make-believe if you tell him yes.*

Shoving that salacious thought to the back of my mind, I shucked out of my joggers and tank top and adjusted the straps of my green bikini. Settling down behind my tail, I pulled on my scuba socks, then got out my lube. Starting just above my ankles, I slathered my way up my calves, over my knees and onto my thighs, leaving behind a glistening, slippery sheen on my skin.

"Looks like I got here just in time."

My hands froze at the sound of Jamie's voice from behind me. Looking over my shoulder, I found him grinning down at me, wearing another one of his tailored suits. I swallowed back my nerves and arched a brow. "In time for what?"

Jamie inclined his head at the bottle of lube. "I finally get to solve the Astroglide mystery." He came around to stand in front of me and cocked his head to the side, considering the bottle. "Although, I have to admit, even now I'm not sure why you use it."

I resumed smoothing the lube up my thighs, unable to deny the hum of satisfaction I felt at how quickly his eyes dropped to follow the movement of my hands. I squirted another generous dose into my palms and rubbed it along the back of one thigh, then the other. From the corner of my eye, I saw Jamie pull his lower lip between his teeth and I couldn't swear to it, but I thought I heard a soft growl.

"As your fake boyfriend," he said, his voice a little rough, "I feel I should know why you're spreading personal lubricant all over your thighs."

The low rumble of his voice did things to my insides. Flippy, floppy, twisty things that made the fake feel much too real as I was half naked and covered in lube while he loomed over me like some sort of dark business overlord. A fantasy I never knew I had until right then.

Without looking directly at him, I grabbed one of the washcloths from my bag and wiped my hands. "Just like I told you at the airport, it's useful for tight tails." I tapped the opening of my silicone tail lightly. "These things are as fitted as a scuba suit, but much more delicate. Getting good and lubed up makes wriggling into it that much easier."

I enjoyed a little too much the choked gargle noise he made in response. Ducking my head to hide a grin, I grabbed two more washcloths and tucked them inside the opening of my tail for handholds, draping one half on the outside of the silicone and one on the inside. His reaction to seeing me oiled up aside, I wasn't thrilled with having to get into my tail in front of Jamie. It was one of the less attractive parts of being a mermaid. Nothing sexy about shoving yourself into a sleeve of silicone like some sort of human sausage.

*Why does it matter if he thinks you're sexy or not? Unless you're thinking of taking him up on his offer* . . . Again, I pushed thoughts of a real affair with Jamie to the back of my mind. Slipping my feet into the tail, I searched blindly with my toes for the monofin at the bottom. Finding it, I pushed my feet into the smooth center slots. Once my heels were hooked in and secure, I began the process of working my tail up my legs.

"Can I . . . help?"

I glanced up at Jamie and couldn't hold back a laugh at the look on his face. Wide-eyed with raised brows, he looked wholly bewildered, as though he had no idea what to offer if I accepted his help. He had no way to know how much easier this was if someone helped tug and smooth out any wrinkles as the tail slowly slid on.

"You could ask Xavier to come help me," I said, jerking my chin in the direction of my mertender.

Jamie followed my gaze to where Xavier was still talking to Lucas. His eyes narrowed and there was a line between his brows when he looked back at me. Crossing his arms, he said, "He looks busy. Is there something I could do?"

*Someone's jealous,* sang a voice in my head. Ignoring it, and the little zing I felt in response to it as best I could, I stopped wiggling with my tail halfway up my thighs. "Ever helped a mermaid put on a tail before?"

"Can't say I have," he replied, then waggled his brows. "Will you be my first time, Coral?"

I rolled my eyes, but grinned up at him. I couldn't help it. The man oozed charisma. "You joke," I said. "But you really do have to be gentle here, okay?"

Sobering, he nodded and stepped closer. "Got it. Just tell me what to do."

I gestured toward the bottom half of my tail. "See those wrinkles?" Jamie nodded. "Well, the last thing we want is a wrinkly mermaid. So, while I pull the tail up, use the palms of your hands to smooth up the silicone, pushing up toward the top, okay? And watch the fluke, please. It won't take much to tear it."

"Er, the . . . fluke?"

I pointed at the broad fins extending from the bottom of my tail. "Fluke." Jamie nodded and toed out of his dress shoes. "What are you doing?" I asked, watching him put his shoes to the side.

He shrugged. "No shoes mean less chance of damaging your . . . fluke."

"Oh," I said, touched by his consideration and struck once more by how thoughtful he was. "Good point."

He went on to divest himself of his suit jacket, then unbutton his cuffs and roll up his sleeves. My mouth went dry at the sight of his forearms. Each roll of the crisp white fabric revealed another few inches of tanned skin over flexing muscles as he adjusted the folds of his sleeve. Muscles that had pressed my naked chest against his when he'd carried me to his bedroom. My fingers twitched with the desire to touch him. Other places twitched with the desire for much, *much* more. *Keep it professional, Coral*, I reminded myself.

"You know, I'm a little surprised you're in your regular suit instead of a bathing suit," I said.

He glanced down at his outfit and then back to me. "You've got your uniform." He pointed to my tail. "I've got mine," he finished, running a hand down the front of his shirt. "Although today, Jocelyn specifically requested I wear a suit."

Crossing the platform, he kneeled in front of me with one knee on either side of my tail, carefully positioning his feet so they didn't touch any part of it. He settled his hands on my calves, and I swore I could feel the heat of them through the silicone. Which was ludicrous.

"This okay?" he asked, blue eyes flicking from his hands to my face.

*Oh boy is it*, I thought and then immediately gave myself a mental slap. "It's fine," I said, the words hurried. Wrenching my gaze from his, I looked down at my tail to resume the slow process of pulling it up my legs. And discovered that with the right person helping, putting on your tail could be the sexiest part of being a mermaid.

I pulled, he pushed, and those damn forearms rippled the whole time. Jamie's hands cupped my tail, working slowly upward to ease out the wrinkles. Strong fingers pressed and slid against the silicone, the pressure of them like a massage over my calves and up my thighs. He kept his eyes down, engrossed in his task. Which made it that much easier to sneak peeks at him as we worked.

He was unfairly gorgeous and each inch he moved up my legs brought that into starker focus. I could see the inky black of his eyelashes against his elegant cheekbones. The firm set of his full mouth. The few recalcitrant locks of blond hair that refused to stay in place. When he lifted his eyes to mine, I blinked away, looking down as I tugged my tail the last of the way up. Which brought Jamie's hands to my hips, his skin a burnished bronze next to the Empress green of my tail. His thumbs worked out the last remaining wrinkle.

Looking up, my gaze crashed back into Jamie's, his face inches from mine. It was like I'd reeled him in, drawing him closer with each pull. And now he was straddling my thighs, hands at my hips and lips close enough to kiss. Neither of us moved. We just stared at each other, exchanging breaths. Jamie's eyes dipped to my mouth, and he licked his bottom lip, drawing it back between his teeth. I swallowed thickly and his hands flexed, fingers pressing into me.

"Not bad for a first time," he said, the words a whisper of sound.

"You're a natural," I whispered back, making him grin. Still, neither of us moved.

"Coral, I th—"

"You sure we can't use some behind-the-scenes stuff, Joss?"

Lucas's question jarred us both from the moment and Jamie released his grip on my hips to rock backward, then stand. I instantly missed his closeness, his touch. Even more so when he stepped further away from me.

"I'm telling you, Joss," Lucas went on excitedly. "These would be perfect images to use in the campaign. I mean look at this chemistry!"

Recovering from my Jamie induced malaise, I looked over to see Lucas and Jocelyn bent over the viewfinder of Lucas's camera. Jocelyn looked up first, a thoughtful glint in her eyes as she glanced from me to Jamie. One side of her mouth lifted in a barely perceptible half smile.

"Sorry, Lucas," she said. "While you may be right, we can't use most of those because we're selling more than chemistry here. We're selling the magic of a mermaid. If we show a mermaid putting on her tail, she stops being a mermaid and becomes a lady wearing silicone. Kills the mystery and the magic. It's a nonstarter."

I heard Jamie exhale and looked back at him. The desire I saw in his eyes almost overrode some secondary emotion. Something that resembled yearning more than simple lust. Like whatever he wanted was behind shatter resistant glass. I swallowed and looked away, unable to maintain eye contact because I was too scared it would pull me in like the power of the tides. That I'd wash right over to him on the strength of his stare alone.

Clearing my throat, I smiled brightly and asked Lucas, "Should I go ahead and dive in, then, or . . ." My voice trailed off, and I gestured generically. "Where do you want me?"

# chapter seventeen

## JAMIE

*Where do you want me?*

Those five words conjured images that were not fit for polite company, much less a room that contained my sister, a photographer, a mertender named Xavier who looked like Lenny Kravitz only somehow cooler and finally the woman responsible for and starring in each of the NSFW images now in my brain. I'd lasted all of thirty seconds before commenting on the lube and not even five minutes before I'd finagled a way to touch her. If I didn't get my libido on lockdown quickly, it was going to be a very long morning.

"How partial are you to that suit?" Lucas asked, and it took me a few seconds to realize he was talking to me.

I glanced down at my clothes. "Uh, excuse me?"

Jocelyn's instructions to be here at ten o'clock had been less than fulsome. As in, she just said, "Be at the tank at ten for pictures. And make sure you wear a suit." So, I'd dressed like I normally did and reported for duty.

I glanced over at her. "You said wear a suit."

She rolled her eyes. "Only you would think I meant a business suit and not a swimsuit for a mermaid photoshoot."

I flushed in embarrassment at my obvious mistake.

Lucas shook his head. "No, no! I think this whole vibe could *work!*" He waved a hand up and down at me. "What you're wearing, how much do you love it, and would you be willing to get it wet?"

Grateful, but still suspicious of the reprieve, I took stock of my Hugo Boss dress shirt and Tom Ford suit pants. "How much of it needs to be wet?"

Lucas considered my question, tapping a finger to his lips. "Just the shirt, really, for what I'm thinking. But it needs to be *wet*, not damp. I'm talking drenched, soaked, drippi—"

"Got it," I choked out. After watching Coral slather lube over her thighs, I did not need any more euphemisms for the word "wet" right then. "I'm good with the shirt getting soaked, that's not a problem. The pants are another story."

He nodded. "Okay, cool. So, lose the pants and we can get started."

My mind skidded like a record scratch, and I stared at him. "I'm sorry, lose the . . . pants?"

Lucas nodded impatiently, rolling his hands in a "get on with it" gesture. "The pants. They can't get wet, so you'll need to take them off."

I looked at Jocelyn, but she shrugged with an evilly sweet smile. "It's a small sacrifice, don't you think?"

Briefly I wondered if I could get away with murdering my sister, before realizing my parents would notice if she didn't show up for the holidays and it would raise too many questions. I glanced over at Coral, who was studying the opposite side of the room and avoiding looking at me. Was I really about to strip down to my underwear right now?

"I've got some trunks you can borrow, man," Xavier said, becoming my singular ally in the room.

Relief at not having to parade around in my briefs buoyed me as Xavier pulled a bag from a locker on the far wall and extracted a wad of black nylon from inside.

"Thanks," I said, catching his toss one-handed.

"No problem," he said. "Showers are back there if you need some privacy."

I headed toward the door he indicated. Beyond it was a generic bathroom with multiple stalls along one wall and a row of showers along the other. After stripping off my socks and folding my pants, I finally took a good look at the suit Xavier lent me. Board shorts it was not. Based solely on his choice of swimwear, Xavier was a man very secure in himself. The only thing trunk-like about it was the truncated length of it. While it wasn't a speedo, it only came to about mid-thigh, barely longer than my boxer briefs. At least, I hoped it would come down that far. I was taller than Xavier by a few inches, and when this little fabric was involved, every inch counted.

*Beggars can't be choosers*, I thought and pulled on the suit. It looked absurd paired with my dress shirt, but it was better than walking back out in my underwear.

"Knock, knock," Lucas called, and I turned to face him. "Oh, yes, that should work nicely. But you'll need to take your undershirt off to get the look we want here."

"And what look is that?" I asked, arching a brow.

He smirked. "I told you. Wet."

"Jesus Christ," I muttered, but obeyed his request and rejoined the party in nothing but a tiny swimsuit and my button down.

Jocelyn laughed and let out a loud whistle. I shot her the bird. It only made her laugh harder. Wearing a scuba mask and holding what looked to be a waterproof camera, Lucas joined Coral and me on the platform.

"Okay, you two, we're going to start in the tank and then get some additional shots on dry land, once we've gotten Jamie here good and wet."

*Did the man not know another word?* I wondered, then processed what he'd said.

"Wait, what?" I asked, looking at the giant aquarium below us. "You want me to get in there?"

"How else did you think you were going to get wet?" Lucas asked. Coral giggled and tried unsuccessfully to cover it with a cough.

"But what about the fish? And the people? They'll see me." *In this nonsensical getup*, I added silently.

Jocelyn chimed in. "No, you'll be in the area blocked by the rock formation, so no one can see you. And absent feeding time, the fish rarely swim up this far, so they're a nonissue."

Before I could say anything, Coral raised her . . . tail and twisted toward the water. There was a slight splash as her fluke disappeared beneath the surface. Easing herself downward, she pushed off the platform and slipped into the water as graceful as a . . . well, mermaid. "C'mon, Jamie," she said, grinning up at me, clearly pleased to have the upper hand. "I promise I'll protect you from all the scary fish."

I glared at her for a moment but knew I had only myself to blame for being in this predicament. There was no sense in being a child about it. I'd agreed to this and, if it went well, had the most to gain, so I had to live up to my side of the bargain. Resigned, I sat on the edge of the platform to lower myself down into the . . . freezing cold water.

"Holy shit!" I hissed through clenched, soon to be chattering teeth. "Why is it so cold?"

Coral laughed, arms moving in smooth arcs to keep herself afloat. "It's cold, Jamie, because this isn't the hotel pool. It's set for the comfort of those with fins, rather than those with feet."

"H-h-how are you not cold?" I asked between shivers.

She flipped her tail at me in a gentle spray of water. "Like I said, fins, not feet." Swimming closer to me, she patted my shoulder. "We won't be in here long." Her eyes flicked to someone behind me, and she smiled. "Right, Xavier?"

"You know the rules," I heard him reply.

A slight splash to my left signaled Lucas's arrival in the tank, complete with flippers and a mask. He held up his underwater camera. "Here's the plan, Coral. Since you're the expert here, we're going to use Jamie as more of a prop than an active participant."

"Gee, thanks," I said, wiggling my fingers in the still frigid water. This whole experience was getting more surreal by the second.

Ignoring me, Lucas kept talking. "I need some shots of you next to him in the water. His shoulders and torso are going to be our money shot, so keep that in mind as you swim. Touch his chest, his arms, his stomach. You know the drill."

Coral nodded as though she caressed half-naked men underwater on the daily. The thought did not sit well with me. But, before I could voice any opinion on the matter, or question what in the hell Lucas meant by "money shot," both of them ducked under the water.

And then I didn't care about anything but the sensation of Coral swimming around me as I treaded water. Whispers of sensation danced over my skin as she followed whatever pantomimed directions Lucas provided. I could feel the brush of her arm, the sight graze of her fingers, the smooth glide of her tail and the satiny slide of her hair as she swam in slow circles around me. Just as she had been the first time I'd seen her perform, she was fluid and graceful, her movements easy and relaxed. I was truly nothing more than a prop, and she was the star.

Her fingers slipped under the hem of my shirt and trailed over my abs, leaving tingles in their wake. Deftly she undid a few buttons before curving nimbly around me in a supple arc, her tail parting the open fabric of my shirt. I had to fight the urge to turn around and watch her, reminding myself of Lucas and his camera.

Once she was behind me, her arms snaked underneath mine and her hands came to my ribcage, fingers splayed. As her hands moved higher, I felt the unmistakable press of her breasts against my back. I clenched my jaw to keep from reacting to the slow slide of her body against mine in the water, now thankful the temperature was cold enough to keep me from embarrassing myself. Reflexively, I covered her hands with mine and Lucas's thumbs up broke the surface of the water along with an excited huff from his snorkel.

Having Coral wrapped around me was exquisitely excruciating. The feel of her against me kicked off a mental highlight reel of our night together. Kissing her, touching her, watching her come apart beneath me. Images of all of it swirled around my brain, each one spurring another until there was no space for anything but her. It was too much and nowhere near enough to have her so close.

I pressed her hands into my chest, and she tightened her arms around me for the span of a heartbeat before letting go and surfacing behind me. Resting her hands lightly on my shoulders, she took a deep gulp of air. Before I could turn and face her, she leaned closer, lips at my ear, and asked, "How are you holding up? We should've had a signal for you to give me if something wasn't working for you."

Lucas surfaced in front of me, spitting out his snorkel. "Don't move, you two. These shots are going to be epic," he said, already moving toward us with the camera. "Coral, drape your arm across his shoulder . . . down his chest . . . Yes! Just like that. Now, Jamie, angle your head away from her just a bit."

I blinked, snared equally in the memory of Coral and her presence behind me in the water. Gentle fingers touched my jaw and nudged it in the direction Lucas had indicated. "I've got you, newbie," she teased in a whisper.

"Ooh, yes, leave your hand there, Coral. Now give me sultry, sexy. C'mon, baby girl, seduce me with those eyes. Yes! That's it! Jamie, touch her forearm where it's across your chest. Curl that big paw around it . . . Yes, right there. Yes!"

"I guess we know it was good for him, huh?" Coral whispered again, her giggle a breath of sound against my neck.

I turned toward her, and my nose brushed hers. Her eyes went wide at our proximity, the water on her lashes reminiscent of the dream I'd had about her. "Somehow," I said, lost in the blue-gray glow of her eyes, "whether it was good for Lucas is the last thing on my mind."

## CORAL

"Okay, Lucas, that's enough in the water for now. No need for Jamie to tire himself out right off the bat."

Xavier's command pieced through my lust-fogged brain, and I snatched my gaze away from Jamie's. Belatedly, I realized I was still draped over him like a human blanket, which meant he was holding both of us, plus the weight of my tail, up in the water. Without even breathing hard, but still it hardly seemed fair. Quickly, I released my grip on his shoulders to slip back down into the tank. Even though I wasn't looking his way, I knew Jamie's eyes remained on me. I could feel the weight of his stare as I swam toward the platform.

Xavier held out a hand, but I shook my head and shifted over. "Let Jamie get out first. He's less used to the water temperature than I am. And he's been treading water the whole time."

"I'm okay," Jamie said from behind me.

"Nah, Coral's right," Xavier said, gesturing for Jamie to climb onto the short ladder extending off the platform. "We need to get you out first."

"I'm good, man," Jamie said stubbornly. "I'll help you get Coral back on the platform."

Xavier looked from me to Jamie and then back again with a knowing grin. "You heard the man, Coral." He held out his hand again as Jamie stood on the bottom rung of the ladder but made no move to go up it.

"Seriously, I'm fine," I said, shooting Jamie an exasperated look. "You really need to get out of the wa—EEP!" Before I knew what was happening, Jamie locked an arm around my waist and hoisted me out of the tank and onto the platform in one fell swoop. Still breathing evenly.

With one hand still on the ladder he'd used for leverage, he loomed over me. His position on the ladder gave his already impressive height an extra boost that was just irritating. I reared back to glare up into his scowl. "That was wholly unnecessary," I said, trying to sound haughty, which was hard to do after being flung bodily onto the platform like some sort of giant tuna.

"But impressive," Xavier said from behind me, making no effort to disguise his laughter.

What was impressive was the insanely attractive way Jamie Standard filled out a wet shirt. Specifically, a *white* wet shirt that clung to every single one of his absurdly sculpted muscles. Tan skin blazed through the soaked sheer fabric in an unfairly erotic display that made it difficult for me to inhale a full breath.

*Look at his face*, I instructed myself. But that wasn't the most helpful advice, either, considering the fact his stupid face was just as delectable as the rest of him. And those eyes. Those devastating blue eyes were now glowing with challenge as they stared down at me. A few drops of water were caught on his inky lashes, which somehow made him even sexier.

He should look silly, not sexy, in his dress shirt and swimsuit combo. Any normal guy would. But Jamie looked . . . God, he looked beyond good. When he'd strolled out of the shower area in those fitted black trunks under that crisp white shirt, my fingers had curled with the urge to climb him like a tree. Not just climb him, but make some sort of human nest in the crook of his arm and live out my days there, surviving on orgasms alone. My plan for only clean thoughts and keeping things professional until I'd had more time to think things through was going *so* well.

"Impressive or not," Jamie said, still glowering as he climbed the rest of the way out of the water. "We'll have to agree to disagree on it being unnecessary, Coral." He gestured back at the tank. "Too much time in water that temperature could result in hypothermia."

If he'd been looming before, now he was positively towering over me. One of the few downsides of being a professional mermaid? The inability to stand up and argue with arbitrary assholes.

Irritation flared at his overbearing attitude. "You're going to lecture me about how much time to spend in an aquarium?" If I could've stood up and flounced away, I would have. But without any real hope for upward movement, I settled for turning up the heat on my glare. "Why do you think I wanted you to get out of the water first?"

I no longer wanted to live in the crook of his arm. I now wanted to kick him in his shins, but again . . . mermaid tail prevented kicking. I considered briefly pushing him back into the tank, but that would only undercut the point I was trying to make. I settled for crossing my arms and making a face similar to that of a sullen mule. "I know what I'm doing in there, Jamie."

Crouching next to me, he replied, "I never said you didn't, Coral." His tone was every bit as snippy as mine. "Which is why you know I'm right. You'll be getting back in that tank well before I will, so you needed to get out first to give your body more time to warm up."

"I hardly think the two minutes it would've taken for you to get out of the tank would have made that much difference," I said, unwilling to concede the point. He was being an imperious ass to me on my own turf and I wouldn't take that from anyone, no matter how obvious it was they never skipped leg day.

Jamie opened his mouth to reply, but Xavier cut in with a hand on each of our shoulders. "Okay, okay, kids. Let's retreat to our neutral corners." Turning to Lucas, he asked, "You ready for the next shot?"

"Absolutely," Lucas called back. "Can you bring Coral over?"

Xavier nodded and turned to get the little cart he'd already positioned at the base of the platform.

"What's that for?" Jamie asked him.

I answered. "It's not like I can walk around in this getup, so I need some wheels."

Understanding dawned and was then replaced by a sly twinkle in his eyes. "Not today, you don't."

"What are you talking about? Of course I d—OH!" One second I'd been sitting on cold metal, the next I was nestled against Jamie's chest. His extremely broad, defined chest.

His biceps flexed against my ribcage and his fingers spanned my ribs just south of the underside of my boob. Hell, his thumb was all but playing underwire to my bikini top. Which my boob took immediate notice of and perked up like a debutante at her come out. We locked eyes, and for a second or two I didn't breathe.

"What are you doing?" I asked once my diaphragm resumed functioning. Regrettably, my question came out in a breathy wheeze that would've embarrassed an asthmatic.

Jamie grinned down at me. "If you have to ask, Coral, maybe we should get you checked for hypothermia. As I understand it, one of the symptoms is loss of cognitive function." Shifting me in his arms, he said, "Put your arm around my neck."

"Excuse me?" I was still reeling from his lifting me into the air as easily as a feather, while also searching for a witty comeback to his hypothermia comment, so I wasn't prepared to take instructions. Had he carried me before? Sure, when I was naked and not wearing an additional forty or so pounds of silicone mermaid tail. But he'd swept me up into his arms with little to no additional effort. I would *not* think about how hot that was.

"You'll be more comfortable that way," Jamie said.

"That would imply there could be anything comfortable about this entire situation. And why are you researching hypothermia symptoms?" Not quite the zinger I was going for, but it would have to do. Being back in Jamie's embrace was worse for my cognitive function than submersing in cold water ever could be. Even dripping wet, he was warm, pumping out body heat like a furnace. And somehow, he still smelled good. As though being dipped in saltwater only enhanced the power of his cologne, soap or stupid male pheromones.

"If I'm a glorified prop for a mermaid, I need to be up to speed on all aspects of the professional mermaid realm. So, I did a little studying last night on the basics," he said. "Now put your arm around my neck and relax, okay?" he said, voice now cajoling instead of an outright command.

"Fine," I replied, giving in, and draping my arm around his shoulders and trying not to think about him researching my job. Or how it made me feel that he had. I relaxed into his arms and grudgingly admitted, only to myself, that it was more comfortable this way.

Satisfied with my compliance, Jamie looked over my head at Xavier. "I've got her."

Xavier, the traitor, chuckled and said, "Certainly looks that way to me."

Jamie hadn't even taken two steps before Lucas was in front of us, snapping away. "This is even better than I'd hoped," he said, the excitement in his voice raising it to a pitch usually reserved for dolphins in mating season.

I wasn't sure I agreed with his assessment, as there was no way my being smashed against Jamie's chest would offer the most flattering angles. Would toting me around make Jamie's biceps pop against the wet fabric of his shirt? Sure. Would it emphasize the breadth of his shoulders? No question there. Would his chest look even broader than it was in real life? A distinct possibility. Would it also round my shoulders, smush my boobs and compress my midsection into a less than complimentary accordion? Again, no doubt about it.

Putting a hand on Jamie's chest, I angled my shoulders back and arched my spine. He faltered a step.

"What are you doing?" he asked.

"The right angle is everything," I replied, looking into Lucas's camera instead of at Jamie. "Not that you'd need to be concerned with that, Adonis. Those cheekbones of yours would look good from any angle."

I felt his chuckle beneath my hand. "Why does that sound like more of an insult than a compliment?"

I laughed and glanced away from the camera lens up to his face. "Just my mere mortal jealousy coming out in the arms of a Greek god."

"Says one of the most beautiful women I've ever met."

His words hovered between us in a frisson of energy that sparked along my skin. Jamie gazed down at me, his heated blue gaze roaming over my face and catching on my lips. Longing burned hot in the depths of his eyes, turning them into deep pools of molten blue. My fingers curled into the fabric of his shirt and my lips parted, which made his pupils dilate and his fingers press more firmly into my side. Our bodies' innate reactions to each other were immediate and so heady I felt a bit drugged. Like I could get a contact high just by being near him.

"Jamie." His name on my lips was more of an exhalation than an actual word, but it elicited a gravelly sound from deep within his chest. Half growl, half muted groan that I felt as much as heard. The sensation of it rippled through me in a heated wave as his arms shifted beneath me, lifting me closer as his head dipped toward mine.

"You two are on fire!" Lucas's enthusiastic shout sliced through the bubble of raw lust around us and the real world came rushing in to remind us we were not alone. Jamie's arms loosened and my hand flattened against his chest as he lifted his chin and looked away, the air around us no longer charged and laden with want. My skin cooled and I couldn't suppress a shiver.

That brought Jamie's eyes back to me, this time laced with concern instead of heat. "Are you cold?"

I shook my head. "No, I'm fine." The rash of goose bumps along my arms prickled in contradiction.

Jamie frowned. "No, you're cold."

"Jamie, really, I'm fi—"

"Let's take a break, Lucas," Jamie said, cutting me off. "Coral needs to get dried off and warmed up."

Lucas lowered his camera and shot me a concerned look. "Are you okay?"

I shoved at Jamie's chest. Not that he could just put me down, but it helped allay some of my frustration. "I'm fine," I said to Lucas.

He looked less than convinced, and a little intimidated by Jamie's glower. The latter must have been more persuasive than my assurances, because he gave a little nod. "Joss and I will review these images and discuss next shots while you two get dry."

When he turned away, I poked Jamie in the chest. "I don't need a keeper."

Jamie snorted and shook his head. "Once again, we'll have to agree to disagree." His grin was impish when he added, "And I thought they were called mertenders."

I rolled my eyes. "Normally, mertenders take orders from the mermaids, not the other way around."

His grin widened and his voice went a little lower. "Coral, didn't we agree the other night that nothing between us would be normal?"

A shiver went down my spine that had nothing to do with being cold. I swallowed roughly. "That does ring a bell."

"And I have to say, so far, abnormal is really working for me," he said. "I mean, I spent the morning swimming with a mermaid and now I've got her in my arms." He tightened his grip around my legs. "Yep, I could get used to this sort of abnormal."

I shifted a little, adjusting my arm around his neck. "It definitely has a few perks," I said, which made him smile. *Just think about what other perks he's offering,* my horny inner voice suggested.

I knew then my response to his offer had been a foregone conclusion. I wanted what he'd outlined just as badly as he did. And if he hadn't been such a bossy bastard about my getting out of the tank, I probably would've told him yes right then and there. But that sort of overstepping didn't deserve to be rewarded, so he'd have to wait a little longer for my answer.

# chapter eighteen

## JAMIE

My phone chimed with an incoming text, pulling my attention from the YouTube video of Coral swimming in some sort of hot spring. We'd wrapped the photoshoot a few hours ago, and I'd come back to my room to try to work, but ended up watching Coral TV instead. Glancing at my phone, I saw it was a group message from Jocelyn to Coral and me. I swiped it open.

Jocelyn: *Thought you might want to see these. You two are really selling the attraction!*

A cluster of photos sat beneath her text like a hand of cards. One tap to the screen brought up a shot of Coral and me that must have been taken right after I helped her put on her mermaid tail. My arms remained braced on either side of her hips, and her face tilted toward mine, a teasing smile playing on her lips.

The next two shots were similar, each one as sizzling a display of attraction as the last. In all of them, I looked ready to devour her, and she appeared willing. I shifted in my seat and swiped to the fourth and final picture.

In it, I held Coral in my arms, clasped to my chest with our faces inches apart. Lucas must've snapped it just after she said my name and I'd almost lost my mind and kissed her right then. The hunger I felt for her in that moment was perfectly captured in the picture, as though every inch of my body was straining toward her. She clutched the front of my shirt and stared at me with hooded eyes.

In the moment, I'd thought she wanted me as much as I wanted her. I'd been sure of it, and now, the proof I'd been right was on the screen of my phone. The desire on her face was so raw and undeniable the sight of it made my hands itch with the need to feel the supple weight of her in my arms. I tapped the screen to save the photos then answered Jocelyn's text.

Jamie: *Thanks for sharing these.*

Bubbles appeared, then her response came in a text separate from the group.

Jocelyn: *Not a problem. At least, I don't think it's a problem.*

*What the fuck?* I squinted down at the phone, then tapped the screen to call her.

"That was fast," she said, picking up on the second ring.

"What do you mean you don't 'think' it's a problem?"

Jocelyn sighed. "Jamie, don't be a moron."

"I'm not being a moron. I'm asking a question."

Another long sigh and then she said, "Jamie, anyone with eyeballs can see the way the two of you are looking at each other in these pictures. Real, physical attraction practically leaps off the screen and slaps you across the face. Which makes me wonder, big brother, just what went down between the two of you over that 'dinner'?"

"I thought our selling a love story was the whole point of this scheme," I dodged. "So, isn't it a good thing if the pictures show two people who are attracted to each other."

Jocelyn hummed into the phone. "Jamie, I know I teased you about Coral when you said yes to this, but now . . ." Her pause stretched too long for comfort, and I couldn't take it.

"Now what?" I asked.

"I just want you to be careful if this romance isn't just for the camera."

"What's that supposed to mean?" I asked.

"If you're into Coral, that's fine. I happen to think she's awesome. But your track record isn't what I'd call the best. If it were, the article wouldn't even have been a possibility. Which means I want you to be careful with her. Make sure the two of you are on the same page about whatever is happening with the two of you. Do not fuck this up for me because you want to cavort with a mermaid while you're in Vegas. Coral is an integral part of what I'm trying to build here, so keep that in mind, okay?"

"Cavort, Joss? Really?" Her warning reinforced what I'd told Coral. There was no way my sister would take my side over Coral's. If anything should go sideways between us, which I still didn't think it would, there wasn't any question at whose feet Jocelyn would lay the blame. Because, as she'd made clear at lunch the other day, she at least partially agreed with Abigail's portrayal of me. Just like I had come to in the last few days.

"You're my brother, so I refuse to use anything sexy to describe whatever it is you and Coral either have gotten or intend to get up to while you're in town. I'm just reminding you that I need her not to regret taking this job. Or listening to me when I pitched the idea of selling the two of you as a couple."

"Joss, listen, I kn—"

She interrupted me, her voice a little less strident. "You and Coral are two consenting adults, I know that. And I'm not trying to play den mother here any more than absolutely necessary. I just want you to keep in mind this show has the potential to do exponential things for my career and hers. Whatever happens between the two of you, don't lose sight of that."

"I won't, Joss. I swear," I said and meant it. The last thing I wanted to do was cause any problems for my sister or Coral, especially when they were trying to help me clean up my own mess.

I decided to test the waters a little. "But weren't you the one who told me I needed to change my priorities? Make space in my life for something other than work?"

"Yes," she said carefully. "I did say that. Barely three days ago." There was a pause, then she added, "And you're what? Going to make room in your life for Coral? Who lives in Vegas?"

"Would that be so wrong?" I asked and she harrumphed.

"Geography aside, it seems like a quick reversal on your part, Jamie. If it's really what you want, I'll support it. But make sure you're doing it for the right reasons and not using Coral to test a theory."

"Test a theory?" I asked, somewhat affronted.

Jocelyn exhaled into the phone. "I'm not trying to be a dick about this, Jamie. But honestly, isn't it a little too meta that the fake love story we're pitching on social media could end up being a real one? It's more realistic for the two of you to be clear this is just a fling and then go your separate ways. Right?"

That was exactly the proposal I'd outlined to Coral, but when Jocelyn framed it out for me, I felt a little twinge in my gut. Now that I'd voiced the idea of something more with Coral, it lodged in my brain. But was Jocelyn right? Had it stuck there because of the article, or because it was something I really wanted?

Before I could respond to Jocelyn or sort through any of that in my head, my phone beeped, signaling another call. Pulling it away from my ear, the sight of Coral's name on the screen made my blood hum a little faster.

"Sorry, Joss, I've got another call coming in," I said. "But I swear I heard what you said and I'm not going to do anything to fuck this up for either of you, okay?"

"Thanks, Jamie," she said. "I'll talk to you tomorrow."

"Bye, Joss," I said and clicked over to take Coral's call.

"Hey Coral," I said.

"Jamie, hey," Coral responded. "I was wondering if you wanted to grab a drink with me," she said, direct as ever.

"A drink?" I asked, then winced. I sounded like an idiot. I needed to get my shit together.

Her laugh coasted out of the speaker. "Yeah, a drink. With me. I got the pictures from Jocelyn, just like you did obviously, and I wanted to talk to you about a couple social media posts before I made them. To make sure you're okay with my ideas."

"Sure," I said, hoping I didn't sound as overeager as I felt. "When and where?"

"How about the Skyway Bar in about an hour?"

"I can make that work," I said, still trying to play it cool.

"Cool," she said. "I'll see you in an hour."

## CORAL

The Skyway was even cooler than the website made it seem. Walking into the place felt like walking out into the sky over Vegas. Definitely not a place for people with a fear of heights, given the strategically placed and hopefully well-reinforced clear floor tiles that let you see straight down to the gardens of the hotel below. In the distance, the faux Eiffel Tower arched up across the Strip, its iron girders illuminated by the multicolored lights of neighboring casinos. The glass ceiling provided an unobstructed view of the inky night sky, interspersed with stars that seemed close enough to touch.

Making my way toward the bar at the back wall, my eyes roamed over the patrons, looking for Jamie. Even in a crowded bar, he was easy to spot. Tall, broad, and wearing his impressively tailored suit from earlier, my eyes picked him out immediately. He was chatting with an attractive brunette at the bar and her interest in him was apparent in the way she leaned toward him, letting her arm brush his in a deliberately incidental way.

Equally obvious was his lack of reciprocal interest. The smile he gave her was a polite curve of his lips that failed to trigger the laugh lines around his eyes. The lines of his body were rigid, from the stiff set of his shoulders to the arm he braced against the bar. There was no welcoming bend to his body, beckoning her closer. If anything, his posture was like a giant "No Trespassing" sign that she failed to read. Abigail Johnson would be so disappointed in her favorite playboy.

Jamie glanced up and spotted my approach. This time, the smile that lit his face pushed the corners of his mouth high enough to release the crinkles around his eyes. Murmuring what had to be a disappointing excuse to his companion, he stepped away from the bar to meet me. Over his shoulder, I saw her dismayed frown and felt a twinge of sympathy as she watched him walk away.

Then he was in front of me, and she faded into the background along with the rest of the patrons. Even if I had weeks, or months of exposure to Jamie, I didn't think I'd ever get used to the way it felt to be the object of his focus. It was more potent than any drug to have the full force of his attention rest solely on you. The way he drank me in, like he was savoring the very sight of me, left me feeling lightheaded.

His hand came to my elbow with a gentle squeeze. "You look beautiful," he said, dusting a kiss against my cheek.

"So do you," I replied, which made Jamie laugh.

"Thank you," he said, using his grip on my elbow to angle me toward a table for two along the wall of windows. "If you'd rather sit at the bar we can, but I thought this would give us a little more privacy."

"A table is great," I said, letting him lead me to it and pull out my chair.

Once the waitress left with our drink order, Jamie sat back in his chair. "I thought the pictures turned out well."

"Well" was an understatement, as far as I was concerned. While I hadn't seen all of them—Jocelyn and I were meeting in the morning to go over the rest of the images and pick which ones we thought would be best for the hotel's campaign—the few she'd sent tonight sizzled. Lucas hadn't been wrong about the chemistry Jamie and I had. Chemistry I still felt bubbling between us at the table. Fueled in large part by his unanswered request to take what had appeared on camera out of the make-believe and into a tangible reality. At least on the physical side. The romance aspect of it was firmly in the land of make-believe.

"Lucas took some great shots," I agreed and pulled my phone out of my purse to bring them up. "This one is the one I'd like to post first."

Setting my phone on the table between us, I turned it toward Jamie so he could see the image of the two of us just as he'd finished helping me put on my tail. It wasn't the sexiest of the pictures, but it was playful and light. A perfect first image to introduce my followers to Jamie. It showcased our differences with me in my mermaid tail and him in his fancy suit pants and dress shirt, while still highlighting a simmering attraction with his hands at my hips and the way my face angled up to his like I couldn't wait for him to kiss me.

"Why this one?" he asked, genuine interest in his eyes.

"Because we're telling a story with this campaign, so we need things to have a beginning." I tapped the screen. "This is a good beginning, because it's flirty and fun. Sexy, but not overwhelmingly so. It's the start of something, and you can see that in the picture."

Jamie nodded, then looked up at me. "Sort of like foreplay for your followers."

I swallowed, my throat suddenly tight at the mention of foreplay. "That's certainly one way to phrase it."

"But picking a picture is only half the job, right?" he asked. "Your caption choice is equally important, isn't it?"

"It is," I said, grateful to dive back into safer waters. "The initial video of us is proof of that. The poster's hashtags helped this thing take off."

"Ah, yes," he nodded with a chuckle. "The illustrious #PrinceEricOnTheProwl was an epic choice."

"If you think that's bad, you haven't been keeping up with the comments on the video," I said, picking up my phone and switching over to Instagram. I'd saved the reel, so it was easy to get to. Scrolling through the comments, I found my favorite section and put my phone back on the table, so we could read at the same time.

SwampRat46: Think he wants to show her his dinglehopper? *fork emoji*

RealyRandy45: This guy is giving me major King Triton vibes in ways I need to discuss with my therapist.

SmutReader35: I feel like I'm watching Disney fanfic come to life right now.

WillyWanda79: I mean . . . I'd be willing to communicate only in body language for that #brunchdaddy

LucyScoreFanGirl88: Think they're off to test her gadgets and gizmos a-plenty, then maybe whip out a whozit or whatzit galore? I hear Ariel's got quite the collection. *eggplant emoji* *peach emoji*

Jamie barked out a laugh. "Good God, people are bizarre." He looked up at me and asked, "Can you explain to me what a #brunch-daddy is?"

I scrolled away from the comments to the reel itself, pausing it when Jamie's profile came into the shot. I pointed at the screen. "That is a #brunchdaddy."

He looked at the image of himself on my phone, then at me. "That is a less than helpful explanation."

Thinking back to our night together and the way he'd owned every aspect of my pleasure, I couldn't help the flush that crept over my cheeks. "Trust me," I said, looking back down at my phone. "You fit the bill perfectly."

I heard the grin in his voice when he said, "Based on how pink your cheeks are getting, I think I should be pleased with that assessment."

The waitress reappeared with our drinks, took one look at the sparks arcing between us and left.

Shifting away from the reel that launched a thousand speculations, I pulled up my Instagram page. "So, you're good if I post this one?"

He nodded. "Who am I to question someone with . . ." He tilted my phone toward him, his brows shooting up. "Two hundred thousand followers?"

"Two hundred thirty-two thousand four hundred and . . ." I checked my phone. "Seven, to be precise."

Jamie held his hands up. "Far be it from me to second guess the expert. If you think that pic is the right one to post, then by all means get it up there."

Laughing, I added the picture with the caption I'd come up with and a slew of hashtags, starting with #ArielandEricTakeVegas. A few more tweaks and it was ready. I passed my phone over to Jamie. "What do you think?"

He took it and when he tapped the screen, Katy Perry sang, "That's what you get for waking up in Vegas." Laughing, he said, "Solid music selection and so is the little GIF of the dancing crab."

"That's Sebastian from *The Little Mermaid*," I said. "Again, you're going to have to brush up on these things to fill the role of mermaid boyfriend. What did you think of the caption?"

Jamie glanced back down at my phone, eyes skimming over the text before meeting mine again above a wide grin. "'My catch of the day at L'Atelier'? Very nice. And I'm honored to be on your menu."

"Glad you approve," I said, matching his smile. I tagged the hotel, skimmed the hashtags once more, and posted it. Within seconds, alerts started popping on my phone to signal likes, comments, and shares.

Jamie's eyes went wide. "That quickly?"

I laughed. "My followers are pretty plugged in to me and with content about a guy . . ." I shrugged. "It's a glimpse into my life they don't normally get, so they're very invested."

"You don't normally post about your relationships?" he asked.

"I, uh, don't usually have much to post in that department," I admitted.

His brows lifted, but he didn't say anything. I sighed. "It's been a while since I've had a serious boyfriend. And the last guy I dated wasn't what you'd call supportive of my career, so he wasn't keen on being featured on my page."

Blond brows dipped down in disapproval. "He sounds like a douchebag."

I laughed. "He was, in fact, a huge douchebag."

"Is he why you haven't dated seriously in a while?"

I shrugged. "Not really." I sipped my drink. "Interestingly, my reason is pretty parallel to your own troubles when I think about it."

"You were featured in a mermaids under forty article?"

I shook my head with a smile. "No, but I get having to dedicate so much to your career that it makes relationships hard. You can't make two things number one in your life, so you have to make choices. Choices that a lot of people don't understand. Which brings the two of us to our current predicaments."

He smiled back at me. "I don't know. I sort of feel like my predicament has been on a consistent upswing since we met."

"I'm glad to know I'm your Gulf Stream current," I said. "And you've certainly made my arrival in Vegas . . . memorable."

"All I get is memorable?" Jamie asked, pouting.

"What about unforgettable, then?" I amended and he grinned.

"Much better." He glanced at my phone as it continued to buzz with notifications. "You're good at this."

"As evidenced by my two hundred thirty-two thousand four hundred and seven followers," I said with a chuckle.

"What made you want to do it?" he asked.

"Post a pic of us on Instagram?" I asked, confused. "Because that's a part of what we agreed to do for the PR campaign."

"No, no," Jamie replied, shaking his head. "How does someone wake up one day and say, 'Hey, I'm going to be a professional mermaid'?"

"Oh." I laughed. "It's not that interesting of a story."

"I find that hard to believe," he said. "I mean . . ." Sitting back in his seat, he took a drink and waved a hand at me. "You're a freaking mermaid. How can the origin story of that not be interesting?"

"I'm not a superhero, so I don't know that you can say 'origin story,'" I protested.

"Sure, I can," he persisted. "Let's hear it."

Relenting, I said, "I guess I'd have to thank the good folks over at TBS for first giving me the idea of it."

Jamie drew back a little. "TBS? Like the channel TBS?"

I nodded. "As you know, *Splash* is my favorite movie."

"That choice makes a lot more sense to me now," he said with a laugh.

I chuckled too, acknowledging that my love for a movie that came out well before I was even born might strike someone as unusual. "TBS was one of my best babysitters growing up. And it was where I first watched *Splash*. Seeing her as a mermaid is where the idea took root, I guess," I said. "And then as I grew up, I was always comfortable in the water. I joined the swim team, worked as a lifeguard in the summers, generally spent as much time in or near water as I could."

"How do you get from swim team to mermaid tails, though? It's not a career option most people latch on to."

"One Halloween in college I dressed as a mermaid to a costume party at a frat house. The DJ saw me and asked if I'd be interested in working a party with him the next weekend."

"That doesn't sound sketchy at all," Jamie said, frowning.

"I was twenty, so naturally I considered myself immortal and immune from anything bad happening. All I heard was a chance to make some cash being a mermaid, so I jumped at it. Luckily, it wasn't at all sketchy. It turned out to be a kid's birthday party. A kid obsessed with mermaids like I had been. Only her family was able to hire one for her birthday. Anyway, in my homemade mermaid tail and bikini top, I was quite the hit and things sort of snowballed from there."

"Let me guess, marine biology was your major."

"Ha! You're so wrong and so cliché," I chided. "I graduated with a degree in history, thank you very much."

"Was your senior thesis on the lost city of Atlantis?" he teased, and I stuck my tongue out at him.

"It was a comparative analysis of ancient mermaid myths from all over the globe," I said pertly.

"So, you're saying there was a section on Atlantis?" His grin widened when I couldn't deny it. "Gotcha."

I chucked a wadded-up cocktail napkin at him, which he caught with ease.

"Well, from kids' birthday parties to your own show in Vegas." Jamie smiled. "I guess it's safe to say you've made it."

I shook my head. "Hardly. I'm just getting to the tough part—proving to your sister she didn't make a mistake in bringing me out here." I took a deep breath, ready to grab the bull by the horns. "Which brings me to the main reason I asked you to meet me."

"I cannot believe you used Instagram subterfuge to lure me to a bar, Coral," Jamie teased, picking up his drink. Over its rim, he said, "What's on your mind?"

"The same thing that's been on my mind since you proposed it—whether we can really pull off a no-strings fling while selling a fake romance on social media."

Jamie's drink paused halfway to his mouth, then he set it down, taking his time to align it perfectly on the square coaster before meeting my eyes. "I wondered if you were ever going to give me an answer, or just pretend like I'd never mentioned it."

I sipped my own drink. "What if I had? Would you have let it fall by the wayside?"

He picked up his bourbon once more, taking a good swallow. I watched his throat work and wondered briefly when the act of taking a drink had become so sexy. Or maybe it was only sexy when he did it. The man could probably make shopping for toilet paper hot.

"There's no good way for me to answer that question," Jamie said with a sly smile. "If I say yes, I would have let it simply slip into the ether, then you'll doubt the sincerity of my interest. If I say no, that I would have pursued you until you answered me, well, at worst I'm a freaking creep who won't take a hint, and at best come off desperate and pathetic." He shrugged and swirled his drink. "It's a lose-lose for me, I'm afraid."

The more time I spent around Jamie, the more we talked, and I saw the man beneath the suit, I understood why so many women wanted more from him. He was much more than a handsome face. His innate sense of self-awareness and the care with which he treated people were so genuine, it made it easy to want to sink into it like a warm bath and luxuriate in the comfort he so readily provided.

"Then I guess it's a good thing I brought it up to save you from all of that."

He tipped his glass toward me in salute. "A truly selfless act on your part." His blue gaze sharpened, and I could almost feel the fine edge of it skimming over my skin when he said, "I can't say it pains me to hear you've been thinking about me, Coral. Considering I haven't stopped thinking about you since the night we met."

"Well," I said, my voice a little too feathery. "We have seen a lot of each other since then."

"We certainly have," he agreed with a smile that would put the Big Bad Wolf out of a job. "But, as I've said, I would like to see . . . more of you."

Jamie wasn't touching me, wasn't even that close to me. There was a whole block of reclaimed wood between us, and we were surrounded by other patrons in the bar. And yet the gravelly timbre of his voice coupled with the weight of his gaze had my blood humming in my veins in a searing pulse. The thrum of it heated my skin with a rosy flush, obvious even in the dim light of the bar.

I took a drink to cool down and refocus. I'd come here with a response to his offer. With guidelines and rules and structure for his idea. Because after obsessing over it, I knew that was the key to my emerging unscathed on the other side of whatever this was. I wasn't going to be another woman bemoaning the loss of Jamie Standard. Once this . . . thing between us ended—because there was no question it was going to end—I would be fine. Thanks to the carefully crafted rules I'd come up with.

# chapter nineteen

## JAMIE

I watched the telltale pink flush creep up the long line of Coral's throat until it dusted her cheeks a rosy hue. I'd seen that flush before—when she'd been naked and sprawled out under the weight of my body. I told myself to calm down, not to get ahead of myself. Not to count naked Corals before they stripped down in my bedroom. She said she had a response, but I'd yet to hear the response. It could be a "please fuck directly off" or a "thanks, but no thanks." Her body's physical reaction to me asking to see more of her didn't necessarily correlate to her acquiescing to that request. If I knew anything from the time I'd spent with her, it was that the unexpected was a much more likely occurrence than anything ordinary.

So, I waited for her response. For her to tell me I wasn't alone in wanting more while it was possible. To tell me she wanted to take full (and naked) advantage of my remaining time in Vegas.

Setting her drink down, she closed her eyes and took a deep breath through her nose. Blowing it out slowly, she regarded me in that steady, forthright way that did strange things to my stomach. Like when I'd eaten a whole thing of Pop Rocks as a kid, only better.

"If we do this," she started, and the Pop Rocks in my gut began rocketing around in earnest. "If we do this, there will need to be rules to make sure we're always on the same page about everything. This cannot be a situation of blurred lines or misread feelings. For this to work out for everyone—you, me, Jocelyn, the hotel, all of us—clarity is key."

I nodded, somewhat bemused by her continued focus on having guidelines or rules for everything. I thought about her saying TBS was her favorite babysitter and that it had been "just her" growing up. She'd mentioned they'd moved a lot, too. And there had been no mention of a dad, just her mom. I wondered if her need for structure sprang from the lack of it in her childhood. Regardless of the reason, it was something she needed, so I didn't fight her on it. "Absolutely," I said.

"Okay, so that means that rule number one is that work—yours *and* mine—comes first. If for any reason it looks like our . . . extracurricular activities are throwing a wrench into the plan, then they stop. Right then, no questions, no buts. It's finished."

Again, I nodded, even as the feeling in my gut changed slightly. Morphing from true excitement to something I wasn't sure how to describe. I flashed back to my earlier conversation with Jocelyn and her disbelief that I was ready to make the change we'd talked about. That this time it would be better to stay true to my habits and put work ahead of everything. I pushed the unfamiliar feeling aside and agreed once more. More because I didn't want to screw things up for Coral and Jocelyn than anything else.

"Of course," I said. "I get how big a deal this is for you and Joss, and the last thing I want to do is take anything away from that."

"And we can't let your deal with Shattucks slip through your fingers," she said. "We've all got a lot riding on this, so it's good to spell it out at the start. Clear lines of communication right from the jump."

"Right," I said, touched by her putting my needs on equal footing with hers.

"Second rule is that we don't have any misconceptions about . . . 'us' continuing after you leave Vegas. This will be the definition of 'what happens in Vegas stays in Vegas.'"

I didn't nod as readily at that. Logistically, her refusal to consider anything more than the present made perfect sense. There was no reason for her to expect anything beyond Vegas to develop for us, because I wouldn't be here. I'd be back in Boston, with no plans to return any time soon. She had no reason to come back east, and even if she did, she'd be too busy putting the new show together to make the trip. Just like once I had Shattucks on board, I'd be in the thick of the Union Square Project. Neither time nor geography would allow for anything outside the two weeks of my stay in Vegas.

And yet, I still hesitated. Long enough for Coral to arch an eyebrow and ask, "Jamie, you still with me?"

It would be foolhardy to try to talk to her about feelings I didn't even understand yet. There would be time later once I had time to think about the reasons for my hesitation. The reasons why the thought of more than just two weeks with Coral was so appealing to me. I lifted my chin. "Yes, sorry, just spaced out there for a second." I smiled to cover my unease. "Staring at you tends to have that effect on me."

Coral frowned, her posture stiffening again. "This is serious, Jamie."

God, I was fucking this up before it even started because I was too much in my own head. "Right, I know. Trust me, I'm with you, I swear. No misconceptions." And I didn't have any misconceptions. I knew where she stood on the subject. It was my own perspective that was unclear.

She nodded, a firmly resolute up and down of her chin. "By then, you'll have Shattucks on board, the show will have a ton of buzz and you and I will have worked each other completely out of our systems."

I highly doubted that would be anywhere close to true. I signaled the waitress for another round. "Let's talk about that last part a little more."

Coral's head tilted, and she squinted suspiciously at me. "The last part?"

"What's involved in our being worked out of each other's systems?" At her still quizzical look, I continued, " I guess I'm asking how long do you expect it to take for me to be out of your system? Think one more night would do it, or is it a more of a 'know it when it happens' amorphous timeline?"

Her mouth opened, then closed, then opened and closed again without her saying anything. She sat back in her chair, brows knitted with thought. Her eyes swung back to mine, twin swirls of uncertain blue-gray. "One night would certainly be . . . neater."

I swallowed a laugh. "True, but . . ." I leaned forward, resting my forearms on the table. "What if it isn't enough? After all, that was true the first time around, right? What makes you think round two will be any different?"

"I'm pretty sure we're up to at least like round five or six at this point," she teased.

"Stuck on semantics, are we? Okay, fine. What makes you think night two of deliriously exhausting sex would result any differently than night one? How can you be so sure I'll be completely out of your system?"

"You make a good point," Coral admitted, tapping a finger against her lips. "Do you have a counterproposal?"

"You speaking boardroom to me should not be as hot as it is," I said, which made her laugh.

"Boardroom talk gets you hotter than the main topic of this discussion? Talk about a freak in the spreadsheets . . ." She leaned closer, which gave me an excellent view of her cleavage. "Detail your strategy for me, Jamie, so we can each attain our mutual goal of total . . . satisfaction."

Jesus. Fucking. Christ. This woman.

Clearing my throat, I adjusted my slacks, which were now noticeably tighter in the crotch. "What I would propose, Ms. Triton, is that we allow this arrangement to be more fluid to allow a chance for each of us to achieve simultaneous satisfaction."

The waitress delivered our next round of drinks. Coral shifted in her seat and crossed her legs in the opposite direction. "And what happens if one party to this agreement finds satisfaction more quickly than the other?"

"You can rest assured I intend to discover just how quickly I can satisfy you, Coral. Repeatedly," I replied, watching her eyes darken and her tongue dart out to wet her lips. "But, if in the event you discover that you've achieved what we'll call 'final satisfaction' and have no further interest in our arrangement, obviously that's your call to make."

"And the same goes for you. Obviously," she said.

The idea it would be possible for me to no longer want Coral was laughable, but I nodded anyway. "I think we can agree that reciprocity on that point is key."

She nodded briskly. "So, rule three is reciprocity—we both must want to continue this and either of us is free to say it's over even before you leave Vegas. And if that happens, it won't have any impact on the PR campaign for either of us."

"None whatsoever," I assured her. "Any other terms you need to outline?"

"There is one," she said, and her eyes went flinty, piercing me with a look. "There will be no more nonsense like there was today in the tank."

Taken aback, I blinked, then shook my head. "Nonsense?" Was she talking about our almost kiss?

Leaning forward, she let her crossed arms rest on the tabletop. "As in when you thought it was a good idea to dictate to me when to get out of the water. And when you essentially overruled me in front of Xavier."

Her hand shot out in a sharp slice. "There will be no more of that crap, understood? Regardless of what happens between us while you're in town, you will absolutely, one hundred percent, *not* undercut me in front of the people I work with, which includes your sister. Are we clear on that?"

She'd leaned even farther forward, poking the table in front of me to make her point. Her cheeks were flushed pink, and her eyes sparked like overheated charcoal. As sexy as she was when she was mad, I felt like an ass for getting her so worked up. Even though I'd technically been right, I'd been highhanded about it. If someone had done that to me, I would have been livid.

Setting my drink down, I said, "I'm sorry about how I handled that, Coral. It won't happen again. You've got my word." Not that I was willing to sit idly by while she risked hypothermia or anything else in that tank. But that was a bridge we could cross later.

Coral blinked at me, as though she didn't think she'd heard me correctly. "Just like that, huh?"

I nodded. "Just like that."

Her features relaxed, and she reached across to take my hand in hers. "That means a lot, Jamie. Thank you."

I brought her knuckles to my lips and brushed a kiss there. "You're welcome." Lowering our hands back to the table, I held hers in mine, enjoying the simple touch. "Anything else we need to cover?"

Taking a sip of her drink, Coral considered my question. I could see the thoughts tumbling through her mind in the way her brows drew down and her lips twisted from side to side. It was equally obvious when she landed upon a topic she wanted to discuss, because her entire body sprang to attention and a spark of humor made those enigmatic eyes of hers practically glow.

"It's not really a term, per se," she said, twisting her drink on its coaster. "It's more of a . . . disclosure."

"A . . . disclosure?" I asked, intrigued as to where this was going. "About what?"

"I read the article," she said with a little wince.

"Oh," I said, although I should've expected it. After all, she'd have been curious about what could've been in it to make the rejuvenation of my reputation necessary in the first place. "Any questions after what had to be scintillating reading?"

Coral laughed. "Questions?" She shook her head, red curls dancing over her shoulders with the movement. "No questions. If anything, it makes this"—she waggled a finger between us—"easier, because I've now read several personal testimonies that prove you'll have no problem following our rules."

The weird feeling in my gut came back, but this time it was slick and oily. I forced a smile. "Right," I said, even as the word tasted sour on my tongue. I had the sudden urge to protest, which would be beyond stupid because I'd just agreed to all her rules. Fuck, my head was all over the place.

Coral's cell phone rang, making her cringe and reach inside her purse. "Sorry, I thought I'd put this thing on vibrate." When she pulled it out, I saw "Mom Cell" on the screen. Coral frowned and hit decline before sliding the phone back into her purse.

"You could've taken that, if you needed to," I said.

She shook her head. "No, it's fine."

There was an uncomfortable pause, and it felt like the dynamic between us had shifted somehow. I wasn't sure if it was the call from her mom, or my own insecurities bleeding into things, but whatever was the cause, I hated it. Hated the way I now felt oddly self-conscious and off-center.

Clearing my throat, I said, "So should we g—"

Right as she said, "Well, I think we shou—"

We both stopped talking and looked at each other, then away. Tonight had gone from smoothly perfect to unbearably awkward in minutes.

"Please," I said. "What were you going to say?"

"Oh," Coral licked her lips and tucked her hair behind her ear. The knuckles of her right hand hovered near her breastbone, but then she immediately lowered it. I wondered if she'd been about to crack her knuckles in the habitual way I'd seen over the last few days.

"I was just going to say we should snap a quick picture up here and then we could . . . head to your room." The inflection of her voice changed at the end, turning into more question than statement. "That is"—she smiled a little hesitantly—"if you're cool with that."

"Of course," I said, relieved that whatever this weird mood was between us, it hadn't yet ruined the rest of the night. I spread my hands wide. "I'm at your disposal, just point me where to stand."

Slipping out of her chair, she came to stand in front of me. "You're good there, that backdrop is gorgeous." Spinning on her heels, Coral leaned in to me, the ocean clean scent of her tickling my nostrils and her hair brushing against my cheek. Instinctively, I turned toward her right as she raised her phone. "Ready?" she asked, the flash a rectangle of pale yellow light as she snapped a selfie of us before I could respond.

We both looked down at the picture on her phone. In it, I was looking at her with a curious half smile, while she beamed into the camera. Behind us, the night sky sparkled, its stars resembling thousands of tiny flash bulbs going off to capture the moment. We looked every inch the happy couple out on the town. The Pop Rocks fizz in my stomach came back with a vengeance.

"I think this is a good one," she said, already swiping something on her phone.

Clearing my throat, I said, "Again, I'm not going to argue with an expert."

After she'd worked her magic on it and posted the picture, I pointed to her half-full glass. "Want to finish that?"

Coral shook her head. "No, I'm good." She gestured to the bourbon remaining in my glass. "But if you want to take a minute to . . ."

Her words drifted off when I lifted the glass to my lips and drained the rest of it, returning the empty glass to the table. "All set," I said, and she chuckled.

"Something tells me that was a bourbon you're supposed to savor, not toss back like medicine."

Throwing a mental blanket over my unruly thoughts I focused on Coral. On the way her lips parted with her smile, the way her hair shimmered reddish gold in the lights of the bar, on the teasing way she looked at me as she laughed, like we were sharing an intimate joke. Drinking her in quieted the storm brewing in my mind. At least temporarily. And when I smiled at her, it wasn't forced. "If there's something I plan to savor tonight, Coral," I said, tossing a few bills down on the table to cover our drinks, "it's not the bourbon."

Her lips parted and those expressive eyes of hers lit with interest as she slipped off her stool and looped her arm through mine.

"Then by all means," her fingers stroked the fabric of my suit jacket. "Let's get to that part of the evening."

# chapter twenty

## CORAL

Yes, I'd caved and read the damn article. I wish I could say I'd stayed strong in my commitment not to give Abigail Johnson any more clicks based on Jamie's embarrassment. Or that I hadn't given it much thought since my initial internet sleuthing. That I hadn't been lured in by the prospect of a little female insight into Jamie Standard. But that would be a bold-faced lie. After spending the day with him in various poses of abject adoration and pining, I couldn't help myself. I needed to know what the deal was with the article. If I were really considering getting even the least bit involved with him, I needed all the facts, right? So, I'd found it online, paid the $3 article fee and read it as soon as I'd gotten back to my room that afternoon.

And now, riding up in the elevator with the Bad Boy of Business standing so close behind me I could feel his chest move against my back when he breathed, I was glad I'd read it. It was a good reminder of what this was and what it couldn't be. Because we were the same. Neither of us had any interest in something long term or serious. It wouldn't fit into either of our lives. We were the perfect release for each other while he was here. And that was all it could be.

I'd needed that reminder again after seeing the pictures Jocelyn sent. Pictures of the two of us looking at each other like there was no one else in the world. Or at least no one else we'd rather be with. I had to remember those pictures were an illusion. A carefully fabricated story we were selling to advance both of our careers.

I had to keep that in mind, because it was awfully easy to get swept up in Jamie Standard. The man had a gravitational pull equal to that of the sun and, as a redhead I was aware of the dangers of overexposure. I could bask in his warmth for the limited time he would be here, but hoping for anything beyond that would get me burned.

Which was why I'd mentioned the article before we'd left the bar. It needed to stay in the forefront of my mind, lest I got carried away. I needed to stick to my tried-and-true method of focusing on the present and enjoying the moment without developing any expectations beyond what was right in front of me. Or, in this case, standing right behind me. Focus on the physical. The solid heat of him at my back, the tantalizingly spicy scent of his cologne teasing my nose and the way his hand at my hip felt as he tucked me close against him in the corner of the elevator.

Jamie shifted behind me, and I realized that while I'd been in my own head about everything, we'd reached his floor. The elevator doors stood open to the familiar muted elegance I'd seen a few nights before.

He squeezed my hip. "Still with me?" His words were low and soft at my ear, sending a shiver through me. Glancing back over my shoulder, my eyes met his, which were dark with both concern and a good dose of lust.

I ignored the twinge in my chest at his look of concern. Heart twinges and swoony feelings had no place in this thing between us. I nodded and pushed my lips into a smile, dusting my fingers over the knuckles of his hand at my hip. "Absolutely."

# JAMIE

Keeping my hands off Coral Triton was a physical impossibility. Earlier at the bar, my mouth had gone dry at the sight of her in a sleeveless emerald green . . . I think it was called a romper . . . that showcased her toned arms and gorgeous legs and set off the fiery cascade of her hair. But as good as she looked downstairs, standing at the sliding glass door of my balcony, silhouetted by the lights of the Vegas Strip stretched out below us, she looked like sin come to life and my hands flexed with the need to touch her.

An image flashed in my brain. Coral naked against the glass with those long legs wrapped around me. Her head tilted back on a moan as I pushed inside her to take what I couldn't stop fantasizing about. My dick throbbed at the thought.

*Down boy, we've got all night.* That mental announcement did nothing but make my dick that much harder.

*Get a hold of yourself, Jameson,* I chastised myself. This wasn't going to be some quick fuck up against the wall. Okay, so maybe that might happen at some point in the evening, but first, I was going to take my time with Coral. I'd meant what I said at the bar. I wanted to savor her. Explore all of her all over again. Rediscover what made her body tremble and her thighs part and find new ways to make her gasp with pleasure.

I was not doing a good job of redirecting the blood flow from my groin to my brain cells. Tonight was about seduction, and that required more finesse. Which required thought before action.

"I have to be honest, Jamie," Coral said, pulling me out of my lust-addled brain. "I figured a guy like you would have a much better poker face." Putting her hands behind her back, she leaned against the glass and crossed her ankles. "That's a real hazard in this town."

I crossed toward her. "What do you mean?"

Watching me approach, she lifted a shoulder with a knowing grin. "One look at your face and I know just what you're thinking."

Reaching her, I couldn't help but put a hand on her cocked hip. "And what am I thinking?"

Coral reached out and ran a finger down the buttons of my shirt. "You're thinking about sex, Jamie. More specifically, you're thinking about sex with me." Her fingers reached my belt, and she teased along the supple leather before pulling the strap free and undoing the buckle. Its metal clink was like a starter's pistol for my eager libido.

From beneath inky lashes, mischievous blue-gray eyes met mine. "Am I right?"

Encircling her wrist with my fingers, I tugged her hand away from my belt and pushed it lower, to where my erection strained against the fly of my pants. Her eyes went even darker as she cupped me through the fabric. Flexing my hips against her hand, I put my lips to her ear. "I've been thinking about sex with you, Coral"—I nipped her earlobe, and she gave a little hum of pleasure—"since the first time you threw a giant bottle of lube at me."

It took a minute for the words to sink in through the haze of lust between us, but when they did she all but howled with laughter. Her hand left my crotch and slid around my waist, pulling me closer and burying her face in the crook of my neck. My hands came to the window behind her for balance. Lifting her head, she looked at me with a smile. "You have to admit, though," she said. "I recovered well from that."

I nodded, smiling back at her. "Epically. I've been thinking of nothing but your tight tail ever since."

"Just my tail?" she asked, her eyes going to my mouth as she licked her bottom lip.

"Among other things," I said, tilting her chin to give me better access to her mouth.

Her phone rang shrilly, breaking the moment, and she cringed. Ducking under my arm, she hurried to grab her purse from the table. "Sorry," she said over her shoulder. "I swear I put it on silent. Just give me one second to . . ."

Coral froze when she pulled her phone out. As in, she went stock still, except for the rapid rise and fall of her chest. She looked over at me. "It's Jocelyn," she hissed, and I could see her starting to panic.

Silently cursing my sister for killing the mood, I said, "Go ahead and answer it." Nodding toward the balcony, I added, "You can step out there if you want some privacy."

Chewing her lip, she shook her head and swiped the screen of her phone. "Jocelyn? Hi, what's up?"

I heard my sister's voice, although her words were too garbled for me to know what she was saying. Coral's eyes went wide. "Really? That's . . . great, right?"

More muted noise from Coral's phone and she nodded, even though Jocelyn couldn't see her. "Yeah, I'm up for it." She snuck a look at me, and her lips twitched a little. "Do you think Jamie will go for it?"

My sister's laughter was tinny, but unmistakable, and Coral giggled in response to whatever Jocelyn was saying. "Okay," she said. "I'll let you broach the topic with him, then."

Jocelyn said something else I couldn't hear, and Coral replied, "Okay, sounds good. We'll talk tomorrow." When she hung up, she made a show of silencing her phone and sliding it back into her purse before turning to face me with a mile wide grin.

I crossed my arms and narrowed my eyes. "You really think you're going to get away with not telling me what that was about?"

Indigo eyes widened in faux innocence. "Your sister wants to be the one to tell you about it, so I don't think it's my place to . . . EEP!"

She yelped as I scooped her into my arms. "I have ways of making you talk, Triton," I said, nuzzling her ear. "And I'm not afraid to play dirty."

Her arms wound around my neck, and she looked up at me. "I thought we agreed work comes first, so I really can't disobey a directive from my boss just because you ask me to."

My phone buzzed in the pocket of my jacket and Coral jumped a little, then chuckled. "Looks like you're about to get your answer."

I lowered her legs to let her feet hit the ground. "I think my method of finding out from you would've been more fun for both of us."

She swatted my chest. "Answer your sister's call, Standard."

With my best put-upon sigh, I pulled my phone out and sure enough, it was Jocelyn calling. "Joss," I said after accepting the call. "Two calls in one day. To what do I owe this honor?"

"You and Coral are going to be on *Waking Up in Vegas* tomorrow, thanks to your brilliant sister's PR work and Coral's Instagram skills," she chirped like a proud robin.

I glanced over at Coral who gave me a double thumbs up. "I'm sorry," I said. "Coral and I are going to do what tomorrow?"

"Our acknowledgment of the initial viral video with a few posts on L'Atelier's socials and Coral's post from earlier tonight have really made the local media take notice of the mermaid love story. The booking agent for *Waking Up in Vegas* called me today about Coral appearing on the show. And when I told them I thought it could be a joint appearance with you, I honest to God thought they were going to swoon. This is the kind of spot that could get picked up by the national media, Jamie. Which means it could even air in Boston markets. I knew we could salvage your image, but I can't believe this stroke of luck."

"You want us to go on a morning show?" I asked, feeling a little prickle of sweat. Social media posts were one thing. But to sit down for an interview with Coral as my girlfriend I was supposed to be head over heels for was quite another. Especially after my last interview had gone so totally off the rails. I swallowed, stomach crawling with nervous energy. "Do you really think we can pull that off so quickly? I mean, this idea only came together a few days ago, Joss. Coral and I barely know each other."

"Not to worry on that front, big brother. I've emailed you both a relationship dossier for you to review and use tomorrow."

My eyes went to Coral, who was watching me intently. I'd heard her half of the conversation, so I knew she was game. But that wasn't a surprise. This woman lived her life out loud for everyone to see and had no qualms about it. While I found it sexy as hell she was so comfortable with it, I wasn't on her level and probably never would be. Airing my love life, fake or not, for public consumption in an interview made me more than a little nervous.

"Jamie?" Jocelyn said, and I realized I'd been silent for too long.

"Yeah, sorry, I'm still here. Just . . . thinking about this."

"This won't be another train wreck like *Boston Commons*, Jamie," Jocelyn said, her voice soft. "I promise you, it's the right move. It's an opportunity for you to show people you aren't the unfeeling jerkface Abigail Johnson made you out to be. You can show them your real personality. And with Coral there next to you, people are going to eat it up. It's going to totally overshadow the *Boston Commons* article, I promise."

"I thought you said my real personality was the problem," I said.

Jocelyn snorted. "Your personality was never the problem. If anything, it's why most women want more than you're willing to give them. You're a good guy, Jamie. And this is your chance to let people know that. It will be ten or fifteen minutes tops. A true fluffy, cuddly love piece on how you and Coral found each other when you slid into her DMs after seeing one of her videos."

"When I slid into her what?" I asked, looking back at Coral, whose eyes had gone wide in surprise. Her mouth fell open into a perfect "O" and I realized what it sounded like from her perspective. I mouthed "DMs" at her, and she relaxed a little.

"I'll explain it to you later," she whisper giggled.

"God, you're old," Jocelyn said with a laugh. "It's all in the dossier I sent you. Listen, I need to call the booking agent back tonight and let them know if you are in. If you aren't, they need to fill the ten a.m. social story with someone else. So, are you in or out, big brother?"

Was I up for this? For going on television and letting people think I was in love with Coral? I thought about how natural things felt with her. How glad I'd been when she'd texted me to meet for a drink. That rush of elation I'd felt when she gave me her number. The way my body responded to her in the tank and, honestly, the way it responded when she simply walked into a room. The woman had taken up residence in my thoughts since the day we'd met. Selling the idea of my being enchanted by her wouldn't be a hardship.

"I'm in," I said, watching Coral smile over at me. It hit me then that the hardship wouldn't be convincing people it was real. No, the hardship would be convincing myself it wasn't.

# chapter twenty—one

## CORAL

Jamie flopped back against the couch, closing his eyes and shoving his laptop to the side with a groan. "No more studying," he whined.

"Does that mean you've got our backstory memorized backward and forward?" I teased from my place on the opposite end of the sectional. "Because I'm still having trouble remembering when you took that summer abroad."

His head lolled to the side, and he cracked one eye open to peer at me. "Smart-ass."

I laughed and set my phone down. Since Jocelyn's call, we'd spent the last couple hours cramming for our interview the following morning. I had to hand it to her, Jamie's sister had put together quite the backstory for our romance. She'd even solved the problem of his lack of social media profiles by using my YouTube channel as the source of our meet cute. Someone had forwarded him a video of me, and he'd been so infatuated with watching me perform, he'd sent me a DM using the Standard Development corporate Instagram account. A very plausible story with no way for anyone to confirm it absent high level hacking skills and I didn't see that being an issue.

I stretched and stifled a yawn. "I have to admit, this is not how I saw our evening unfolding."

He snorted and sat forward, resting his elbows on his knees and regarding me with interest. "And just what did you envision for tonight?"

"We were a lot more naked," I said. "Although I guess I should be flattered that you took your suit coat off for me. Do you seriously own nothing but suits?"

Jamie glanced down at his still perfectly pressed pants. "You don't like my suits?"

I shook my head, because his suits were sexy as hell, and he wore the hell out of them. There was something about knowing underneath the pristine suit with a crisply knotted tie lurked a guy who could be dirty in all the best ways. The idea of it made me shiver with anticipation.

"Are you cold?" he asked, standing. "Let me grab a blanket out of the linen closet."

I held up a hand to stop him. "No, no. I'm good. But I agree with you, I think I'm done with studying for the night." I stood up and stretched more fully than I could've on the couch, working out a crick in my back.

Glancing over at Jamie, I didn't miss the way his eyes roamed hungrily up my legs, taking in my hips and lingering hotly on my cleavage before coming up to my face. "I haven't had a real opportunity to appreciate this outfit," he said.

"Are we moving on to the Fashion Police part of the evening, then?" I asked, coming to stand next to him. "I think there are better ways for us to entertain ourselves tonight, don't you?"

Blue eyes heated as he reached for me, settling his hands on my hips and giving them a rough squeeze. "I can think of a few, yeah." His voice was a husky rasp that made my body pulse in response.

I put my hands on his chest, enjoying the solid feel of him beneath my fingers. Sliding my hands up over his shoulders, I clasped my fingers behind his neck. One more step brought our bodies flush against each other, all my curves pressed into his chiseled hard planes.

And then he kissed me and nothing else mattered but the warm press of his mouth to mine. My lips opened on a sigh, and he took full advantage, deepening the kiss to tease and taste. Big hands slipped over my hips to cup my ass and then he lifted me into his arms with such ease it felt like I was floating. Fingers teased under the hem of my romper, brushing the curve of my bottom.

When my legs came around his waist, his grip tightened, fingertips digging into the soft flesh of my thighs and dragging me against the rigid erection currently trying to fight its way out of his slacks. It was my turn to make an animalistic sound as he ground me against him.

Tearing his mouth from mine, he grinned at me. "Like that, sweetheart?"

"I'd like it better if we were naked," I said, and nipped at his bottom lip.

His grin was sin itself. "That can be arranged."

Expecting him to hoist me higher in his arms and head for his bedroom, I was surprised when he kept one hand on my ass while grabbing the chair at the head of the dining table. Pulling it out, he flipped it to face the wall of glass.

I looked at him quizzically. "Uh, what are you doing?"

His answer was a sizzling grin as his hands came to my waist and lifted me away from his body. Also known as not the direction I wanted to go. But I wasn't going to hang on to the man like some sort of barnacle if he wasn't into it, so I let my legs drop from his hips. Gently, he set me on my feet in front of him and the chair.

"Like I said, I haven't had a real chance to appreciate this outfit."

"I thought we agreed we had better games to play than Fashion Police," I said, reaching for his belt.

He caught my hand and *tsked* me. "So impatient. I told you I planned to take my time tonight and, despite your best efforts to tempt me otherwise, that's what I'm going to do."

Releasing my hand, he lifted his suit coat from where he'd draped it over a chair. Sliding back into it, he moved to stand in front of the chair, making a show of adjusting the creases in his slacks before sitting down. Crossing an ankle over one knee, he leaned one elbow on the armrest of the chair, looking every bit the insolent king of the boardroom.

Irritated by his layering up instead of stripping down, I put a hand on my cocked hip, knowing full well it drew the already short hem of my outfit that much higher. "And I'm just supposed to . . . what? Strut the catwalk in your hotel suite so you can critique my outfit?"

A flare of his nostrils proved he noticed the extra inch of thigh. He rubbed a hand over his jaw, eyes dragging slowly over every inch of me. "Turn around, Coral. Let me get a good look at you."

The command was gravelly and low and targeted my lady bits like a guided missile. Butterflies flittered low in my belly as I obeyed, spinning in the slowest pirouette possible until I faced him once again.

"You're a goddamn vision in green," Jamie said, his gaze lit with a dark intensity.

"Glad you approve," I said. "But wasn't there an earlier discussion of nudity that you sa—"

"Strip," he barked, interrupting me.

I blinked. "What?"

"Take. Off. Your. Clothes," he said, enunciating each word as though it were its own sentence.

I couldn't help but cast a glance over my shoulder to the wall of glass, which made him chuckle. A low rasp of sound that made my knees weak. "Don't worry, gorgeous, these windows are one way," Jamie said. "No one gets to watch but me."

The possessive edge to his voice sent shockwaves through me. It also triggered a new response in me, one I'd yet to experience. The desire to obey. To give myself over completely to Jamie's control and follow his every demand. Heat swirled through me at the thought.

With only the barest tremble to my fingers, I found the zipper on the side of my romper and eased it down. The only sounds in the room were the hiss of the zipper and Jamie's deep inhalation as he watched. Once it was unzipped, it took only a breath of movement for the rich green fabric to slide from my shoulders into a silky pool around my stilettos.

"Fuuuccckkk," Jamie ground out, no longer so relaxed in his seat. I was currently receiving a standing ovation from within his trousers.

Emboldened by his response, I drew my hands up my sides, letting the backs of my fingers brush the sides of my bra and then up over my chest. The touch may have been designed to tease Jamie, but it sent goose bumps rippling across my skin. My hands reached my neck and then my hair, drawing it off my shoulders to give him a better look before letting it fall back into place.

"Do you need me to turn around again?" I asked, my own voice now low and seductive.

Shifting in his chair, he asked, "Are you asking if I want to see your perfect ass in the tiny excuse for underwear you're wearing?"

I nodded, my hand drifting over the slope of one breast.

Jamie's hand fisted on the arm of the chair, and I bit back a smile. Not quickly enough, though, because in one smooth movement he was out of his seat to stand before me. He took my hand in his, running his thumb over my knuckles. "Something amusing you?"

I shook my head, but he was having none of it. "I don't think I believe you, Siren."

Lifting my hand, he pirouetted me to face the glass. Our reflections were superimposed over the lights of Vegas. He was a brooding force behind me in his dark suit and crisp white shirt. A sharp contrast to the gossamer lace bra and panty set I was wearing.

I watched him in the glass as he reached for me, fingers grazing my hips before skimming up my ribcage and disappearing. His touch slid along the band of my bra to its clasp in the center of my back.

"As pretty as this is," he murmured just behind my ear, sending shivers racing down my spine. "I prefer what's underneath it." One nimble flick of his fingers and the clasp was undone.

I swallowed a moan as Jamie reached around me and hooked a finger between the lace cups. One tug made the straps slide down my arms, and then I was topless. He rubbed a thumb against the silky lace in his hand, meeting my eyes in the glass.

"Did you think about me when you put this on tonight?"

I swallowed, arching my back the tiniest bit. My shoulder blades brushed his dress shirt and my nipples tightened. He noticed and grinned. "I guess I have my answer."

That smug smirk should not be turning me on, but damn if it wasn't.

"Are you complaining I thought about you while selecting lingerie?"

Jamie stepped closer, pressing his fully clothed chest to my bare back. "Complaining?" He dipped his head to kiss my shoulder before meeting my reflection's gaze. "Siren, I'm thanking my lucky fucking stars."

I arched a brow even as I melted back against him. "Siren?"

He pushed my hair to one side and kissed up my neck. Reaching my ear, he said, "Seems appropriate, don't you think? After the way you've enchanted me."

I reached back and wove my fingers into his hair, tugging him closer to encourage his kisses. "Aren't you scared I've lured you to your demise?"

His lips dusted the shell of my ear. "Ah, but what a way to go."

My laughter was cut short when Jamie cupped my breasts. I arched into his touch with a groan and felt his appreciative hum in response.

My head fell back against his shoulder as he stroked the undercurve of my breasts, fingers teasingly close to where I ached for his touch.

"Look at us, Coral," he said, fingertips moving higher. "Open your eyes and look at how fucking gorgeous you are right now."

Lifting my head, I saw my body on wanton display. Even in the imperfect reflection, I could see the flush of my cheeks, the subtly eager pout on my lips, the arch of my spine thrusting my breasts forward and my hands clasped around Jamie's neck. I watched his hands moving over my body. Saw him caressing my breasts in long lingering strokes that had my shoulders pressing back against his chest and my fingers tightening in his hair. He brushed the pads of his fingertips over my curves, then traced the valley between them. He worshipped every inch of my breasts in slow, tantalizing circles, never quite reaching my now painfully tight nipples.

"Jamie," I whined, tugging at his hair. "Please."

"I don't think you understand what that word on your lips does to me," he said, the words a dark whisper as he pressed himself against my backside.

I ground back against him. "I'm starting to get the general idea."

His answering chuckle was wicked. "Happy to hear that, sweetheart. But don't worry . . ." One hand left my breast and ghosted down over my stomach to tease the waistband of my panties. "By the end of tonight, you'll know the precise effect all your little sounds have on me. Right now, though . . ." He sucked gently on my neck before continuing. "I'm more interested in finding out what my touch does to you."

Jamie flattened his hand against my stomach, letting the tip of one finger delve just beneath the top of my panties. "At this point," I said, rolling my hips to encourage that finger to come closer, "you're already well aware of what your touch does to me, Jamie Standard."

"I'm a man who likes to be thorough in his research," he said, nipping my earlobe and pushing his hand all the way into my panties to cup my sex while the fingers of his other hand closed over my nipple in the roll-ing pinch I'd been desperate for since he'd divested me of my bra.

The simultaneous stimulation of my overwrought erogenous zones made my entire body jolt as though there were a live wire running straight from my nipple to the throbbing ache between my thighs. "Ohmigod," I gasped out, unable to stop myself from writhing against his hand.

Jamie groaned and used the hand in my panties to pull me tighter against him, even as he teased one finger through my folds. Through his pants, his erection pressed between my cheeks, hard and insistent. For a brief second, I debated suggesting we get to the main event for his sake as well as my own. But then his middle finger pushed inside of me and curled forward in the most delicious stroke of my g-spot and all conscious thought fled my brain.

There was only sensation. The feeling of being wound tighter and pushed higher with every drag of his finger against that sensitive spot. Jamie's touch was rhythmic agony, timed perfectly with the pinch and release of my nipple still trapped between the fingers of his other hand. My body tightened around his finger in a greedy vise as my hips bucked and jerked against his hand.

"That's it, sweetheart," he said, his voice rough and uneven. "I could watch you fucking my hand all night. Taking what you need."

"I . . . I want . . . I need . . ." My stuttering sentence ended with a keening noise instead of any real plea for what I wanted. My brain was too overloaded with the feel of being surrounded by Jamie. His touch was everywhere all at once, and it overwhelmed any power of speech I possessed.

Luckily, the man remained so in tune with my body that I didn't need words for him to know what I needed. "I've got you, baby," he said. "I know what you want." A second finger joined the first, and I moaned in appreciation at the welcome stretch it provided.

Giving me a moment to adjust to the fullness, Jamie redoubled his stroking thrusts and my knees almost buckled. "That feels . . . oh God, Jamie. That feels . . ." Again, words failed me because there was no way for me to verbalize the intense waves of pleasure flowing through my body with his touch. Tingles of pure bliss radiated through me in warm, liquid spirals. Spirals that exploded into fireworks when Jamie pressed the heel of his palm against my clit. I cried out as the orgasm took hold and rolled over me in sharply cresting waves.

This time, when my knees did give out, Jamie was there to hold me up. One arm banded tightly around me while he continued to work his magic with deftly timed strokes of his fingers and rolling presses of his palm designed to wring out every last luxurious drop of my orgasm.

"So fucking gorgeous," he rasped against my ear. "So. Fucking. Gorgeous."

My head lolled back to his shoulder and my arms dropped from around his neck. Jamie's hand was still in my panties, and something about seeing his knuckles stretching the fabric of my underwear was just so hot. We both watched as he slowly slipped his hand free, his fingers sending quivering aftershocks through me with their slow retreat.

Without breaking eye contact, Jamie lifted his hand to his mouth and my mind flashed to our first night together. Two fingers disappeared between his lips, and he hummed with approval before pulling them out.

"Did you just . . ." My question trailed off when he grazed my nipple with the tip of one still wet finger.

"If you still don't believe me about savoring you, then I guess I've got some work to do," Jamie said, sweeping me back into his arms and marching toward the bedroom.

# JAMIE

A sliver of pale gray morning light woke me before my alarm. I'd been so zeroed in on Coral that I'd neglected to close the blackout curtains all the way. Grumbling at the intrusion of the early hour, I rolled over and stretched out a hand, expecting to find Coral but only touching soft cotton. A sickening feeling of déjà vu crept over me until I noticed the sheets beneath my hand were still warm. As though they'd been tucked around the heat of her body not that long ago. Then I heard a cabinet open and close from somewhere else in the suite and relaxed a bit. Rubbing my eyes, I pushed up to a sitting position and saw one of Coral's heels lying next to my suit pants by the bed. The presence of her footwear confirmed she had not slunk out in the middle of the night. The rest of the weight pressing down on my chest lifted with the knowledge she was still here. Tossing the covers back, I grabbed a pair of joggers from the bureau, a Listerine strip from the bathroom, and went to find her.

The vision that greeted me when I rounded the corner into the kitchen was one I could get used to. Coral—wearing my dress shirt and, I prayed to all the unholiest of gods, nothing else—was reaching for a mug. Given her height, she didn't have to stretch, but the simple act of lifting her arm resulted in a corresponding lift of the hem of my shirt. Which gave me a delicious glimpse of toned thighs and a brief peek at the curve of her—thank you, pagan gods of horny men everywhere—bare ass.

I watched her putter around the kitchen for a moment or two. Her hair was a riotous mass of red that fell around her shoulders in thick waves. Fresh faced and just out of bed, wearing only my shirt she looked adorably soft. Vulnerable, even, a descriptor that surprised me as it popped into my head.

"Good morning, gorgeous," I said, which made her jump with surprise.

She whirled around, coffee cup clutched to her chest. "Jesus, Standard, you scared the shit out of me."

"Sorry," I said, coming into the kitchen. "But it's only fair, since I got a scare of my own when I woke up alone." I gave her a pointed look. "Again."

She flushed a little, then spread her arms wide, and I still didn't hate it that any move she made hiked up the hem of that shirt. "Relax, Jamie. I'm standing right here. Searching for coffee in this hovel."

"Let me help you with that," I said, pulling open the drawer next to her hip to reveal a wide variety of coffee beans.

Coral blinked down at it, then back at me. "So, yeah . . . I'm a mermaid, not a barista. Not sure what you want me to do with . . ." She waved a hand at the drawer. "All of that."

With a laugh, I asked, "What sort of coffee do you like? Bold and dark, or more fruity florals with a lighter finish?"

"Ummm, the kind that has caffeine in it and tastes good with cream and sugar?"

"I see it's a good thing I found you when I did," I teased. "We seem to have a bit of a coffee emergency on our hands here."

Coral rolled her eyes. "I think you meant to say we have a bit of a coffee *snob* on our hands here."

I grabbed my chest. "Moi, a snob?"

She tapped one of the bags of beans. "The evidence speaks for itself, Standard. You sir, are a coffee snob."

"I prefer the term connoisseur, please," I corrected, plucking a medium Colombian roast from the drawer. "And you should be thanking me for expanding your coffee horizon rather than calling me names."

Handing me her mug, Coral levered herself onto the counter. And, once more, I did not hate the raised hemline that move created. I was truly enjoying the game of peekaboo her thighs and I were playing this morning, even if she were unaware of it. She crossed her legs and smirked at me. Okay, maybe not as unaware as I'd thought.

"You said cream and sugar?" I asked her, and she nodded. "Flat white okay? Or would you prefer something more like a macchiato?"

Her eyes rounded. "Did I say 'coffee snob'? What I meant was that I do accept you into my heart as my one true coffee lord and savior."

I laughed and opened the fridge. "Coffee is the way to your heart, huh? Good to know." I hid behind the fridge door in the uncomfortable silence that followed. The words had been out of my mouth before I'd even thought about them. About how *not* appropriate they were to say. Hearts had no place in what we were doing. What she'd outlined, and I'd agreed to. Which made what I'd just verbalized the equivalent of a loud fart in church while seated next to your grandmother in the third pew. *Shit!*

I needed to say something. Regroup somehow, but my mind had gone painfully blank. No words would come to mind. Except for the idiotic words I'd just said that seemed to be hanging in the air in front of me. *Shit, shit, shit!*

"Please tell me you're not in there actually milking some sort of tiny arctic cow whose milk comes out mocha flavored," Coral said from her side of the stainless-steel wall I was hiding behind.

I barked out a laugh and looked at her around the door. "What?"

She shrugged. "It was either that or you'd licked the shelf, and your tongue was stuck to it. The only two rational explanations for why you'd be taking so long in there."

"No," I said. "No, I was just . . . never mind." I pulled the milk out and closed the door. If she was cool with just skating right past that awkward patch, then so was I. I brandished the milk carton like a conquering hero. "So, flat white, or something else?"

She smiled at me and the remaining tension over my miscue drained away. "Flat white sounds amazing."

# chapter twenty—two

## JAMIE

"What's the story behind this?" Coral asked, perched on the counter and sipping the coffee I'd just made her. I knew we didn't have much time before we needed to get ready for our close-up, so to speak, but I was enjoying the simple pleasure of this moment of domesticity with her.

I leaned a hip against the cabinet next to her. "Story behind what?"

She pointed first to the coffee maker on the counter, then to the now closed drawer of beans. "Neither of those things are standard hotel issue. And while L'Atelier is not your average hotel, I find it hard to believe that even on the floors so high they require additional oxygen to be pumped in that a drawer full of coffee beans is customary."

Laughing, I nodded as I drank my own coffee. "True. I think it counts as one of the perks of being related to someone in management. Jocelyn takes good care of me. Plus, I think she's still got some of that younger sibling competition in her blood and wants to show off."

Coral smiled. "It must be nice to always have someone like Jocelyn in your corner."

"Yeah, for a pain in the ass baby sister, she's pretty great. Without Jocelyn, I wouldn't have gotten into half as much trouble as a kid. Or had nearly as much fun. Either way you phrase it, my mother would say we terrorized her and half of Boston with our antics."

"So, you grew up in Boston?" she asked, sipping her coffee.

I nodded. "Born and raised. And still terrorizing the city to some extent, I suppose."

"Oh, I've read," Coral teased, and I groaned.

"Guess I walked into that one. That fucking article." I dropped my head back and pouted, which only made her laugh.

"Okay, Standard," she said, crossing her arms and leaning back against the cabinet. The shirt inched higher, then she also crossed her legs at the knee. Jesus, those *legs*. She was saying something, and I tore my eyeballs away from my new favorite way to measure three and a half feet.

"I'm sorry, what did you say?"

Coral slowly raised one brow, then pointedly pulled the hem of my shirt down. It didn't do much good, but it did get her point across. "Sorry," I mumbled, not entirely meaning it.

She laughed again. "At least now I know how to make you look like an anvil fell on your head."

"I believe the word you're looking for," I said, coming to stand in front of her while gripping the counter on either side of her thighs. "Is stupefied."

Putting one hand on the center of my chest, she gave a little shove. "We're having a conversation, Standard. Not counter sex."

"Counter sex is wholly off the table?"

Her eyes twinkled with her smile. "I'm starting to wonder if I have any hard limits with you."

That news shot straight to my groin, and I moved forward, but she stiffened her arm to keep me at a distance while she shook her head. "I'm serious, Jamie."

Sighing, I held up my hands and retreated around to the other side of the island. "Fine, but I'm considering counter sex merely tabled for further discussion at a later date."

"I'll make sure that appears in the minutes," she said with a smile. "Anyway, I as I was saying before your mind went . . ." She flicked a hand through the air. "Wherever it went. Tell me what you wanted to be in that article."

I wasn't expecting that. "What?"

She lifted a shoulder, and her cheeks went a little pink, as though she were embarrassed for asking. "I've gathered you had something else in mind when you agreed to the interview, right? So, what did you want people to know about Jamie Standard?"

I leaned onto my elbows on the cool granite surface of the island, considering her question. "Well, I'd planned to address the importance of green space in development. Especially in cities like Boston."

Coral made a rolling motion with her hand. "Go on."

"Are you sure you want to hear this?" I asked, unable to hold in a nervous chuckle. "It's not exactly . . . interesting to everyone."

"Let me worry about what I find interesting," she said. "If I get bored, we can always re-introduce the topic of counter sex."

I laughed. "Good enough. Well, first, have you ever been to Boston?"

"Only once, but it's been a while."

I had the inane thought of taking her there to show her all my favorite spots. Starting with the park in Boston Common. The idea held way more allure than it should have, given our arrangement.

Pushing that aside, I said, "Okay, but you've heard of Boston Common, right?"

"The big park in the middle of the city, not the magazine currently the bane of your existence?"

I laughed and nodded. "Correct. It's the oldest park in America, since it was founded in 1634. And the thing I love about it is that in a city that is so cramped together they had to build roads underground, for three hundred and fifty years, no one has ever touched fifty acres of pristine green space in the city center. And any suggestion of ever doing so would probably result in the advocate for it being run out of town. Which is amazing, if you think about it. Fifty acres sitting untouched in a major urban area is a true feat."

"I can see that," Coral said.

"Boston Common is what made me want to get into development."

"A park made you want to build skyscrapers?" she asked. "I need to hear more."

"A park made me want to change the way people build skyscrapers. Not just skyscrapers, but anything. The incorporation of green spaces into development gives people within that development a better sense of community. Not just with each other, but with the land itself. It gives people a place to come together and enjoy the outdoors, even if they're in downtown Boston. Sure, you're ringed in by the city, but the park itself provides a sort of sanctuary."

"I like that," she said. "I bounced around a lot as a kid, but my favorite places were the ones with public parks. Even if we were in a shitty apartment, I could escape to the park for a few hours."

"Exactly," I said, getting excited. "Which is why at Standard we focus on incorporating as much land planning as possible to provide things like pocket parks and walking trails, or public gardens in all our developments. And if you can use those to connect your development to other areas, like linking the walking trails with a network of existing trails, even better. You're providing links between communities."

"You've got a real passion for this," Coral said.

I nodded, "I minored in landscape architecture in college and got even more hooked."

"Well," she uncrossed her arms and smiled. "That would've been a much better article." Her grin turned impish. "I do have to agree with the writer on some points, though. Your eyes are quite dreamy. And the physique." She kissed the tips of her fingers. "Absolute perfection."

I grumbled into my coffee, but that only made her laugh. Glancing at the clock on the microwave, she slipped off the counter. "We need to get a move on if we're going to get presentable before meeting Jocelyn to head over to the studio."

With a hand at her hip, I guided her closer. Her arms came around my waist and she smiled up at me. "I happen to think you look more than presentable right now. In fact, I'd use words like 'delectable' or 'irresistible.'"

She giggled and kissed my chin. "That's sweet." Her fingers trailed under the waistband of my pants. "I like you like this too. Until you came into the kitchen this morning in sweatpants, I was honest to God questioning whether you owned anything other than suits."

"Technically, these are called joggers," I corrected. "Sweatpants are for old men in their BarcaLoungers."

Coral stepped back a little and blue-gray eyes trailed lazily down my torso, stopping pointedly at my crotch. "Jamie, honey, I have news for you. You are wearing gray sweatpants, and those sweatpants belong on the Insta page of @hotguysingraysweats for all the world to enjoy."

I shook my head in confusion. "I'm sorry, did you just lapse into some weird female language that I cannot comprehend as a cis-het white guy? What is the deal with gray sweatpants, er, joggers?"

Coral laughed and grabbed her phone off the counter. "You're adorable." I watched her open Instagram. She typed a few keys and then turned her phone toward me. It was on the aforementioned page of

@hotguysingraysweats and I was instantly confronted with the outlines of *so* many dicks.

I blinked, then rubbed my eyes, but the smorgasbord of manhood contours and silhouettes were still there draped in varying qualities of gray fabric. I wanted to look away. I needed to look away. But my eyes stayed glued to her screen. Finally, I found my voice. "What am I looking at?"

Coral laughed. No, that wasn't right. She chortled, or maybe even guffawed. Whatever you wanted to call it, she did it for an inordinate amount of time before recovering enough to answer me. "What you're looking at, my dear, is proof positive that cis-het men aren't the only ones with the ability to be raunchily inappropriate when it tickles their fancy."

"So, you're saying these are just random pictures of . . ." My voice drifted off, and I was embarrassed to admit I felt my cheeks get hot.

"Dicks in gray sweatpants?" Coral asked and nodded. "Yes, that is precisely what they are. Not all of them are random. Some are anonymous boyfriend or husband or partner appreciation posts. But they most certainly are all pictures of men's junk."

Tugging her lower lip between her teeth, she gave me another slow once-over. "You'd have been a shoo-in for Dick of the Week and easily in the running for Cock of the Month."

My cheeks got warmer. "Cock of the . . ." I shook my head. "Never mind. I don't want to know."

Coral came closer, sliding her arms around me once again. "On second thought, you in a suit is probably safer for the female population."

I raised a brow. "Oh? You don't think I look good in a suit?"

"I think you look better than good in a suit, Jamie." Her mouth turned up in a wicked grin. "But in these sweatpants . . . I'm sorry 'joggers'. . ." She shook her head and made a little hum in the back of her throat that shot straight to my groin. "You're positively lethal." Pushing on to her toes and putting her lips within a millimeter of mine, she added, "But like you said, what a way to go."

# CORAL

"You look amazing," Jocelyn said for the third time in as many minutes as she flitted around the back of the director's chair I sat in while an aesthetician put the finishing touches on my makeup. I don't think Jocelyn sat down once since we'd arrived backstage at *Waking Up in Vegas* an hour and a half ago.

"Thanks," I said, careful not to move my lips too much and interrupt the pinky-nude liner being applied to them. The makeup artist smoothed a rich gloss over the stain she'd already applied to my lips and stepped back to appraise her work. With a brisk nod, she told me to break a leg and hustled out of the little alcove where I'd been deposited by the show runner.

Jocelyn met my eyes in the lighted mirror. "What do you think?"

"It's surreal," I answered honestly, taking in my overly glam appearance. "It's my first time on a morning show, so I'm still wrapping my head around it."

She put her hands on my shoulders and gave me a reassuring squeeze. "I have no doubt you're going to do great out there today. You're a natural performer, so this is going to be like a walk in the park for you." Her head tilted a bit. "Or should I say swim in a lake?"

I laughed, thinking of my earlier conversation with Jamie. "I'll take either one at this point."

Glancing around to see if anyone was in earshot, she leaned closer and lowered her voice. "I hope those relationship profiles I sent you and Jamie weren't too much for you to download in such a short time."

"Um, no," I said, trying to play it cool as the sister of the man I was growing more obsessed with by the hour started to coach me on our fake relationship. Talk about surreal.

"I've talked with Sam, the show runner, and she knows to keep things light and not delve too deeply into anything. No one wants any sort of deep dive here, so if you keep things simple everything should be fine."

"Coral and I have this well in hand, Joss," Jamie said from somewhere to my left, making both Jocelyn and me jump.

He came into view in the mirror, looking just as dapper as he had on the car ride to the studio. His suit was still impeccable, not a wrinkle in sight. But he'd added a blue tie that did wonders for his eyes. A crisply knotted sapphire blue tie spotted with tiny . . . I squinted into the mirror.

"Are those mermaids on your tie?" I asked.

He lifted the end of the tie to study it before grinning cheekily at me in the mirror. "Seems appropriate, don't you think? I saw it in the wardrobe racks after you were whisked off to makeup. I thought Sam was going to swoon when I asked to wear it. I think her exact words were 'So fucking Gucci.' Not sure what she meant, but she did give it to me, so I think it was a positive interaction."

"You're so old," Jocelyn teased him, tweaking the knot of the tie.

A production assistant came up on our collective right with her hand over the mouthpiece of her headset. "Your segment is up in three minutes, so if you'll follow me, I'll take you over to the set."

I slipped off my chair and smoothed down the front of my aquamarine dress. The handkerchief skirt swirled around my legs and showcased my gold sandals. The same sandals I'd worn the night Jamie and I met.

Jamie gestured for me to follow Jocelyn and when I did, his hand settled at the small of my back. Its warm, reassuring presence was becoming familiar in a way I both loved and hated. Waking up next to him that morning had been wonderful in the thirty seconds before reality intruded. I was his fake girlfriend, so I didn't need to read anything into the way his long arms had wrapped possessively around me. Or the way he'd sleepily nuzzled his face in my neck. While the sex might be real, the rest of it wasn't. Including the calming stroke of his thumb against my spine. That, and everything else that would happen in the next thirty minutes, was all for show. None of it was real, that was for the best and I had to remember that.

"You ready for this?" Jamie whispered, the warmth of his breath coasting along the shell of my ear.

"I think so," I whispered back, telling myself the way I swayed toward him just helped sell our story that much more. "Are you?"

"With you on my arm, gorgeous, I'm ready for anything," he replied, and my insides melted. At this point, I was going to have to get *Not Real* tattooed inside my brain. Because the truth of it was, against my own better judgment, I was starting to feel very real things for Jamie Standard. Very real, very dangerous feelings that would offer cold comfort when he left me behind in just over a week.

I was saved from responding by the PA saying, "You're on in twenty seconds." She bustled around, hooking up our mics and swiping down any stray hairs or flyaways.

From her place center stage on a tall, high-back stool, the host, Analise McCord, said, "And I'm so excited to welcome our next guests, Coral Triton and Jamie Standard, although I think most everyone on the internet knows them as the latest Eric and Ariel!"

At the nudge from the PA, we headed out from the wings and into the bright lights of the stage. Just before we came into view, Jamie took my hand and I felt the warm, encouraging clasp of it curl all the way around my heart. I was so screwed.

# chapter twenty—three

## JAMIE

My heart hammered in my chest, but I plastered on my best smile and waved at the audience as Coral and I walked out to join Analise who'd hopped down from her stool to give us both air kisses. The way she wriggled back up there in her tight pink pencil skirt was impressive. When I assisted Coral onto the stool closest to our host, the crowd let out a collective "Aww!" and I felt the tips of my ears go pink.

Once she was settled, I took the seat next to her, trying to appear as relaxed as possible. Which was difficult since, despite my earlier assurance to Coral, I was petrified this was all going to go horribly wrong. I'd talked with Davidson briefly that morning and he'd been cautiously on board with things. "While I have every confidence in Jocelyn's ideas, it's up to you not to screw this up," he'd said in a super supportive pep talk.

"Welcome, welcome, you two!" Analise trilled, hooking one stiletto on the rung of her stool and leaning forward. "I'm so glad you could join us this Friday morning." Her shoulder-length blond bob swayed gently with the force of her greeting.

"We are too," said Coral, reaching over and interlacing our fingers. Earning another "Aww!" from the audience.

Analise faced the camera and said, "For those of you who've been living under a rock for the last week or so . . ." She looked over at Coral. "Or maybe I should say at the bottom of the ocean!" Then laughed heartily at her own joke. Coral laughed politely, and I managed a smile that I hoped looked more genuine than rictus induced.

"Anyway, these two beautiful people are the latest viral sensation, due in large part to this clip!" A screen dropped down behind us and the initial video of me stalking after Coral played for the audience and, presumably, on TV screens across Vegas.

"And if you thought that was steamy," Analise fanned herself with a cue card. "Look at this Insta post from Coral's account @QueenTriton."

The picture Coral had posted the night before flashed on the screen to several wolf whistles and catcalls from the audience. It still blew my mind how quickly this had all been put together. Coral and Jocelyn were social media wizards.

"So, tell us, Coral, how did you and Jamie first get together?"

With admirable poise, Coral detailed our meet cute in so much detail I almost believed it was true.

"Jamie just swam right into your DMs?" Analise tittered and Coral again laughed politely at the lame mermaid joke.

"He certainly did," she said, looking over at me with a fond smile, which I easily returned.

"We'll circle back to you two lovebirds in a second, but first, tell me about this show you're putting together at L'Atelier. A choreographed mermaid show? I need to hear more, please!"

Coral flushed a little, then launched into a description of what she, Jocelyn and Xavier had planned for the upcoming show at L'Atelier.

"Thanks so much for your interest, Analise," Coral said, like a seasoned talk show professional. "I'm just so grateful to Jocelyn and L'Atelier for giving me this opportunity to work and create with someone as talented as Xavier Raulston. It's an honor to share the tank with someone like him and to get to work with him on the choreography is almost unbelievable. But his involvement with the show guarantees it's going to be unlike anything anyone has ever seen. We're still in the early stages and I don't want to give too much away, but I think I'm safe in revealing we plan to use a tank that's roughly the size of a boxcar for the underwater portion of the performances. We'll have multiple merfolk participating in the show, with changing themes throughout the year. We're shooting for an opening night in October and I'm most excited about our ideas for Halloween, because the skeleton makeup is unreal. Parts of the show will feature our finned friends and parts will be mainly underwater choreography. There's talk of some aerialists joining in the future, so I'm keeping my fingers crossed for that."

A growing sense of pride started unfurling in my chest as I watched Coral positively light up as she talked. Her excitement for the show itself and the opportunity it offered practically radiated off her. It was exhilarating to hear her talk about it, so I could only imagine how riveting the actual show would be in the coming fall. I reached out to squeeze Coral's shoulder in a move that was for her, not the cameras trained on us. I wanted her to know how impressive she was. How much I enjoyed listening to her passion. The small squeeze wasn't nearly enough, but it would have to do on live television.

"Well, if it looks anything like this reel L'Atelier posted this morning, I can't wait to see it," Analise said, cuing up another video clip. This one Lucas must have taken while Coral and I were in the pool. Images of her hands on my stomach, her hair trailing across my chest, a close-up of her tail dragging my shirt open. It was sexy as hell.

"Whew," Analise fanned herself dramatically. "Talk about hot!" The crowd hooted in approval.

"There's no question this production sounds like quite the undertaking," Analise said to Coral. "And like you'll be a Vegas resident with us for some time to come."

"That's the plan," Coral said. She looked out at the audience and gave them a megawatt smile. "Which means I need all of you to go to the L'Atelier website and pre-order those tickets!"

The audience cheered its approval and Analise even clapped along before turning to me. "How do you feel about that, Jamie, since you're based out of Boston? That's quite the long-distance relationship, isn't it? How do you see that working long term?"

That question had *not* been in Jocelyn's carefully prepared portfolio, and it interrupted the warm, squishy feelings expanding behind my sternum. Joss promised we'd get softballs about the show and how we met and that was it. Nothing about how Coral and I would make things work in the long run.

Forcing my lips into a smile, I let my arm drape over Coral's shoulders. She met my gaze, and I caught the barest hint of alarm in her eyes. I said, "Well, Analise, first I want to say how proud I am of Coral and what she's going to accomplish here in Vegas. She's been dedicated to her career for over a decade and come a long way from playing kids' birthday parties in a homemade mermaid tail, wouldn't you say?"

The crowd applauded, but I could tell they were waiting for me to answer Analise's questions.

"Her success is what's most important to me. She's worked hard to get here and I'm so happy for her and would never be anything but supportive. And sure, long-distance relationships can be hard, but when you're as committed to one another as we are, you find ways to make it work. It won't be any hardship for me to travel back to Vegas to see my girl do her thing. I'm excited for our future together and being able to celebrate Coral making L'Atelier even more of a must see in Vegas."

As I said the words, the truth of them sank in. I did want to see Coral's dreams become a reality. I wanted to be here on opening night cheering her on. I wanted to support her in any way I could.

"Aw," Coral said, putting her head on my shoulder for a second. "That's so sweet, babe." I leaned in to the moment and dropped a chaste kiss on her upturned lips, which the audience loved.

Irritation and something darker flickered in Analise's eyes, as though she hadn't expected me to field her question so well. When her smile turned sharper and she angled forward like a cat about to pounce, I knew whatever came next wasn't going to be good. My pulse picked up, and I felt a trickle of sweat run down my back. She had something up her sleeve and was about to spring it on us.

"Coral," she said, reaching out to touch Coral's arm. "It must make you feel pretty special to have Boston's Bad Boy of Business so smitten with you. Especially given his playboy past."

*Oh, fuck.*

My shirtless picture from the *Rakes* article flashed onto the screen behind us, much to my dismay and the simultaneous delight of the audience. More catcalls and woo-hoos sounded from beyond the stage lights.

*Fuck, fuck, fuck.*

Analise's smile widened when she looked into the camera. "One of our eagle-eyed fans pointed out this wasn't the first time Jamie here had gone close to viral recently and was kind enough to pass along the link to a fascinating article." She pointed to my larger-than-life shirtless image behind us. "I mean the pictures alone are worth the download cost!"

Turning back to Coral, she asked, "Have you read the article, Coral?"

"I have, Analise, have you?" Coral asked, her tone calm and conversational while her polite smile never wavered.

Analise's smile faltered a little. "Of course. Scintillating reading, wouldn't you agree?"

Coral lifted one shoulder in a careless shrug. "Honestly, I'm not that into ambush journalism, Analise. Or when a reporter twists quotes to fit the narrative they prefer. I don't want to take anything away from the experience of the women quoted in that article. I certainly wasn't there and can't speak for them. And maybe their quotes weren't taken that far out of context. But what I can say is that Jamie Standard has never been anything but honest and upfront with me about everything, including how important his work is to him. And I admire that because I feel the same way. Sure, we use it in completely different areas, but we share the same work ethic and dedication to a job we love. And as someone who has clawed, scraped and busted their a--, er, fanny to forge a career, I have a lot of respect for everything Jamie has accomplished in such a short period of time."

She paused to give Analise a sugary smile. "And I'm sure you know about the awards he's received from the U.S. Green Building Council, not to mention the preservation work Standard Development has done down in North Carolina, while simultaneously revitalizing a small downtown."

"Well, I—"

Coral rolled right over whatever Analise was going to say. "One of the things I love most about Jamie is the way he tries to incorporate green spaces into all his developments. You might be wondering why a mermaid would care about green space, but I can tell you the more green space we have, the better it is for our planet. Including the oceans, lakes and rivers that are near and dear to my heart. Jamie's dedication to preserving the natural landscape where he can is so important. And it's not just that. He works to create a sense of community, not just a grouping of build-ings, and I find that sexy as hell. I love his unwavering commitment to his company and his vision for what he wants that company to be. And I know that it won't reach the goals he has for it unless he gives it all the time it needs. I know that, because the same is true for me. And, as you just heard him say, Jamie respects and applauds that about me." Reaching over, she took my hand once more and gave me a beatific smile. "To find a true partner who is driven to succeed, but also values your career goals is rare and I consider myself lucky that Jamie found his way to me."

The audience roared its approval as I stared somewhat dumbfounded at Coral. Her takedown of Analise had been the stuff of legend, evidenced by the way Analise sat sputtering next to us. Her plan to bump her ratings by fluttering the pages of the *Boston Commons* article in my face on live television had bombed abysmally. Thanks solely to Coral.

## CORAL

"Remind me never to get on your bad side," Jocelyn said with a laugh when she met me offstage. "I think Analise is still wiping the smoke off her face from that spectacular on-air backfire."

Still a little jittery from my wrangle with the morning host, I managed a shaky chuckle. "Sorry if that was too much," I said. "But she was ju—"

"Too much?" Jocelyn's eyes went wide. "Are you serious? That witch just tried to slut shame my brother on live television. It wouldn't have been too much if you'd shoved her off her stool. I cannot believe she pulled that crap after I went over what was off-limits with Sam before we agreed to this interview. You better believe I'm going to give the station an earful about that, trust me."

"My hero," Jamie said, joining us. His mic clip had gotten stuck, so he'd been delayed in his escape.

I flushed a little in the brilliance of his wide smile. "How could I let her try to besmirch the man who'd just sung my praises for all of Las Vegas?"

Warm wispy feelings had unspooled within me as Jamie told Analise how he was proud of me and was looking forward to see what we put together. Sure, it wasn't true that he was coming back to visit. That part was all part of our act. But the way he'd taken pride in my devoting myself to my dream . . . Suffice it to say that it had been a long time since someone outside the pod had viewed my career with anything more than wry amusement. It was a far cry from my mother's disinterest and occasional disbelief that I'd ever make it. Jocelyn had given me a chance, but Jamie gave me confidence that chance wouldn't be wasted.

"All I did was tell the truth, Coral," he said, and I did my best to smoosh down the stupidly swooning part of me that wanted to believe it. That wanted the fiction of his return to Vegas to be a reality.

"Ready to get the hell out of here?" he asked us, and I nodded.

"You two go on ahead," Jocelyn said, looking past me. I glanced behind us to see what she was looking at and saw Sam approaching. She looked as though she were about to face a firing squad and, given the simmering glint of anger in Jocelyn's eyes, she wasn't far off. I felt a pang of sympathy for her, both for having to face Jocelyn's fury and having to work with an insipid twit like Analise.

"No bloodshed, sis," Jamie cautioned, his lips kicking up into a smirk.

"No promises," she responded, still watching Sam. "You guys take the SUV back to the hotel. Carlos can circle back to get me once Sam and I have finished our . . . discussion."

Leaving Sam to her fate, Jamie and I made our way back to the car. Relaxing back into the cool leather of the back seat, I closed my eyes and blew out a breath. The adrenaline from our live appearance ebbed away, like air leaving a balloon. I felt Jamie's hand on my knee, the press of his fingertips gentle and warm. I let my head loll against the headrest and opened one eye to find Jamie smiling over at me.

"Some morning, huh?"

"Not exactly how I prefer to wake up in Vegas," I said.

He laughed, leaning back into his seat. "I think Analise would share that sentiment today."

I snickered. "Probably Sam, too, once Jocelyn is finished with her."

"So, I have a question," Jamie said, angling toward me on the bench seat.

"Which is?"

"I don't remember mentioning anything to you about the USGBC, or our development down in North Carolina. Which leaves me wondering . . . did you google me, Coral Triton?"

The heat of a blush crept over my cheeks. "And if I did?"

He spread his hands out and grinned wider. "*If* you had, given the fact you just saved my ass on a local television spot we hope goes national on the backs of influencers invested in our fake relationship? I'd be very, *very* glad."

The word "fake" echoed around in my brain, boomeranging back and forth into every nook and cranny. Which was good. I needed that word to take up constant residence and drive out any other stupid thought in there. Especially thoughts about anything real between Jamie and me.

Focusing on that thought, I shifted to face him. "Well, in that case . . . yes, I did google you."

"Are you, the woman who refused to learn my last name the night we met, telling me that you actually went in search of information about me?" He put a hand to his chest and fluttered his eyes at me. "Coral, I'm honored."

I shoved his knee, unable to hide a smile. "Don't make this any more weird than it has to be."

"It's not weird in the least that instead of asking me whatever you wanted to know you typed my name into a search engine," he teased.

I groaned, which only made him laugh. "If I'm being honest, you using internet fodder about me to shut Analise down isn't the only reason I'm glad you googled me."

"Okay," I said, stretching the word. "What's the other reason?"

He shifted a little, adjusting his tie and rolling his shoulders. "Well, again, if I'm honest . . . you googling me makes it a lot less weird that I . . . watched multiple YouTube videos of you."

"Is that so?" I ignored the surge of pleasure at his admission.

The tips of his ears went pink and the sight of it pushed at a tender spot behind my ribs. "It is," he replied, meeting my eyes. "You're a real talent, Coral. And Jocelyn is lucky to have you."

I refused to be carried away by the tide of feelings that rushed through me in response to his praise. It didn't matter that we weren't on stage any longer and that his words were just for me. Nothing had changed. We weren't a real couple, and we wouldn't be. Because we'd both agreed that was how things had to be. How we both wanted them to be.

"Thanks," I said. "That means a l—"

My phone vibrated with a bizarre metallic sounding whine that made us both startle. Concerned, I opened my purse to see what was happening. Rather than being in its rightful place in what I thought of as the phone pocket in the side of my bag, somehow my phone had gotten wedged through the metal ring of my keys—Why were those even in my bag?—and each pulse of the vibrations of the incoming call sounded like a weed whacker attacking a chain-link fence.

"Sorry," I said to Jamie, as I tried to work it free to silence it.

"I'm just glad we aren't under some sort of alien attack," he said, not even attempting to smother a laugh as he watched me try to wrestle the phone free of its purse trap.

"Wouldn't that mean your phone would be making the same noise?"

He snorted. "Please, my phone hasn't made noises since I last paid for a ringtone in college."

With one final tug, the phone tumbled free of its circular prison with the exuberance of a spring breaker released after a night in the drunk tank. Which was unfortunately timed perfectly with the SUV bouncing over what had to be a world record pothole. The combination of the two sent my phone flying out of my purse. Lurching as far forward as my seat belt would allow, I grabbed for it, catching it between my thumb and forefinger. Only to have it slip sideways in my grip, with my thumb tracking right over the slider to answer the FaceTime call from my mother.

# chapter twenty—four

## JAMIE

Finally, Coral! I honestly thought I was going to have to call the law to track you down!"

Coral's eyes flew wide with panic, and she pressed the phone into her chest. "My mother," she whispered so quietly it was more like she mouthed the words than actually said them. "On FaceTime!" The last part was a frenzied hiss. I heard muffled words from where the phone was pressed against her top.

Stifling a laugh, I whispered back, "Sounds like you better talk to her, otherwise you can expect a visit from 'the law.'" I made air quotes around "the law."

Her head dropped back, and she let out a silent scream, mouth open and eyes squeezed shut. Lifting her head, she opened and closed her mouth a few times, as though warming up the muscles she needed before plastering on a smile and raising the phone.

"Hey, Mom," she said. "Sorry about that, I'm actually in the middle of someth—"

"Oh, I saw with my own two eyes what you're in the middle of," her mother snapped, and I winced at the irritation in her tone. It was obvious she was pissed.

Coral's brow wrinkled. "What?"

"How do you think I felt, Coral, when Darlene rushed over to my chair at work today to tell me my daughter was on *Waking Up in Vegas* with her *boyfriend*?"

She'd almost spat the last word she was so mad. Coral paled and swallowed, and I resisted the urge to put an arm around her. This was uncharted territory and, given the venom in her mother's voice, I needed a better read on the situation before acting. The last thing I wanted to do was make things worse.

"You saw the show?" Coral asked and her mother responded with an irritated splutter, like an angry baby blowing raspberries.

"Obviously, I saw the show, Coral. I saw the show because *Darlene*, not my own flesh and blood daughter, told me to watch it. Darlene, not the daughter I spent twenty-two and a half hours in labor with. And not only did my daughter not tell me about the show, she failed to mention she now has a serious boyfriend. But then it's hard to mention anything to your mother when you don't take her calls and barely respond to her texts."

It was a torrent of words unleashed in a maelstrom of disapproval. Coral's smile frayed a little at the edges. "I'm sorry, Mom. It's all been sort of a . . ." She flicked a look at me. "The thing is, I'm . . ." Her eyes came to mine again, churning with panic, then darted back to the phone as she floundered for an excuse.

Without giving it much thought, I unbuckled my seat belt and slid across the seat until we were hip to hip. I felt rather than heard Coral's surprised gasp. I was barely out of the frame of her phone's camera, but I could see the screen. An older version of Coral looked out of it with a deepening frown. Her hair was shorter and her eyes a lighter, colder blue, but the cheekbones looked like the mold Coral's were made from.

With what I hoped was a reassuring glance at Coral, I cupped my hand around hers and angled the phone to show my face. "My apologies, Mrs. Triton. I'm afraid all of this is my fault."

Giving Coral's mom my best boardroom smile, I said, "I'm Jamie Standard, Coral's boyfriend." The last part tripped so easily off my tongue it startled me. It must have also shocked Coral, because she made an odd gurgling sound and her hand tightened around the phone.

From its screen, her mother's eyes moved from my face over to Coral. "This is how you introduce your mother to your boyfriend?"

Coral swallowed but kept smiling. "Well, now you can see why I tried to call you ba—"

Her mother interrupted again. "Nonsense." Her gaze came to me. "Jamie, it's nice to meet you, although I'd prefer if it were in person and before you announced it on the local news." She side-eyed Coral before continuing, "I'm Coral's mother, Evangeline Triton."

"Very nice to meet you as well, Mrs. Triton," I said, smiling even more broadly.

"Please, call me Eva," she said with a demure flutter of her lashes. "I haven't been Mrs. Triton in years."

Coral made another noise in the back of her throat, but I kept my eyes on the screen. "Of course, Eva."

Eva's eyes moved to her daughter with a knowing smile. "I guess now I know who's been keeping you so busy you haven't been able to answer my phone calls. Or give me a date you can come home for dinner."

I glanced over at Coral. The flush on her cheeks had spread down her neck to her chest, and her smile tightened. "I've been busy with my new job, Mom. The one I just started, remember? It's not like I can take time off work in my first week."

Eva huffed her displeasure. "All I'm asking is for you to give me a date you *can* come home, Coral. There's no way you're working twenty-four seven for the next however long. Even mermaids get days off."

Her gaze came back to me, although her next words were still directed at Coral. "And you could bring Jamie with you for a proper introduction. FaceTime may be enough for your generation, but I need more of the human touch."

As she spoke, the inflection in her voice changed into something more . . . deferential was the only way I could describe it. The shift was subtle, but noticeable if you were paying attention. Which Coral obviously was by the way her shoulders stiffened and the hand holding her phone went white at the knuckles.

"Mom, Jamie is even busier than I am, okay?" Coral said, her voice strained as though she were making an effort not to snap at her mother. "He doesn't have time for a visit right now."

Unsure of the dynamic playing out before me, but wanting to be supportive, I put an arm around her and gave her shoulders a squeeze. "I'm sure we can work something out that is convenient for everyone, Eva. Coral and I will chat and figure out a time for us to come for a visit, okay?"

Coral relaxed into my embrace, and I felt like I'd taken some unseen weight off her shoulders. Her mother was a real piece of work, that much was clear. I thought again about the "just me" way Coral had described growing up. An image of what that meant was taking shape in my mind, and I didn't like it.

"This Sunday would be convenient for me," Eva said, totally ignoring my offer to compromise and steamrolling right along with her plan. "Tex loves to barbeque on Sundays, so that would be perfect. Let's plan on around six, okay? We'll see you two then. Bye now!"

The phone went dark, and I stared in disbelief at the small black square in Coral's hand. Had that really just happened? And who, or what, was Tex and why did his preference for barbeque Sundays factor into anything?

"Evangeline Triton, ladies and gentlemen," Coral muttered, then dropped her phone back into her purse and threw her head back with a groan. "Damn my sausage fingers for swiping my mother into this!"

I choked out a laugh, still somewhat shellshocked by her mother's complete disinterest in anyone's schedule but hers. "I happen to be quite fond of your fingers. Although the timing on my meeting your mother could have been a little better, I'll admit."

Lifting her head, she chuckled. "Rest assured, Jamie, having you and my mother on FaceTime was the furthest thing from my mind today." Her eyes warmed as she put a hand on my knee. "Thanks for jumping in when you did, though. I was a few seconds away from just throwing my phone out the window. So, not only did you try to save me from my mother, you also kept me from having to deal with my cell phone company. A true win-win if there ever was one."

"Happy to be of service," I replied.

"And don't worry, I'll come up with a reason we can't make it on Sunday."

"What?" I asked.

Her brows knit together in confusion. "What do you mean what?"

"I mean . . ." I pushed a hand through my hair. My knee-jerk reaction was to protest her doing anything of the sort. I waited for that to change. For my standard aversion to meeting the family to rise up and announce its appearance. But . . . it didn't.

Coral was still looking at me, so I said, "I mean, why do that?"

"Why do . . ." She shook her head, letting out a rueful laugh. "You don't know my mother, Jamie. If I don't come up with something, she will expect me to arrive on the doorstep of her house with you in tow."

"Would that be so bad?" The words tumbled out before I could stop them, and then they were just sitting between us like the flashing Welcome to Las Vegas sign on the other end of the Strip.

"Would that be so . . ." Coral blinked, then shook her head. She gave me a confused half smile. "You can't actually *want* to meet my mother."

"What if I do?" *What the fuck was I doing? Was that an actual thought in my brain? Something I seriously wanted to do? When was the last time I'd met a girl's parents, for God's sake?* And yet, despite those inner what the fucks, I really wanted to hear Coral's answer to the question.

"Jamie," she said with a huff of nervous laughter. "That's not what this"—her hand flipped between us—"is about." With a glance at the front seat, she lowered her voice. "My mother isn't a part of the PR campaign. There's no reason for you to meet her. And trust me, it's an experience you won't regret missing out on."

## CORAL

Jamie shook his head. "I didn't offer to meet your mother because I thought it was part of the PR campaign. I offered to meet your mother because it seems like it would help you out. Nothing in your rules prevents me from doing something nice for you, Coral."

I blinked owlishly at him. "What?"

Strong hands cupped my arms, and his thumbs stroked my biceps. "I'm not going to pretend I understand the dynamic between you and your mother by witnessing a single, short FaceTime call, but I get the sense my coming home with you would help in some way. A way I might not completely understand, but it's enough for me to know that I could help you. And that's good enough for me."

"But . . . why would you do that for me?" The idea of Jamie, with his close-knit family complete with a perfect grandpa, meeting my train wreck of a mother made my skin go clammy. Not only that, if he did come with me, it could also result in the further blurring of certain lines that were already fuzzy. At this point, snow angels in seventy-five degree weather were more clearly defined than how I felt about things between us. Taking him home with me would only exacerbate that. But his offer was so sweetly genuine, I couldn't help but consider it.

Jamie laughed and bumped my chin with his knuckle. "As we've already established, Coral, I enjoy your company. I genuinely like spending time with you. I like you as a person. If I didn't, we couldn't have pulled it off this morning." Blue eyes twinkled when he grinned at me. "That's a long way of saying I'd do this for you because I like you."

I quashed the little flutter in my chest at that, even as his words worked like a giant eraser on the line between what parts of us were real and which ones were fake.

At my lack of response, he continued. "If you're not comfortable with the idea, I won't offer again. But it's honestly not a problem for me."

"It's not that I'm uncomfortable with it," I responded. "It's just I . . ."

Maybe it was the way his eyes went soft when they looked at me, or the comforting stroke of his fingers on my arm, or the honest way he'd said he liked me. Whatever it was released a torrent of feelings within me that burst out in a waterfall of words.

"I try to avoid setting expectations for people, because in my experience they rarely live up to them." I shook my head. "No, that's not exactly true. What I normally do is set a negative expectation for people and wait for them to meet it. I guess it's a sort of defense mechanism honed by a childhood spent meeting too many of my mom's boyfriends. None of whom ever measured up to the expectations she had for them. But you, Jamie Standard, seem intent on continually defying the low expectations I set for you."

"Uh, thank you?" he said, with a half smile.

I laughed. "It was a compliment, I promise. What I'm saying is that it's hard for me to go against instinct here, no matter how badly I might want to." I put a hand on his knee. "But every day I spend with you makes me want to try that much harder."

Telling him that wasn't in line with what we'd said this was, but I couldn't hold it in. I had to let him know how much his actions over the last few days meant to me. Since the night we met, he'd been just what I needed when I needed him. Saying *that* would have been way too much, but I had to say something.

Jamie's hand covered mine, and he cupped my cheek with his other hand, thumb stroking my cheekbone. "Expectations aren't something to be scared of, Coral. So long as you have them of the right person. And I promise you can expect me to be there for you, okay? Whether it's dinner with your mother, chasing off dimwitted douchebags in bars, or fitting into that tight tail squeeze, I'll be there for you."

I mentally added "for the next few days" to what he'd said, then forced myself to erase it. No need to think about that now, because he was right here, touching my cheek and smiling at me like I was everything.

I smiled back at him, then turned to kiss his palm. "You're an excellent negotiator, you know that?"

He brushed my hair off my shoulder, letting his hand rest there. "Only when there's something at stake worth the effort."

I swallowed thickly. "And dinner with my mother is an example of that?"

Jamie's blue eyes grew serious. "You're an example of that, Coral. And it's a travesty you don't already know it."

Coral: *This is an all-points bulletin, red flag emergency best friend situation and I need you to answer your phone.*

Five minutes later.

Coral: *I'm really freaking out here, Cam. I need you to talk me down, okay? Call me back as soon as you can.*

Fifteen minutes later.

Coral: *Cameron Eunice Decker! Why are you not answering your mother ducking phone???*

Coral: *We both know that should NOT have said "ducking."*

Cam's return phone call came two hours later, while I was in the middle of reviewing mermaid résumés with Xavier. My phone vibrated angrily on the table next to my elbow, making him glance up from a stack of headshots.

He nodded toward the phone. "Do you need to get that?"

I absolutely did need to answer Cam's call and unload the entire whirlwind of the last few days onto her so she could help me parse through what was real and what wasn't. Why a guy who'd proposed a fun Vegas fling to me was now saying things that wove around me like rainforest vines. Threading their way into the tiny cracks of the strategically designed walls I'd built to keep any expectations for the future from crowding into our present. Pushing those cracks into widening fissures with words like "lucky to have you" and "because I like you," until the whole flimsy mess threatened to cascade down around my ears in a shower of rubble and I was awash in a sea of expectations and hopes for more with Jamie. A sea I could very easily drown in if I didn't get myself back under control and face the reality of our situation.

So, yeah, I needed to answer Cam's call, but there was no way I could do that in front of Xavier. Coaxing my features into something at least moderately close to casual, I shook my head. "No, it's just Cam. I'll give her a call when we're done here. No worries."

Xavier gave me a long look that let me know my attempt at casual fell well short of the mark. But he didn't push it, just nodded and went back to the assortment of glossy, hopeful 8×10s he was sorting through.

My phone buzzed again, signaling a voicemail, then once more with an incoming text message.

Cam: *I know you did not "Eunice" me in a panic and then send me to flipping voicemail, Coral Elizabeth Triton. What the actual duck?*

I swiped to answer her before she could correct "duck."

Coral: *In a meeting with Xavier. Will have to call you later.*

In my head, I could hear her irritated huff as she read that, but all she sent back was a thumbs up emoji. Just knowing she'd be available to talk later helped quiet my mind and mend my frayed concentration. As all-consuming as things with Jamie had become, I couldn't let it affect my work. Within these piles of photos, listings of experience and references, we'd find the people we needed to make this show come to life. That deserved all my attention, not some half-cocked fantasy about maybe, just maybe, Jamie and me lasting longer than his vacation.

For the rest of the afternoon, Xavier and I worked through the stack of merfolk prospects, separating résumés and headshots into piles of definite auditions, possible Zoom interviews and rejections. It sucked being the one standing between someone and their dream job and it was difficult to shift my performer perspective to one of producer or director. It wasn't that long since I'd been where these hopefuls were now, and I knew the sting of rejection. But, I had to focus on what was best for the show rather than my instinct to play mother hen to the applicants.

When I put the last résumé onto the Zoom pile, I slumped back into the conference room chair and released all the air in my lungs in a deep *whoosh!*

Xavier laughed. "It's tough being the boss, isn't it?"

"And I'm just one of many underbosses," I said. "I can't imagine Jocelyn's load."

His dark eyes sparked a little at the mention of her name. "She's something else, all right."

"Absolutely," I said, resisting the desire to tease him about his obvious interest in her.

The spark shifted to something more inquisitive when he said, "Her brother doesn't seem half bad, either."

"Mm-hmm," I said, noncommittally. The chemistry between Jamie and me was obvious, and Xavier was in on the PR plan. But he didn't know anything else, and I wasn't about to volunteer anything about what Jamie and I had going behind the scenes. Especially given the thought tornadoes that started spinning in my brain at the mere mention of him.

With a chuckle, he held up his hands. "I'm not prying, Coral. What you do on your own time is wholly your business. And we all deserve to have a little fun when we can find it, right?"

The blush that crept up my face might as well have been a neon sign that said, "Jamie and I are SO DOING IT!"

A knowing grin stretched across his face. "Well, then, I'll take the definites up to Jocelyn for her to look over and drop the Zoom stack off with Meredith to set up the interviews. I'll see you in the pool tomorrow morning at ten for choreography?"

"You know it," I said, just as his phone chimed with an incoming text.

Pulling it from his pocket, he glanced at the screen and his smile softened a little. "There's the big boss now," he said, typing out a reply and tucking the phone back into his jeans. Oh yeah, Xavier Raulston had it *bad* for Jocelyn. And it was beyond adorable.

I tucked the two stacks of paperwork he needed into separate folders and handed them to him. "Don't want to keep her waiting."

When the door to the conference room clicked shut behind him, I grabbed my phone. Reaching Cam was easiest when you texted her to let her know to expect your call. She viewed calling without texting first as something akin to guerrilla warfare.

But before I could type anything, my phone buzzed in my hand with a text from Jamie. No matter how hard I tried, I couldn't net and subdue the swirl of butterflies in my stomach at the sight of his name on my screen.

Jamie: *Congratulations, Coral.*

I frowned at the text. Congratulations? For what? Which is exactly what I typed in response.

Jamie: *You haven't seen it?*

Again, I typed exactly what I was thinking.

Coral: *Seen what?*

Bubbles appeared, then a hyperlink to a well-known entertainment site. Before I could click on it, my phone rang and Jamie's name appeared on the caller ID. The butterflies flapped their wings with the exuberance of Penelope's fan in *Bridgerton*.

"I can't even click the link that fast, much less read whatever it is you sent me," I said.

His rich laugh tumbled out of the speaker. "Sorry, I couldn't help myself. Your takedown of Analise has gone national, Coral. Davidson texted me earlier to let me know it's even been picked up by *Boston Commons* of all places."

"Are you serious?" I asked. "Why on earth would they do that?"

Jamie snorted out a laugh. "Because it let them continue the theme of the article and they're trying to ride the wave with us. Only now, hang on, I don't want to get this wrong." There was a muffled tapping, and I assumed he was pulling something up on his phone. "Yeah, here it is," he said and cleared his throat and in a breathy tone he continued,

"'Ravishing Rogue, or Reformed Rake? Has Jamie Standard gotten lucky in love in Las Vegas?'"

"Really leaning in to the alliteration there, aren't they?" I asked with a laugh.

"I didn't even read you the part about the 'mythical mermaid' who's 'bewitched one of Boston's Business Bad Boys.'"

"Oh, my God," I choked out as laughter overtook me.

Laughing with me, Jamie said, "I know, right? It's all so over the top, but in the perfect way. It's almost as good as a retraction or apology and I have you to thank for it! Let me take you to dinner tonight to celebrate. Anywhere you want. Nowhere is too good for my enchantress." He paused for a second, then added, "Is it corny to tell a professional mermaid the world is our oyster?"

I giggled. "Yes, it's definitely corny, but I'll accept my reward nonetheless."

"Perfect," he said. "Text me your room number and three places you want to try, and I'll swing by to collect you around seven thirty, if that works."

"Why three places?" I asked.

"Because that way it will still be sort of a surprise," he said, and I could hear the grin in his voice. "I'll see you then, Siren."

# chapter twenty—five

## CORAL

Wait, what?" Cam almost shrieked through the phone. I winced and adjusted the volume. "Did I just hear you say you're taking the hottie home to mama?"

"You heard me say he offered," I hedged. "I haven't said yes yet."

Cam and I had been on the phone since I'd gotten back to my room about an hour ago. I'd given her the entire rundown on Jamie and me. Including my growing difficulty in knowing where the fake part stopped and the real part started. Which segued nicely into his offer to join me for family dinner on Sunday. Because he wanted to be there for me. Because he wanted me to know I could count on him. Because I was worth it. Not sentiments usually associated with a no-strings fling.

"So, you're *not* going to take him to dinner with your mother?" Cam pressed, skepticism obvious in her tone and downward slash of her perfect brows.

"I . . . I don't know," I admitted. "Don't you think that's pushing things a little too far in the direction of real?"

Her shoulder lifted inside the square of my screen. "So what if it is?"

"So what if it . . ." My voice drifted off as I stared at her. "Have you not been listening to me?"

"Oh, I've heard every word you've said," Cam replied. "Which is how I know there is nothing fake about your feelings, Coral. You are head over heels for this guy, honey. That much is obvious, based on that glow you've got and that you're spending every waking moment with him."

I opened my mouth to deny catching feelings for the man. But I couldn't. Because having a semi-constant infusion of Jamie in my life since getting to Vegas had done nothing but make me want more of him. There was no such thing as overexposure where he was concerned. And that was a problem because it meant I'd gotten in over my head. That all my rules and structure hadn't saved me from falling for him. And that when he left, it was going to hurt like hell.

"Even if you're right, it doesn't matter," I said.

"How could the way you feel about him not matter?" Cam asked, incredulity etched in her tone.

"Because, Cam, regardless of how amazing things are in this weird bubble we've created, it's not realistic to think that can last outside of it. He's here on vacation. I'm here for the long term . . . hopefully. This was only supposed to be a fun vacation romance, nothing serious."

"Things change, Coral," Cam said, like it was the simplest thing in the world.

"Our zip codes haven't," I said. "And they aren't going to, Cam. Once he's gone, he's gone." Back to a life that didn't include me.

"How do you know he doesn't feel some of the same things you do? Have you talked to him about it?" she asked.

"We've . . . talked around it, I guess you could say." Which was the only way to categorize the conversations Jamie and I had. There were inklings of feeling, but no set declarations of any kind. *He thinks you're worth it*, my inner voice reminded me. I ignored her.

Cam threw up her hands. "Well, until you talk *about* it, how can you be so sure the two of you can't find a way to make this work? What do you have to lose? If this really is just a Vegas vacation story for him, then you're no worse off than you are now. But if it's not . . ."

For a few seconds, I gave in to that idea. Let the picture of Jamie and me having something more than a fling take shape. Leaned in to the way my heart fluttered when it saw him, and the warmth that spread through me when he smiled. *You can expect me to be there for you.* My heart twisted with the force of how badly I wanted that to be true.

"Just talk to him, Coral," Cam said softly. "Based on what you've told me, I don't think you'll be disappointed."

A little bubble of hope formed in my chest at her encouragement as I considered it. Her advice dovetailed nicely with the promise Jamie and I had already made to each other. Clear communication was something we'd both insisted on, so technically I owed it to him to come clean about how I felt. And what better time than tonight, when we were celebrating our big win?

"Okay," I said, unable to keep from smiling.

## JAMIE

"Shattucks has agreed to a meeting."

Davidson's announcement made me stop switching dress shirts back and forth in the mirror. I'd been vacillating between the dove gray and the business blue for the last twenty minutes. Which was unfortunate, given I needed to be at Coral's room in the next half hour and couldn't afford to waste any more time.

His news sent a jolt of excitement racing through me. It was a familiar sensation, one I felt every time things got close on a deal. The thrill of the chase was at its pinnacle—the quarry was in sight and victory was within our grasp.

"Jamie, did you hear me?" he asked.

"Yeah, sorry, just took me off guard," I replied, dropping the business blue in favor of the dove gray. I put the phone on speaker and slid my arms into the shirtsleeves. "When and where?"

"That part is a little unorthodox," Davidson said, then paused. "He's invited us to a dinner on Monday, as in this Monday. But he doesn't only want to meet with us."

The elation I'd felt ebbed slightly. "Is there another bidder for the property?"

"What? No, nothing like that," Davidson replied, sounding reluctant to continue.

"For fuck's sake, man, spit it out. You've got me on pins and needles here. Who else does he want to meet?"

"Coral," Davidson said, and my hands paused mid buttoning.

"Did you say . . ."

"Coral, yes," Davidson confirmed I hadn't misheard him. "He wants to meet your fake girlfriend."

The words "fake girlfriend" scraped over my skin like a thorny vine. Nothing between Coral and me felt fake, no matter how many times either of us said the word aloud. But that was not something I was prepared to get into with Davidson. Telling him I'd developed feelings for a professional mermaid that lived across the country needed to be done at the right time, which was not this call.

Tabling my discomfort with his characterization of my relationship with Coral, I considered Shattucks's request, then asked, "Think that's a good sign, or a bad sign?"

"I think it's a sign this guy is an eccentric old coot and also that your sister is terrifyingly good at assessing a situation. I mean, who in their right mind comes up with concocting a fake relationship to close a land deal?" I could hear the dazed admiration in his voice.

"Not exactly the question I was asking, man," I said. "But I'll let Jocelyn know you're in awe of her talents."

Davidson chuckled, but did finally answer my question. "I hardly think the guy would invite the two of you to some sort of dinner meeting just to get you to sign the cover of *Boston Commons* magazine. He asked for you because he knows you're the one who spearheaded this project from the jump. You're the guy, Jamie, so he wants you there. And he wants Coral there to see if the two of you are the real deal." Davidson chuckled drily. "To see if she's tamed Boston's Business Bad Boy or whatever the fuck that article said."

"That's Boston's Bad Boy of Business, thank you very much," I said with a laugh, shocked by my ability to laugh at the article I'd feared just a week ago would ruin everything.

"Whatever," Davidson said. "The real question is whether you think Coral will go for it."

Given it was Friday night and we'd been invited to dinner at her mother's house on Sunday, I wasn't sure if Coral would be up for flying across the country with me the following day. To be fair, I wasn't sure she'd be ready to fly across the country for me at all. Or if she even could do that, given she'd just finished her first week at L'Atelier. I knew Jocelyn was all in on helping me seal the deal with Shattucks, but that didn't mean she could spare Coral from whatever it was they'd be doing on Monday.

"I can ask," I said. "But she does have a job here, so it will depend on her schedule."

"Assuming she can work it out, do you think she'll come? I need to get back to Shattucks's assistant on this sooner rather than later."

Logistics aside, I wasn't sure if Coral would come. It was a big ask. I thought about her reticence to accept my offer to go to dinner with her mother. Her questioning why I would agree to do that. Maybe she'd be more comfortable with the idea if she felt like she returned the favor by meeting Shattucks.

"I may have a way to get her on board," I said, letting the concept tumble around in my head.

"Great," he replied. "Let me know as soon as you can."

I knocked on Coral's door at precisely 7:30, inexplicably excited at the prospect of seeing where she'd been staying. It wasn't as though this was her house. It was just a staff room at a hotel. But still, the concept of seeing her at home, even a temporary one, set off a curiosity within me I hadn't experienced before.

"Hey," she said, opening the door and beckoning me inside. "C'mon in, I just need to grab my shoes and we can hea—"

"Holy shit," I said, momentarily taken aback by the line of multi-colored silicone mermaid tails standing sentry between the two queen beds. At first glance, I'd thought she was entertaining some sort of rainbow army.

She glanced over her shoulder, then back at me with a grin. "Sorry, that must look pretty weird to someone who isn't used to it."

Blinking at the row of disembodied tails hanging upside down from some sort of wooden rack, I shook my head. "No, it's not that." It absolutely *was* that. "I just . . . didn't know you had so many of them."

Coral laughed. "Says the man with a suit for every possible occasion. My tails are like your suits, Standard. I need more than just one, so Jocelyn was kind enough to arrange transport of them through a bonded shipping company. I wasn't going to trust FedEx to get them here unscathed." She glanced around the room, frowning slightly. "Although I hadn't factored in the space they'd take up. It made me realize we'll need a good storage system in the dressing rooms for the show." Her room wasn't small, but the addition of seven person-sized mermaid tails did shrink it a bit.

"Makes sense," I said, walking over to get a better look at them. The silicone shimmered in varying colors of pinks, purples, and reds. The green one I'd seen her in was on a separate rack, positioned over a small box fan. "What's with that one?"

She looked up at my question, the zipper of her black knee-high boots pausing halfway up her calf. "I can't toss them in the dryer after rinsing them out. And you don't want to risk mildew or mold by just hanging them up. So, the box fan is a necessity in any mermaid's toolkit."

"I didn't know you'd been in the tank today." If I had, I would've made a point of seeing her perform.

Coral shrugged. "I wasn't. But I was a bit keyed up after our interview this morning, so I got in a swim in the pool before meeting Xavier to review résumés."

"You could've called me," I said. "I would've been happy to mertend for you."

She finished zipping up her boots. "I'll keep that in mind for next time."

"And I'm sorry if this morning was a little much for you. I hate that you got put in that position."

Her laugh made her eyes twinkle. "I think my being put in that position was the entire point of Jocelyn's PR plan. And most of the reason we were interviewed in the first place." She picked up her purse from a small side table, then shot me a saucy look. "Besides, I liked sticking up for you, Standard. From what I've seen, you're worth the effort, too."

Setting aside the myriad of tingling sensations her words cut loose in my chest, I grinned back at her. This was the perfect opening to bring up Shattucks's request to meet her. "Funny you should mention effort, Siren."

Coral's eyes narrowed. "Why do I feel like I just unwittingly opened the door to something?"

I looped her arm through mine. "Relax, I promise it's nowhere close to deserving of that level of suspicion."

"Boston? You want me to fly back to Boston with you on Monday? Monday as this coming Monday?" Coral's eyes were wide, and her brows flirted with her hairline as she stared at me from across the white linen tablecloth.

"You make it sound like I asked you to join me on the moon," I teased, taking a sip of wine. "It's nothing that complicated. Assuming your schedule would allow it, we'd fly out Monday morning, go to whatever Shattucks has set up that night, and you could head right back to Vegas on Tuesday. I know you'd need to get back as soon as you could for work, so I'd only impose on you for a day."

The mention of her return trip was like pressing a bruise I hadn't known was there, the discomfort of it startling in its intensity. Because if things were moving forward with Shattucks, that meant my vacation in Vegas—and my time with Coral—would be cut short. *Unless you tell her how you've started to feel about her.*

But I couldn't combine the two topics. I couldn't make her think my asking to take the fake completely out of our relationship had anything to do with meeting Shattucks. I couldn't afford for her to view my growing feelings for her as transactional.

So, I needed to get her on board with meeting Shattucks, because our timeline was tight. And then, I could tell her how I felt without her thinking I'd was just trying to manipulate her into agreeing to the meeting. It was better to wait and tell her after she'd agreed.

Coral chewed on her lip. "I'll have to talk to Jocelyn and Xavier, of course, but if it's just one day, I think they'll be cool with it. After all, Jocelyn is the one who came up with this idea, so I don't think she'll have an issue with it."

"That was my thought as well," I said, lining up my silverware in a show of nonchalance. "And it would let you return a favor."

Red brows dipped down in consternation. "And how do you figure that?"

I shrugged. "I'll be your buffer for your mom on Sunday, then you can come with me to meet Shattucks on Monday."

When I said it out loud, it didn't sound as good as when I'd come up with the idea earlier. The words felt wrong. Because I didn't view going to dinner with her mother as a favor that needed to be repaid. I'd meant what I said to her. I'd offered to go because I wanted to be there for Coral, not because I wanted to stock up on IOUs.

It hit me then that I wanted her to come to Boston for largely the same reason. Yes, Shattucks had been the impetus, but for once it wasn't just the deal that had me excited. It was the girl and the prospect of taking her to see my home. Having her meet my friends. Seeing the life I'd built for myself. Convincing her to consider becoming a part of it in whatever way she wanted. And instead of saying that, I'd made it sound like some sort of trade-off.

Something that looked a lot like disappointment flashed in her eyes and I wanted to kick myself for putting it there. I needed to fix this, and quickly.

"Coral, I th—"

"Well played, Standard," she said, looking away from me and taking a drink. When her eyes came back to mine, there was a cool detachment in them that skewered me. "Like I said, you're one hell of a negotiator."

"Coral, I don't think I phrased things in the bes—"

She waved a hand to cut me off. "I figured a Bad Boy of Business like you would know not to keep selling once someone's already on the hook. Assuming Jocelyn and Xavier are cool with it, I'm in, Jamie. I'll come back to Boston with you and do the romance dog and pony for Shattucks and then fly back the next day."

The relief I should have felt never materialized, because I could see her pulling back from me. The easy, relaxed manner she'd developed around me was gone, like each of my idiotic words was a building block of a wall now separating us. I tried again to make it right. "That's amazing, Coral. Thank you. And I didn't mean to make it seem . . ." Words failed me, but not Coral.

"Beneficial for both parties?" she asked, picking up her wine. "It's fine, Jamie, seriously. So long as you're cool with my posting from whatever soiree we're attending. Gotta keep those followers in the know of our romance, right?"

Her flippant response cut me to the quick. I'd hurt her by asking her the way I did, and she was striking back the best way she could. It didn't make it hurt any less.

"Coral, I think y—"

She interrupted me once more. "Plus, I can guarantee you my first class overnight to Boston is a much better deal than your drive over for a barbecue in Searchlight, Nevada."

# chapter twenty—six

## CORAL

My heart thudded a wounded beat in my chest. When Jamie'd first asked me to fly back to Boston with him, I'd been shocked, of course. But also thrilled by his asking me, because I thought it meant he was on the same page I was. That it could be a way to see if things between us could exist outside our little bubble here in Vegas. Hearing he viewed it as a tit-for-tat scenario sliced through me in a long, hot stroke. Had I misread things between us that badly? When he'd said he wanted to be there for me, had he only meant as a friend? I struggled to reconcile that with the way he'd looked at me.

But then again, we had outlined and negotiated a whole plan over what this thing between us would be and what it wouldn't be. And the number one thing we'd agreed on was that work came first. So, who was I to get my feelings hurt when all Jamie did was stick to the plan we'd outlined? It didn't make him the bad guy, because all he was doing was following the rules *I'd* made for us.

And, if I were honest with myself, there was at least a part of me that was relieved by not baring my feelings to him. As exciting as the idea had been, it was equally terrifying. Thank God I hadn't led with that tonight.

How humiliating would it have been to make that declaration and be rejected? I would have curled into a ball and died. His reminder of what we were to each other saved me from that indignity.

"Searchlight?" Jamie asked, pulling me out of my own thoughts.

I nodded, forcing myself to meet his eyes and shelve the disappointment I couldn't quite shrug off. "That's where my mom's lived for the past . . ." I tapped my fingers on my wineglass as I thought about it. "Four years, I think?"

"You . . . think?" Jamie looked confused, as though the idea of not knowing how long your parent had lived somewhere was beyond his comprehension.

For once, I was grateful for the distraction of my family disfunction. My relationship, or lack thereof, with my mother was guaranteed to monopolize conversation once the topic came up.

"I don't have the sort of relationship I think you have with your family, Jamie. That safe, secure family dynamic you can depend on? It's not something with which I have any experience." I huffed out a laugh. "Honestly, I'm a little envious of the easy relationship you have with your family. How invested you all are in each other. It's nice."

His forehead wrinkled. "Your mom seemed pretty invested earlier today."

I shook my head. "It's not the same as what you have, so I doubt you could understand."

Jamie pushed his wine to the side and leaned forward. "Then enlighten me, Coral."

His eyes were soft, and I could tell from his posture he wanted to reach across the table for me, shifting forward in his seat with one broad hand flexing against the tabletop. I was torn between the desire to reach for his hand and the knowledge that if I did, if I accepted the comfort he so obviously wanted to give in this moment, it would just muddle things further for me. I tucked my hands beneath my thighs and kept talking.

"My dad was the first in a long line of men who left," I said, the ache in my chest at the memory now a dull throb instead of a sharp slicing pain. "We lived in Ohio at the time. I was seven and had just gotten my first real Barbie. Sparkle Beach Barbie, who came with a bracelet for you to wear. I was so excited about that damn bracelet." I watched a bead of water slide down the side of my water glass and then looked at Jamie. "Funny how you remember stuff like that, huh?"

I didn't wait for him to respond. "It was so confusing to me that he would leave, because seven-year-old Coral saw her mother as the most beautiful woman on the planet. I couldn't understand how my dad could leave her and never look back."

"He left both of you, Coral," Jamie said quietly.

I shook my head. "Not to my mother. To my mother, he left *her*. And once he did, she began her never-ending quest to fill the space he left. She became some sort of silly putty person that would conform around that emptiness to fit whoever filled it. She tried to become the ideal woman for every man she dated after my dad left. If one liked bowling, she joined a bowling league. If another liked the Yankees, she hated the Red Sox. And when things didn't work out, we'd head out for greener pastures. By the time I was in high school, we'd moved at least six times. Always on the hunt for Mr. Right and always willing to be whoever they wanted her to be. Like if she morphed into someone close enough to their dream girl, they would stick around. I watched her change and reinvent herself so many times, it's hard for me to remember who she was—who she is—at the core of it all. Sometimes I wonder if she even knows—or cares—who she is without a man there to tell her."

It was as unflinchingly honest as I'd ever been about my mother. Even more so than with Cam. She knew of our strained relationship, of course, but I'd never laid all of this . . . feeling about it out there to her or anyone else. Maybe it was because I'd been so geared up to tell Jamie how I felt that the need for some sort of emotional release boiled over into this disclosure. I couldn't reveal my feelings for him, so instead I unloaded all this crap about my mom. But whatever made me do it, there was something freeing about it. So, I kept talking.

"Before I was old enough to push back, I was expected to be as big a chameleon as she was. To reflect back at all these possible dad-replacements what they wanted to see, even if it had little to no resemblance of who I was."

Jamie made a disgusted sound but didn't interrupt.

"I recognized it was a problem in high school when my boyfriend asked me what my favorite food was, and I couldn't tell him the answer. I'd never given it any thought, because my choices hadn't mattered enough to result in my having a favorite anything. Once I started making my own choices and becoming my own fully dimensional person instead of a reflection of someone else . . ."

I shrugged. "Things at home got more complicated between mom and me. She couldn't process my need to be a separate person and I couldn't stomach the way she lost herself in relationships. We just sort of . . . coexisted until I left home after graduation and now I can't even say we do that. The only time I really hear from her anymore is when she's got a new man in her life who shows some indication he's interested in meeting her daughter. That's when I come in handy, so she gives me a call."

"So, this dinner on Sunday . . ." Jamie cocked an eyebrow.

"You got it. Not only will you get to meet my mother, *we'll* also be meeting Tex."

"And that's not her lab mix who loves to play fetch?"

I laughed. "Not that I know of."

"How disappointing," he said with a grin. "Although your mother doesn't strike me as a dog person."

"Unless the guy she's dating is," I quipped, but it lacked any real humor.

"You know," Jamie said. "When I went through something crappy recently, this smart, beautiful woman simply told me, 'I'm sorry that happened to you.' She didn't offer a solution, or rail against the injustice of it. She just commiserated with me for a moment. And that made me feel so much better than anything anyone else had to say." He reached across the table and I put my hand in his. "I'm really sorry that happened to you, Coral."

I felt the burn of tears prick the back of my eyes as I looked down at his large hand covering mine. Even if I couldn't have what I wanted with Jamie, it didn't stop the warmth of his quiet concern spreading slowly to warm parts of me that had been cold for a long time.

## JAMIE

"Tonight is going to be fine," I said, sneaking a glance over at Coral's profile from the driver's seat. According to the GPS, we were just a few minutes from her mother's house. I hadn't been able to talk to her about what I was really trying to say on Friday night. Saturday had been a clusterfuck, with me being tied up in discussions with Davidson and Gideon for Monday's meeting with Shattucks. And once I'd wrapped up, she'd been doing the first round of Zoom interviews of potential merpeople—a sentence I never thought I'd have in my lexicon—followed by a satellite radio interview with Jocelyn and an appearance at a local club. I'd offered to go with her, but she'd declined.

"There's no reason for you to be there, Jamie," she'd assured me when I'd called to volunteer. "I'll be in my tail for most of it. They've set up a small tank for me, so I'll be fine on my own."

I could've pushed the issue then, but didn't feel right having the conversation over the phone. I needed to apologize to her in person. Get her to see I'd phrased it like a trade-off for her comfort, not any hesitation on my part. So, I'd backed off.

And now, we were on the way to her mother's house, and I still hadn't found the right time to bring it up. She was already on edge, that much I could tell from her posture and the way she kept popping her knuckles. I didn't want to add to her stress by forcing the point on our drive.

She turned to me, face illuminated briefly by oncoming headlights. "Easy to say that in the safety of a vehicle not yet pulled into my mom's driveway," she said, trying for teasing but not quite making it.

"Coral, I don—" I said, but was interrupted by the English accented voice telling me to turn left, followed by the next right. I followed instructions and piloted the car onto a tree-lined street with modest size homes.

"Your destination is on the right," trilled our British navigator as we approached a small Spanish-style home with a tiled roof and circular drive.

"Here we are," Coral said, plucking at the hem of her skirt and shooting me a nervous smile.

I pulled into the driveway and parked behind a pickup truck with a personalized plate that read, "TXHLDEM."

"How perfect," Coral said and rolled her eyes.

"At least we now have a conversation starter," I said, and she laughed.

"You're really Mr. Brightside, aren't you?"

I shrugged. "What can I say, you bring out the best in me."

A complex expression passed over Coral's features and she started to say something, but the door of the house flew open to reveal her mother dressed in what appeared to be a black velour tracksuit while wearing a frilly apron and brandishing a spatula. She waved to us with her free hand while whirling the spatula in rolling gesture with the other.

"No backing out now," Coral said and returned her mother's wave with a fraction of her enthusiasm. She made a move to open her door, but I put a hand on her knee. Glancing down at my hand, then back to my face, she arched an eyebrow.

"I'm nothing if not the full-service experience," I said, keeping my tone light. "Let me get the door for you, sweetheart."

I opened my own door and slid from the car before she could answer, giving her mother a polite wave as I made my way around the hood of the car to open Coral's door. Extending a hand to her, I helped her from the car and pulled her against my side as we both faced the front door of the house.

"Ready?" I asked from the corner of my mouth.

"No, but we don't have a choice at this point," she responded, shoving the corners of her mouth into a smile as we made our way up the walk to the front steps.

Eva beamed down at us, the picture of beatific maternal happiness. "You made it," she exclaimed, bringing Coral into a hug before turning to me with open arms. "So nice to meet you in person, Jamie."

"Likewise, Eva," I said, right before being pulled down into an embrace the strength of which I wasn't prepared to face. A heady floral fragrance invaded my nostrils, and I held in a cough while Eva thumped me heartily on the back. Finally releasing me, she held open the glass storm door of the house. "Come in, come in. Dinner is almost ready."

"You cooked?" asked Coral with palpable skepticism.

Eva cut her a look, but male laughter forestalled any response on her part.

"Eva acted as my sous chef tonight," said a tall, barrel-chested man standing in the small foyer of the house and wiping his hands on a dish towel. Eva floated over to him, and he looped a long arm over her shoulders, tucking her firmly against his side. He regarded us with an easy smile that reached his light brown eyes and enhanced the weathered lines of his face. Holding out a hand to Coral, he said, "I'm Grant Kelly, but everyone calls me Tex."

"Nice to meet you, Tex," Coral replied, taking his proffered hand in a short shake. "Based on the license plate, I'm guessing you're a poker player?"

His grin turned rueful. "Guilty as charged." Turning to me, he said, "You must be Jamie."

"Yessir," I replied, shaking his hand. "It's a pleasure to meet you. Thank you both for inviting me tonight."

"Happy to do it," Tex said, squeezing Eva a little tighter. "It's nothing fancy, but I hope you brought your appetites."

I smiled at him. "We sure did." I mimicked his position with Eva, putting an arm around Coral and holding her close. "People can be a little skittish about making dinner for Coral, like it's some sort of hardship." I felt her stiffen but kept going. "It means a lot to both of us that you've made sure we'd have a gluten-free meal tonight. I can't wait to try it."

Tex's smile wavered, and he looked down at Eva, who no longer looked that pleased to see me. "Uh, gluten free?"

I nodded, keeping my smile firmly in place and my arm wrapped around Coral. "Yeah. I'm sure Eva mentioned that Coral is celiac, given how badly she wanted you two to meet over dinner."

Tex shifted on his feet and for a second I almost regretted ambushing him. But I'd already decided I needed to set the tone—and some boundaries—with Eva. Starting with treating Coral as a person and not some accessory to trot out and then put away when she was through. If Eva considered tonight a legitimate introduction, Tex would have already been well versed in Coral's celiac. Especially if he'd been drafted to act as chef while Eva preened in an apron that still sported its packaging folds. His reaction told me I'd been right in my assumption she'd done nothing of the sort.

"It's not that big of a deal, honey," Eva said to Tex, while giving me a smile in name only.

"Only because Coral manages it so well," I said, giving her a squeeze. "She never wants to make anyone feel bad about it, but I have to take care of my girl, right? Surely you can understand that, Tex?"

"Of course," Tex replied. "Completely understandable." He looked at Coral, forehead creased with worry. "I made grilled skirt steak with poblano mac and cheese and hatch chile rice with a garden salad. Is that okay?"

"It's fine," Eva answered before Coral could. She narrowed her eyes at her daughter. "Isn't it Coral? After all, Tex worked hard on this meal and we'd hate for him to think it's unappreciated, wouldn't we?"

Coral gave me a gentle elbow in the ribs when I opened my mouth to say it didn't matter how hard Tex had worked on anything if it would make Coral sick. But I swallowed my own protest and waited for her to respond.

"We do appreciate you making dinner," she said to Tex. "The skirt steak and salad sound great. I'll have to pass, regretfully on the mac and cheese, unless the macaroni is gluten free and, while the hatch chile rice sounds amazing, I'll need a rundown on the ingredients to make sure I can eat it. I'd hate for my sensitivities to ruin tonight for everyone."

Every fiber in my being wanted to correct her and say that it wasn't her "sensitivities" that would ruin tonight, but her mother's lack of any sensitivity at all. All Eva had to do was tell Tex what Coral could and couldn't eat and this whole situation would've been avoided. The fact he seemed more upset about it than Eva made me even angrier.

"See," Eva said, patting Tex's chest. "Like I said, it's nothing to get worked up about. Coral should probably stick to salad and steak anyway." She shot Coral an appraising look. "After all, she's got her performances to think about. I wouldn't imagine there's a huge demand for chunky mermaids."

I wouldn't have noticed Coral's flinch but for my arm being around her. I wanted to strangle her mother and then scoop Coral into my arms and head back to Vegas as fast as humanly possible.

"Actually, Mom," Coral said, her voice calm and steady. "Mermaids come in all shapes and sizes. And those without celiac can eat as much mac and cheese as they want to, just like anyone else."

# chapter twenty—seven

## CORAL

I could feel my mother's irritation like a living, breathing thing standing next to me. I'd been invited here to play a part, and she wasn't pleased with my performance thus far. It would never occur to her that belittling my celiac diagnosis only to follow up with a healthy dose of fat shaming wasn't the best way to ensure a solid evening of family fun.

But even that couldn't dull the shine of having Jamie wade into things on my behalf. I wasn't prepared for how nice it felt to have someone else looking out for me. To not have to be the one to question what was in something or how something was made. The gentle weight of his arm around me offered its own additional comfort as well, as did the solid strength of his body next to mine.

I'd been a little worried things would be awkward, given how I'd avoided him yesterday. I needed some time away from him to get my emotions back under control. I'd been so ready to tell him how I felt that night that I was worried it might just spill out of me if I were around him too soon afterward. I didn't want to embarrass either one of us with that. Thankfully, we'd both had full days yesterday, and that had given me the chance to get a better handle on things.

And I should've known better than to think Jamie would be anything other than what I needed. He'd never been anything else in the time I'd known him. And tonight wasn't any different. He was more than a buffer or a shield for me, he was a sword cutting through my mother's bullshit and putting her in her place. In such a charmingly polite way, she had no choice but to accept it or look like an asshole.

My mother smoothed her already satiny hair and schooled her features to a pleasant smile before saying to Tex, "I bet Coral is the first professional mermaid you've ever met, isn't she, honey? I mean, it's still hard for me to believe it's a real job."

I tried my best to mask the responsive wince, which should have been easy to do at this point. It wasn't the first time Eva made her feelings known on my job, but the dig still found its mark.

Jamie's arm tightened around me. "Good thing you'll have the chance to see Coral perform," he said, voice pleasant. "Now that she's so close by. I'm sure you're excited for the chance to see just how talented she is." To someone who hadn't spent the better part of the last week with him, Jamie's smile seemed genuine. But I saw the sharper edges of it when he added, "But then, as her mother, I'm sure you already know that."

Eva's eyes flickered, like she knew somehow she'd been insulted, but couldn't quite pinpoint where it was in the words Jamie used. "Of course," she said. "And I'm so happy Coral is finally close to home."

Tex nodded, giving me a bright smile. "Well, I'm tickled to death to be able to meet her." To Jamie, he said, "How'd you meet Coral? Fishing trip?"

Jamie smiled politely at the dad joke and said, "I met her at the hotel where she works." He looked down at me, rubbing my shoulder with his thumb. "It's safe to say I was smitten at first sight."

Tex laughed and looked down at my mom. "I can relate to that. Guess it's true what they say." At Jamie's quizzical expression, he added, "Like mother, like daughter."

*Oh, Tex,* I thought. *How wrong you are.*

"Indeed," Jamie said neutrally.

As though he suddenly realized we were all still in the foyer, Tex said, "No need to stand on ceremony. Come on in and make yourselves comfortable. Would you like a drink, Jamie?"

My mother didn't bat an eye at Tex assuming the role of the man of the house, even though we were standing in her house instead of his. Unless he'd already moved in, which wouldn't be that much of a stretch given her history.

Jamie pointed a thumb over his shoulder. "I'll just grab the wine and dessert out of the car first."

Tex handed the dish towel to my mother. "I'll give you a hand," he said and bustled out the door behind Jamie.

The door had barely shut before my mother pinched the underside of my arm.

"Ouch!" I cried, rubbing the red spot left by her fingers.

"You're not even here two minutes and you've already made me look bad," she snapped, hands on hips.

"It's my fault you didn't tell Tex about my gluten issues?"

She threw up her hands in exasperation. "How is that even still a thing for you? Can't you get it under control?"

"Yes, Mom," I said, fighting to keep my voice level. "I keep it under control by eating the right things. Things that don't trigger a reaction. You know this. You've known it since my diagnosis as a kid."

Eva waved me off. "It is what it is," she said, and I wasn't sure if she was talking about my diagnosis, or my refusal to risk a trip to the hospital by consuming any of Tex's mac and cheese. "Tex is important to me, and I need him to see me in the best light, okay? Which he won't if he thinks I don't know about my own kid's allergies."

I didn't waste my breath saying it wasn't an allergy, because to Eva it made no difference. Either way, it wasn't "normal" which had always been a problem. Not for Eva directly, but she'd never liked explaining it to anyone. Especially not men, because she'd been so scared they'd see it as a reason to go. That it would give them the out she thought they were always looking for.

With a sigh, I said, "Tex seems like a nice guy."

My mother lit up like a sparkler on the Fourth of July, practically beaming. "He really is," she said. "I think there could be something real here, you know? Something that lasts and becomes something more."

And there it was. Confirmation that my mother's everlasting quest to find someone to give her that elusive "more" remained ongoing.

Her sparkle dimmed slightly when she added, "I just need to be who he wants me to be, and we'll get there."

My anger drained away, replaced by pity. The refrain was painfully familiar. I'd spent my childhood listening to it. If only she'd been taller, thinner, funnier, smarter or any other number of things she thought a particular man wanted, then he would've stayed. She'd always seen it as her own personal failure, not theirs, when they made the decision to walk away. That she was lacking something and if she could put her finger on what it was and how to fix it, things would be different.

"Mom," I said, touching her elbow. "Shouldn't it be enough for you to just be you? And if it isn't, then it's his loss, not yours."

Eva snorted derisively and rolled her eyes. "Right, because that's how it is these days with men and women. We can just be our true selves and they'll come running." She shook her head. "Nothing could be farther from the truth, Coral. They want someone to fit into their life, not the other way around. And if you don't fit, they aren't going to adapt the space to accommodate you. They'll find someone else to slot in there before your car is even out of their driveway."

The storm door screeched, and the return of Tex and Jamie cut off any reply I could've given. But it didn't stop me from mentally acknowledging that in the entire time I'd known Jamie, he'd never asked me to be anything other than my authentic self.

"Miss me?" Tex asked my mom with a laugh.

She giggled coquettishly and kissed his cheek. "Every time you walk out of the room."

Tex blushed, and seeing his reaction made it easier to resist the urge to vomit at her remark.

From behind me, Jamie leaned close and whispered, "What about it, Siren, did you miss me?"

*Not yet,* I thought, *but I know I will soon.*

I pushed that thought away. "I'm not sure which is more likely to make me throw up, Tex's mac and cheese or the saccharinely sweet way my mother will fawn over him all night."

Jamie's laugh tickled my ear. "Well, we're in this together. So just let me know if I need to hold your hair back."

The flip-flop of my stomach had nothing to do with nausea and everything to do with the man standing next to me. I glanced back at him, taking in his easy smile and the way his eyes crinkled at the corners and my heart squeezed in my chest. "Good to know," I managed to say.

"How about that drink, Jamie? Coral?" Tex asked, breaking the moment only I was aware of. "What can I get you kids?"

## JAMIE

Based on its inauspicious beginning, I'd worried dinner with Coral's mother and Tex would be on par with a colonoscopy, or worse, because I'd be conscious for the dinner. As it turned out, it wasn't half bad. Eva dialed things down a bit, seeming to take most of her cues from Tex. He'd meticulously listed every ingredient in his hatch chile rice and was delighted when Coral not only tried it but took a second helping. I'd declined his mac and cheese with a brief explanation that as good as it looked, I'd rather be able to kiss Coral later without any concerns.

"Who am I to stand in the way of young love?" Tex asked with a wink.

Coral almost choked on her bite of steak at the mention of the word "love." And, yeah, it was way too soon for anyone to toss around the "L" word for us, but playing the part of Coral's doting boyfriend for her mother and Tex only fueled what was becoming a familiar desire to make things much more real with her. To see where things between us could go if we eliminated the limits I'd stupidly agreed to place on our relationship.

The feelings I had for Coral were anything but fake. They were so real it was frightening to consider the speed with which they'd developed. It was far outside the norm for me to fall this hard this fast. But then, as Coral liked to say, our relationship was anything but normal, so why wouldn't my feelings for her develop at hyper speed?

Admitting it to myself was one thing. Telling Coral was quite another. After meeting Eva, the origin of her aversion to setting expectations for anyone was crystal clear, as was her dogged resistance to relying on anyone but herself. I hated the thought of a young Coral feeling like she had no one in her corner. And how it had shaped her into someone so reluctant to put her faith in others. Including me.

But then, I hadn't given her that many reasons to, had I? Agreeing to a sexy Vegas fling without batting an eye didn't scream "Trust me with your feelings!" Nor had categorizing tonight as some sort of bargaining chip for her to agree to meet Shattucks. Doing that had obviously set things back for me, and I had a lot of work to do to overcome that misstep.

To convince Coral there could be an "us" after Vegas, I needed to be the first to open up to her. Have an honest conversation with her about how I hated it when she used the word "fake" to describe anything between us. That I wanted to see what we could be together. To see if we could make this work, despite living across the country from one another. And maybe it was a pipe dream, maybe it would all implode in spectacular fashion. But I was willing to take that risk, because she was worth it.

Except . . . I didn't want her to feel uncomfortable with any aspect of our trip tomorrow. She was already doing me a huge favor by flying across the country and back in the span of twenty-four hours right in the middle of starting a new job. It wasn't great timing to drop anything else on her, especially not something as big as the feelings I'd developed for her. No, I was already toeing the line of impossible by getting her to agree to come to Boston. Any big reveal would have to wait until we got through the meeting with Shattucks. Once that was behind us, I could tell her how I felt about her.

"Jamie?" Coral broke into my thoughts as we were on the road back to Vegas.

"Hm?" I said, easing off the highway.

"Thank you for tonight," she said, giving me an almost shy smile.

I glanced over at her. "For tonight?"

She nodded. "I know it was a lot. I know my mother is a lot. But having you there with me. . ." Coral rolled her lips between her teeth and looked away. I waited, sensing she had to work her way around what she wanted to say.

"One of the things I hate about visiting my mother is how alone I feel after I leave. But tonight, I don't feel like that. Because I had you with me and you were so . . ." Her laugh was so soft it was more of a sigh. "I don't even know how to describe it other than saying you were you. Which was perfect, because you were who I needed to get through tonight. And for the first time in a long time, I don't feel worse after leaving her house. I don't feel like a disappointment or a burden or anything like that."

Her hand came to rest on my leg. "You make me feel like I'm enough, Jamie. And I can't explain how much that means to me, or come close to telling you how glad I am I agreed to your sister's crazy plan."

Giving my leg a squeeze, she moved her hand back to her lap. "I definitely had my doubts we'd be able to pull this off at first, but now . . . We've gotten almost too good at faking it, right? I mean, my mom and Tex completely bought our fake relationship. And don't worry, I plan to return the favor when I meet Shattucks. I'm going to make him think we are so loved up he'll expect an invitation to our wedding. He'll never suspect it isn't real."

What I'd been about to say died on my tongue, each letter of the words turning to ash and putting a foul taste in my mouth. Had I misread what I'd seen as disappointment Friday night? When she'd started talking, I'd seen it as my perfect opportunity to tell her how I felt. That I no longer needed to wait to say I wanted more. But now . . . uncertainty lumbered forward in great silencing strides.

"Right," I said, somewhat halfheartedly.

A horn blared, making both of us jump. The light had changed without me noticing. I accelerated and put my signal on to turn in to L'Atelier. I needed to say something more to her. I wasn't sure what, just that I needed to say something other than "Right." But before I could formulate a coherent sentence, the valet was at her door.

"Welcome back, miss," he said, extending a hand to help her from the car. Inwardly I cursed the efficient luxury of this place as I hurried around the hood of the car after tossing yet another valet my keys.

The lobby was bustling, which made conversation difficult. We reached the bank of elevators for my floor. Pushing up on her tiptoes, she kissed my cheek.

"Thanks again for tonight, Jamie," she said.

"Wait, you're not coming up with me?" I asked, confused.

She shook her head. "I want to. Believe me, I want to. But I need to make sure I've got everything packed for tomorrow's flight." Her smile was a tad forced. "You sprung Boston on me a little last minute, Standard, and I want to make sure I make a good impression on Shattucks. But I'll see you in the morning, okay?"

"Oh, yeah," I said lamely. "Sure, I'll see you in the morning."

"Good night," she said, and then she was gone.

# chapter twenty—eight

## CORAL

There was no way I could've spent last night with Jamie without spilling my guts to him about how I felt. And there was no way I was going to dump that on him the night before one of the most important days in his career. It wouldn't be fair to him. And I wasn't going to do that to him after what he'd done for me by coming to Searchlight.

I'd meant what I said to him on the way home. For the first time in as long as I could remember, there wasn't a dark cloud lingering over me as I left her house. The emptiness I normally experienced wasn't there. Because Jamie had filled it with his distinct brand of charisma and forthrightness. His presence made the night more than bearable. It was almost enjoyable.

The only downside was that it made the feelings I'd developed for him expand almost exponentially. To the point where every time I opened my mouth, I worried they would tumble out with no warning. So, I'd done my best to bottle them up until after tonight.

It sounded like a good plan, until we were midway through our flight to Boston, and I was nothing but a pulsing mishmash of swirling thoughts. Of whether we could really make this dual time zone romance last. Or if I was only kidding myself that he'd even be interested in something more with me.

A warm hand wrapped around my knotted fingers in my lap.

"You don't need to be nervous about tonight," Jamie said, misreading my apprehension as over the dinner party with Shattucks.

"Nervous? Why would I be nervous?" I asked. "It's only the future of one of the most important projects you've worked on that's riding on tonight. What is there to be nervous about?"

I ignored the twinge of guilt for not letting him know what was really bothering me. But now wasn't the time to get into that. He had too much on his plate right now for me to add my insecurities as a garnish. We'd have time to talk about everything once things were on solid ground with Union Square.

"Then it's a good thing I've got you on my arm tonight. You'll have Shattucks eating out of the palm of your hand in no time." He untangled my clutched fingers and lifted one hand to his lips to kiss my knuckles. "Just relax, Coral. Everything is going to be fine."

"Easy for you to say," I replied. "You go to stuff like this all the time. The only time I've been to a party thrown by the upper echelon, I was wearing a tail and floating in a giant martini glass."

"I hate to have missed that," he said with a grin. "They're going to love you, Coral. And, according to Jocelyn, they're going to love our story. So, we've got nothing to worry about, okay?"

I swallowed, because now that we'd been talking about it, I *was* starting to get nervous for tonight. Everything hinged on Shattucks believing Jamie and I were a couple. Which we weren't. But I wanted us to be so badly. What if my concerns over that bled into tonight? What if Shattucks could tell we were lying? Fooling my mother was one thing, but this guy was a whole other story.

"Jamie, I . . ." The words caught in my throat. Was I really going to unload all of this onto him now? Mere hours before we were supposed to convince people we were totally in love?

"Coral?" Jamie said, when I didn't continue.

"I . . ." Again, everything I wanted to say tangled in a knotted mass of thoughts that lodged in my chest, choking off my words. Clearing my throat, I smiled at him. "Nothing, just a few more jitters." We'd talk later, I promised myself. After we got through tonight.

Leaning over, he kissed my cheek. "It's going to be fine, I promise."

I hoped he was right on so many levels.

"Welcome to my humble abode," Jamie said, opening the door to his condo and stepping aside to let me walk in first. The layout was open, with a kitchen immediately to the right and a living room with pale-colored walls and sleekly modern furniture arranged in front of a bank of windows overlooking the Harbor. I crossed to the sliding glass door and stepped onto the balcony, the tang of frigid ocean air teasing my nose as I looked down at the boat slips below us.

Jamie stepped out to join me at the railing, pulling my coat tighter around me. "This is the best part of the place," he said. "Perfect for watching the sun set." Grinning down at me, he added, "Better in the spring and summer, though."

"I can imagine," I said as he took my hand to usher me back inside.

"Let me give you the rest of the tour." Leading me through the living room, he pushed open a closed door I'd passed to reveal the master bedroom. The focal point of which was a huge bed with a cool gray comforter, on which sat a giant gold box tied with a red ribbon.

I glanced over at Jamie. "Someone left you a present."

His grin was boyish as he shook his head. "I don't think what's in there is going to fit me."

Girlish excitement bubbled up within me. "Oh no?"

"Nope," he said, tugging me closer to the edge of the bed. "But I know a gorgeous redhead it would fit perfectly."

"You do, huh?" I asked, fingering the soft velvet of the bow.

Sitting next to the box, he nudged it toward me. "Don't keep me in suspense, Coral. Open it."

Grasping the end of the ribbon, I undid the elegant bow and lifted the lid of the box. Pushing aside gold foil paper, I sucked in a breath. The lid tumbled from my hands to the floor as I stared down at the most beautiful dress I'd ever seen. The blue-green of the fabric was almost iridescent, shimmering within the carefully wrapped confines of the box. When I took it out, the skirt floated down in a cascade of silk.

A full-length mirror hung on the wall next to the bed and I couldn't resist holding the dress against me. Jamie appeared behind me in the reflection.

"It made me think of the first time I saw you as a mermaid," he said quietly, touching the skirt of the dress with gentle fingers. And I realized he'd found a dress that mimicked my Empress mermaid tail, from its unique color to the fit and flare cut of it.

"Do you like it?" he asked.

I met his eyes in the mirror. "Like doesn't even begin to cover it, Jamie," I said, pressing the dress to my chest. "It's beautiful, thank you!"

His grin was wide and pushed the adorable crinkles up at the corners of his eyes. "But that's not all," he said, turning back to the box and lifting out a pair of strappy gold heels interspersed with jewel toned studs. They looked impossibly delicate dangling from his big hands, and I couldn't wait to put them on.

"I feel like Cinderella," I said, overwhelmed by his thoughtful generosity.

Stepping closer, he put his free hand on my waist and pulled me back to him. Nuzzling my ear, he gave a low chuckle. "Wrong princess, sweetheart," he said, nipping my earlobe. "Haven't you been keeping up with the gossip columns? It's Ariel who reformed this rake, not Cinderella."

Tears pricked at the backs of my eyes as I stared at us in the mirror. This man, this unbelievably thoughtful man saw me in a way no one else ever had. Going to the lengths he did to find a dress so undeniably me stole my breath and made my heart swoop down to my toes.

"Well," I said, trying to keep my voice from going watery. "It's some reformation, because we are definitely entering Prince Charming territory."

He grinned at me in the mirror. "At your service, milady." And when he kissed my cheek, I felt like a real princess adored beyond measure. No matter how the rest of the evening played out, I knew I'd remember this moment for the rest of my life. A life that hopefully would include Jamie by my side.

## JAMIE

I adjusted the cuffs of my shirt until the correct amount of white showed beneath the sleeve of my jacket. Smoothing down my pocket square—a discreet emerald and blue herringbone—I turned from the hallway mirror in time to see Coral step out of the bedroom. The sight of her in that dress made it hard to breathe. The silk molded to her long, lithe body, the side slit in the skirt offering peeks at her toned thigh as it rippled around her legs. She'd piled all her glorious hair into a loose waterfall of curls down her back, wispy tendrils framing her face. Darkened lashes looked even longer around her eyes, their unique color enhanced by whatever makeup she'd applied.

Slowly she spun in a circle, the dress fluttering around her ankles and the studs of her shoes glittering in the dying sunlight. "What do you think?"

I thought she looked like a queen, and I was ready to drop to my knees and swear an oath of fealty. But that seemed over the top, so I settled for, "You're the most beautiful thing I've ever seen." I tapped a finger to my lips to hide a smile. "But there does seem to be something missing."

Frowning, she looked down at the dress, patting it protectively with her fingertips. "Well, there was nothing else in the box. I'm wearing everyth—"

The objection died on her lips as I pulled out a velvet box from the middle drawer of the table below the mirror. The only sound in the room was the slight creak of the box's hinge as I lifted the lid to reveal a delicate necklace of layered golden ropes from which hung graduated sizes of emeralds, culminating with a teardrop stone on the longest strand.

The refrigerator hummed quietly in the silence as Coral stared down at the necklace, her mouth slack and eyes huge with surprise. Slowly, she pulled her gaze from the glitter of the jewels to my face. "Jamie, I . . . I don't know what to say."

"You don't have to say anything," I replied. "All you have to do is turn around and let me help you with the clasp."

I'd seen the necklace when I'd gone engagement ring shopping with Gideon a few months ago. And remembered it when my assistant sent me the link for the shoes to match Coral's dress. Luckily, the jeweler had a special place in his heart for us after what Gideon dropped on Everest's doorknocker of a ring. He'd been only too happy to have it delivered to my condo earlier that morning.

The thin filigreed chains lay perfectly along Coral's collarbones, the jewels at each of their centers creating a dazzling path down her chest. The last, largest stone rested perfectly at the start of her cleavage. She exhaled slowly as she shifted her curls to the side to let me fasten the necklace at the nape of her neck, and I couldn't resist placing a kiss there.

She lifted a hand to touch the necklace, then turned to face me. "Jamie, all of this is just so . . ." Her hand fluttered to the side as she shook her head. "I can't even describe it."

I kissed the tip of her nose. "Even if you could, we don't have time. The car's already downstairs."

Thankfully, traffic was light as we made our way out of the Seaport District and over to Beacon Hill. Although less than three miles separated them, the drive was often much longer than the fifteen minutes it took us to reach Shattucks's rowhouse on Brimmer Street.

As I'd been informed by email from Shattucks's secretary, tonight would be a "small, but elegant gathering of a few friends" designed to let Gabriel Shattucks "evaluate the possibility of a partnership in a less formal setting." If pretention were a power source, the wording of the email could've lit up the entire city of Boston for the better part of a week.

I helped Coral from the car, taking care her heels didn't snag on the cobblestoned sidewalk. We made our way down the wide masonry stairs leading to the arched doorway of the brick and stone house. Before even ringing the bell, the door swung open and an honest to God butler greeted us.

"Good evening," he said, with a short bow. "Mr. and Mrs. Shattucks are entertaining their guests in the family room. Allow me to take your coats."

Turning to allow him to help her with her coat first, Coral mouthed, "A freaking butler?" to me and I had to swallow a laugh. We made our way to the expansive family room, complete with soaring twelve-foot ceilings, marble fireplace, and glass paneled French doors that opened to a balcony overlooking the Charles River. Well-dressed guests holding flutes of champagne chatted as waiters carrying trays of hors d'oeuvres milled around.

"*This* is a gathering of a few friends?" Coral asked out of the side of her mouth.

I snagged two glasses of champagne from a passing waiter. "To misquote Fitzgerald, 'The rich are different.'"

She touched her necklace. "*You're* rich."

I laughed and handed her a glass. "Not to these people. I'm afraid we have now entered the land of the not just rich, but the unbearably wealthy."

"Good to know," she muttered, taking a sip of her champagne.

Davidson approached, holding his own glass of champagne. Before I could make any introductions, he leaned in and gave Coral the barest of side hugs, "Coral, good to see you again."

"You too," said Coral, giving him a wide smile and a pat on the back with her free hand.

"Don't look so surprised," Davidson said to me in a low voice. "If the two of you have been dating for months, this isn't the first time I've met Coral."

"Right, right," I said, having momentarily forgotten we'd sold a completely different backstory of our relationship. I needed to get my head in the game before totally cocking this up.

"Have you seen Shattucks yet?" I asked him, and he angled his glass toward a group of men by the patio doors.

"He's holding court with his cronies in that corner. I was waiting on the two of you before I approached him." He smirked at me. "After all, I'm not the one he's so anxious to meet."

I drained my glass and held out an arm to Coral. "No time like the present, right?"

# chapter twenty—nine

## CORAL

Looking at the diminutive man with white sideburns so long they qualified as muttonchops, it was difficult to believe he was the key to a multimillion-dollar land deal. His suit was well tailored, but obviously a few seasons old. I could see a small threadbare spot on the collar of his starched shirt that would be a hole after a few more trips to the cleaners. His white hair was combed back and tamed into what would have been a distinguished style if it hadn't been just a shade too long. But his smile was wide and welcoming when the three of us descended on his little gaggle of admirers.

"Well, well," Shattucks boomed rather than said, inquisitive dark eyes shining. "If it isn't Boston's Bad Boy and the mermaid who harpooned him!" He guffawed at his own joke while the rest of the men in his group smiled politely.

Jamie's ears were pink and irritation at Shattucks prickled my insides.

"Don't believe everything you read, sir," Jamie said with a wry grin.

One of Shattucks's bushy white brows lifted. "Oh? Then I shouldn't buy into this love story of yours that's been plastered all over every website from BuzzFeed to that ridiculous rag *Boston Commons?*"

*This guy read BuzzFeed?*

Jamie laughed. "I said not to believe *everything*. One of the few kernels of truth in that morass is how I feel about Coral." His words wrapped around my heart as swiftly as the arm he put around my waist. "Gabriel Shattucks, this is Coral Triton, professional mermaid extraordinaire."

"A pleasure to meet you, sir," I said, extending my hand. He took it in a hand that was oversized for the rest of him. With our height difference, it was almost like shaking hands with Papa Smurf.

"The pleasure is mine, my dear," Shattucks said, pumping my hand up and down. "I was so glad you could join us today."

"Gabriel, darling, there's no need to pump the poor girl's arm like you expect water to come out of her ears."

I turned to find an elegantly dressed older woman standing at my elbow, smiling indulgently at Shattucks.

He let out another hearty chuckle at her chastisement. "Right as usual, my dear," he said. "Coral, Jamie, allow me to present my wife, Katherine Shattucks."

"Please, call me Kitty," she said as we shook hands.

"Nice to meet you," I said.

"You as well," she said. She was taller than her husband, but several inches shorter than me. And yet still managed to look perfectly at ease looping her arm through mine. "Let's leave them to whatever boring business deal they've come together to broker this afternoon. You and I have more interesting things to discuss."

I looked fleetingly at Jamie. "Uh, we do?"

Her smile made her light blue eyes sparkle. "We certainly do," she said, leading me toward the patio doors. "Starting with who designed this gorgeous gown you're wearing."

"Oh, well, I . . ." I cast another helpless look Jamie's way, but I was already locked into Kitty's orbit and there was nothing he could do.

She pushed open the glass doors, and I braced for a blast of frigid February air, but we stepped out into a temperate space.

"Whoa," I said, walking further onto the balcony.

Kitty laughed, a dainty sound that contrasted sharply with her husband's braying laughter from earlier. The two of them made quite the pair.

"Years ago, I mentioned to Gabriel how I hated not being able to use this space in the winters. So, he surprised me by glassing all of this in. The windows are retractable for spring and summer, so now I can enjoy my balcony year-round." She glanced back through the patio doors. "You wouldn't know it, but the man is a romantic."

*That's what we're counting on*, I thought. The small space was feminine to the extreme, with overstuffed white chairs flanked by huge potted ferns. A spiral staircase led downward in one corner.

"That's to our lower patio," Kitty said, when she saw me glance at the stairs. "We've got a walled garden down there. Not much to look at in the winter, but delightful in the spring and summer months."

"I'm sure," I said, looking down into the now dormant space. It wasn't difficult to picture it in full bloom around the brick patio below.

"Your dress is truly exquisite," Kitty said.

Reflexively, I touched the halter neckline. "Thank you, it was a gift from Jamie." My fingers brushed against one of the stones of my necklace. "This whole ensemble was, actually."

Her eyes dropped to my necklace, and she smiled. "He has excellent taste."

I returned her smile. "I like to think so."

"He also seems quite taken with you, Coral. At least according to the internet." Kitty laughed, the sound tinkling around us.

Glancing back through the glass doors, I saw Jamie and Davidson talking with Shattucks, watching the way Jamie's eyes lit up as he laughed at something the older man said. There were those damn eye crinkles again and that mischievous schoolboy grin. A lethally handsome combination.

"And I see he's not the only one who's smitten," Kitty said, bringing my attention back to her.

"Oh, I . . ." I blushed at being caught ogling my date. "That obvious, huh?" It felt good to give in to the feeling and admit it to someone.

"Only to anyone with eyes," she said, but her voice was kind. "I remember that feeling well." It was her turn to look over at the group of men. "I felt the same way the first time I met Gabriel. My whole world stopped and then started spinning the wrong way. Totally upended me, I have to admit."

I laughed. "That's a very good description of how I feel right now."

Kitty grinned and touched my arm. "Well, that's how you know it's real. When the pull you feel to be near them has the power to flip the axis of your world, it's safe to say you're a goner."

Her smile turned a little sly. "But it's important for women like us to remember no matter how they might flip it, it's still our world and they're lucky to be in it." She glanced back at Jamie. "Something tells me, though, that young man is well aware how lucky he is."

"You think?" I asked, unable to stop myself.

Kitty patted my arm in reassurance. "I do, my dear. He looks at you like you hung the moon and arranged all the stars. You can't fake that sort of adoration."

My hand went to my chest, but my knuckles brushed the emeralds lining my sternum, an elegant reminder this was not the place to pop them. Kitty was right. I was totally gone for the man. I just hoped she was also right that he felt the same for me.

"Ladies," Jamie said, making both of us turn to where he stood in the doorway. "I hate to interrupt." His smile was devastating, and my stomach dropped to my toes when he turned the full force of it on me.

Kitty didn't let him finish. "No need to apologize, I need to check in with the kitchen to confirm dinner remains on schedule." She took my hand in hers. "So lovely to have met you, Coral. We'll talk more over dinner."

Jamie held the door open for Kitty and then closed it behind her. In two strides he was beside me, arms slipping around my waist to bring me closer. My hands landed on his lapels. "Looks like you've made a new friend," he said. I could feel the heat of his hands through the thin fabric of my dress.

"All going according to plan on my end," I replied. "How about you? Looks like you and Shattucks are getting along famously."

"He's not what I expected," Jamie said, a thoughtful expression on his face. Then he shook his head and chuckled. "I guess neither one of us should believe everything we've heard about the other."

He reached up to tuck an errant curl back into place, fingers lingering on my cheek. "Thank you for this, Coral. I know it was very last minute and inconvenient, but it really helped me out for you to be here. I think this dinner is going to seal the deal for us with Shattucks. And I couldn't have done that without you. So . . . thank you."

I tried to focus on what he said, rather than the tender way he touched me. Because what he said was *Thanks for holding up your end of the deal.* But the way he touched me hinted at more. That soft caress wasn't for show, since it was just the two of us. It was sweet and caring and fueled my desire to tell him how I felt about him. That I didn't want to let him go. But the place to do that was not a dinner party full of strangers on Beacon Hill.

So, I swallowed the words that threatened to tumble out and settled for, "You're welcome, Jamie."

He grinned and stepped back. "Now, let's go finish this thing out, okay?"

I returned his smile and let him lead me back inside, my world's axis tumbling backward the entire way.

## JAMIE

"You were . . ." I shook my head and laughed. "I don't even have words for the way you captivated the entire room at dinner."

Before meeting Coral, I'd never brought a woman to a business dinner. Sure, there were dinner parties and the like, but those were tangentially related to business. I'd always assumed having a date at something like tonight would be a distraction from what was important.

But, once again, Coral had shown me the error of my ways. Her being there not only made the night more fun, but it brought things into sharper focus for me. She asked questions about our project that I never would've thought to bring up. Or pointed out benefits that I couldn't. She added a perspective to things I'd never imagined, but now couldn't imagine being without.

From her seat next to me in the back of the car, Coral blushed and said, "Captivated might be taking things a bit far, don't you think?"

"Not at all," I disagreed. "Shattucks was practically hanging on your every word."

She laughed. "Well, if nothing else, being a mermaid gives you great stories to tell at parties."

*And I want to hear all of them*, I thought.

"Coral, I . . ."

"Jamie, I . . ."

We broke off with sheepish laughter.

"I'm sorry," Coral said. "What did you want to say?"

I had so much to say to her I didn't have any idea where to start. So, I delayed once more and said, "No, I'm sorry. You go ahead."

Reaching into her clutch, she pulled out her phone. "I was just going to say a post from tonight would be a good way to cap off the evening. I've already put some stuff on my story, but the first visit to a boyfriend's hometown is something that deserves an actual post."

"Oh," I said. "Yeah, that's probably a good idea." Then I thought about what she'd said. "Wait, you said you already posted some things?"

She nodded while looking down at her phone. "Mm-hmm, just a few snaps from today."

I hadn't even noticed her taking pictures. "Mind if I see what you posted?"

Looking up with a grin, she said, "You could've already seen it if you had your own Instagram account."

"There are limits, Coral, even where you're concerned. Social media is your gig, not mine."

Laughing, she passed me her phone. "Okay, old timer. Just tap that circle there and it will play my story from today."

Ignoring her dig, I did as instructed. Instrumentals from a pop song started playing and a picture of our gate from the airport this morning appeared. In looping typescript, Coral had written, "Boston bound with my baby." The song changed with the image, female Motown singers crooning about their man as a picture of me in profile appeared. She'd taken it midflight and I was staring down at my laptop, readers on the tip of my nose. Over the screen, she'd typed, "It's the glasses for me," with a GIF of a woman biting her lip. That image bled into the view from my balcony, but cut smoothly to the gold box Coral's dress had come in, followed by an image of the tissue paper folded back to show the dress itself. All backed by a woman singing about being swept off her feet. Then there was Coral herself, looking as she had at the start of the night, standing in front of my bedroom balcony doors and framed by the sunset, its fading rays turning her hair into a golden copper while Taylor Swift asked you to remember her standing in the sunset in a nice dress. Coral had added #WildestDreams.

The screen went dark, and I stared down at it, then over at Coral, who nervously bit her lip and toyed with her necklace. "Sorry if that was too much, but I cou—"

My lips crashed against hers, cutting off whatever it was she'd been about to say. I'd just watched a love letter she'd written for me in pictures set to music and there was no way I could find words that would convey how it made me feel. So, I did the only thing I could think of to show her she wasn't alone in this. That I was right there with her, teetering on the edge of the unknown and willing to fall together into an uncertain future, so long as she was with me.

I pushed everything I'd kept bottled up into the press of my lips to hers. Pouring into the kiss everything I'd wanted to say but couldn't. My hands clutched at her hips, but the seat belt kept me from dragging her onto my lap. The hum of her laugh made me draw back with a ragged inhale.

"What was that for?" she asked, her words coasting over my lips in a breathless whisper.

A throat clearing interrupted the raw haze of want in the back seat of the car. I turned, my nose brushing Coral's as I looked at the driver. Who was politely idling in the circular drive of my building.

Coral's giggle dusted against my cheek, and I had to bite back my own laugh at our making out in the back seat like teenagers. I would need to give this guy an obscene tip. With a murmured apology, we got out of the car and headed inside the airy lobby, trading touches like teenagers.

An elderly couple joined us at the elevator and their presence was the only thing that kept me from getting a letter from the POA about illicit elevator activities. But it didn't stop me from slipping a hand just inside the back of Coral's dress, fingers teasing along her lower ribs. She shot me a look, eyes flicking between my face and the couple in front of us. I just winked, which made her snort and cover it with a cough when the lady of the pair looked over her shoulder.

They got off on the floor below mine and the doors barely shut behind them before I'd pulled Coral in for a kiss.

"Cameras, Standard," she said against my lips. I could give a fuck less about the cameras at that point, but drew back at the ding of the elevator and practically yanked her out after me in my haste to get home.

I had to punch in my door code twice, which only made Coral laugh. Finally, the door beeped, and I shoved it open. Her giggles ended on a gasp as I pushed her against the wall of the entry and pressed our bodies together, her height letting every single inch of us line up perfectly. We were so close, I could see the stormy swirl of passion in her blue-gray eyes, feel every heave of her breathing against my chest.

"What's going on right now, Jamie?" she asked, head dropping back against the wall. "Not that I'm complaining, but this feels like we've unlocked some other level."

I laughed and tightened my grip on her hips, the silk crumpling under my fingers. "Sorry, I've just been trying to figure out the best way to tell you something."

"Tell me what?" she asked, arching a brow.

*No turning back now*, I thought. Pushing a hand through my hair, I sighed. "To tell you that I made a mistake."

Coral blanched, recoiling against the door. "A mistake? Doing what?" Her eyes flew wide. "Asking me to come here?"

"What? No! God, no. That's not . . ." I let out a frustrated groan. "Jesus Christ, I'm fucking this up. Just like I fucked up the other night."

She shook her head, copper curls dancing with the movement. "What are you even talking about, Jamie?"

I drew in a deep breath, focusing on what she'd posted. The emotion I'd seen behind everything she'd put into it. "When I said coming here could repay the favor of me going to Searchlight." My hands found her hips once more, my grip desperate. "This wasn't some trade-off, like I made it sound. Yes, I wanted you to come to Boston to help with Shattucks, but that's not the only reason. I wanted you to come to Boston because I wanted to show you my town, introduce you to my friends, have you with me. And, even if you hadn't agreed to come, I would've gone to dinner with your mother. Because I wanted to be there for you. To be with you. Not because of anything related to the article, or a project or publicity for your show. Just because if you're somewhere, that's where I want to be. Because I want to be with you, Coral."

Blinking wide eyes at me, she said, "You want to . . . be with me? As in, really with me?"

I nodded. "And I know that sounds crazy, because we live on opposite sides of the country. And I have no idea how it would work, or if it will work at all. But I know what doesn't work for me any longer and that's letting things end between us without at least trying for more."

"You don't know how happy I am to hear you say that," she said, fingertips dusting over my cheek. "Because it's a version of what I've wanted to say to you for days."

"It is?" My heart swelled with the knowledge she felt the same.

"It is," she said with a shaky laugh. "But I . . . You're . . . We're . . ." She spluttered the words then took a breath. "We're so different, Jamie. And my life isn't . . . normal. It isn't quiet and staid, but solidly in the limelight. Social media and public interest are central to how I make a living. A living I don't just love, but one I've worked hard to get and don't want to give up. One I won't give up. Even for someone like you." She fell silent, waiting for me to respond.

My gut twisted at the knowledge she thought I'd expect her to change anything about herself for me. But it wasn't a shock after meeting her mother. Old wounds ran deep for anyone, and Coral was no different.

"Coral, I'd never ask you to change who you are." I smiled. "I like that you live your life just the way you want. I loved seeing the way you see us when I watched what you posted. It's what gave me the courage to tell you how I feel about you. Why in the hell would I want to change that?"

She frowned and shook her head. "Believe it or not, it was something Kitty said. She reminded me that just because you burst into my world with the force of a freight train, it's still my world you'll be a part of. I want to make sure you're going into this with your eyes open to what that means. My social media presence is convenient now, because you need a good PR boost. My job is a bonus because it attracts attention. But what about when it isn't? What about when you no longer need to sell the love story? What happens then?"

Glancing away, she exhaled slowly and closed her eyes. When she turned back to me and opened them, her expression was guarded. Those striking eyes a dark swirl of color, like an angry sky. "I'm not my mother, Jamie. I won't morph into something I'm not for a guy."

"I'd never ask you to," I said. "And I don't give a shit about selling a love story. I saw what you posted, Coral. That's about us, regardless of who else saw it. It's a story about how you feel about me. I can see that, and I love that you're willing to put it out there for anyone else to see. I love the way you live out loud in every aspect of your life and I'd never ask you to change that, baby. I'm not asking you to give any of that up. I'm letting you know that in a week, or a month or a year, I won't be anywhere near ready to give you up."

Her smile contained all the hope I felt. Slender arms slid around my neck, and she asked, "Did you just go all in on me?"

My heart sped up, the delighted thump of it thundering in my ears. "I think I did," I said.

"Well, then," she said, leaning toward me until our lips were almost touching. "How's a Vegas mermaid supposed to resist a gamble like that?"

My gaze dropped to her mouth, then back up to the deep navy of her eyes. With Herculean effort, I resisted the urge to kiss her. I needed her to say it. To say she wanted more. To say she wanted me. "Is that a yes?"

# chapter thirty

## CORAL

I nodded and whispered, "That's a yes." The word barely passed my lips before Jamie covered them with his in a kiss that seared its way into my memory. I imagined I could feel his conviction in the eagerly desperate way he kissed me. Like he wanted to kiss away any doubts I had about us, or the way he felt about me.

His lips left mine to trail kisses along my jawline, pausing at the tender spot just behind my ear he'd discovered and now loved to tease. I shivered at the slight graze of his teeth there and felt his smile, then the barest brush of his tongue, before he swept me into his arms. The ease with which he lifted me and the tender way he held me would never get old.

My skirt fanned out over his arms as he walked into his bedroom and laid me gently onto the bed. He sank to his knees at the end of the bed, hands dipping under the hem of my skirt.

I put a heel on his shoulder. "While I adore the idea of you diving under my skirts, wouldn't it be better for me just to take off the whole dress?"

His indigo eyes went molten, and Jamie shot to his feet, grabbing my hands and pulling me with him. Large hands fumbled at my back. "Where's the mother fucking zipper on this thing?"

Laughing, I guided his hands to the small hook just below my shoulder blades and he grumbled in relief as he worked it free, then slid the zipper down as I undid the two buttons at the nape of my neck. The dress slid to my feet in a pool of liquid silk.

Jamie's nostrils flared as he inhaled sharply at the sight of me in nothing but a tiny pair of panties. "Christ Almighty, Coral. You're fucking perfect."

He reached for me, but I grabbed his wrist. "Your turn," I said, tugging at his jacket.

In a flash, he'd pulled it off and tossed it over his shoulder. With a grin, he loosened then shed his tie, unbuttoning a few buttons of his shirt. And then he pulled that sexy as hell move where he reached behind his head with one hand, gripped the collar of his shirt and slid it off in one smooth move. Why was that so hot? My guess was it had a lot to do with what was revealed when he divested himself of the shirt in question. Broad shoulders, sculpted chest and abs that rippled as he took off his socks.

I tsked. "How do you get through life being so scrawny? I mean, you're like Steve Rogers's before picture in Captain America. You should really consider lifting wei—" The rest of my tease ended in a muted yelp when Jamie lunged and tumbled us both onto the bed. His hand cupped the back of my head protectively as he took care not to land on me.

"You were saying?" he asked, while doing a pushup on top of me.

I rolled my eyes. "Now you're just showing off."

His eyes shone with a wicked gleam. "Not yet, but I plan to."

Settling back onto his forearms, Jamie stroked my cheekbones with the pads of his thumbs. He dipped his head and brushed a soft kiss over my mouth, then another and another. Each one with a little more pressure, a little more need until I parted my lips to allow his tongue entrance as I groaned into his mouth. I felt the vibration of his answering growl and pushed my fingers in his hair, clinging to him as he kissed me, deep and thorough, until we were both breathless and gasping.

With Jamie braced above me so as not to crush me, our torsos were aligned in a perfect press of skin on skin. Again, the unfamiliar sensation of feeling small flooded through me. His shoulders spanned wide enough I could wear him like a great coat and have room for another person. The man was unnaturally big—a sexy, immaculately groomed Viking. Like if Leif Erikson ever stumbled into a salon.

I reached out and traced the lines of his face. The smooth slope of his brow. The straight blade of his nose. The sharp angles of his cheekbones. The soft swell of his lips that curved into a smile at my touch. He kissed the tips of my fingers and brushed the hair back from my forehead.

"I think this 'more' thing is working out so far," he said.

"They say the first five minutes of anything is the true test," I replied.

"Then we're golden," Jamie said with a laugh, before leaning down to nuzzle my neck.

"Mm-hmm," I agreed as he kissed his way down my throat to my collarbone. My fingers trailed lazily through his tousled blond hair as his light stubble scraped a tantalizing path down to my breasts . . . and kept going. I protested their neglect with a whine, which made him grin up at me as he continued to leisurely kiss his way down my body. Tracing the slope of my ribcage with his tongue, sucking lightly on the curve of my hip as he pulled down my underwear. I lifted my hips to help him slide them the rest of the way off, and then I was naked. Jamie rocked back on his heels and raked his eyes over me, cataloging every inch.

An unexpected sense of shyness bloomed inside me, which was crazy given the fact I'd been naked around the man more than I'd been fully clothed. But tonight, as he gazed down at me with those sizzling blue eyes, it felt different somehow. The weight of his gaze was heavy on my skin, like an imprint or a brand that I'd wear forever.

"You're so beautiful, Coral," he said, fingertips sketching an unseen pattern on my inner thighs. His touch was light and sent pulses of electricity skittering along my nerve endings, lighting me up from the inside until I was certain my skin was glowing. Warmth pooled low and heavy within the innermost reaches of my body as his touch became more deliberate, more demanding.

Jamie's fingers stopped their featherlight touch and took a more purposeful grasp, with the flat of his palms resting on the innermost point of my thighs. "Open for me, gorgeous," he said, using his grip to guide my thighs open wide enough to allow room for him to lie between them on his belly. From there, he draped first one, then the other of my legs over his shoulders. He shimmied down a bit farther, then hummed with approval. "Fucking perfect," he said, voice deeper than before. I didn't know if he was talking to me or having a private conversation with my vagina.

Then he parted me with his thumbs and kissed my center and I no longer cared what part of me he wanted to speak with, so long as he didn't stop.

"Jamie." I gasped, writhing under his touch. His fingers tightened their grip, digging into my ass and holding me in place. I grunted with irritation at my immobility and felt him smile against my sex. Jamie hummed against me as his fingers dug into the flesh of my ass. With a flex of his forearms, he lifted my hips to meet the first rolling thrust of his tongue. My legs tightened, and I clawed at the comforter beneath me. He held me in place as his tongue fluttered over my clit, then down to lap at the already soaked seam of my sex.

"Oh my God," I said, feeling every pass of his tongue as it dragged over what felt like the entirety of the nerve endings between my legs. I tried again to roll my hips, to get more of the exquisite pleasure he was doling out on his own schedule. And again, he held me where he wanted with a warning growl and a pinch of my ass.

The man was an edging master, holding the release I wanted, the release I needed, that my whole body ached for, just out of reach. Pressure built and built with each talented thrust of his tongue. It swirled and rolled in a rising wave that almost crested, only for him to change the angle or ease back and tease until I wanted to scream in desperation.

His holding me still was frustratingly sexy, because he knew what I wanted. What I needed. How much and where to apply pressure, which delicate flickers of his tongue would make my eyes cross, what angle would make my thighs clench around his face and my back bow. He knew all of this, which meant he also knew how to bring me to the brink but ease off the exact moment before I tumbled into ecstasy.

And that was what he was doing while holding my ass in his hands. He licked and sucked and lapped at me until I was a panting, desperate mess at the edge of oblivion. And then he'd retreat, ease off or change from a hard suck to a smooth stroke with the flat of his tongue. Only to follow up with a devastating swipe over my clit that sent me spiraling back up.

I was so focused on the slide of his tongue that I failed to realize he'd completely released his grip on my ass until I felt the press followed by the opulent pressure of his finger deep inside me. I gasped and widened my thighs. Jamie responded by adding another finger to join the first, spreading his fingers and me with them. The euphoric stretch as his hand pumped in and out in rhythm with his sucks of my clit pushed me higher and higher. His fingers curled and stroked inside me right as his tongue pressed and rolled heavily at my clit.

He lifted his mouth from me and blew a warm stream of air directly across my clit and my hips jerked at the sudden change in stimulation. My inner walls clamped around his fingers in satisfaction, and I felt the huff of his laugh ghost over my throbbing clit. The next rough swipe of his tongue made my breath catch. I could feel my pulse in my core as he began to lick and suck in earnest. I bit back a cry and worked my hips in time with his tongue, so grateful for the ability to move and chase the flutters dancing across the bundle of nerves.

"Jamie, please," I murmured, releasing the death grip I had on the sheets to push my hands into his hair and pull him closer. "Please, Jamie, I need to come, baby."

I pulled his hair again and a few low, dirty words escaped his lips as he pressed his fingers deeper inside me, curling up in an immaculate stroke that brought my hips off the bed and had me biting my lip to hold in a moan. And then his tongue was moving in small, tight circles right where I wanted it and I felt my body contract, winding tighter and tighter with each thrust of his fingers and flit of his tongue. Until I was on the edge once more, primed and aching to fall.

Lifting my head, I looked down my body and met Jamie's eyes. They burned into me, scorching me with the intensity of his desire. The intimacy of it, how he watched my face while he worked my body with single-minded focus on my pleasure, sent me over with a raw cry that I couldn't hold in. My climax crashed over me in wave after wave of sensation until I was utterly spent. My legs that had been locked around Jamie's head and shoulders went limp and slid down his back. My head dropped onto the bed with a whimper as I shoved weakly at Jamie, who was still moving his fingers through my folds in languid strokes.

"No more," I slurred. "I think you just killed me."

Lifting my head, I looked down at him. His hair was ravaged from the fierce grip of my fingers and his lips glistened as he grinned back at me. I watched as he wiped a hand over his mouth, then licked his fingers one by one. This man was positively filthy in all the best ways.

Jamie chuckled and rubbed his cheek against my thigh. "Death by orgasm, huh? Sounds like something I'd like to experience."

I roused myself enough to push up onto my elbows. "Well, I'd hate to die alone."

"Yeah?" Jamie asked, rising from the bed to unbuckle his pants. Leaving the belt dangling, he undid his fly and shoved his trousers and underwear down. Freed from the confines of his briefs, his erection bobbed up against his stomach. Keeping his eyes on me, he used the hand whose fingers had just been inside me and stroked himself. One, two, three rough pulls and a low groan rumbled out of him that had my sex clenching in anticipation.

Snatching up the strip of condoms he'd located in the nightstand, he tore one off and tossed the rest aside. "I can't tell you how happy I am to hear you say that." Wrapping a hand around his cock, he gave it a few more wicked strokes while he opened the wrapper with his teeth. Watching him sent lust searing through me once more. The confident set of his shoulders, the flex of his forearm and biceps, the proud jut of his erection gripped in his hand as he watched me. It was such a primally masculine display that my lady parts quivered with greedy anticipation. When Jamie rolled the latex down his shaft, I had to squeeze my thighs together. He noticed and shot me a cocky smirk before grabbing my ankles and dragging me to the edge of the mattress.

"Hm," he said, looking down at me. "This is one of the rare occasions you're not quite tall enough."

I laughed as he grabbed a pillow with one hand and lifted my hips with the other to slide it under my ass. "Perfect," he said, hooking my legs over his forearms and spreading them wide.

The head of his cock dragged against me, and I shuddered when he groaned. "Fuck, Coral," he said, taking himself in hand and sliding against me again.

I dug my heels into his ass, urging him forward. He let out a rough chuckle. "There's my greedy girl," he said, and I decided to live up to the nickname. Curving my hand over his, I guided him to my entrance and tilted my hips up. His snapped forward in a reflexive thrust and we each moaned softly at the prolonged contact.

"Yes," he said, pressing forward and finally working his way inside in an agonizingly slow push. The angle created by the combination of him standing and the pillow beneath my hips let the entire length of him coast along the front wall of my core, sending a shower of sensation through my clitoral network. I gasped and clutched his forearms at the unexpected intensity of it.

"Coral?" My name was a guttural noise from Jamie. "Do I need to st—"

"Stop and I'll kill you," I said, nails digging into his arms. "Keep, oh God, keep going," I said, locking my calves around the back of his thighs and pulling his hips flush against my thighs.

After a sharp inhale, Jamie swore darkly and gripped my hips with bruising force. His hands were big enough I'd have fingerprints on my ass after this, but I did not care. He could've tattooed his name across my pubic bone in that moment and I wouldn't have cared, just as long as he stayed where he was. Like, forever.

And then he moved his hips, and I felt like champagne—all lightness and fizzy effervescence. Each thrust and dragging retreat of his shaft created a friction within me that I'd never experienced. It was all at once too much and nowhere near enough. I wanted him to go faster and slow down all at the same time. "Jamie." My voice was raw, and he reacted to the untethered need in it by increasing his pace, snapping his hips forward in an almost punishing rhythm.

I was leaving half-moon incisions in his forearms from digging in my nails, but I couldn't seem to stop. I had to hold on to him, ground myself in the moment so I wasn't completely lost to the spiraling pleasure.

"Coral, sweetheart," Jamie gritted out, abs flexing and hips driving. "I'm so close. Tell me what you need to get you there. I'm not going without you. Tell me, baby, please. I'm . . . fuck . . . I'm close." His grip on me tightened further, and he swiveled his hips against mine.

"Oh, Jesus," I said. "That, keep doing that. Oh, God."

Jamie doubled down and rutted his pelvis against mine and I felt that telltale tightening in my core. "Yes, right there," I arched up to meet him and bit down on my lip to hold in the litany of sounds that threatened to tumble out as my orgasm crashed over me in another crushing wave.

"Fuck, sweetheart," he said as his movements became more sporadic. His head dropped back with a low groan, and he joined me in bliss with one more deep thrust.

Those large hands slipped from my hips and the skin there tingled with relief and regret at the loss of his touch. Jamie collapsed on top of me, nestling his head between my breasts as his hips slowed to a stop. I wrapped my arms around him and stroked his back, noting that each of us were coated in a thin sheen of sweat.

"That was . . . I don't know what that was," he said to my left breast.

"When you figure it out, please let me know," I said, moving a hand up and stroking my fingers through his hair. "Because I'd like to request a repeat."

His laugh rumbled out, and he nuzzled the underside of my breast. "Just give me five minutes to lie here."

I joined his laughter. "Okay, I'm setting a timer."

Still laughing, he said, "Wait, wait. Let me at least get all the way into the bed for my rest."

Peering around him, I saw that only his top half was on the bed, and he was half standing, half leaning against the edge of the bed. "How do your legs still work? Mine are like overcooked spaghetti, and all I did was wrap them around yours."

"Trust me," he said, kissing the center of my chest. "My hamstrings and I both noticed."

I laughed. "Sorry, but you have only yourself to blame for my clutching you like a sexual life raft."

Jamie raised his head and lifted a brow. "Sexual life raft, huh?"

I shoved at his shoulder. "You know what I mean."

With a soft groan, he rose to his feet and headed into the bathroom to deal with the condom. "I don't," he said over his shoulder. "But I look forward to your explanation upon my return."

When he did return, he lifted me into his arms and cradled me to his chest, drawing a blanket over us. His heart thrummed beneath my ear, and I sighed in contentment. His hand came to my hip and mine rested against his stomach.

"This is nice," I said.

"Definitely something I could get used to," he replied.

"I'm kicking myself for missing out on the past two nights," I said.

He shifted a little and I could feel him looking at me. "Mind if I ask why? Because I know it had nothing to do with your club appearance or having to pack."

"Are you sure you want to know?" I asked.

A finger under my chin tilted my head back to look at him. Serious blue eyes stared down at me. "I wouldn't ask if I didn't want to know, Coral."

Seeing I had no choice but to come clean, I sighed and said, "The night you told me about Shattucks, I'd decided to tell you I was developing feelings for you. That things weren't 'fake' for me anymore. That I wondered if they ever had been anything but real."

Jamie groaned. "And then I made that ridiculous favor swap comment. Fuck me."

I laughed. "Yeah, sort of killed any romantic grand gesture on my part. But the feelings were still there and so close to the surface, so I was worried without some distance I'd just blurt them out. And I didn't want to pile that on you with the Shattucks meeting looming so large in the background."

"I'm an idiot," he said. "A complete fucking idiot."

I smacked his chest. "Hey, that's my man you're talking about."

His arm tightened around me. "Your man, huh?"

"My man," I repeated, loving the way it sounded.

# chapter thirty—one

## JAMIE

*Ping, ping!*

I groaned and rolled over, fumbling on the nightstand for my phone before it could wake Coral up.

*Ping, ping!*

I blinked into full consciousness, fingers wrapping around the phone as it alerted once again.

*Ping, ping!*

I flicked it to silent, then glanced over to make sure Coral was still sleeping. But she wasn't there.

"Coral?" I called. No answer. I reached up and turned on the bedside lamp.

"Coral?" I called again and was once more met with silence.

Anxiety spiked deep within me as my eyes darted around the room. Coral's dress wasn't on the floor where we'd left it, and her suitcase was no longer in the corner of the room. I could feel the heavy pulse of blood thrumming in my veins as my anxiety turned to panic.

She couldn't have just left. That made no sense.

Throwing back the covers, I surged from the bed calling for Coral in what I instinctively knew would be a fruitless move. But a tiny part of me clung to the hope she'd be sitting in the kitchen waiting patiently for me to take her to breakfast.

"Coral," I said as I pushed open the bedroom door. No answer and the yawning emptiness of my living room hit me like a sucker punch.

My phone buzzed in my hand, and I glanced down at it. Multiple text alerts from Davidson crowded the screen. Whatever he wanted could wait. Clearing the screen, I pulled up Coral's contact and was about to call her to ask what the hell was going on when my eyes snagged on the square of paper resting on the bar. A white noise hum sounded in my ears as I crossed the room, déjà vu creeping over me with each step. The paper felt sticky beneath my hands, and I realized my palms were sweating. With fumbling fingers, I unfolded it to read the one handwritten line

*I'm so sorry.*

That was it, no signature, no explanation, just an apology I didn't understand. My stomach dropped and then roiled. For a moment, I thought I was going to vomit into the sink. Last night had been . . . my brain tripped over the word "amazing" since that had been penned in Coral's last note to me. But, fuck me, it *had* been amazing. Every part of it. And yet, she left with an unprompted one-line apology?

My phone buzzed in my hand and my heart lifted with the briefest hope it was Coral. Instead, it was another text from Davidson. Still reeling, I swiped up to at least see what the hell he wanted.

I scrolled through his texts, each one more direct than the next.

Davidson: *We need to talk.*

There was a link attached to it.

Davidson: *Call me ASAP.*

Davidson: *For fuck's sake, Jamie, CALL ME.*

Davidson: *Call me NOW you asshat!*

First Coral left for no reason and now Davidson was about to shit himself about something. What the fuck was going on? My phone rang in my hand, Davidson's contact flashing on the screen.

Swiping to answer it, he was already talking when I brought it to my ear. "Did you watch the fucking video?"

"What are you talking about?" I rasped out, slumping against the counter, Coral's note still in my hand.

"The video I sent. Did you watch it?"

"No, I didn't watch it. Listen, I've got bigger prob—"

"Watch it, Jamie," Davidson cut in. "Watch it right fucking now and call me back."

He hung up. Apprehension worked its way up my spine, sliding past the despair and confusion over Coral's unexplained departure. Davidson never panicked. Ever. But there had been a definite unhinged tinge of it in his voice. I pulled up his text and clicked the link.

Analise McCord's syrupy smile spread across the screen of my phone. "Hello out there, everyone! Analise McCord here. I know you're not used to seeing me in the evenings, but this story couldn't wait for tomorrow. You may remember our special guests from Friday's show, Coral Triton and Jamie Standard?"

"What the fuck?" I said aloud.

Analise continued talking, "Well, I know how much we all loved their story. How Jamie saw her perform and couldn't help but shoot his shot through her YouTube channel. And I mean, is there a more modern-day romance?"

Her smile shifted into something more like a leer. "Or is it?"

My hand tightened on the phone and the sick feeling re-opened in my stomach.

"I have someone here with me who has a little different version of this love story," Analise said as the camera panned to . . . a rat-faced guy with slicked back hair and an oily smile. He looked strangely familiar, and then it hit me.

"Oh shit," I murmured, recognizing the weasel who'd hit on Coral my first night in Vegas.

"I hear you have a different version of this story, Mr. Donaghey. Is that right?" Analise asked, and the way she was salivating made it clear she already knew the answer.

"I certainly do, considering I was with Coral her first night in Vegas," he said, his signet ring winking in the studio lights as he adjusted his tie.

I wanted to punch the guy through the phone.

"You were?" Analise sat forward.

Donaghey looked into the camera and his smile faltered a little. "Well, uh, I would have been. Absent Standard's interruption. But that's not the real point, Analise. That whole story they're selling about how they've been together for months? How he slid into her DMs, or whatever, and now they're so in love?" His laugh was like someone playing a broken clarinet with their nose.

"You're saying that's not true?"

The human equivalent of the poop emoji nodded excitedly in response to Analise. "It's all bullsh—" He winced a little, looking directly into the camera. "Sorry, what I meant to say was that it's absolutely not true. They met that same night, after I turned her down."

"I'm going to find him and make him eat that stupid signet ring," I said to the empty condo, my grip on the phone threatening the viability of the screen.

"You're saying they met a week ago?" Analise asked, eyes wide with faux shock.

"Exactly," Donaghey nodded like a puppet. "It was just a Vegas hookup they're trying to pitch into something more to drum up publicity for that mermaid show."

"So, all of this she and the hotel have been posting was just a PR stunt for her show?" Analise shook her head in disgust. "The lengths people will go to for fame. Thank you so much, Mr. Donaghey, for coming on with me tonight to bring this to our viewers' attention. The public has a right to know when they're being conned."

The screen went dark, and I stood there stunned. I went to rub my face, but still held Coral's note. Realization hit me like a sledgehammer and my knees wobbled.

*I'm so sorry.*

"Oh, Coral," I said, grasping the meaning of the apology. She must've already seen this video and now saw this whole thing as somehow her fault. It didn't take a genius to know she'd bolted back to Vegas. Most likely to try to fix this on her own, because she'd been relying on just herself for too long. The insanity of her taking the blame was that if it weren't for me, none of this would've happened. And I knew she was the one probably bearing the brunt of the reaction to this, because she was the one with a public persona. I didn't even want to think about the comments that were probably flooding her social media pages right now.

My brain hiccupped over the words "social media," and then a thought blazed into the forefront with the speed of a bullet train, screeching to a halt and shouting a possible solution to this mess.

"Fuck," I said, and called Davidson back, still piecing together what I hoped would end up being a brilliant idea.

He answered on the first ring. "Who the fuck is this guy, Jamie? And what the fuck is he ev—"

"I don't have time to explain any of that right now," I said. I felt the familiar buzz of excitement at putting together a deal proposal flood my system, amping me up. "I need a flight to Vegas."

There was a pause, then Davidson said, "A flight to Vegas. That's your number one concern right now?"

"That and I need you to round up some of the Gen Z interns and figure out which of them have the best social media skills."

The pause that followed that request was even longer. "Please don't take this the wrong way," Davidson said. "But are you on some sort of hallucinogenic drug?"

I ignored the dig, riding the buzz as my idea took root and grew while we talked. "No, listen man, I'm working on a plan to deal with this. It's a little unorthodox, bu—"

"Says the man who is fake dating a mermaid," Davidson said drily.

"Yeah, we'll need to have a longer discussion about that at some point, namely that it's not fake and there's a good chance I'm in love with her. But there's no time for that now. Flight and a person under thirty, those are the things I need from you right now. Social media moves too fast for us to delay anything. We've got to get on this now."

"For Christ's sake." Davidson groaned. "At what point in this whatever the fuck you're doing are we going to deal with Shattucks?"

"I'll deal with Shattucks, but Coral is in crisis right now and I've got to help her first."

"Her crisis is more important than securing the final piece of the Union Square project?"

"Without a doubt, man."

## CORAL

Cam had sent me the link to the *Waking Up in Vegas* exclusive interview with the rodent-faced suppository, the soft chime of her text rousing me from sleep in the cocoon of Jamie's arms. Her message sent a chill through me. *The trolls are running with this.*

Slipping carefully out of bed, I'd watched the video in the bathroom, pushing a fist to my mouth to cover the choked gasp of outrage. In that moment, I felt my entire world slipping away. Everything I'd worked to build and all the things I had planned for my life in Vegas sliding through my fingers. Cam had been right about the trolls, of course. They'd picked up the scent of scandal and humiliation and were now jubilantly running with it in all their hatemongering glory.

The deluge of online vitriol aimed at my and Jamie's fake relationship rained down across all my social media platforms in a hurricane of hateful comments and hashtags. I couldn't stop myself from scrolling through the nastiness on my way to the airport. People were incensed with both of us, but since Jamie didn't have any social media presence, I was the easy target. They used all the same hashtags Jocelyn and I had on our posts, which meant the video of that turd muffin's interview was now linked with all our posts. It was a PR nightmare of epic proportions.

By some miracle, I managed to get on an eleven thirty flight out of Logan. I had no cuticles left by the time I landed in Vegas a little after one. I hadn't dared to turn my phone off airplane mode during the flight, because I couldn't stomach any more notifications about how I was a #liar or #fraud or #publicitywhore. And those were the tame ones.

I'd also been too scared to hear from Jamie. Things were awful for me, but this bad publicity could ruin things for him. I couldn't face him and see the disappointment on his face at the way everything had cratered around us. Because of me. Because I'd been the one to say this was a good idea. I'd told him it could work, and he'd believed me. He was in this mess because I'd convinced him to do it. So, I'd crept out with an even shorter note this time and that only made me feel worse, if that were even possible.

When I finally turned my phone on to use my ride service app, the ping and chirp of my alerts almost drowned out the slot machines around me. I quickly set it to silent and turned my social notifications off. After ordering a car, I opened up my texts and found a message from Jocelyn.

Jocelyn: *Come straight to my office when you land.*

I texted her back to let her know I had an earlier flight and would be there soon, then I turned my phone back off. I dreaded the conversation with her almost as much as the one I'd avoided with Jamie. There was no way the hotel could keep me on after this shitstorm. They'd have to cut ties with me to salvage the show. My stomach clenched and my hands were clammy. Vomiting felt like a real possibility, as did the demise of my career in Vegas before it even got off the ground.

Meredith was grim-faced when I got to Jocelyn's office. "Go right in, Coral," she said.

I knocked on the open door and Jocelyn looked up from her computer. Seeing it was me, she jumped out of her seat and hurried over to me. I wasn't sure what to expect from her, but it definitely wasn't the hug she gave me, or the apology that followed it.

"Oh my God, Coral, I'm so sorry," she said, giving me an extra squeeze before letting me go.

Startled, I asked, "Um, for what?"

She unwrapped a muffin from the tray on her coffee table and took a huge bite. Speaking as she chewed, she said, "For getting you into this mess in the first place. If I hadn't convinced you to help out my dumbass brother, none of this would be happening!"

"Well, that's not necessarily tru—"

Jocelyn shook her head violently, spraying crumbs down the front of her fuchsia blouse. "No, it is true. But I'm going to make it up to you, okay? I've already had security pull the footage from L'Andier the night that asshat says he met you. And, big surprise, it shows that he is completely full of shit. Side note, we've also got an incident report that night from Mr. Donaghey being tossed out of a VIP poker room for trying to feel up a waitress. I've already got our PR folks working on a press release to contradict everything that imbecile said and legal is sending me a draft of the letter to *Waking Up in Vegas* demanding a public apology and a retraction."

She sucked in a breath and took another enormous bite of her muffin. The iron twist ties of tension that had been wrapped around me since checking my phone in Boston started to loosen.

"So . . . I'm not fired?" I asked. My jangled nerves rattled in response to one more emotional shift. I'd been on quite the roller coaster since being jolted awake by a stream of online hatred. At this point, I wasn't sure if my equilibrium would ever recover from the last twenty-four hours.

Jocelyn's eyes went round as saucers and she coughed, then swallowed, then took a long drink of water. "Fired? Coral, no! Like I said, none of this is your fault. And we are going to make things right. I know it's hard to get the cat back in the bag on social media, but I promise you we're going to do everything in our power to fix this."

A huge breath whooshed out of me, but then I remembered what all of this negativity would mean for the show and my gut gurgled with renewed anxiety. "I appreciate that, Jocelyn. Really, you can't imagine how much. But I don't want this thing to interfere with the show. And if that means you need to let me go, I completely understand. Honestly. Because I'm just not sure how much good a press release is going to do in convincing people." I gave her a sheepish smile. "After all, Analise wasn't completely wrong."

Jocelyn waved a hand in dismissal. "Analise is a fame-thirsty bitch who is angling for a job in a larger market and she's willing to step on whoever she has to on the way." She pointed at me. "You're not going to be her stepping-stone to an anchor desk in New York."

Meredith knocked on the doorframe. "Jocelyn?"

"Did that email from legal come in?" Jocelyn asked.

She shook her head. "No, but there is something you need to see." Her lips twitched as she looked at me. "Actually, it's something you *both* need to see."

I groaned and slumped down onto Jocelyn's sofa. "I don't know that I can handle seeing anything else today."

"Oh, I think you'll want to see this," she said and handed me her phone. YouTube was open on it and . . .

I blinked, because there was no way what I was seeing was real. Jocelyn sat next to me and peered at the screen, then gasped. "What in the world?"

Meredith reached between us and hit play.

"Hi," Jamie said, looking both handsome and uncomfortable as he smiled out from the screen of Meredith's phone. He was sitting at the counter in his condo back in Boston. "I'm not exactly sure how this is supposed to work, but my girlfriend, Coral Triton, is pretty popular on here. At least she was until I came along and screwed things up for her. So, now I'm here to set the record straight."

"What is he doing?" Jocelyn asked.

"I have no idea," I replied, watching as Jamie adjusted his tie.

"Did I slide into Coral Triton's DMs a few months ago after watching one of her videos on here?" He shook his head. "No, I didn't. I'm a thirty-nine-year-old man, which means I'm not even one hundred percent sure what it is I just said. So, yeah, that part of our story isn't true."

Giving the camera a shy smile, he said, "The truth is I saw her across a crowded room and, while we're being honest here, started falling for her right then and haven't stopped since. Except I didn't have the guts to tell her that right away and instead convinced her to participate in a PR campaign to improve my reputation. The whole fake relationship was my idea, not hers, and it was to help me, not her or her career. And yeah, now I know that was incredibly stupid and I just should have told her how I felt from the start."

My pulse thudded in my ears as I listened to Jamie take all the blame for the scheme we'd hatched. Excitement over his being willing to do that for me warred with guilt over what it could mean for him with Shattucks. I was, it seemed, destined to experience every possible emotion in a very short period of time.

With a sigh, he ran his hands through his hair. "It might not be the social media love story you all wanted, but I promise you there's nothing fake or phony about my feelings for Coral. I'm crazy about her and have been since the moment we met. That's the real, unvarnished truth of it and the good news is that I finally got the courage to tell her."

His grin was lopsided as he added, "The craziest part is that I have you all to thank for it. It was the posts she made for you that helped give me the courage to tell her, because through those I could see she felt something real for me, too. That I wasn't alone in the way I felt about her. So, I guess for me this is part confession, part apology and part thank you. And now that we've cleared the air on a few things, how about you all cut my girl some slack, okay? It's not her fault I'm an insecure dumbass."

The screen changed to a paused video of a sneezing baby panda as next in Meredith's viewing que. I handed her phone back to her.

"I'm not sure if you noticed," she said into the stunned silence. "But his video has already gotten like thousands of views. And he just posted it this morning."

"Oh my God," Jocelyn said, cutting me a look.

"Jocelyn, I can expl—"

She let out an excited squeal and pulled me in for a hug. "I knew there was more than just chemistry between the two of you! This is so great!" Drawing back, she added, "And if he screws up, just let me know and I'll kick his ass."

"But what about Jamie and this whole thing with Shattucks?" I asked, still seized by the guilt that had plagued me all the way back from Boston.

Jocelyn patted my leg reassuringly. "Jamie's a big boy, Coral. If he made the decision to shoulder this, that's on him. And, if you think about it, that's where the blame should rest, don't you think? I mean, I'll admit to my fair share of it too, but in the grand scheme of things, you are the innocent party here. None of this was your idea."

"But I . . ."

She shook her head. "But nothing. Jamie did what he felt was the right thing for all of us, and he did it because he wanted to. On that, you can trust me."

# chapter thirty-two

## CORAL

As much as I wanted to believe Jocelyn about Jamie's motivation, I couldn't without talking to him. I needed him to tell me things weren't ruined for him and his partners. Because as sweet as it was for him to swoop in to save me from internet trolls, I couldn't stomach his sacrificing his career for mine. I couldn't take solace in his selflessness until I knew what it cost him.

So, I'd called him as soon as I left Jocelyn's office and got his voicemail. And continued to get his voicemail over the following hour and a half. It was driving me crazy, and I was wearing a hole in the carpet of my hotel room pacing and waiting to hear from him. The fifth time his voicemail picked up, I flung my phone onto the bed with a frustrated groan. Where was he? He had to have expected to hear from me after that video, so why wasn't he picking up? I wanted to throw myself onto the bed kicking and screaming like a toddler.

"Screw it," I said and jerked a plain black one piece from my dresser. Swimming was the only thing that calmed me when I was this worked up, the soothing silence of the water cutting out everything else while I worked through whatever was bothering me. It had worked throughout my life, and I hoped it would work its magic today before I exploded.

Leaving my phone in my room, I made my way to the indoor pool, which was quiet at 4:15 on a Tuesday afternoon. Dropping my towel on a chaise, I dove into the water, arms slicing through the surface and legs churning as I swam off the emotional upheaval I'd experienced since waking up that morning.

I settled into a rhythm, the turbulence of my thoughts easing as my body relaxed into the familiar motions. Stroke, kick, breathe. Stroke, kick, breathe. My muscles lengthened and my mind began to clear as the tension ebbed away. I barely registered the splash of someone getting in the pool across from me. And I probably would have ignored it, except they were in my lane. And wearing dress pants.

Sputtering to a stop, I stood up and jerked my goggles off, wiping my eyes with the heels of my hands. When I dropped my hands, the first thing I saw was Jamie's cocky grin from halfway across the pool.

"Hey, Siren," he called, slogging toward me. "You weren't answering your phone."

"You're here," I said stupidly as he continued his waterlogged approach, coming to a halt just in front of me.

"I am," he agreed and lifted me out of the water.

Instinctively, my arms went around him. "You're ruining your suit." Man, I was on fire with my obviousness.

Jamie just laughed and turned toward the stairs. "I tried to get your attention, but you were in the zone, so I had no choice but to dive in."

"Most would disagree that was the obvious choice," I said, laughing as he carried me from the pool like Poseidon wearing Tom Ford. "What are you doing here?"

Sitting on a lounger, he draped my legs over his lap and pushed a few wet strands of hair off my face. "My girl had a rough day, so I needed to make sure she was okay. Xavier clued me in to you most likely seeking solace in the water, which is how I found you here."

Warmth bloomed within me like spring roses opening to the sunshine. "By flying across the country after . . ." The video!

I clutched the soaked front of his shirt. "What did Shattucks say about everything?" I shook him a little, or at least tried to. The man was an immovable mass. "And why weren't you answering the phone? I've been freaking out since I saw your video."

"We'll get to that, Coral. But first we need to chat about why you thought it was a good idea to just bolt this morning instead of talking to me. I thought we'd agree to give this thing a chance, that we were together. And then at the first sign of trouble, you bail on me?"

"I . . . I wasn't bailing on you," I protested. "I was trying to protect you."

"By leaving me a one sentence note and flying across the country without talking to me?" Jamie's narrow-eyed look let me know exactly what he thought of that plan.

And if I were honest, it didn't sound great when I said it out loud. "I wanted to try and fix things."

"I'm sure you did, sweetheart. But when are you going to realize you don't have to do everything by yourself? I'm here for you, Coral. That was the whole point of last night. Those weren't just words. They're how I feel about you and I need more than you just saying you feel the same way. I need to know you trust me when I say I'm going to be there when you need me. What else do I need to do to get you to believe that?"

"I . . ." My voice trailed off, because he was right. Jamie had never done anything but show up for me since the night we met. If I needed him, he was there. I'd been the one pushing him away, not the other way around. I'd been the one whose fear of being open and honest with him almost ruined things.

It occurred to me that I'd spent so much time cultivating my independence, so I didn't repeat my mother's mistakes, that instead of independence what I'd really cultivated was isolation. And it was really fucking lonely.

"There's nothing else you can do," I said, and his face fell.

"But, Coral, I don—"

I put a hand to his lips. "There's nothing else you can do, because you've already done enough. I was just too scared to see it. Too scared to believe it was true, so I ditched and ran. But I don't want that to be my first impulse anymore. Because you make me want to trust you. To trust in what we have and what we can have. Assuming I haven't completely ruined things?"

Jamie smiled down at me and kissed my forehead. "And here I thought you'd watched the video I made." His eyes were warm as he touched my chin. "Nothing's ruined, sweetheart. Things are just getting started."

He lowered his head, but right before our lips met, I remembered his dodging my question about Shattucks. My hand hit his chest with a wet splat.

"Jamie, wait! What about Shattucks? There's no freaking way that video helped anything. After you've worked so hard and were so close to getting everything you wanted, how could you risk throwing it all away?"

His laughter surprised me. Readjusting me on his lap, he said, "Believe it or not, if anyone could appreciate a grand romantic gesture, it's Gabriel Shattucks," he said. "I talked to Shattucks before the video went live and told him the truth."

"You did?" I asked, fingers burrowing back into his shirt. "What did he say?"

Jamie sobered slightly. "He wasn't thrilled about being hoodwinked— his word, not mine—but said he admired my creativity almost as much as my choice of accomplice. And then he told me to go get my girl. Seems as though you've got a real fan in Gabriel Shattucks, Coral," he said with a grin. "I think my screwing things up with you would be the one thing he couldn't forgive."

"Wait, does that mean he's on board?"

Jamie's grin was infectious when he nodded. "We're still hammering out details, or rather Davidson is, but yeah, in essence it's a done deal. The first of many, we hope."

"Jamie that's amazing!" I threw my arms around him, soaking the last remaining dry parts of him with my enthusiasm.

He laughed and pried my arms from around his neck to see my face. "You asked me how I could throw it all away. Even if Shattucks had turned us down, I wouldn't have seen my coming clean about my feelings for you as throwing anything away."

Taking my hands in his, he said, "I told you I'd never ask you to change who you are. Well, that's not precisely true, because I want to change your warped misconception about expectations. Like with the fallout from this fake dating debacle. You expected to have to deal with it alone. You expected me to choose my work over yours. You expected to be the one who had to make the sacrifice and then pick up the pieces when it was over. I want you to expect more from me, because you deserve it, Siren. You deserve to be someone's priority and so much more, and I want to be the man who gives it all to you."

Heart in my throat, I tried to think of something to say, some way to respond to the beautiful promises he'd just made me. But all I could say was, "Oh?"

Jamie laughed softly and lowered his face to mine, bringing our lips close. "I told you before, Coral. You're who I want. Just as you are, wherever you are, with or without fins. You're it for me."

"You know," I said, reaching out to touch his cheek. "You could've texted me some of that earlier and saved me the beginnings of an ulcer."

His laugh was low and soft as he shook his head, grazing my nose with his in the process. "I couldn't do this in a text." And then he kissed me.

# *epilogue*

# OCTOBER

## JAMIE

**W**ill you relax, man?" Gideon asked, his arm draped casually around Everest. "Someone would think you're getting ready to strap on a tail and dive into that thing." He pointed over at the massive tank, dimly visible in the lowered stage lights.

"You pull on a tail, you don't strap into it," I corrected, pushing down the nerves I felt for Coral's opening night. She'd worked so hard on this show, and I wanted it to go well. Not just for her, of course. I also wanted my baby sister's first big solo production to do well. But, for Coral, this was something she'd dreamed about her whole life and there was nothing more I wanted than for it to be a success. If I thought putting on a merman costume would ensure that, I'd be in that tank in a hot second.

"Excuse my ignorance," Gideon said with a grin. "I forgot you were an expert on all things mer-related these days." He smirked at me. "At least based on the billboard of you and Coral I saw on the Strip." His eyebrows waggled. "Hubba hubba, Standard."

Jocelyn had used some of the earliest shots of Coral swimming around me for the billboard ad. A video billboard, so realistic you could almost feel the slide of her tail against my torso. Thankfully, she'd cropped it, so it didn't show anything above my chin. But the guys knew it was me and had given me immortal hell about it since.

Everest elbowed Gideon. "We're here to support, not antagonize, West," she said. "This is a big moment for Coral and it's sweet Jamie's so nervous."

Seeing that her calling me "sweet" simply gave Gideon additional ammo, she cut him a look that could curdle milk. He rolled his lips between his teeth and stayed silent.

Davidson slid into the vacant seat on the other side of me. "Sorry I'm late," he said. "Call ran long."

Before I could respond, the house lights came up, illuminating the aquarium with an eerie greenish glow.

"Welcome everyone!" I recognized Xavier's voice as it boomed through the speakers. "To L'Atelier's *Mer Spectaculaire!* Thank you so much for joining us tonight at our inaugural performance. I promise you're all in for a treat . . . Or is it a trick?" The opening strains of "Thriller" started to play as Xavier gave a ghoulish laugh. The tank went dark, then in a flash five mermaids appeared in glowing skeleton body paint.

My heart did a quick somersault as it always did when I first spotted Coral in her element. She was at the center of the mermaids, red hair floating out around her in a red crown. The five of them moved together in a series of loops and twirls synchronized to the beat of the music. Music I knew they could hear thanks to the tiny waterproof earpieces Xavier helped design.

I watched, enthralled with the rest of the crowd, as the pod executed flawless choreography, timing their puffs on the breathing tubes perfectly. It was a beautiful display of underwater acrobatics, and the longer I watched the more my nerves eased. She'd done it. Just a few minutes into the first performance, I knew the show would deliver on everything it promised and then some. Pride threatened to crack my chest wide open as the first routine ended and the crowd surged to its feet in appreciation of my girl.

## CORAL

The pop of a champagne cork greeted Cam and me as we stepped off the elevator arm in arm into the Skybar like triumphant heroes coming home. Jocelyn spotted us first and rushed up, champagne flutes in hand. "There they are, my two shining stars!" she crowed, thrusting the flutes into our waiting hands before gathering us both into a three-way hug that threatened the integrity of my ribcage.

Cam's wheezing laugh let me know she was being equally crushed by our overenthusiastic boss. Pulling back, Jocelyn was practically bouncing in her stilettos, the metal fringe of her one-shouldered black minidress cha-chaing with her excitement. "Tonight was unreal, you two. I knew it was going to be, but to see it all come together like that . . ." Her words tapered off into an exuberant shriek that made me laugh.

Jocelyn's reaction summed up the way I was feeling—the human equivalent of steam being released from a kettle. After months of planning and hard work, tonight's performance had gone off without a hitch. And the crowd's reaction had been one for the ages. I could ride the high of this performance well into the next week.

"I'm so glad everyone enjoyed it," I said. Looking at Cam, I added, "I know we had a blast putting it all together."

Cam smiled, but shook her head. "Don't be so modest, girl! I showed up, tailed up, and performed. You and Xavier were the ones who put this whole thing together. So, stop trying to shy away from the credit you're due!"

"Did I hear my name?" Xavier asked, coming up behind Jocelyn and snaking an arm around her waist. She giggled and melted back into him. They were too precious, now that they'd gotten the HR stamp of approval on being together.

Xavier clinked his glass to mine, then Cam's. "Congratulations, ladies. Tonight was one hell of an opening night."

"Oh, I think we both know who deserves the most credit, and that's you," I said, taking a sip.

Warmth at my back and an accompanying tingle down my spine alerted me to Jamie's presence seconds before his arms wrapped around me and pulled me against his chest. I luxuriated in the feel of him as his lips landed on my bare shoulder before coming to my ear.

"Hi," he said, voice low and that one word sent pinwheels of anticipation down my back.

"Hi yourself," I replied, angling away a little to meet his eyes.

"You were spectacular, tonight, Coral," Jamie said, pride shining brightly in his eyes. "Simply spectacular."

"I think you mean Spectaculaire," Jocelyn cut in, making everyone laugh.

Jamie released me from the hug, but kept an arm around my waist, hand splayed over my hip. He nodded contritely. "Apologies, baby sister. Of course I meant to say Spectaculaire." Looking over at Cam, he added, "And you certainly live up to the hype, Cam."

She gave him a little salute. "Why thank you, Jamie." Eyeing him in his suit, she added, "And believe me, so do you."

"Hey," I said, giving her a little shove. "Eyes on your own paper."

With a laugh, Cam glanced behind Jocelyn. "I think I see my cheat sheet now," she said, making eye contact with Jarrod, a merman from

Dallas she'd hit it off with immediately upon getting to town. "If you'll excuse me." Cam cut through the crowd without a backward glance.

"May I get you another drink, Joss?" Xavier asked and led her away before she could answer, leaving Jamie and me as alone as two people could be in a crowded after party.

Turning on my heels, I put my arms around Jamie's neck and smiled. "Hi," I said again.

He smirked, hands finding the small of my back, thumbs rubbing the bare skin revealed by the cutout of my dress. "Hi there," he said.

"So, you liked the show?"

His smirk became a wide, guileless grin. "Liked doesn't even begin to cover it, Siren."

Happiness uncorked in my chest like the champagne that greeted my arrival that night, bursting outward in a kaleidoscope of joy that zipped all over my body. "That means a lot, coming from you," I said.

"I'm glad to hear you say that," Jamie replied, reaching inside his jacket pocket to pull out what I recognized as a card key for L'Atelier.

I laughed. "I assumed we'd be going back to my place instead of you getting a room."

Once things had solidified with *Mer Spectaculaire*, I'd broken the lease on my old apartment and was now living at L'Atelier full-time. At some point, I'd find an apartment in Vegas, but for now the convenience of living on-site outweighed my need for a true place of my own.

Jamie smiled, fingers of one hand flexing along my spine. "What if I said I wanted to go back to our place tonight?"

Frowning, I looked at the black and purple key card in his hand, then back at his face. "Our place?"

He nodded. "You know I'm always on the lookout for a good investment. And Vegas has become a place I'm very, very invested in." That statement was punctuated by the press of his fingers into my skin.

"So, when Jocelyn told me the hotel was selling some of the top floor units in this tower as residences . . ." One of his broad shoulders lifted under my hands as my heart flew into my throat. "What could I say other than, 'Where do I sign?'"

"You bought a condo? In Vegas?" The last part came out as a squeak.

"How can we be a true bicoastal couple if we don't own a place on both coasts?" Jamie said, bopping my nose with the key card.

"Technically, Vegas isn't on the coast," I said, barely able to squeeze the words past the lump in my throat.

"Always so exacting," he replied, leaning closer. "I guess I need to be crystal clear, you know, to make sure there's no blurred lines or miscues on this."

"Never a bad idea," I said, voice a little breathless.

"Yes, I bought a condo in Vegas. Yes, I'm keeping my condo in Boston." He stroked my cheek. "But without you in them, neither place is a home for me. My home is with you, wherever you are, Coral. And if that means I'm eventually buying a place in San Diego, or New York, or Bermuda, or wherever my mermaid swims to, I'm good with that. So long as wherever I am, I'm with you."

He tilted my chin up until our mouths were a breath away and I felt the whisper of his next words on my lips. "I'm yours, Siren. You own every bone in my body and each breath in my lungs belongs to you."

"And here I thought you'd gone all in back in Boston," I said, breath hitching.

Jamie smiled, his huff of laughter skating over my skin. "I guess you could say I've doubled down."

"Then I guess there's just one thing left to do," I said.

"What's that?"

"Collect your winnings," I replied and pulled his lips to mine.